EMPIRE OF THE WOLVES

Jean-Christophe Grangé was born in Paris in 1961. Formerly an independent international reporter, he worked with magazines all over the world as well as with various press agencies before setting up his own news agency. *Blood-red Rivers*, his second novel, was made into a film – directed by Mathieu Kassovitz – with the title *The Crimson Rivers*.

Jean-Christophe Grangé

EMPIRE OF THE WOLVES

TRANSLATED FROM THE FRENCH BY
Ian Monk

VINTAGE

Published by Vintage 2005

2 4 6 8 10 9 7 5 3 1

First published with the title *L'Empire des Loups* by
Éditions Albin Michel, 2003

First published in Great Britain in 2004 by The Harvill Press

Vintage
Random House, 20 Vauxhall Bridge Road,
London SW1V 2SA

Random House Australia (Pty) Limited
20 Alfred Street, Milsons Point, Sydney
New South Wales 2061, Australia

Random House New Zealand Limited
18 Poland Road, Glenfield, Auckland 10, New Zealand

Random House (Pty) Limited
Isle of Houghton, Corner Boundary Road & Carse O'Gowrie,
Houghton, 2198, South Africa

The Random House Group Limited Reg. No. 954009
www.randomhouse.co.uk/vintage

A CIP catalogue record for this book is
available from the British Library

This book is supported by the French Ministry of Foreign Affairs, as
part of the Burgess Programme headed for the French Embassy in
London by the Institut Français du Royaume-Uni

ISBN 0 099 46666 X

Printed and bound in Great Britain by
Cox & Wyman Limited, Reading, Berkshire

For Priscilla

I

CHAPTER 1

"Red."

Anna Heymes was feeling increasingly ill at ease. The experiment was danger-free, but the idea that someone could read her mind at that very moment deeply disturbed her.

"Blue."

She was lying on a stainless-steel table, in the middle of a shadowy room, her head inside the central opening of a white, circular machine. Just above her face was a mirror, fixed at an angle, with small squares being projected onto it. All she had to do was announce what colour they were.

"Yellow."

A drip was slowly pouring into her left arm. Dr Eric Ackermann had briefly explained to her that it was labelled water, allowing blood flows to be located in the brain.

Other colours appeared. Green. Orange. Pink . . . then the mirror went dark.

Anna remained still, her arms by her sides, as though in a coffin. A few yards to her left, she could make out the vague, aquatic glassiness of the cabin where Eric Ackermann was sitting beside her husband, Laurent. She pictured the two men staring at the observation screens, observing the activity of her neurons. She felt spied on, pillaged, as though defiled in her closest intimacy.

Ackermann's voice echoed in the transmitter fitted in her ear: "That's fine, Anna. Now the squares are going to start shifting about. You just have to describe the movements. Just use one word at a time: right, left, up, down . . ."

The geometrical shapes immediately started moving, forming a

3

brightly coloured mosaic, as vibrant and fluid as a school of tiny fish. In the mike attached to her transmitter she said: "Right."

Then the squares rose to the top of the frame.

"Up."

The exercise went on for a few minutes. Slowly, monotonously, feeling more and more drowsy, the heat the mirror adding to her torpor. She was about to drift off to sleep.

"Perfect," Ackermann said. "This time, I'm going to present you with a story told in a variety of different ways. Listen to each one carefully."

"And what am I supposed to say?"

"Nothing. Just listen."

A few seconds later a female voice echoed in her receiver. It was speaking in a foreign language, with an Asian or perhaps oriental tonality.

A short silence followed. Then the story started again in French. But the syntax was all wrong. The verbs were all in the infinitive, the articles did not agree, the liaisons were incorrect . . .

Anna tried to decipher this pidgin, but then another version started up. This time, nonsense words cropped up in the tale . . . What did it all mean? Suddenly, silence filled her ears, making the cylinder feel even darker.

After a time, the doctor said: "Next test. When you hear the name of a country, give me its capital."

Anna was about to agree, but the first name was already ringing in her ears: "Sweden."

Without thinking, she replied: "Stockholm."

"Venezuela."

"Caracas."

"New Zealand."

"Auckland, no, Wellington."

"Senegal."

"Dakar."

The capitals came to mind easily. Her answers were automatic, and she was pleased with the result. So her memory had not been completely lost. What could Ackermann and Laurent see on the screens? Which zones were being activated in her brain?

"Last test," the neurologist announced. "Some faces are going to appear. You must name them as quickly as you can."

4

She had read somewhere that a simple sign – a word, a gesture, a visual detail – could trigger a phobia. It was what psychiatrists called an anxiety signal. Signal was the right word. In her case, the very word "face" was enough to make her uneasy. She immediately felt she was suffocating, her stomach became heavy, her limbs stiffened, and a burning lump filled her throat . . .

A black-and-white portrait of a woman appeared in the mirror. Blonde curls, sultry lips, beauty spot above her mouth. Easy.

"Marilyn Monroe."

An engraving replaced the photograph. Dark look, square jaw, wavy hair.

"Beethoven."

A round face, as smooth as cellophane, with two slanting eyes.

"Mao Tse-tung."

Anna was surprised that she could recognise them so easily. Others followed: Michael Jackson, the *Mona Lisa*, Albert Einstein . . . It felt as though she was looking at the bright projections of a magic lantern. She replied unhesitatingly. Her uneasiness was receding.

Then suddenly, a portrait brought her to a halt. A man aged about forty, but with still-youthful looks and prominent eyes. His fair hair and eyebrows added to his look of an indecisive teenager.

A sensation of fear went through her, like an electric shock. Pain pressed down on her chest. The face looked familiar, but she could put no name to it. It evoked no precise memories. Her head was a dark tunnel. Where had she seen this man before? Was he an actor? A singer? An old acquaintance? The picture was replaced by a long face, topped with round glasses. Her mouth dry, she answered: "John Lennon."

Che Guevara then appeared, but Anna said: "Eric, wait . . ."

The show went on. A self-portrait of Van Gogh glittered with its sharp colours. Anna gripped the microphone.

"Eric, please!"

The image froze. Anna felt the colours and heat refract on to her skin. After a pause, Ackermann asked: "What?"

"Who was the person I didn't recognise?"

No reply. The differently coloured eyes of David Bowie glimmered on the angled glass. She sat up and spoke more loudly. "Eric. I asked you a question. Who was it?"

The mirror went black. In a second, her eyes grew accustomed to the darkness. She saw her livid, bony reflection in the titled rectangle. A death's head.

The doctor finally replied. "It was Laurent, Anna. Laurent Heymes. Your husband."

CHAPTER 2

"So how long have you been having these fits of abstraction?"

Anna did not reply. It was almost noon. She had been having tests all morning: X-rays, scans, the MRI and, finally, those tests in the circular machine . . . She felt empty, worn out, lost. And this office made her feel no better. It was a narrow, windowless room, too brightly lit, with stacks of files everywhere, in the metal cabinets, on the floor. The pictures on the wall depicted open brains, shaved scalps with dotted lines, as though ready to be cut up. That was all she needed . . .

Eric Ackermann repeated: "How long, Anna?"

"For over a month."

"Be more precise. You can remember the first time, I suppose?"

Of course she could remember. How could she ever forget?

"It was on 4 February. In the morning. I was coming out of the bathroom and I bumped into Laurent in the corridor. He was on his way out to the office. He smiled at me. I jumped. I didn't know who he was."

"Not at all?"

"Not at that moment. Then everything came back together again in my mind."

"Can you describe exactly what you felt at that moment?"

She shrugged in hesitation under her black and bronze shawl.

"It was a weird, fleeting sensation. Like something I had already experienced. But it only lasted a moment." She clicked her fingers. "Then everything went back to normal."

"What did you think at the time?"

"I put it down to tiredness."

Ackermann jotted down something on the pad in front of him.

"Did you tell Laurent about it that morning?"

"No. I didn't think it was serious."

"When did the second fit happen?"

"The following week. It happened again several times."

"Always with Laurent?"

"Yes, always with him."

"But every time you ended up recognising him?"

"That's right. But as time went by, it seemed to take longer for the penny to drop . . ."

"Did you tell him about it then?"

"No, I didn't."

"Why not?"

She crossed her legs and laid her slender hands on her dark silk skirt, like a brace of pale birds.

"I thought talking about it would make the problem worse, and then . . ."

The neurologist looked up. His red hair reflected in the rings of his glasses.

"Then what?"

"Well, it isn't something that's easy to admit to your husband. He . . ."

She felt Laurent's presence, standing behind her, leaning on the metal cabinets.

"Laurent was becoming a stranger to me."

The doctor seemed to sense her uneasiness. He changed tack. "Have you had the same difficulty recognising other faces?"

"Sometimes," she hesitated. "But it's extremely rare."

"Who with, for example?"

"In the neighbourhood shops. At work, too. I don't recognise some of the customers, even though they're regulars."

"What about your friends?"

Anna gestured vaguely. "I don't have any friends."

"And your family?"

"My parents are dead. I just have some uncles and aunts in the South-West. But I never see them."

Ackermann continued writing. His face gave nothing away. It looked as though it was set in resin.

Anna hated this man, a family friend of Laurent. He sometimes came to have dinner with them, but he always remained as cold as ice. Unless, of course, the conversation turned to his field of research – the brain, cerebral geography, the human cognitive system. Then there was a transformation: he became animated, enthusiastic, beating the air with his long brown arms.

"So it's Laurent's face that poses the biggest problem for you?" he resumed.

"Yes. But then he's also the closest to me. The person I see most."

"Do you have any other memory problems?"

Anna bit her lip. Once again, she hesitated. "No."

"Problems of orientation?"

"No."

"Of elocution?"

"No."

"Do you have difficulties making certain movements?"

She did not answer. Then she smiled weakly. "You think I have Alzheimer's disease, don't you?"

"I'm checking, that's all."

It was the first explanation that had occurred to Anna. She had gathered information on the subject and consulted medical dictionaries. Failure to recognise faces was a symptom of Alzheimer's.

As though talking to a child, Ackermann added: "You're not nearly old enough. And anyway I would have noticed at once during the tests. A brain afflicted with a degenerative disease has a quite specific morphology. These are just questions I have to ask you if I'm going to make a full diagnosis, do you understand?"

Without waiting for a reply, he went on: "So do you or do you not have difficulties making certain movements?"

"No."

"Any trouble sleeping?"

"No."

"Any inexplicable weariness?"

"No."

"Do you get migraines?"

"Never."

The doctor closed his notepad and stood up. This movement always created the same surprise. He stood at almost seven feet, but weighed just ten stone. A beanpole in a white coat which looked as if it had been slung there to dry.

He was a real, flaming red-head. His wiry unkempt locks were the colour of burning honey. Ochre freckles covered his skin, even his eyelids. His face was angular, decked with metal glasses as thin as blades.

His physiognomy seemed to have removed him from time. He was older than Laurent, about fifty, but he still looked like a young man. Wrinkles had formed on his face, but without attacking the essential: his eagle-like features, sharp and inscrutable. Only acne scars marked his cheeks, giving him real flesh and a past.

He paced up and down in his tiny office for a moment in silence. The seconds ticked by. Anna could take no more. She asked: "For God's sake, what's wrong with me?"

The neurologist fiddled with a metallic object in his pocket. Presumably his keys. But it was the sound that seemed to set him talking at last.

"Let me start by explaining the experiment we've just conducted."

"It's about time."

"The machine we used is a positron camera. What specialists call a Petscan. It uses Positron Emission Tomography, or PET for short. It allows us to observe zones of mental activity in real time by localising concentrations of blood in the brain. I wanted to conduct a sort of general check-up on you, by looking at several large areas of the brain that have been positively localised. Such as vision, language and memory."

Anna thought back over the various tests. The squares of colour, the story told in various ways, the names of capital cities. It was easy to see how each exercise fitted into the context. But Ackermann was off: "Take language for instance. Everything happens in the frontal lobe, in a region which is itself subdivided into sub-systems devoted to aural comprehension, vocabulary, syntax, meaning, prosody . . ." (He pointed at his skull.) "It is the association of these zones that allows us to understand and use language. Thanks to the various versions of my little tale, I stimulated each of these subdivisions in your brain."

He continued to pace up and down his tiny room. The pictures on the wall appeared and disappeared as he moved. Anna noticed a strange engraving of a coloured monkey with a large mouth and huge hands. Despite the heat of the strip-light, her spine was frozen.

"And so?" she murmured.

He opened his hands in what was meant to be a reassuring manner.

"So, everything's fine. Language, vision and memory. Each region was activated normally."

"Except when I was shown the portrait of Laurent."

Ackermann bent down over his desk and turned his computer screen around. Anna discovered the digital image of a brain. A luminous green transverse section. The inside was totally dark.

"This is your brain when you were looking at the picture of Laurent. No reaction. No connections. An empty image."

"What does it mean?"

The neurologist stood up and put his hands back into his pockets. He stuck out his chest in a dramatic manner. The moment had come for the verdict.

"I think you have a lesion."

"A lesion?"

"Which is specifically affecting the zone dealing with the recognition of faces."

Anna was stupefied.

"There's a zone . . . for faces?"

"That's right. There's a specialised neuronal system for that purpose, in the right hemisphere, at the back of the brain in the ventral temporal cortex. It was discovered in the 1950s. People who had suffered from a vascular incident in that region could no longer recognise faces. Since then, thanks to Petscan, we have localised it even more precisely. For example, we know that the region is particularly highly developed in people who watch the entrances of night clubs and casinos."

"But I recognise most people's faces," she broke in. "During the tests, I identified all of the portraits . . ."

"All except the one of your husband. And that's a vital indication."

Ackermann placed his two index fingers on his lips in a sign of deep thought. When he was not icy cold, he was expansive.

"We have two sorts of memory. There are the things we learn at school, and the things we learn in our daily lives. And they don't use the same path in the brain. I think you're suffering from a faulty connection between the instant analysis of faces and their comparison with personal memories. A lesion must be blocking the route to this mechanism. That's why you can recognise Einstein, but not Laurent, who belongs to your personal archives."

"And . . . is there a cure?"

"Indeed there is. We can move the function to another, healthy part of your brain. Adaptability is one of the mind's strong points. To achieve this, we'll have to conduct some therapy. A sort of mental training, with regular exercises backed up by the right medication."

The neurologist's grave tones undermined the good news.

"So what's the problem?" Anna asked.

"Where the lesion came from. There I have to admit that I've drawn a blank. There's no sign of any tumour, or neurological anomaly. You haven't had any head injuries or suffered from a stroke, which could have stopped irrigation of that part of the brain." He clicked his tongue. "We'll have to carry some further, more detailed tests in order to diagnose the origin."

"What sort of tests?"

The doctor sat down behind his desk. His glassy stare fell on her.

"A biopsy. A tiny sample of cortical tissue."

It took Anna a few seconds to understand, then a wave of terror crossed her face. She turned towards Laurent, but saw that he was already looking in agreement at Ackermann. Her fear was replaced by anger. They were in it together. Her fate had been decided. Probably that very morning.

Words trembled out from her lips. "No way."

For the first time, the neurologist smiled. The smile was meant to be reassuring, but looked totally false.

"There's nothing to worry about. We'll perform a stereotaxic biopsy. It's just a little probe which . . ."

"No one's touching my brain."

Anna got to her feet and wrapped herself up in her shawl: wings of a raven lined with gold. Laurent broke his silence: "Don't take it like that. Eric has assured me that . . ."

"So you're on his side, are you?"

"We're all on your side, Anna," Ackermann purred.

She pulled back to get a better look at this pair of hypocrites.

11

"No one's touching my brain," she repeated in a stronger voice. "I'd rather lose my memory completely, or die from the disease. I'm never setting foot here again."

Suddenly in the grip of panic, she yelled: "Never, do you hear me?"

CHAPTER 3

She ran along the deserted corridor, leapt down the stairs, then came to a halt in the doorway of the building. She felt the cold wind calling to her life blood. Sunlight flooded the courtyard. It made Anna think of the clearness of summer, without heat or leaves on the trees, which had been frozen for better conservation.

On the far side of the courtyard, Nicolas the chauffeur noticed her and jumped out of the saloon car to open the door. Anna shook her head at him. With a trembling hand, she rummaged through her bag looking for her cigarettes, lit one, then savoured the acrid smoke that filled her throat.

The Henri-Becquerel Institute was made up of several four-storey buildings surrounding a patio dotted with trees and dense shrubs. The dull grey or pink façades were decked with warning sings: NO UN-AUTHORISED ENTRY, MEDICAL STAFF ONLY, DANGER. In this damned hospital, the slightest detail seemed hostile to her.

She breathed in another throatful of smoke. The taste of the roasted tobacco calmed her, as if she had cast her anger into its tiny flames. She closed her eyes, abandoning herself to its heady odour.

The sound of footsteps behind her.

Laurent walked past her without looking round, crossed the court-yard, then opened the rear door of the car. He waited for her, tapping the concrete with his brightly polished moccasins, his features tense. Anna threw away her Marlboro and went over to him. She slid onto the leather seat. Laurent walked round the car and got in beside her. After this little silent routine, the chauffeur pulled away and drove down the slope of the car park with all the majestic slowness of a space ship.

Several soldiers were on guard duty in front of the white and red barrier at the gate.

"I'll go and get my passport back," Laurent said.

Anna looked at her hands. They were still trembling. She took a compact from her bag and observed her face in its oval mirror. She was almost expecting to see marks on her skin, as though her internal upheaval had been like a violent punch. But there was nothing. She still had the same bright, regular features, the same snowy whiteness, framed with Cleopatra-style hair; the same dark blue eyes rising up towards her temples, their eyelids lowered slightly with the languidness of a cat.

She saw that Laurent was coming back. He was leaning over in the wind, lifting up the collar of his black coat. She suddenly felt a warm wave of desire. She observed him: his fair curls, his prominent eyes, that torment creasing his brows . . . He pulled his coat closer to his body with the uncertain movement of a cautious, timid child, which sat strangely with his power as a top-ranking civil servant. It was like when he ordered a cocktail and described with little pinches the proportions he wanted. Or when he slid his hands between his thighs and raised his shoulders to show he was cold or else embarrassed. It was this fragility that had appealed to her, the weaknesses and failings that contrasted with his real power. But what remained of her love for him? What could she remember of it?

Laurent sat back down by her side. The barrier rose. As they passed, he directed a firm salute at the armed men. This gesture of respect irritated Anna once more. Her desire faded. She asked coldly: "Why all these policemen?"

"Soldiers," Laurent corrected her. "They're soldiers."

The car slipped into the traffic stream. Place du Général-Leclerc in Orsay was tiny and immaculately groomed. A church, a town hall, a florist's shop: each element clearly stood out.

"Why these soldiers?" she pressed him.

Laurent replied absently.

"It's because of the Oxygen-15."

"The what?"

He did not look at her, his fingers were tapping the window.

"Oxygen-15. The labelled water that was injected into your blood for the experiment. It's radioactive."

"How nice."

Laurent turned towards her. He was trying to look reassuring, but his eyes revealed how annoyed he was.

"It's not at all dangerous."

"Which explains why there are all these guards I suppose?"

"Don't be stupid. In France, any activity using nuclear materials is supervised by the Atomic Energy Commission. And this implies the presence of soldiers, that's all. Eric has no choice but to work with the army."

Anna could not help sneering. Laurent stiffened. "What's the matter?"

"Nothing. You just had to find the only hospital in the Paris region that has more khaki uniforms than white coats."

He shrugged and stared at the countryside. The car had already turned on to the motorway, and was heading into the Bièvre valley. Dark brown and red forests rose and fell away into the distance.

The clouds were back. Far away, a pale light was struggling to make its way through the low wisps in the sky. Yet it still felt as if the heat of the sun was about to take command and inflame the countryside.

They had been driving for over a quarter of an hour before Laurent opened his mouth again. "You should trust Eric."

"No one is going to touch my brain."

"Eric knows what he's doing. He's one of the best neurologists in Europe."

"And a childhood friend. As you keep telling me."

"You're lucky he's treating you. You . . ."

"I'm not going to be his guinea-pig."

"His guinea-pig?" Laurent clearly articulated each syllable. "His *guinea-pig*? Whatever do you mean?"

"Ackermann was observing me. My condition interests him, that's all. He's a researcher, not a doctor."

Laurent sighed. "You're being paranoid. Really, you are . . ."

"So, I'm mad, am I?" Her mirthless laughter fell like an iron curtain. "That's hardly news is it?"

This outbreak of lugubrious merriment made her husband even angrier. "And so? Are you just going to sit there and wait while the disease gets worse?" He was writhing on his seat.

"You're right. I'm sorry. I've been talking nonsense."

Silence once more filled the car.

The countryside looked increasingly like a blaze of damp grasses, reddish, sullen, mingled with grey mists. The woods continued as far as the eye could see, at first indistinct then, as they drew nearer, in the shape of crimson claws, fine carvings, dark arabesques . . .

From time to time a village appeared, with a rural church steeple jutting up. Then a spotlessly white water tower trembled in the hazy light. It seemed unbelievable that they were just a few miles from Paris.

Laurent launched his last distress flare. "Just promise me you'll agree to have more tests done. And I don't mean a biopsy. It will only take a few days."

"We'll see."

"I'll go with you. I'll devote all the time we need. We're with you, you do understand that?"

Anna did not much like the word "we". Laurent was in full association with Ackermann. She was already more of a patient than a wife.

Suddenly, from the top of the hills of Meudon, Paris appeared in a flash of light. The entire city lay there, with its endless white roofs, glittering like a lake of ice, stuck with crystals, peaks of frost and clumps of snow, while the skyscrapers of La Défense stood like icebergs. Gleaming with clarity, the city was burning in the sunlight.

This dazzling sight cast them into a dumb stupor. They crossed the pont de Sèvres then drove through Boulogne-Billancourt without exchanging a word.

When they were approaching Porte de Saint-Cloud, Laurent asked: "Shall I drop you off at home?"

"No, at work."

"You told me you were taking the day off." His voice was tinged with reproach.

"I thought I'd be more tired than this," Anna lied. "I don't want to leave Clothilde on her own. On Saturdays the shop's taken by storm."

"Clothide and the shop . . ." he repeated sarcastically.

"What about it?"

"This job, I mean . . . It's beneath you."

"Beneath *you*, you mean."

Laurent did not reply. Maybe he had not even heard her last comment. He leant forward to see what was happening in front of them. The traffic had ground to a halt on the ring-road.

Impatiently he asked the driver to "get us out of here". Nicolas got the message. From the glove compartment he produced a magnetic flashing light, which he placed on the roof of the car. With its siren blaring, the Peugeot 607 pulled out from the traffic jam and sped away again.

Nicolas kept his foot down. His fingers gripping the back of the front seat, Laurent followed each turn, every twist of the wheel. He looked like a little boy concentrating on a video game. Anna was always amazed to see that, despite all his qualifications and his job as Director of the Ministry of the Interior's Centre des études et bilans, Laurent had never forgotten the excitement of the beat, the call of the street. "Lousy cop," she thought.

At porte Maillot, they turned off the ring-road and into avenue des Ternes, where the driver at last switched off the siren. Anna was back in her universe. Rue Saint-Honoré and its precious window displays; the Salle Pleyel with its high bay windows through which, on the first floor, slender dancers could be seen moving around; the mahogany arcades of Mariage Frères, where she bought her special teas.

Before opening the door, she picked up the conversation where the siren had interrupted it.

"It's not just a job, you know. It's my way of staying in contact with the outside world. Of not going completely nuts in that flat."

She got out of the car, then bent down towards him. "It's that or the lunatic asylum, you understand?"

They exchanged a final look and, in a twinkling of an eye, were allies once more. She would never have used the word "love" to describe their relationship. It was based on complicity and sharing, which lay beyond desire, passion or the fluctuations caused by days and moods. They were calm, underground waters mixing deeply. They could then understand each other, reading between their words, between their lips . . .

Suddenly, she felt hopeful once more. Laurent would help her, love her, support her. The shadow had now lightened. He asked: "Shall I pick you up this evening?"

She nodded, blew him a kiss, then headed towards the Maison du Chocolat.

CHAPTER 4

The bell on the door rang as though she were an ordinary customer. Its simple, familiar notes reassured her. She had applied for this job a month before, after seeing it advertised in the shop window. At the time she had just been looking for something to take her mind off her obsessions. But she had in fact found far more.

A refuge.

A magic circle protecting her from her anxieties.

At two in the afternoon, the shop was empty. Clothilde must have taken advantage of this quiet moment to go to the stockroom.

Anna crossed the floor. The entire shop looked like a chocolate box, wavering between brown and gold. In the middle, the main counter rose up like an orchestra, with its black or cream classics in squares, circles and domes. To the left, on the marble slab of the till, were the "extras", the small delights customers picked up at the last moment while paying. To the right were the by-products: fruit jellies, sweets, nougat, like a series of variations on a theme. Above, the shelves contained more gleaming delicacies, wrapped in cellophane, whose bright glints were even more appetising.

Anna noticed that Clothilde had finished the Easter window display. Woven baskets contained eggs and hens of every size; chocolate houses with caramel roofs were being watched over by marzipan piglets; chicks were playing on a swing, in a sky of paper daffodils.

"Is that you? Great! The assortments have just arrived."

Clothilde appeared on the goods lift at the back of the shop, which was worked by an old-fashioned hoisting winch, and allowed them to bring goods up directly from the car park on square du Roule. She leapt off the platform, strode over the piles of boxes and stood radiant and breathless in front of Anna.

In just a few weeks, Clothilde had become one of her reassuring landmarks. She was twenty-eight, with a small pink nose, and light brown hair which fluttered in front of her eyes. She had two children, a husband "in the bank", a mortgage and a destiny that had been traced out with a set-square. She lived in a world of certain happiness that amazed Anna. Being with her was both comforting and irritating. Anna just could not believe this faultless scenario devoid of any surprise. There was a kind of obstinacy or underlying falsehood in such a credo. In any case, it was an inaccessible mirage for her. At the age of thirty-one, Anna was childless and had always lived in an atmosphere of malaise, uncertainty and fear of the future.

"It's been a hell of a day. I haven't stopped."

Clothilde picked up a box and headed towards the stockroom at the back of the shop. Anna slipped her shawl over her shoulder and did likewise. Saturday was such a busy day that they had to make the most of the slightest lull to prepare new trays.

They went into the windowless room, ten yards square. Piles of cardboard and layers of bubble wrap were already cluttering the floor.

Clothilde put down her box, pushed her hair back and pouted.

"I forgot to ask you. How did it go?"

"They made me take tests all morning. The doctor said something about a lesion."

"A lesion?"

"A dead area in the brain. The region that recognises faces."

"That's crazy. Is there a cure?"

Anna put down her box and repeated parrot-fashion what Ackermann had told her. "Yes, there's going to be treatment. With memory exercises and medication to shift that function to another, healthy part of my brain."

"That's marvellous!"

Clothilde was smiling broadly, as though she had just learned that Anna had completely recovered. Her reactions rarely fitted the situation, and revealed a profound indifference. In reality, Clothilde was oblivious to other people's misfortunes. Grief, anxiety and doubt slid off her like drops of water on an oilskin. Yet, at that moment, she seemed to sense her mistake.

She was saved by the bell.

"I'll go," she said, turning on her heel. "Make yourself comfortable. I'll be back."

Anna pushed aside some boxes and sat down on a stool. She started laying out some "Romeos" on a tray – squares of fresh coffee mousse. The room was already full of the heady odours of chocolate. At the end of the day, their clothes and even their sweat smelt of it, and their

18

saliva was saturated with sugar. It is said that barmen get drunk from breathing in vapours of alcohol. Do chocolate sellers get fat from being around such delicacies?

Anna had not put on an ounce. In fact, she *never* put on any weight. She ate like a pig, but the very food seemed to avoid her. The glucosides, lipids and fibres went through her without touching the sides.

While she was arranging the chocolates, Ackermann's words came back to her. A lesion. An illness. A biopsy. No. She would never let them slice her up. And especially not him, with his cold gestures and insect eyes.

In any case, she did not believe in his diagnosis.

She just could not believe it.

For the simple reason that she had not told him a tenth of the truth.

Since the month of February, the fits had become far more frequent than she had admitted. These moments of emptiness now came upon her at any time, anywhere. A dinner party with friends, a visit to the hairdresser's, when buying a magazine. Anna now often found herself surrounded by strangers, with nameless faces, in the very heart of her daily life.

Even the nature of the attacks had changed.

It was no longer just a question of names slipping her mind and of fits of abstraction. She also had terrifying hallucinations. Faces went hazy, trembled, then altered before her very eyes. Expressions and looks began to waver and float as though seen through water.

Sometimes they looked like faces made of burning wax, which melted and folded into itself, creating demonic grimaces. On other occasions, features vibrated and shook, until a series of different expressions became simultaneously juxtaposed. A cry. Laughter. A kiss. They all merged together in a single physiognomy. A nightmare.

Anna lowered her eyes when walking in the street. At parties, she never looked at the person she was speaking with. She was becoming nervy, timorous and scared. The "others" now just reflected back the image of her own madness. A mirror of terror. Nor had she really described the sensations she experienced concerning Laurent. In fact, her uneasiness never went away, never completely disappeared after a fit. There was always a trace left, a hint of fear. As though she no longer really recognised her husband. As if there was a voice whispering to her: "It's him, but it isn't him." Deep down, she sensed that Laurent's appearance had changed, that it had been altered by plastic surgery.

Ridiculous.

This craziness had an even more absurd aspect. While her husband was becoming ever more a stranger to her, one of the shop's regular customers was starting to feel strikingly familiar. She was sure that she had already seen him somewhere . . . It was impossible for her to say where or when, but her memory lit up in his presence, with an electrostatic tingle. And yet, this spark never led to a precise memory.

The man came once or twice a week and always bought the same Jikola chocolates – squares filled with marzipan, rather like oriental delicacies. He in fact spoke with a slight, perhaps Arabic accent. He was about forty, always dressed in the same way, in jeans with a threadbare corduroy jacket buttoned up to his neck, like an eternal student. Anna and Clothilde had nicknamed him "Mister Corduroys".

Every day they looked out for him. It was a game of suspense for them, an enigma, a pleasant way to pass the time. They often elaborated hypotheses. He was a childhood friend of Anna's, or an old boyfriend, or instead a furtive pick-up merchant and she had caught his eye at some cocktail party . . .

Anna now knew that the truth was far simpler. This reminiscence was just another sort of hallucination set off by the lesion. She should not focus on what she could see, or what she felt about anybody's face, because she no longer had a reliable system of references.

The door of the shop opened. Anna jumped – she realised that the chocolates were melting in her clenched hands. Clothilde appeared in the doorway. She whispered between her curls: "It's him."

Mister Corduroys was standing beside the Jikolas.

"Good afternoon," Anna said at once. "Can I help you?"

"Two hundred grams, as usual please."

She slipped behind the main counter, picked up the tongs and a Cellophane bag, then started to fill it with the pieces of chocolate. At the same time, she looked round at the man, her eyes veiled by her eyelashes. First she saw his large leather shoes, his over-long jeans crinkling up like an accordion, and then his saffron-yellow corduroy jacket, worn down in places into a threadbare lustrous orange.

Finally, she dared a glance at his face.

It was uncouth, square, framed with dishevelled brown hair. More the face of a peasant than of a refined student. He was frowning in an expression of annoyance or else concealed anger.

Yet Anna had already noticed that when he opened his eyelids they revealed long feminine eyelashes and violet irises, ringed with gilded black: the back of a bumblebee flying over a field of dark violets. Where had she seen that look before?

She placed the packet on the scales.

"Eleven euros please."

The man paid, picked up the chocolates and spun round. A second later, he was outside.

Despite herself, Anna followed him to the door. Clothilde joined her. They watched the figure crossing rue du Faubourg-Saint-Honoré, then diving into a black limousine with frosted windows and foreign number plates.

They stayed there on the doorstep, like two crickets in the sunlight.

"So?" Clothilde finally asked. "Who is he? Don't you know yet?"

The car vanished into the traffic. In answer, Anna said: "Got a cigarette?"

Clothilde removed a crumpled pack of Marlboro Lights from her trouser pocket. Anna inhaled the first drag, finding the same soothing sensation as she had experienced that morning in the hospital courtyard. Clothilde said, sceptically: "There's something wrong about your story."

Anna turned round, elbow raised, cigarette pointed like a weapon. "What?"

"Let's suppose that you once knew this person, and he's since changed."

"Well?"

Clothilde puckered up her lips, making the sound of a beer bottle being opened. "Well, why doesn't he recognise you?"

Anna watched the cars driving beneath the dull sky, splashes of light criss-crossing their bodywork. Further on, she could see the wooden façade of Mariage Frères, the icy windows of La Marée restaurant and its doorman who was staring at her placidly.

Her words vanished into the blue-tinted smoke: "Crazy. I'm going crazy."

CHAPTER 5

Once a week Laurent met up with the same "pals" for dinner. It was an unchanging ritual, a sort of ceremony. They were not childhood friends, or members of any particular circle. They had no shared passion. They were simply part of the same corporation: policemen. They had met at various stages of their careers and today each of them had reached the top of his speciality.

Like the other wives, Anna was excluded from these get-togethers, and when the dinner was held in their flat on avenue Hoche she was asked to go to the cinema.

Then, three weeks before, Laurent had asked her to join them at their next meeting. First she refused, especially as her husband had then added in his male nurse tones: "You'll see. It'll take your mind off things." But she relented. She was in fact rather curious to meet Laurent's colleagues, and to be able to see at first hand other examples of top-ranking policemen. After all, he was so far the only model she knew.

She had not regretted her decision. During the party, she got to know men who were hard, yet passionate, who talked to each other without fear or reserve. She felt like the queen of the group, the only woman on board, in front of whom the police officers competed with one another to find the best stories, feats and revelations.

Since that first evening, she now attended all their dinners, and had got to know them better. She had spotted their tics and strong points – and also their obsessions. These parties provided her with a real image of the universe of the police force. A black-and-white world of violence and certainty, both clichéd and fascinating.

The guests were always the same, barring the occasional exception.

Generally it was Alain Lacroux who led the conversation. This thin, tall, upright fifty-year-old punctuated the end of each of his sentences with a stab from his fork or the wag of his head. Even the lilt of his southern accent added to this art of finishing, of chiselled expression. Everything about him sang, rippled, smiled – no one would ever have suspected his real responsibilities. He was second in command of Paris's Affaires criminelles.

Pierre Caracilli was his opposite. Small, squat and dark, he was constantly grumbling in a slow almost hypnotic voice. It was this voice that had put to sleep many a criminal's defences and extracted confessions from the hardiest of them. Caracilli was Corsican. He held an important position in the Direction de la Surveillance du Territoire (or DST).

Jean-François Gaudemer was neither upright nor laid-back: he was a compact, solid, stubborn rock. Beneath his high, balding forehead his eyes glistened with a darkness that seemed to announce an approaching storm. Anna pricked up her ears whenever he spoke. What he said was cynical, his stories were terrifying, but you experienced a sort of gratitude in his presence; the ambiguous feeling that a veil had been lifted on the hidden workings of the world. He was the head of OCRTIS or Office Central de Répression du Trafic Illicite des Stupéfiants. France's Mister Dope Trade.

But Anna's favourite was Philippe Charlier. This six foot four colossus was squeezed into his expensive suits. Nicknamed "The Jolly Green Giant" by his colleagues, he had the head of a boxer, which was as dense as a stone and edged by a grey-flecked moustache and mop of hair. He spoke too loudly, laughed like a car engine starting on a cold morning and forced his listeners into sharing his funny stories by taking them by the shoulder.

To understand him, you needed a sexual glossary. He called an erection a "bone in the pants", described wiry hair as "bollock fur" and, when he spoke about his holidays in Bangkok, summed them up as follows: "Taking your wife to Thailand is like taking beer to Munich."

Anna found him vulgar, off-putting, but irresistible. He gave off an animalistic power which was extremely "police". You could not imagine him anywhere other than in an ill-lit office, dragging confessions out of suspects. Or else, in the field, commanding men armed with assault rifles.

Laurent had told her that Charlier had cold-bloodedly killed at least five men during his career. His field was terrorism. He had fought the same war in a number of different units, such as the DST, the DGSE and the DNAT. Twenty-five years of undercover operations and raids. When Anna asked for more details, Laurent waved her questions away: "It would only be the tip of the iceberg."

That evening the party was being held at his flat on avenue de Breteuil. It was a huge old Parisian apartment with varnished parquet floors, full of colonial knick-knacks. Anna's curiosity had pushed her into exploring those rooms that were accessible. There was not the slightest trace of a female presence. Charlier was a confirmed bachelor.

It was eleven p.m. The guests were slumped in nonchalant post-prandial positions, encircled by the smoke of their cigars.

In this month of March 2002, just a few weeks before the presidential elections, they were rivalling one another with their predictions and forecasts, imagining the changes that would take place in the Ministry of the Interior depending on which candidate won. They all seemed ready for a great battle, but unsure whether they would participate.

Philippe Charlier, who was sitting next to Anna, whispered to her: "Aren't you as pissed off as I am with their pig shop talk? Do you know the one about the Swiss man?"

Anna smiled. "You told me it last Saturday."

"What about the Hillbilly at the train station?"

"No."

Charlier leaned his elbows on the table. "There's this Hillbilly about to take the train for the first time. So he stands right on the platform edge waiting for it. An inspector sees him and goes: 'Watch out, if the express comes along it'll suck you off.' And Hillbilly goes: 'Come along train!'"

She took a second to get it, then burst out laughing. Policemen's jokes never got higher than the belt, but at least she had not heard most of them before. She was still laughing when Charlier's face started to distort. Suddenly his features became unclear. They were quite literally undulating across his face.

Anna looked round at the other guests. Their features also seemed dislocated, forming a wave of monstrous, contradictory expressions, mingling flesh, grins and screams . . .

A spasm gripped her. She started breathing through her mouth.

"Are you OK?" Charlier asked.

"I'm . . . I'm hot. I'm going to freshen myself up."

"Shall I show you the way?"

She laid her hand on his shoulder and stood up. "It's OK. I'll find it."

She edged along the wall, leaned on the corner of the mantelpiece, then bumped into an occasional table setting off a chorus of tinkling.

When she reached the door, she glanced round. The sea of faces was still rising in a dance of cries and mingling wrinkles, distorted flesh reaching out to follow her.

Holding back a scream, she left the room.

The hall was unlit. The hanging coats formed disturbing shapes, the half-open doors revealed rays of darkness. Anna stopped in front of a mirror framed with old gold.

She stared at her reflection: a pallid parchment, a ghostly gleam. Beneath her black woollen sweater she seized her trembling shoulders.

Suddenly, a man appeared behind her in the mirror.

She did not recognise him. He had not been there at the dinner. She turned round to face him. Who was he? Where had he sprung from? He looked threatening.

Something twisted and disfigured hovered about his features. His hands gleamed in the shadows like a pair of steel weapons . . .

Anna pulled back, sinking into the hanging coats. The man stepped forward. She could hear the others talking in the next room. She wanted to cry out, but her throat was lined with burning cotton. The face was now just a few inches from her. A reflection from the looking glass glittered in her eyes, dazzling her pupils with a golden flash . . .

"Do you want to go home now?"

Anna stifled a groan. It was Laurent's voice. His face immediately recovered its usual appearance. She felt two hands holding her up and realised that she must have fainted.

"Jesus," Laurent said. "What's the matter with you?"

"My coat. Give me my coat," she demanded, freeing herself from his arms.

The malaise did not diminish. She did not completely recognise her husband. Once again she felt sure that his features had changed, that his face was different, that a secret lurked there, a zone of darkness . . .

Laurent handed her her duffle-coat. He was trembling. He was clearly scared for her, but also for himself. He was worried that his friends would see what was happening. One of the top people in the Ministry of the Interior had a wife who was loony.

She slid on her coat, savouring the feel of the lining. If only she could wrap herself up completely in it and vanish . . .

Bursts of laughter could be heard from the lounge.

"I'll go and say goodbye for both of us."

She heard tones of reproach, then more laughter. Anna looked one more time in the mirror. One day soon, when faced with these features she would ask: "Who is this?"

Laurent came back. She murmured: "Take me home. I want to sleep."

CHAPTER 6

But the fit pursued her in her sleep.

Since the beginning of her attacks, Anna had had the same dream. Black-and-white images paraded before her at various speeds, like in a silent movie.

The scene was also identical. Hungry-looking peasants were waiting at night on the platform of a station. A goods train arrived in a cloud of steam. A sliding door opened. A man wearing a cap appeared and leaned down to take a flag that was being handed to him. The standard bore a strange device: four moons arranged in a star pattern.

The man then stood up, raising his extremely dark eyebrows. He harangued the crowd, waving the banner in the air, but his words were inaudible. Instead, a sort of blanket of noise was created: an awful murmur, made of sighs and children sobbing.

Anna's whispering then mingled with that terrible chant. She spoke to the young voices: "Where are you? Why are you crying?"

In reply, the wind rose on the platform. The four moons on the banner started to glow as if they were fluorescent. The scene descended into pure nightmare. The man's coat opened, revealing a bare chest that was sliced in two and emptied. Then a gust shattered his face. His flesh fell away like ash, starting from below his ears, revealing dark bulging muscles . . .

Anna woke up with a start.

Eyes wide open in the darkness, she recognised nothing. Not the bedroom. Nor the bed. Nor the body sleeping beside her. It took her several seconds to familiarise herself with these strange forms. She leaned back on the wall and wiped the sweat from her face.

Why did this dream keep recurring? What did it have to do with her illness? She felt sure that it was another aspect of what was wrong with her: a mysterious echo, an inexplicable counterpoint to her mental decay. In the darkness, she called out: "Laurent?"

His back turned, her husband did not move. Anna grabbed his shoulder.

"Laurent, are you asleep?"

There was a slight movement, a rustling of the sheets. Then she saw his profile stand out in the shadows. She repeated softly: "Are you asleep?"

"Not any more."

"Can I . . . can I ask you something?"

He half sat up, and leaned his head on the pillows. "Go on."

Anna spoke even more softly – the sobbing from her dream was still echoing in her mind.

"Why . . ." She hesitated. "Why don't we have any children?"

For a second, everything was still. Then Laurent pulled aside the sheets and sat on the side of the bed, turning his back to her. The silence suddenly seemed full of tension and hostility.

He rubbed his face, then announced: "We're going back to see Ackermann."

"What?"

"I'll call him. We'll make an appointment at the hospital."

"Why are you saying this?"

He said over his shoulder: "You lied. You said you didn't have any other memory problems. That there was only the problem of faces."

Anna realised that she had made a mistake. Her question revealed a fresh gulf in her head. All she could see was the nape of Laurent's neck, his vague curls, his straight back. But she could guess how low he felt, and also how angry.

"What did I just say?" she hazarded.

Laurent turned a few degrees towards her.

"You never wanted a child. It was a condition when we married," he raised his voice and lifted his left hand. "Even on our wedding night you made me promise that I'd never ask you for that. You're losing your mind, Anna. We have to do something. We have to have those tests done. To understand what's happening. For Christ's sake, we have to stop it!"

Anna curled up on the far end of the bed.

"Just give me a few more days. There must be another possibility."

"What possibility?"

"I don't know. Just a few days. Please."

He lay down again and hid his head in the sheets. "I'll call Dr Ackermann next Wednesday."

There was no point in thanking him. Anna did not even know why she had asked for this reprieve. Why deny the obvious? Her illness was gaining ground, neuron by neuron, in each region of her brain.

She slid beneath the covers, a good distance from Laurent, and thought over this mystery about having children. Why had she demanded such a promise? What had motivated her at the time? She had no answers. Her own personality was turning into a stranger.

She thought back to her marriage. Eight years ago. She was then just twenty-three.

What could she really remember about it?

A country manor in Saint-Paul-de-Vence, palm trees, broad lawns yellowed by the sun, the laughter of children. She closed her eyes and tried to recover those sensations. A circle of Chinese shadows lengthening across the grass. She could also see bunches of flowers and white hands . . .

Suddenly, a tulle scarf floated into her memory. The material danced before her eyes, disturbing the circle, reducing the greenness of the grass, picking up the light with its fantastic movements.

The material came nearer, until she could feel its weave on her face, then around her lips. Anna opened her mouth in laughter, but the cloth pressed into her throat. She was panting, as it now stuck to the roof of her mouth. And it was not tulle, it was gauze. Surgical gauze that was suffocating her.

She screamed into the night. Her cry produced no sound. She opened her eyes. She had fallen asleep, her mouth pressed into the pillow.

When would it all end? She sat up and felt the sweat on her skin once more. It was this sticky veil that had set off that suffocating feeling.

She got up and went to the bathroom, next to the bedroom. On tiptoes, she found the way inside and closed the door before switching on the light. She pressed the switch then turned towards the mirror over the basin.

Her face was covered with blood.

Red streams covered her forehead, there were scabs beneath her eyes, by her nose, around her lips. Her first thought was that she had hurt herself. But when she took a closer look she saw that she had just had a nose bleed. By wiping her face in the darkness, she had covered herself with her own blood. Her sweat-shirt was soaked in it.

She turned on the cold tap and put out her hands, flooding the basin with a pink whirlpool. She was sure of one thing: this blood symbolised a truth which was trying to wrench itself free from her flesh. A secret that her consciousness refused to recognise or formulate, but which was escaping in an organic flood from her body.

She dipped her head beneath the cool flow, mixing her sobs with the translucent water. As it flowed, she continued to whisper to it: "What's the matter with me? What's the matter with me?"

II

CHAPTER 7

A little golden sword.

That is how he saw it in his mind's eye. In reality he knew that it was only a copper paperknife, with a Spanish-style carved pommel. At the age of eight, Paul had just stolen it from his father's workshop and had then concealed in his bedroom. He could perfectly remember the atmosphere at the time. The closed shutters. The stifling heat. The calm of the siesta.

A summer afternoon like any other.

Except that these few hours would alter the course of his life for ever.

"What are you hiding in your hand?"

Paul tightened his fist. His mother was standing at his bedroom door.

"Show me what you're hiding."

Her voice was calm, with just a hint of curiosity. Paul tightened his grip. She advanced into the half-light, the sunbeams filtered through the slats of the shutters, then she sat down on the edge of the bed and gently opened his hand.

"Why did you take the paperknife?"

He could not see her face in the shadows.

"To defend you."

"To defend me against who?"

Silence.

"Against your dad?"

She leaned over him. Her face appeared in a ray of light. It was swollen, covered with bruises. One of her eyes, white and full of blood, was staring at him like a porthole. She repeated: "To defend me against your dad?"

He nodded. There was a moment of uncertainty, of stillness, then she hugged him in a wave of abandon. Paul pushed her back. It was not tears and pity that he wanted. All that mattered was the coming battle. The promise he had made to himself the previous evening, when his drunken father had started beating his mother until she fainted on the kitchen floor. When the monster had turned round and seen him, a little boy trembling in the doorway, and had warned him: "I'll be back. I'll be back to kill both of you!"

So Paul had armed himself and was awaiting his return, sword in hand.

But he never did come back. Not the next day, nor the day after that. By one of destiny's coincidences, Jean-Pierre Nerteaux was murdered on the very night that he had made his threat. His body was discovered two days later, in his own taxi, near the petrol warehouses in the port of Gennevilliers.

When she learned of the murder, his wife Françoise reacted in a strange way. Instead of going to identify the body, she wanted to go to the place of the crime in order to check that his Peugeot 504 was still in one piece and that there would be no problems with the cab company.

Paul remembered the slightest details: the bus ride to Gennevilliers, the mutterings of his devastated mother, his own apprehension faced with something he did not really understand. But, when they reached the warehouses, he was struck with amazement. Huge crowns of steel rose up from the wasteland. Weeds and shrubs sprouted between the concrete ruins. Steel rods were rusting like metal cactuses. It was a landscape for a Western, like the deserts in the comic books he read.

Under a sweltering sky, the mother and child crossed the storage areas. At the far end of these abandoned fields, they found the Peugeot, half sunk into the grey dunes. Paul soaked up everything that an eight-year-old could understand. The police uniforms, the handcuffs glinting in the sunlight, the muted explanations, the black hands of the break-down men in white light as they bustled about the car . . .

It took him a while to understand that his father had been knifed at the wheel. But only a second to see the lacerations in the back of the seat, through the half-open rear door.

The killer had attacked his victim *through* the seat.

The child was at once struck by how coherent the event was. A day before, he wanted his father to die. He had armed himself, then revealed his criminal plans to his mother. This confession had acted like a curse: some mysterious force had made his wish come true. He might not have held the knife himself, but it was he who had mentally ordered the murder.

From that moment, he had no more memories. Not of the funeral, nor of his mother's complaining, nor of the financial difficulties that marked their daily lives. Paul was completely drawn in on this truth: he was the real murderer.

The true organiser of the massacre.

Much later, in 1987, he enrolled in the law department of the Sorbonne. By doing odd jobs, he had managed to save enough money to rent a room in Paris, away from his mother, who now drank all the time. As a cleaning woman in a supermarket, she was thrilled at the idea that her son was to become a lawyer. But Paul had other ideas.

When he passed his master's degree in 1990, Paul joined the Cannes-Ecluse police academy. Two years later, he was first in his class and could have chosen one of the jobs most coveted by apprentice police officers: the Office Central de Répression du Trafic Illicite de Stupéfiants (or OCRTIS), the temple of dope chasers.

His career looked set. Four years in a central office or an elite unit, then he could take the internal examination to become a commissioner. Before he was forty, Paul Nerteaux would have a top-ranking job in the Ministry of the Interior, on place Beauvau, among the gilded panelling of headquarters. A triumphant success for a boy who had, as they said, a "difficult background".

But Paul was not interested in such a career. His vocation as a policeman lay elsewhere, still linked to his feelings of guilt. Fifteen years after the expedition to Gennevilliers, he was still haunted by remorse. His career was guided by the sole desire to wash away his crime and recover his lost innocence.

He had had to invent personal techniques and secret methods of concentration to master his anxiety attacks. Thanks to this discipline, he had found the means to become an unbending copper. In his "company" he was hated, feared and sometimes admired, but never liked. Because no one understood that his inflexibility and desire to succeed were his defences, a security barrier. It was the only way for him to control his demons. No one knew that in the right-hand drawer of his desk, he still kept a copper paperknife . . .

He tightened his grip on the wheel and concentrated on the road.

Why was he digging up that shit again now? Was it the influence of the rain-soaked landscape? Because it was Sunday, the day of death for the living?

On either side of the motorway, all he could see were the dark furrows of ploughed fields. The horizon itself looked like a final furrow, opening out on to the nothingness of the sky. Nothing could ever happen in this region, except for a slow descent into despair.

He glanced down at the map on the passenger seat. He now had to turn off the motorway and take the A road towards Amiens. After that, he had to take the D235. Ten kilometres later, he would be there.

So as to chase away his dark thoughts, he focused his mind on the man he was going to see: probably the only policeman he did not really want to meet. At the Inspection Générale des Services he had photocopied his file and could now recite his CV by heart . . .

Jean-Louis Schiffer was born in 1943 in Aulnay-sous-Bois, Seine-Saint-Denis. Depending on the context, he was nicknamed either "the Cipher" or "Mister Steel". The Cipher because of the impenetrable mysteries that surrounded the cases he dealt with; Mister Steel because of his reputation of being implacable – and also for his silvery hair, which was long and silky.

After his leaving certificate in 1959, Schiffer was called up for military service in Algeria, in the Aurès mountains. In 1960 he retuned to Algiers where he became an intelligence agent and an active member of the DOP (Détachements Operationnelles de Protection).

In 1963 he returned to France, ranked sergeant. He then joined the police force. First as an ordinary officer, then a sergeant in the Brigade territoriale in Paris's sixth *arrondissement*. He rapidly became noticed for his instinctive street savvy and liking for infiltration. In May 1968 he dived into the throng and mixed with the students. At the time he wore his hair in a ponytail, smoked dope and discreetly noted down the names of the ringleaders. During the clashes on rue Gay-Lussac, he also saved a riot policeman from under a hail of paving stones.

His first act of bravery.

His first distinction.

But this was only the beginning. After being recruited by the Brigade criminelle in 1972, he was made inspector and continued to act heroically, fearing neither fire nor combat. In 1975 he received a medal for bravery. It seemed that nothing could stop his ascent. But then, in 1977, after a short period spent in the famous "anti-gang" squad, he was suddenly transferred. Paul had found a report written at the time and signed by Commissioner Broussard in person, who had noted in the margin "unmanageable".

Schiffer then found his true hunting ground in the First Division of the Police Judiciaire in Paris's tenth *arrondissement*. Refusing all offers of promotion or transfer, for twenty years he dominated the west of the sector, imposing law and order in an area running from the central boulevards to the Gare du Nord and the Gare de l'Est, including part of Sentier, the Turkish quarter with its high immigrant population. During that time he headed a network of informers, and put a check on illegal activities – gambling, drugs and prostitution – while maintaining ambiguous but effective relations with the leaders of the various communities. He also obtained a record success rate in the solving of cases.

According to a widely held opinion in high places, it was thanks to him and him alone that a relative calm reigned in that part of the tenth *arrondissement* from 1978 to 1998. Jean-Louis Schiffer even enjoyed the exceptional honour of prolonging his time on the force from 1999 to 2001.

In April of that year, he finally retired officially. He had been decorated five times, including the Order of Merit, and could boast of two hundred and thirty-nine arrests and four deaths by shooting. At the age of fifty-eight, he had never risen higher than the rank of inspector. He was a copper on the beat, devoted to fieldwork in a single territory.

So much for Mister Steel.

His Cipher side emerged in 1971, when he was caught beating up a prostitute on rue de Michodière, by La Madeleine. The official inquest and investigations by the vice squad led to nothing. No one wanted to testify against the man with silver hair. Another complaint was made in 1979. It was rumoured that Schiffer was racketing whores on rue Jérusalem and rue Saint-Denis.

Another inquiry, another failure.

The Cipher knew how to cover his tracks.

Things turned really serious in 1982. A stock of heroin disappeared from the Bonne-Nouvelle station, after the rounding-up of a network of Turkish dealers. Schiffer's name was on everyone's lips. He was put under investigation. But a year later, he was cleared. No proof, and no witnesses.

As the years went by, suspicions mounted: percentages gleaned from protection rackets, or from illegal gambling syndicates, fiddles involving local bars, or pimping . . . Apparently, he had a finger in every pie, but no one managed to trap him. Schiffer had his sector in a grip of steel. Even inside the force, internal investigators were confronted by the silence of their fellow officers.

Yet everyone still saw the Cipher more as Mister Steel. A hero, a champion of law and order, with a prestigious career behind him.

But one last scandal nearly brought him down. In October 2000, the body of Gazil Hemet, a Turkish illegal immigrant, was found on the tracks of the Gare du Nord. The day before he had been arrested by Schiffer himself as a suspected drug dealer. When accused of "excessive violence", Schiffer riposted that he had freed the suspect before the end of the legal period of detention – which was rather unlike him.

Had Hemet been beaten to death? The autopsy gave no clear answer, because the body had been torn to pieces by the ten past eight express from Brussels. But an independent forensic report spoke of mysterious "wounds" on the Turk's body, which could have been caused by torture techniques. This time, it looked as though Schiffer's career was going to finish behind bars.

Then, in April 2001, the prosecutor decided to drop the charges. What had happened? Who was pulling strings for Jean-Louis Schiffer? Paul had questioned the officers charged with the internal police investigation. They were so disgusted they did not want to reply. Especially because, a few weeks later, Schiffer personally invited them to his farewell drinks party.

He was bent, a bastard and cocky with it.

Such was the shit that Paul was about to encounter.

The motorway exit to Amiens brought him back to the present. He turned off, and took the A road. There were just a few more kilometres to do before he saw the sign to Longères.

Paul drove down the side road as far as the village. He crossed it without slowing down, then spotted another road that led into a waterlogged valley. While driving between the tall grasses, brilliant from the rain, he had a sort of revelation. He suddenly realised why he had thought of his father while driving to meet Jean-Louis Schiffer.

In his own way, the Cipher was the father of all coppers. Half-hero, half-demon, he alone incarnated the best and the worst, rigour and corruption, Good and Evil. A founding father, a Grand Old Man, whom Paul admired despite himself, just as he had admired, from the depths of his hatred, his violent alcoholic father.

CHAPTER 8

When Paul saw the building he was looking for, he nearly burst out laughing. With its enclosing wall and two clock towers shaped like look-out posts, the Longères police officers' retirement home looked just like a prison.

On the other side of the wall, the comparison became even clearer. The yard was surrounded by three main buildings, laid out like horseshoes, each pierced by galleries with dark arcades. Some men were braving the rain and playing *boule*. They wore overalls that recalled the dress of the inmates in all the world's prisons. Just near them, three uniformed officers, presumably visiting a relative, were playing the part of wardens.

Paul savoured the irony of the situation. Longères, financed by the National Police Mutual Association, was the largest retirement home open to officers. It welcomed all ranks so long as they "suffered from no psychosomatic disorder based on or resulting in alcoholism". He now discovered that this famous haven of peace, with its enclosed spaces and masculine populace, was just another prison house. "Return to sender," he thought.

Paul reached the entrance of the main building and pushed open the glass door. A very dark, square hall led to a staircase topped with a dormer window of frosted glass. The place was as hot and stifling as a vivarium, and it stank of medication and urine.

He turned towards the swinging doors to his left, from which a strong smell of food was wafting. It was noon. The inmates were presumably having lunch.

He discovered a refectory with yellow walls and a floor covered with blood-red lino. On the long lines of stainless-steel tables, the plates and cutlery were carefully arranged. Vats of soup were steaming. Everything was in place, but the room was deserted.

Noises came from the next room. Paul approached the din, feeling his heels sink into the sticky floor. Every detail added to the overall atmosphere of gloom. He felt himself age with every step he took.

He passed the doorway. About thirty pensioners in shapeless track-suits were standing with their backs to him, concentrating on the TV. "Now Hint of Joy has gone past Bartok . . ." Horses were galloping across the screen.

As Paul approached, he noticed a single old man sitting in another room to the left. Instinctively, he craned his neck to get a better look at him. Slumped over his plate, the man was toying with a steak at the end of his fork.

Paul had to face facts: this debris was his man.

The Steel and the Cipher.

The officer with two hundred and thirty-nine arrests.

He crossed the room. Behind him, the commentary was blaring: "Hint of Joy, it's still Hint of Joy . . ." Compared with the last photos Paul had seen of him, Jean-Louis Schiffer had aged twenty years.

His regular features had shrivelled over his bones, as though stretched on the rack. His grey, scaly skin hung loose, especially around his neck, making him look like a reptile. His eyes, which had once been chrome blue, were barely visible beneath his heavy eyelids. The former officer no longer had the long hair that had made him famous. It was now short, almost in a crew-cut. The silvery mane had given way to an iron skull.

His still-powerful frame was obscured in a royal blue overall, whose collar divided into two wavy wings over his shoulders. Beside the plate, Paul spotted a stack of betting slips. Jean-Louis Schiffer, the street legend, had become the bookmaker of a load of retired traffic cops.

How had he ever imagined that such a wreck could help him? But it was too late to turn back now. Paul adjusted his belt, gun and handcuffs, and put on his most impressive look – eyes ahead, and jaw clenched. The glassy eyes had already located him. When he was only a few paces away, the man said straight off: "You're too young to be a copper's cop."

"Captain Paul Nerteaux, First Division, tenth *arrondissement*."

He rattled this off in a military tone which he at once regretted.

"On rue de Nancy?"

"That's right."

This question was an indirect compliment. It was the address of the neighbourhood station. Schiffer had recognised the investigator in him, the cop on the beat.

Paul grabbed a chair, glanced round automatically at the gamblers, who were still stuck in front of their television. Schiffer followed his eyes and laughed.

"You spend your life putting crooks behind bars, then what happens? You end up doing porridge yourself."

He raised a piece of meat to his lips. His jawbones went to work beneath the skin like fluid, alert machinery. Paul revised his judgement. The Cipher was not as far gone as all that. All he had to do was blow the dust off the mummy.

"What do you want?" the man asked, after swallowing his meat.

Paul adopted his most modest tone. "I've come to ask you for some advice."

"What about?"

"About this."

He removed a brown-paper envelope from the pocket of his parka, and placed it next to the betting slips. Schiffer pushed aside his plate and unhurriedly opened it. He took out a dozen colour photographs.

He looked at the first one and asked: "What is it?"

"A face."

He turned to the next pictures. Paul added: "The nose was sliced off with a cutter. Or a razor. The lacerations and tears on the cheeks were made using the same instrument. The lips were cut off with scissors."

Without a word, Schiffer turned back to the first snap.

41

"Before that," Paul went on, "there was a beating. According to the forensic scientist, the mutilations were done post-mortem."

"Who was she?"

"We don't know. Her fingerprints aren't on record."

"How old was she?"

"About twenty-five."

"What was the actual cause of death?"

"You've got a choice. Blows. Wounds. Burns. The rest of the body's in the same state as the face. Apparently, she underwent more than twenty-four hours of torture. I'm expecting more details. The autopsy's being carried out now."

The old man raised his eyes.

"Why are you showing me this?"

"The body was found at dawn yesterday, by Saint-Lazare Hospital."

"So what?"

"So, that was your territory. You spent over twenty years in the sector."

"But that doesn't make me a pathologist."

"I think the victim is a Turkish working girl."

"Why Turkish?"

"Firstly because of the area. Then there are her teeth. They have traces of gold fillings which are now used only in the Near East." He then added: "Do you want the names of the alloys?"

Schiffer moved his plate back in front of him and started eating again. "Why an immigrant worker?" he asked after a long chew.

"Because of her fingers," Paul replied. "The tips are criss-crossed with scars typical of certain types of sewing work. I've checked."

"Does her description match anyone reported missing?" The old man was pretending not to understand.

"No reported disappearance," Paul muttered patiently. "No one came asking after her. She's an illegal alien, Schiffer. Someone with no official status in France. A woman no one will come to the police about. The ideal victim."

The Cipher slowly and calmly finished his steak. Then he dropped his knife and fork to pick up the photos again. This time, he put on his glasses. He observed each image for a few seconds, attentively examining the wounds.

42

Paul could not help looking down at the pictures. Upside down, he saw the dark sliced opening of the nose, the lacerations in the face, a purple, horrific harelip.

Schiffer laid down the packet and picked up a yoghurt. He carefully raised the top, before plunging in his spoon.

Paul sensed that his reserves of calm were quickly running out. "I've been doing the rounds," he went on. "The sweatshops, the homes, the bars. Nothing doing. No one's gone missing. Which is normal, because no one really exists. They're illegal aliens. How can you identify a victim in an invisible community?"

Schiffer silently scooped up his yoghurt. Paul pressed on: "None of the Turks have seen anything. Or else they won't tell me. In fact, no one's been able to tell me anything. Because none of them speaks French."

The Cipher continued toying with his spoon. Finally, he deigned to add: "And so, someone mentioned me . . ."

"Everyone mentioned you. Beauvanier, Monestier, the inspectors, the boys on the beat. If they're to be believed, you're the only person who can make this damned case advance."

Silence again. Schiffer wiped his lips with a serviette, then grabbed his little plastic pot again.

"That's all a long time ago. I'm retired and I've got other things on my mind." He pointed to the betting slips. "I now devote myself to my new responsibilities."

Paul grabbed the edge of the table and leaned over it. "Listen, Schiffer. He smashed her feet to pulp. The X-rays show over seventy shards of bone sticking in her flesh. He sliced off her breasts so that you can now count her ribs through her skin. He rammed a bar covered with razor blades into her vagina." He banged the table. "He's got to be stopped!"

The old cop raised an eyebrow. "Got to be stopped?"

Paul wriggled on his seat, then clumsily removed the file which was rolled up in the inside pocked of his parka.

Reluctantly, he added: "We've got three of them."

"Three?"

"The first one was found last November. Then a second in January. And now this one. Every time in the Turkish quarter. And always tortured and disfigured in the same way."

43

Schiffer stared at him in silence, spoon in mid-air. Paul started yelling, drowning out the cries from the race course.

"Jesus Christ, Schiffer, don't you understand? There's a serial killer in the Turkish quarter. Someone who only attacks asylum seekers. Women who don't exist in an area which isn't part of France any more!"

At last, Jean-Louis Schiffer put down his yoghurt and took the file from Paul's hands. "You should have come to see me before."

CHAPTER 9

Outside, the sun had come out. Silvery puddles enlivened the large gravel courtyard. Paul was pacing up and down in front of the main entrance, waiting for Jean-Louis Schiffer to finish packing.

There was no other solution. He had realised that right from the start. The Cipher could not help from a distance. He could not advise him from his retirement home, nor help him out over the phone when Paul had run out of inspiration. No. It was necessary for the former officer to question the Turks alongside him and exploit his contacts by returning to the neighbourhood he knew better than anyone else.

Paul shivered at the possible consequences of what he was doing. No one had been informed, neither the magistrate nor his superiors. And it was not on just to let loose such a bastard, known for his violent, unrestrained methods. He was going to have to keep him on a very short leash.

He kicked a pebble into a puddle, thus disturbing his own reflection. He was still trying to convince himself that he had had the right idea. How had he come to this? Why was he so obsessed by this case? Why, since the first murder, had it seemed that his entire existence depended on the outcome?

He thought for a moment while staring at his troubled image, then had to admit to himself that this rage had one sole source.

Everything had started with Reyna.

Paul had started out in the drug squad. He was getting good results in the field, leading an ordered existence, revising for the examination to become commissioner – and was even noticing that the lacerated leatherette seating was sinking into the depths of his consciousness. His copper casing was acting as a solid defence against his old panic attacks.

That evening, he was transferring a North African dealer, whom he had questioned for over six hours in his office in Nanterre, to the Paris Prefecture. A routine procedure. But when he arrived at head-quarters he discovered total chaos. Black Marias were arriving in droves, containing hoards of screaming and gesticulating youths. Riot police were running around in all directions along the riverbank, while sirens constantly blared as ambulances surged into the courtyard of the Hôtel-Dieu.

Paul asked around. A demonstration against a job reinsertion scheme – a proposed minimum wage for young people – had degen-erated. On place de la Nation there were apparently over a hundred policemen wounded, plus several dozen demonstrators and millions of francs' worth of damage to property.

Paul grabbed his suspect and legged it down to the basement. If he could not find any room downstairs, then he could always go to the Prison de la Santé, or even further afield, with his prisoner handcuffed to his wrist.

The detention centre greeted him with its usual din, but this time multiplied a thousandfold. There were insults, screams, spitting. Demonstrators were hanging off the bars, yelling out curses, to which the police replied with their truncheons. He managed to offload his dealer and left at once, fleeing the racket and spittle.

He was about to leave when he spotted her.

She was sitting on the floor, arms wrapped around her knees, appar-ently disdainful of the surrounding chaos. He went over to her. She had prickly black hair, an androgynous form, a sort of Joy Division look straight from the 1980s. She even had a blue-checked head-scarf, like the ones only Yasser Arafat still dares to wear.

Beneath her punkish hair, her face was of a startling regularity: as even as an Egyptian figurine, cut in white marble. Paul thought of the sculptures he had seen in a magazine. Naturally polished shapes, both heavy and soft, ready to slip into the palm of your hand or stand up on a finger in perfect balance. Magical stones, signed by an artist called Brancusi.

He talked with the jailers, checked that the girl's name had not yet been put in the day-book, then took her to the drug squad offices on the third floor. While climbing the stairs, he mentally went through his good and bad points.

In terms of strengths, he was reasonably good-looking. That was at least what he heard from the prostitutes who whistled at him and called to him when he went through the red-light districts looking for dealers. He had the smooth black hair of an Indian. His features were regular, his eyes brown. A dry yet vibrant figure, not very tall, but poised on thick-soled Paraboots. As he looked so cute, he had adopted a harsh stare, which he worked on in front of his mirror, and a three-days' growth that concealed his boyish looks.

In terms of weaknesses, there was just one. A huge one. He was a cop.

When he checked the girl's records, he realised that this obstacle was likely to be a major one. Reyna Brendosa, aged twenty-four, living at 32 rue Gabriel-Péri in Sarcelles, was an active member of the extreme wing of the Ligue Communiste Révolutionnaire. She had links with the Tutte Bianche, or "White Overalls", an Italian anti-globalisation group which practised civil disobedience. She had been arrested several times for vandalism, disturbing the peace, and assault and battery. A real hell-raiser.

Paul turned from his computer and looked once more at the vision staring back at him from the other side of his desk. Just her dark irises, emphasised by eyeliner, knocked him out more thoroughly than the two Zairian dealers who had given him a beating at Château-Rouge, one evening of inattention.

He toyed with her identity card, as all cops do, and asked her: "So you like smashing things, do you?"

No answer.

"Isn't there a better way to put over your ideas?"

No answer.

"You get off on violence, do you?"

No answer. Then, suddenly, a slow deep voice: "Private property is the only real violence. The robbing of the masses. The alienation of minds. And worst of all, written down and authorised by law."

"Those ideas are a bit past it. Hasn't anyone told you?"

"Nothing and nobody will prevent the fall of capitalism."

"In the meantime, you're in for three months behind bars."

Reyna Brendosa smiled: "You're playing at soldiers but you're only a pawn. If I blow, you'll vanish."

Paul smiled back. Never had he felt such a mixture of irritation and fascination for a woman; such a violent desire, mingled with fear.

After their first night, he asked to see her again. She called him a "fucking pig". A month later she was sleeping at his place every night, so he asked her to move in with him. She told him to go fuck himself. Even later, he mentioned marriage. She burst out laughing.

They got married in Portugal, near Porto, in her native village. First at the communist town hall, then in a little church. A syncretism of socialism and sun. It was one of Paul's best memories.

The following months were the happiest in his life. He was constantly amazed. Reyna seemed ethereal, immaterial, then a moment later a gesture or expression gave her an unbelievable presence and an almost animalistic sensuality. She could spend hours talking about her political ideas, her utopian dreams, quoting philosophers he had never heard of. Then, with just one kiss, remind him that she was a full-blooded, organic, vibrant being.

Her breath smelt of blood – she kept biting her lips. Wherever she went she seemed to capture the spirit of the world, to move with nature's fundamental mechanics. She had a sort of internal perception of the universe: something hidden, an underground stream that linked her to the vibrations of the earth and the instincts of the living. He loved her slowness, which gave her the gravity of a death knell. He loved her suffering when faced with injustice, misery, the desperation of humanity. He loved the martyr's life she had chosen and which raised their daily existence to the level of a tragedy. Living with his wife was like asceticism before an oracle. A transcendently religious path of discipline.

Reyna, and a life of fasting . . . This feeling was a hint of the future.

At the end of the summer of 1994 she told him she was pregnant. He felt betrayed. His dream had vanished. His ideal had now sunk into the banality of bodies and family life. Deep down, he sensed that he was going to lose her. At first physically, then emotionally. Reyna's vocation was obviously going to change. Utopia for her was going to reincarnate itself in her internal transformation . . .

And that was exactly what happened. From one day to the next, she turned over in bed and refused his touch. She reacted only vaguely to his presence. She became a kind of forbidden city, closed around her one idol – her child. Paul might have been able to follow this shift, but he then sensed a deeper lie that he had been blind to before.

After the birth, in April 1995, their relationship froze for ever. They both stood there on either side of their daughter like strangers. Despite the presence of their new-born baby, the morbid atmosphere of a funeral parlour hung around them. Paul realised that he had now become totally repulsive for Reyna.

One night, he could no longer stop himself from asking: "You don't want me any more?"

"No."

"You never will again?"

"No."

He hesitated, then asked the fatal question: "And you never have?"

"No, never."

His policeman's flair had deserted him on that score . . . Their meeting, life together, marriage had been a pure fraud, an illusion.

A set-up with the sole aim of having a child.

The divorce took only a few months. In front of the judge, Paul felt as if he was hovering. He heard a raucous voice being raised in the office, and it was his. He felt sand-paper biting into his face, and it was his own beard. He was gliding through the room like a ghost, a phantom in a comedy. He said yes to everything, to the alimony and custody, he did not put up the slightest fight. He did not give a damn, and instead dwelled on how much he had been taken in. He had been the victim of a rare form of collectivisation: Reyna the Marxist had taken over his sperm. She had practised a communist-inspired *in vivo* fertilisation.

The funniest thing of all was that he could not bring himself to hate her. On the contrary, he admired her as an intellectual, free from desire. He was sure that she would never again have a sexual relationship. Neither with a man, nor with a woman. And the idea of this idealist who wanted quite simply to give life, without the slightest physical pleasure or desire, left him drained, without any idea about what she was doing.

It was then that he started to drift, like waste water looking for its sea of sludge. At work, he began to wander. He never showed up at his office in Nanterre. He spent all his time in the dodgiest neighbourhoods, hanging around with the lowest of the low, smoking endless joints, spending his time with pushers and druggies, sinking into the dregs of humanity . . .

Then, in the spring of 1998, he agreed to see her.

She was called Céline and she was three. The first weekends were terrible: parks, rides, candyfloss, terminal boredom. Then, bit by bit, he discovered an unsuspected presence. Something transparent in the child's movements, face, expressions, with their supple bounding whimsical shifts, whose turns and turns-about he observed. A tightly clenched fist to emphasise what was obvious, the way she leaned forward then rounded off the movement with a cheeky grin, her husky voice with its own special charm that made him tingle as though touched by some material or bark. A woman was already there lurking within the child. It was not her mother – absolutely not – but another unique, sparkling being.

There was something new under the sun: Céline was there.

Paul changed completely, and now started to relish the time they spent together. Those days with his daughter brought him back to life. He struggled to regain his self-respect. He dreamed of himself as a hero, an untouchable super-cop, washed clean of any stain.

A man whose gaze would make his morning mirror glisten.

For this recovery, he chose the only territory that he knew: crime. He forgot about taking the exam to become a commissioner, and instead applied for a job in Paris's Brigade criminelle. Despite his period of drifting, he became captain in 1999. He then turned into a determined, inspired investigator. And started to hope for a case that would take him to the top. The sort of inquiry that all motivated officers long for: the pursuit of a beast, a face-to-face duel with an enemy who was up to his expectations.

It was then that he heard about the first body.

A red-head who had been tortured and disfigured then dumped in a doorway off boulevard de Strasbourg on 15 November 2001. No suspects, no motive, and an almost non-existent victim . . . The body did not match any person who had been reported missing. The finger-prints were not on record. The squad had already closed the case. Just another bust-up between some whore and her pimp. The red lights of rue Saint-Denis were not even two hundred yards away. But Paul instinc-tively sensed that there was something else. He read the file – the witness who had found the body, the forensic report, photos of the stiff. At Christmas, while his colleagues were with their families, and Céline had gone to see her grandparents in Portugal, he studied the file in detail. He immediately saw that this had been no usual murder. Neither the diversity of the torture nor the mutilations to the face fitted with the idea that it had been a pimp. What was more, if the girl had really been on the game, then her fingerprints would have been identified – all the whores of the tenth *arrondissement* were on record.

He decided to keep an eye on events in the Strasbourg-Saint-Denis area. He did not have to wait long. On 10 January 2002, a second body was found in the courtyard of a Turkish sweatshop on rue du Faubourg-Saint-Denis. The same type of victim – a red-head who had not been reported missing, the same marks of torture, the same lacer-ations to the face.

Paul forced himself to stay calm, but he was sure that he now had "his" serial killer. He rushed round to see Thierry Bomarzo, the inves-tigating magistrate, and was put in charge of the case. Unfortunately, the leads were already cold. The local coppers had made a mess of the scene of the crime, and forensics had found nothing.

Deep down, Paul sensed that he should track the killer on his own turf, by infiltrating the Turkish community. He got himself transferred to the local police station on rue de Nancy and demoted to the rank of plain sergeant in the Service d'Accueil de Recherche d'Investigation Judiciaire (the SARIJ). He rediscovered the routine of a lowly copper, dealing with burgled widows, shoplifting in grocery stores and neigh-bours from hell.

The month of February passed by. Paul was champing at the bit. He was both fearing and hoping for another corpse. His life alternated between moments of excitement and days of utter gloom. When things could not get any worse, he used to visit the anonymous tombs of the two victims in their paupers' grave in Thiais, Val-de-Marne.

While staring at the stone slabs with just a number on them, he swore that he would avenge them and find the madman who had massacred them. Then, in the back of his mind, he also made a promise to Céline. Yes, he would catch the killer. For her. For himself. So that everyone would see what a great cop he was.

On 16 March 2002, at dawn, another body was found.

The boys on night duty called him up at five in the morning. The dustmen had phoned in: they had come across a corpse in a ditch by Saint-Lazare Hospital, a disused brick building off boulevard Magenta. Paul ordered that no one should go there for another hour. He grabbed his coat and headed for the scene of the crime. He discovered a deserted zone, without a single officer or flashing light to disturb his concentration.

It was a miracle.

He was going to be able to sniff out the trace of the killer, to enter into contact with his scent, his presence, his craziness . . . Once again he was disappointed. He had been hoping for some material clues, a particular disposition that would reveal a *modus operandi*. But all he had was a corpse in a concrete trench. A livid, mutilated body topped by a disfigured face beneath a ginger mane.

Paul realised that he was caught between the silence of the dead, and the silence of the quarter.

He went back home in desperation, even before the police van arrived. He wandered down rue Saint-Denis and watched Little Turkey wake up. The shopkeepers opening their stores, the workers running to their sweatshops, the thousand and one Turks going about their business . . . He felt sure that this immigrant neighbourhood was the forest in which the killer was concealed, a dense jungle where he had fled to seek refuge and security.

There was no way Paul could unmask him alone.

He needed a guide to light the way.

CHAPTER 10

Jean-Louis Schiffer looked better in civvies.

He was wearing an olive-green Barbour hunting jacket and lighter green corduroy trousers that tumbled down over his Church's-style shoes, which shone like chestnuts.

These clothes conferred a certain elegance on him, but without diminishing the brutality of his figure. His broad back and chest along with his arched legs gave him an aura of power, solidity and violence. Someone who could certainly take the recoil from the official Manhurin 38 without budging an inch. His posture even suggested that he had already taken its recoil and incorporated it into his gait.

As though reading Paul's mind, the Cipher lifted his arms: "Search me if you want, kid. I'm not carrying."

"I hope not," Paul replied. "Just remember, there's only one serving officer around here. And I'm not a 'kid'."

Schiffer clicked his heels together to mimic standing to attention. Paul did not even grin. He opened the car door, got in and pulled off at once, trying to swallow his apprehensions.

The Cipher said nothing during the journey. He was absorbed in the photocopy of the file. Paul knew it off by heart. He could recite everything that was known about the bodies which he had now baptised his "corpuses".

When they had reached the outskirts of Paris, Schiffer asked: "Searching the scenes of the crimes didn't turn up anything?"

"No."

"Forensics didn't find a single dab, a single trace?"

"Not one."

"Not on the bodies either?"

"Especially not on the bodies. Forensics thinks the killer cleans them with industrial detergent. He disinfects the wounds, washes their hair and cleans under their nails."

"And what about your neighbourhood inquiries?"

"I've already told you. I've questioned workers, shopkeepers, whores and the dustmen near the scene. I've even spoken to tramps. No one's seen anything."

"What do you reckon?"

"I think the killer goes round in a car, and dumps the bodies as soon as he can, at dawn. A lightning raid."

Schiffer flicked through the pages. He stopped at the photos of the corpses.

"What do you reckon about the faces?"

Paul took a deep breath. He had thought about those mutilations for nights on end.

"There are several possibilities. Firstly, the killer might just be trying to throw us off the track. The women knew him, and if we identify them then we could get to him."

"Why not mess up their teeth and fingers then?"

"Because they're illegal immigrants and not on any records."

The Cipher accepted this point with a nod of his head.

"And secondly?"

"A more . . . psychological motive. I've read a few books on the subject. According to the specialists, when a murderer destroys the means of identification, it's because he knows his victims and can't stand the way they look at him. So he takes away their status as a human being. He keeps them at a distance by reducing them to mere objects."

Schiffer leafed through the papers again.

"I'm not much of a one for the trick-cyclists. And next?"

"The murderer has a thing about faces in general. Something in the faces of these red-heads scares him, brings back a trauma. He has to kill them, but also disfigure them. I reckon these women looked alike. It's their faces that spark off the attack."

"That sounds even more iffy."

"You haven't seen the bodies," Paul replied, raising his voice slightly. "This is a real sicko. A pure psycho. So we've got to think as crazy as he does."

"And what's this here?"

He had just opened a final envelope, which contained photographs of antique sculptures. Heads, masks and busts. Paul had cut them out of museum catalogues, tourist guides and magazines such as *Archaeologia* and the *Bulletin du Louvre*.

"It's an idea I had," he replied. "I noticed that the cuts look like

53

cracks, notches, marks in stone. Then there's the fact that the noses and lips have been sliced off and the bones filed down, as though worn by time. I wondered if the killer might be inspired by old statues."

"Come off it."

Paul felt himself blush. His idea was a little far-fetched and despite all his research he had never managed to find a single detail that was in any way reminiscent of the wounds of the corpuses. Nevertheless, he blurted out: "For the killer, these women are maybe goddesses, to be hated but also respected. I'm sure he's Turkish and up to his eyes in Mediterranean mythology."

"You've got too much imagination."

"Haven't you ever followed your intuition?"

"I've never followed anything else. Just take my word for it. All this psycho stuff is off the point. What we have to do is concentrate on the technical problems he has."

Paul was not sure if he understood correctly. Schiffer went on: "We have to think through his *modus operandi*. If you're right, and these women really are illegal immigrants, then they're Muslims. And not Muslims from Istanbul in high heels. They're peasants, timid souls who keep themselves to themselves and can't speak a word of French. To catch them, you need to know them. And speak Turkish. Our man maybe runs a sweatshop. Or else is a shopkeeper. Then there's the question of timing. These working girls live underground, in cellars and hidden workshops. The killer must grab them when they resurface. When? How? Why do they agree to go with him? It's by answering questions like those that we'll identify him."

Paul agreed. But such questions merely revealed the depth of their ignorance. Quite literally, anything was possible. Schiffer took a different tack: "I suppose you've checked out any other similar homicides."

"I've looked at the new Chardon archives. And also Anacrime, the gendarmerie's records. I've quizzed everyone in the squad. There's never been anything this weird before in France. I also checked out the Turkish community in Germany. Nothing doing either."

"And in Turkey itself?"

"Zero there too."

Schiffer changed subjects. He wanted a full situation report: "Have patrols been increased in the area?"

"We made an agreement with Monestier, the commissioner at Louis-Blanc. There's an increased police presence, but a discreet one. We don't want to panic everyone."

Schiffer burst out laughing. "Don't be daft. All the Turks know what's happening."

Paul paid no attention.

"In any case, up till now, we've avoided any media attention. That's the only guarantee I have if I want to go it solo. If word leaks out, then Bomarzo will put other people on the case. Right now, it's just a business with Turks, so no one gives a damn. I've got a free hand."

"Why isn't the Brigade criminelle on a case like this?"

"That's where I used to be. And I still have contacts there. Bomarzo trusts me."

"And you haven't asked for more men?"

"No."

"You haven't set up a team?"

"No."

The Cipher could not help smirking. "You want him just for yourself, don't you?"

Paul did not reply. Schiffer brushed some fluff from his trousers.

"Never mind what you want. Never mind what I want either. We'll nail him. I promise you that."

CHAPTER 11

On the ring-road, Paul drove west, towards porte d'Auteuil.

"Aren't we going to La Râpée?" Schiffer asked, surprised.

"The body's in Garches. At Raymond-Poincaré Hospital. There's a forensics unit there that does autopsies for the courts in Versailles . . ."

"I know. Why there?"

"For reasons of discretion. To avoid the hacks and amateur profilers that are always prowling round the Paris morgue."

Apparently Schiffer was no longer listening. He was observing the traffic in fascination. Occasionally he would half-close his eyes, as though getting used to the light. He looked like a con on conditional release. Half an hour later, Paul crossed the Suresnes bridge and drove up boulevard Sellier and boulevard de la République. He then went through the town of Saint-Cloud before reaching the outskirts of Garches.

The hospital finally appeared at the top of the hill. Fifteen acres of buildings, surgical theatres and white rooms. It was like a town, inhabited by doctors, nurses and thousands of patients, most of them victims of car accidents.

Paul drove towards the Vésale Unit. The sun was high and sparkled off the fronts of the brick buildings. Each wall offered a fresh tone of red, pink or cream, as though they had been carefully baked in the oven.

As they went on, they passed groups of visitors carrying flowers or cakes. They walked with stiff, almost mechanical seriousness, as though they had been contaminated by the surrounding *rigor mortis*.

They had now reached the inner courtyard of the unit. The grey and pink building, with its porch supported by thin columns, looked like a sanatorium, or a spa concealing mysterious curative powers.

They walked into the morgue, following a corridor of white tiles. When they got to the waiting-room, Schiffer asked: "Where are we now?"

It was not much, but Paul was pleased he could pull a little surprise on him.

A few years before, the Garches forensic unit had been renovated in rather an original way. The first room was painted entirely turquoise. The colour covered indifferently the floor, walls and ceiling, thus wiping out any sense of scale or reference points. It was like plunging into a crystal sea, giving off a tonic limpidity.

"The quacks in Garches called in a contemporary artist," Paul explained. "We're not in a hospital any more, we're in a work of art."

A male nurse appeared and pointed to a door on their right.

"Dr Scarbon will join you in the departure hall."

They followed where he led, through further rooms which were also blue and empty, sometimes topped by a rim of white light, projected a few inches away from the ceiling. In the corridor, marble vases had been placed high on the walls, providing an array of pastel shades:

pink, peach, yellow, ecru, white . . . Everywhere, there seemed to be a strange desire for purity at work.

The last room made Schiffer whistle in admiration.

It was a single rectangle of about a hundred square yards, absolutely empty and covered entirely in blue. To the left of the entrance, three high bay windows brought in light from outside. Facing these luminous forms, three arches had been cut into the opposite wall, like vaults in a Greek church. Within, a line of marble blocks, like huge ingots, which had also been painted blue, seemed to rise directly out of the floor.

On one of them, the shape of a body could be seen beneath a sheet.

Schiffer went over to a white marble basin which stood in the middle of the room. Heavy and polished, it was full of water and resembled a plain holy-water basin of classical design. Moved by a pump, the sparkling water spun round giving off a scent of eucalyptus, intended to lessen the stink of death and the smell of formaldehyde.

The officer dipped his fingers into it.

"All this doesn't make me feel any younger."

At that instant, Dr Scarbon could be heard approaching. Schiffer turned round. The two men looked each other up and down. Paul at once saw that they knew each other. When he had phoned the doctor from the retirement home, he had not mentioned his new partner.

"Thank you for coming, doctor," he said, saluting him.

Scarbon nodded curtly, without taking his eyes off the Cipher. He was wearing a dark woollen coat and was still holding his kid gloves in his hand. He was old and emaciated. His eyes were constantly blinking, as if the glasses he wore on the tip of his nose were of no use to him. His bushy moustache allowed his Gallic tones to filter through in a drawling voice, as though from a pre-war movie.

Paul gestured towards his protégé.

"Let me introduce you to . . ."

"We know each other," Schiffer butted in. "Hi, doctor."

Without answering, Scarbon took off his coat and put on one of the white coats that were hanging beneath an arch, then he slipped on some latex gloves whose pale green colour went well with the surrounding blue.

Only then did he fold back the sheet. The smell of decaying flesh spread through the room, driving everything else out of their minds.

Despite himself, Paul turned away. When he had worked up the courage to look, he stared at the heavy white body, half-hidden by the folded sheet.

Schiffer had stepped under the arch. He was now slipping on his surgical gloves. Not a trace of disgust could be seen on his face. Behind him, a wooden cross and two black iron chandeliers stood out against the wall. He murmured in hollow voice: "OK, doctor, you can begin."

CHAPTER 12

"The victim is a Caucasian female. Her muscular tonicity indicates that she was aged between twenty and thirty. Rather plump. One hundred and fifty-four pounds and five foot three inches tall. If we add that she has the white pigmentation characteristic of red-heads, and the hair to go with it, then it can be asserted that physically she matches the profiles of the first two victims. That's the way chummy likes them: thirty-ish, plump red-heads."

Scarbon's voice was monotonous. It sounded as if he were mentally reading out the pages of his report, lines written during a sleepless night. Schiffer asked: "No distinguishing sign?"

"Like what?"

"Tattoos. Pierced ears. Traces of a wedding ring. Things the killer couldn't get rid of."

"No."

The Cipher grabbed the corpse's left hand and turned it over, palm up. Paul shivered. He would never have dared do such a thing.

"No traces of henna?"

"No."

"Nerteaux tells me that her fingers show that she was a seamstress. What's your opinion?"

Scarbon nodded. "These women had all clearly been doing manual work for some time."

"Do you agree that it was sewing?"

"It's hard to be really precise. There are marks of pinpricks in the lines of the fingers. There are also calluses between the thumb and the index. Maybe from using a sewing machine, or an iron." He looked up across the slabs. "They were found in the Sentier area, weren't they?"

"So?"

"They're Turkish workers."

Schiffer paid no attention to the certitude in his tone. He was staring at the corpse.

Paul managed to force himself to approach. He saw the dark lacerations covering the flanks, the breasts, shoulders and thighs. Several of them were so deep that they revealed the whiteness of the bones.

"Tell us about all this," the Cipher ordered.

The doctor quickly flicked through a set of stapled pages.

"In this case, I counted twenty-seven wounds. Some are superficial, others are deep. It looks as if the killer intensified the torture as time went by. There were about the same number on the other two." He lowered his report to look at his questioners. "In general, everything I am now going to say applies to the previous victims too. The three women were mutilated in the same way."

"With what sort of weapon?"

"A chrome-plated combat knife, with a jagged edge. The marks of the teeth can be seen on several of the wounds. For the first two bodies, I ordered some research to be done into the size and positioning of the teeth, but we didn't come up with anything of interest. It was standard military equipment, matching dozens of different models."

The Cipher bent down over the wounds that spread out over the chest – there were strange black halos there, suggesting love-bites. When Paul had noticed this detail on the first body, it made him think of the Devil. A creature of fire who had salivated over this innocent form.

"What about those?" Schiffer pointed. "What are they exactly? Bites?"

"At first sight, they do look like love-bites. But I've found a rational explanation for them. I think the murderer uses a car battery to inflict electric shocks. To be more precise, I reckon he uses standard serrated clips on them. The marks have been left by their teeth. In my opinion, he probably dampens the body to increase the power of the shock.

Which would explain these black marks. There are over twenty of them on this one. It's all in my report."

He brandished his wad of paper.

Paul already knew this. He had read the first two autopsies over and again. But every time he felt the same disgust, the same rejection. There was no way of entering into empathy with such craziness.

Schiffer stood beside the victim's legs – her bluish-black feet were bent at an impossible angle.

"And this?"

Scarbon moved to the other side of the corpse. They looked like two topographers studying the contours of a map.

"The X-rays are spectacular. The tarsi, metatarsi and phalanges have all been shattered. There are approximately seventy shards of bone stuck in the flesh. No fall from any height could have done such damage. The killer went at her feet with a blunt object. An iron bar or a baseball bat probably. The other two got the same treatment. I checked. This is a specifically Turkish torture technique, called felaka or felika. I can't remember."

In a guttural accent, Schiffer spat out: "Al-falaqua."

Paul remembered that the Cipher spoke fluent Turkish and Arabic.

"From memory," he went on, "I could cite ten countries that use this method."

Scarbon pushed his glasses back up his nose.

"Yes, well. It's all highly exotic, anyway."

Schiffer moved up towards the abdomen. Once again, he seized one of the hands. Paul saw the blackened, puffy hands. The expert said: "The nails were torn out with pliers. The tips were burnt with acid."

"What sort?"

"Impossible to say."

"It was something done after death, to remove the fingerprints?"

"If it was, then the killer messed up. The dermatoglyphs are perfectly visible. No, I think it was more like another form of torture. This killer isn't the sort who messes up anything."

The Cipher laid the hand back down. All of his attention was now focused on the gaping vagina. The doctor also looked at the wound. The topographers were now starting to look like vultures.

"Was she raped?"

"Not in the sexual sense, no."

For the first time, Scarbon hesitated. Paul lowered his eyes. He saw the gaping, dilated, lacerated orifice. The internal parts – labia majora, minora and the clitoris – were all turned inside out, in an unbearable twisting of flesh. The doctor cleared his throat and started: "He pushed in some kind of truncheon, covered with razor blades. You can see the lacerations here, inside the vulva, and there, along the thighs. It's absolute carnage. The clitoris was severed. The labia cut away. It set off internal bleeding. The first victim had exactly the same kind of wounds. But the second . . ."

He hesitated once more. Schiffer tried to meet his stare.

"What?"

"With the second one, it was different. I think he used something . . . that was alive."

"Alive?"

"Yes, a rodent. Or something like that. The internal genitalia were bitten and torn as far as the uterus. Apparently torturers use this kind of technique in Latin America . . ."

Paul's head was spinning. He knew every detail, but each of them hurt him, made him want to be sick. He walked back to the marble basin. Absent-mindedly, he dipped his fingers in the scented water, then remembered that his partner had done just the same a few minutes before. He quickly removed them.

"Go on," Schiffer ordered in a husky voice.

Scarbon did not reply at once. Silence filled the turquoise room. The three men seemed to realise that there was no going back. They now had to confront the face.

"This is the most complex part," the expert at last went on, framing the disfigured face with his two index fingers. "There were several steps to the violence."

"What do you mean?"

"First there's the haematoma. The face is one big bruise. The killer beat her savagely for some time. Perhaps with a knuckleduster, and certainly with something metallic and more accurate than a bar or truncheon. Then there are the cuts and mutilations. The wounds did not bleed. They were made post-mortem."

They were now standing by the mask of horror. They could see the depth of the wounds in all their savagery and without the distance of the camera. Cuts crossed the face, making stripes on the forehead and temples, crevasses in the cheeks; and the mutilations, the sliced-off nose, the split chin, the blackened lips . . .

"You can see as well as I can what he cut, filed and tore off. What is interesting is how applied he was. He took time over his work. It's his signature. Nerteaux thinks he's trying to copy . . ."

"I know what he thinks. What about you?"

Scarbon retreated slightly, his hands behind his back.

"The murderer is obsessed with these faces. For him, they are both a source of fascination and fury. He sculpts them, and fashions them, while at the same time destroying their humanity."

Schiffer's shrug showed his scepticism.

"In the end, what did she die of?"

"I've told you, internal haemorrhaging set off by the butchering of the sexual organs. She must have bled dry onto the floor."

"And the other two?"

"The first, also from internal bleeding, unless her heart gave out before. As for the second, I'm not exactly sure. Probably quite simply from terror. To sum up, you can say that all three of them died in agony. We're analysing her DNA, but I don't think it will tell us any more than for the previous victims."

Scarbon pulled the sheet back up, with an over-hasty yank. Schiffer paced up and down for a moment before asking: "Can you deduce a chronology of events?"

"I couldn't give you a detailed timetable, but I would say she was kidnapped three days ago, on the evening of Thursday. She was probably going home after work."

"Why?"

"Her stomach was empty. Like the first two. He must jump them on their way home."

"Let's leave your suppositions out of it."

The doctor puffed with irritation.

"Then she endured from twenty to thirty hours of non-stop torture."

"How can you judge the duration?"

"She struggled. Her bonds made friction burns on her skin, and bit into her flesh. The wounds went septic. We can gauge the time thanks to the infection. If I say between twenty and thirty hours, then I can't be far from the mark. In any case, at such a pitch, that's the limit of human endurance."

As he walked, Schiffer stared at the blue mirror of the floor. "Do you have any indication of the scene of the crime?"

"Maybe."

Paul butted in: "What?"

Scarbon clicked his lips, like a clapperboard. "I had already noticed it with the first two. But with the third, it's even more obvious. The victim's blood contains nitrogen bubbles."

"Meaning?"

Paul took out his notepad.

"It's rather odd. It could mean that, while still alive, the body was subjected to a greater air pressure than that of the surface of the earth. Like the pressure found at the bottom of the sea."

It was the first time that the doctor had mentioned this particularity.

"I'm no diver," he went on. "But it's a well-known phenomenon. The deeper you go, the higher the pressure is. The nitrogen in the blood stream dissolves. If you go up again too quickly, without respecting levels of decompression, then the nitrogen suddenly turns back to gas and forms bubbles inside the body."

Schiffer looked extremely interested.

"And that's what happened to the victim?"

"All three of them. Nitrogen bubbles have formed and exploded throughout their organisms, causing lesions and, of course, more suffering. This is by no means sure, but these women may well have got the bends."

While jotting this down, Paul asked: "They were immersed at a great depth?"

"I didn't say that. According to one of my assistants, who goes diving, they must have undergone pressure of at least four bars. Which corresponds to a depth of about a hundred and twenty feet. It seems to me a bit tricky finding so much water in Paris. So I think they were in fact placed in a high-pressure chamber."

Paul was writing feverishly.

"Where do you find things like that?"

"You'll have to ask around. There are tanks that professional divers use to decompress, but I wouldn't think there are any in the Paris region. There are also chambers used in hospitals."

"In hospitals?"

"That's right. To oxygenate patients suffering from bad circulation. Diabetes, high cholesterol . . . High air pressure makes it easier to distribute oxygen in the organism. There must be three or four machines like that in Paris. But I shouldn't think your killer had access to a hospital. You'd do better to check out industry."

"What sectors use this kind of technology?"

"No idea. You'll have to find out. That's your job. And don't forget, I'm not sure about all this. These bubbles might have a completely different explanation. But if so, I don't know what it is."

Schiffer said: "And there's nothing about the three bodies that gives us any physical information about our man?"

"Nothing. He washes them down carefully. Anyway, I'm sure he wears gloves when he's at work. He doesn't have sex with them. He doesn't caress them. That's not his thing. Not at all. He's more clinical. Robotic, even. This killer is . . . inhuman."

"Does the madness increase with each murder?"

"No. Each time, the tortures are carried out with the same rigour. He's an evil obsessive, but he never loses his cool," he smiled wearily. "He's an orderly killer, as the text books put it."

"What do you reckon turns him on?"

"Suffering. Pure suffering. He tortures them diligently, obsessively, until they die. It's their pain that excites him, that he feeds off. Deep down, he has a visceral hatred of women. Of their bodies, and their faces."

Schiffer turned towards Paul and sneered: "Looks like I'm up to my ears with trick-cyclists today."

Scarbon flushed.

"Forensic science always involves psychology. The acts of violence we examine are just the symptoms of diseased minds . . ."

The officer nodded, but continued to smile. He picked up the wad of typed pages which had been placed on one of the slabs.

"Thanks, doctor."

He headed for the door which stood out beneath the three bays of light. When he opened it, a violent burst of sunlight shot into the room, like a flood of milk across the blue sea.

Paul grabbed another copy of the autopsy report.

"Can I take this one?"

The doctor stared at him silently, then said: "Do your superiors know about Schiffer?"

Paul grinned back: "Don't worry. Everything's under control."

"It's you I'm worried about. He's a monster."

Paul shivered. The scientist went on: "He killed Gazil Hemet."

The name brought back memories. October 2000. The Turk crushed by the Brussels express, Schiffer accused of murder. Then April 2001. The charges were mysteriously dropped. He replied in a frozen voice: "The body was flattened. The autopsy didn't prove a thing."

"It was me who gave the second opinion. The face bore terrible wounds. An eye had been torn out. The temples had been drilled open." He pointed at the sheet. "It was just as bad as her."

Paul felt his legs go weak. He could not admit such a suspicion about the man he was now working with.

"The report just mentioned some lesions and . . ."

"They suppressed my other findings. They covered for him."

"Who do you mean by 'they'?"

"They were scared. All of them were scared."

Paul stepped back into the whiteness outside. Claude Scarbon inflated then removed his elastic gloves.

"You've teamed up with the Devil."

CHAPTER 13

"They call it the Iskele. Pronounced is-kay-lay."

"What?"

"You could translate it as 'jetty' or 'departure quay'."

"What are you talking about?"

Paul had joined Schiffer in the car, but had not yet pulled away. They were still in the courtyard of the Vésale Unit, in the shadow of its slender pillars. The Cipher went on: "It's the main mafia organisation behind getting illegal Turkish immigrants into Europe. They also help get them work and accommodation. They try and organise it so that there are groups from the same region in each workshop. Some sweat-shops in Paris contain the entire population of a village in the back-waters of Anatolia."

Schiffer came to a halt, tapped his fingers on the glove compart-ment, then continued: "The price varies. The rich take the plane and bribe customs guards. They arrive in France with a fake work permit or false passport. The poor go in cargo boats via Greece, or in lorries via Bulgaria. Whichever way, you have to pay at least two hundred thousand francs. The family in the village chip in and get together about a third of that amount. The worker then slaves away for ten years to pay off the rest."

Paul observed Schiffer's clear profile against the brightness of the window. He had been told dozens of times about these networks, but it was the first time he had been given so many details.

The silver-headed cop gave him more: "You have no idea how well organised they are. They keep records. Everything is written down: each immigrant's name, origin, workshop and outstanding debt. They communicate via email with their opposite numbers in Turkey, who keep up the pressure on the families. Meanwhile, they deal with every-thing in Paris. They look after sending money orders or giving phone calls at lower prices. They replace the post office, the banks and the embassy. You want to send a toy to one of your kids? You ask the Iskele. You need a gynaecologist? The Iskele provides you with the name of a quack who's not too bothered about your legal status in France. You've got a problem with your workshop? The Iskele will sort it out. Nothing happens in the Turkish quarter without them knowing about it, and putting it in their records."

Paul at last realised where the Cipher was heading.

"You think they know about the murders?"

"If those girls really were illegal immigrants, their bosses will have contacted the Iskele first. One, to find out what happened. Two, to get replacements. More than anything, murdered girls means wasted money."

A hope began to form in his mind.

"You . . . you think they could identify the girls?"

"Each file contains a photograph of the immigrant. Their Paris address. And their employer's name and address."

Paul hazarded another question, but he already knew the answer: "And you know these people?"

"The head of the Iskele in Paris is called Marek Ceziüs. But everyone calls him Marius. He has a concert hall on boulevard de Strasbourg. I was present when one of his sons was born."

He winked at Paul: "Are you starting this car, or what?"

Paul stared at Jean-Louis Schiffer for a moment. *You've teamed up with the Devil.* Maybe Scarbon was right. But for the kind of game he was after, what better partner could he hope for?

III

CHAPTER 14

On Monday morning, Anna Heymes discreetly left her flat and took a cab to the Left Bank. She remembered that there were several medical bookshops grouped together around the Odéon crossroads.

In one of them, she browsed through various studies of psychology and neurosurgery in search of information about biopsies performed on the brain. The expression Ackermann had used still echoed in her mind: "stereotaxic biopsy". She soon found some photographs and a description of the technique.

She saw the patients' heads, shaved, inserted in a square casing. A sort of metal cube that was screwed onto their temples. The frame was topped by a trepan – like a drill.

She followed the illustrations of each step of the operation. The bit piercing the bone, the scalpel entering the opening and in turn penetrating the dura mater that encircled the brain, the hollow-headed needle going inside the cerebrum. In one of the photographs the pinkish colour of the organ could even be seen, while the surgeon was extracting the probe.

Anything but that.

Anna had made a resolution. She had to get a second opinion, and quickly, find another specialist who would suggest a different treatment.

She rushed into a café on boulevard Saint-Germain, ran downstairs to the phone and thumbed through the directory. After several fruitless requests to absent or overbooked doctors, she finally came across a certain Mathilde Wilcrau, a psychiatrist and psychoanalyst, who was apparently available.

The woman's voice was deep, but her tone light, almost mischievous. Anna briefly mentioned her "memory problems", and insisted on how urgent the situation was. The psychiatrist agreed to see her at once. Near the Panthéon, just five minutes away from Odéon.

Anna was now sitting alone in a small waiting-room full of old, carved and varnished furniture that seemed to come straight from the Château de Versailles. She looked at the photographs on the walls. They depicted images of sporting exploits in the most extreme conditions.

In one of them, someone was taking wing from the side of a mountain, suspended on a hang-glider. In the next, a hooded climber was ascending a wall of ice. In another, a marksman dressed in a cagoule and ski suit was taking aim at an unseen target.

"My exploits of yesteryear."

Anna turned round towards the voice.

Mathilde Wilcrau was a large broad-shouldered woman with a radiant smile. Her arms burst out from her suit brutally and almost incongruously. Her long, slender legs were curvaceously muscular. "Between forty and fifty," thought Anna, as she noticed her wrinkled eyelids and crow's-feet. But this athletic woman was to be evaluated in terms of energy, not age. It was more a question of kilojoules than years.

The psychiatrist moved aside.

"Step this way."

The consulting room matched the antechamber: wood, marble and gold. Anna sensed that this woman's true nature lay more in the photographs of her exploits than in these rather precious furnishings.

They sat either side of the flame-coloured desk. The doctor picked up a fountain-pen and jotted down the usual information on a cross-ruled notepad: name, age, address . . . Anna was tempted to give a false identity, but she had sworn to herself to be completely open.

While answering, she observed the woman in front of her. She was struck by her brilliant, ostentatious, almost American manner. Her brown hair glistened on her shoulders. Her broad, regular features scintillated around her extremely red, sensual mouth, which drew your eyes. She thought of crystallised fruit, full of sugar and energy. This woman inspired immediate trust.

"So what's the problem?" she asked merrily.

Anna tried to be brief.

"I have memory gaps."

"What sort of gaps?"

"I don't recognise familiar faces."

"None of them?"

"Especially my husband."

"Be more precise. You don't recognise him at all? Never?"

"No. They come in short fits. Suddenly, his face means nothing to me. A complete stranger. Until recently, these attacks only lasted a second. But they seem to be getting longer."

Mathilde tapped the page with the nib of her pen: a black lacquered Mont Blanc. Anna noticed that she had discreetly taken off her shoes.

"Is that all?"

Anna hesitated.

"The opposite also sometimes happens . . ."

"The opposite?"

"I think I recognise strangers' faces."

"For example?"

"In particular, with one person. I've been working in the Maison du Chocolat, on rue du Faubourg-Saint-Honoré, for the last month. There's a regular customer. A man in his forties. Every time he comes into the shop, I get the feeling I know him. But I've never managed to locate a precise memory."

"And what does he say?"

"Nothing. Apparently he's never seen me anywhere but behind my counter."

Beneath the desk, the psychiatrist was wriggling her toes in her black tights. There was something wickedly sparkling about her entire being.

"So to sum up, you don't recognise the people you should recognise, but you do recognise the people you shouldn't, is that it?"

She lengthened the final syllables in a strange way, like the vibrato of a cello.

"Well, yes, you could put it like that."

"Have you tried a good pair of glasses?"

Anna suddenly felt furious. A burning sensation rose up her face. How could she make fun of her illness? She got to her feet and seized her bag. Mathilde Wilcrau grabbed her arm.

"Sorry, I was only joking. It was silly of me. Please, do stay."

Anna froze. That red smile was enveloping her like a benevolent halo. Her resistance faded. She allowed herself to drop down on to the chair.

The psychiatrist went back to her place and her modulating tones returned: "So, shall we proceed? Do you sometimes feel uneasy in front of other faces? I mean, the ones you pass every day, in the street, in public places?"

"Yes. But that's a different sensation. I suffer from . . . some kind of hallucinations. On the bus, at a dinner party, anywhere. The faces mingle together, mixing and forming hideous masks. I no longer dare look at anyone. Soon I won't be able to go out . . ."

"How old are you?"

"Thirty-one."

"And how long have you been suffering from these symptoms?"

"For about six weeks."

"Are they accompanied by a physical malaise?"

"No . . . Well, yes. Signs of anxiety mostly. Trembling. My body becomes heavy. My limbs freeze. Sometimes it feels as though I'm suffocating. Recently, I got a nose bleed."

"But otherwise you're in good health?"

"Fine. Nothing wrong at all."

The psychiatrist paused. She was writing on her notepad.

"Do you suffer from any other memory blocks? About your past life for instance?"

Anna nodded rapidly and replied: "Yes. Some of my memories are losing their consistency. They seem to be drifting away, fading . . ."

"Which? Ones about your husband?"

She stiffened against the wooden back of the chair.

"Why are you asking me that?"

"Apparently, it's mostly his face that sparks off the attacks. Your past life with him may be posing the problem."

Anna sighed. This woman was talking to her as if her state might have been provoked by her feelings or subconscious. As if she was willing away certain parts of her memory. This idea was totally different from how Ackermann saw the problem. But wasn't it just this that she had come to hear?

"That's true," she conceded. "My memories of being with Laurent are breaking up and vanishing."

74

She paused for a moment, then continued more firmly: "But in a way, that's logical."

"Why?"

"Laurent's the centre of my life and of my memory. Most of what I can remember involves him. Before the Maison du Chocolat, I was just a housewife. Our married life was my sole preoccupation."

"You've never worked?"

Anna adopted a bitter, self-disparaging tone: "I've got a law degree, but I've never set foot in a solicitor's office. I have no children. Laurent is my 'one and all', if you like, my sole horizon . . ."

"How long have you been married?"

"Eight years."

"Do you have normal sexual relations?"

"What do you call 'normal'?"

"Dull. Tedious."

Anna did not understand. The smile grew broader.

"Another joke. All I want to know is if you have sex regularly?"

"Everything's fine in that department. On the contrary, I . . . I feel a great desire for him. Increasingly so, in fact. It's strange."

"Perhaps not as strange as all that."

"What do you mean?"

Silence was all she got in reply.

"What's your husband's job?"

"He's a policeman."

"Sorry?"

"At the Ministry of the Interior. Laurent directs the Centre des études et bilans. He oversees thousands of reports and statistics about criminality in France. I've never really understood what he does exactly, but it sounds important. He's very close to the minister."

Mathilde then asked, as if the question followed logically: "Why don't you have any children? Is there a problem?"

"Not a physical one, at least."

"So, why not?"

Anna hesitated. Saturday night came back to her: the nightmare, Laurent's revelations, the blood on her face . . .

"I don't know actually. Two days ago, I asked my husband. And he told me that I'd never wanted any. That I even made him swear not to ask. But I can't remember that." Her voice went up a tone, detaching each syllable. "How can I have forgotten that? I just can't remember!"

The doctor jotted something down, then asked: "What about your childhood memories, are they fading too?"

"No, they seem more distant, but still present."

"And your memories of your parents?"

"None. I lost my family very young. In a car crash. I was brought up in a boarding school, near Bordeaux, with my uncle as my guardian. I don't see him any more. I've never seen much of him, in fact."

"So what can you remember?"

"The countryside. The huge beaches of the South-West. Pine forests. Images like that are still intact in my mind. Right now, they're even getting clearer. Those landscapes seem more real to me than the rest."

Mathilde continued to write. Anna noticed that in fact she was doodling. Without looking up, the specialist went on: "How's your sleep? Do you suffer from insomnia?"

"The opposite more like. I sleep all the time."

"When you make an effort to remember, does it make you feel sleepy?"

"Yes, I get a feeling of torpor."

"Tell me about your dreams."

"Since the beginning of my illness, I've been having a strange dream."

"Go on."

She described her recurring nightmare. The station and the peasants. The man in the black coat. The flag decked with four moons. The sobbing children. Then the terrible gust of wind, the hollowed torso, the face in ribbons . . .

The psychiatrist whistled in admiration. Anna was not sure if she appreciated her familiar manner, but she felt comforted by her presence. Suddenly, Mathilde froze her heart.

"You've consulted someone else, I suppose?"

Anna trembled.

"A neurologist?"

"I . . . what makes you think that?"

"Your symptoms are rather clinical. Those memory blocks and hallucinations bring to mind a neurodegenerative disease. In such cases, patients generally consult a neurologist. A doctor who directly pinpoints the cause and treats it with medication."

Anna gave in: "He's called Ackermann. A childhood friend of my husband."

"Eric Ackermann?"

"You know him?"

"We were at university together."

Anna asked anxiously: "And what do you think of him?"

"He's brilliant. What was his diagnosis?"

"He just made me run tests. Scanners. X-rays. An MRI."

"Didn't he use a Petscan?"

"Yes. We did the tests last Saturday. In a hospital full of soldiers."

"Val-de-Grâce?"

"No, at the Henri-Becquerel Institute in Orsay."

Mathilde jotted down the name on a corner of her paper.

"And what were the results?"

"Nothing very clear. Ackermann thinks I'm suffering from a lesion in the right hemisphere, in the ventral temporal cortex . . ."

"The region that recognises faces."

"That's right. He reckons it must be a tiny necrosis. But the machine failed to localise it."

"And according to him, what caused the lesion?"

Anna spoke quickly, feeling good that she was making a clean breast of it: "That's the problem. He doesn't know. So he wants to carry out more tests . . ." Her voice broke. "A biopsy to analyse that part of my brain. He wants to study the nervous cells, or something. I . . ." She paused for breath. "He says that he needs to do that in order to treat me."

The psychiatrist laid down her pen and crossed her arms. For the first time, she seemed to be looking at Anna with neither irony or cheekiness.

"Did you tell him about your other problems? Your memories fading away? Faces mixing together?"

"No."

"Why don't you trust him?"

Anna did not answer. Mathilde pressed the point: "Why did you come to see me? Why tell me all this?"

Anna gestured vaguely, then, her eyes lowered, she said: "I refuse to have the biopsy. They want to enter inside my mind."

"Who do you mean?"

"My husband and Ackermann. I came here in the hope that you'd have a different idea. I don't want them to make a hole in my head!"

"Calm down."

She looked up, on the verge of tears.

"Can I . . . can I smoke?"

The psychiatrist nodded. She lit up at once. When the smoke cleared, the smile had returned to the face in front of her.

Inexplicably, a childhood memory came to mind. Long walks on the moors with her class, then back to the boarding school, her arms full of poppies. They were then told they should burn the stalks of the flowers to make their colours last longer . . .

Mathilde Wilcrau's smile reminded her of that strange alliance between fire and life in the petals. Something had burned inside that woman and was keeping her lips red.

The psychiatrist paused once more, then asked calmly: "Did Ackermann tell you that amnesia can be set off by a psychological shock, and not necessarily by a physical lesion?"

Anna exhaled abruptly.

"You mean . . . my problems could have been caused by a traumatic experience?"

"That is possible. Violent emotions can lead to memory loss."

A wave of relief invaded her. She knew that she had come there to hear those words. She had chosen a psychoanalyst in order to return to the purely mental side of her illness. She could barely contain her excitement.

"But this shock," she said between puffs, "I'd remember it, wouldn't I?"

"Not necessarily. Amnesia generally wipes out its own source. The founding moment."

"And this trauma might have something to do with faces?"

"That's likely. Faces, and also your husband."

Anna leapt to her feet.

"What do you mean, my husband?"

"To judge by the signs you mentioned, they seem to be the two main blocks."

"You think Laurent caused an emotional shock?"

"That's not what I said. But in my opinion, everything is connected. The shock you had, if there was one, has brought about an association between your amnesia and your husband. That's all I can say for now."

Anna was silent. She stared at the glowing tip of her cigarette.

"Can you gain some time?" Mathilde asked.

"Gain time?"

"Before the biopsy."

"You . . . you'd agree to treat me?"

Mathilde picked up her pen and pointed it at Anna.

"Can you put off the biopsy, yes or no?"

"I think so. For a few weeks. But if the attacks . . ."

"Do you agree to dive into your memory using language?"

"Of course."

"Do you agree to come here on an intensive basis?"

"Yes."

"To use techniques of suggestion, such as hypnosis, for example?"

"Yes."

"And injections of a sedative?"

"Yes, yes, yes."

Mathilde dropped her pen. The white star of the Mont Blanc was glittering.

"Trust me. We'll decipher your memory."

CHAPTER 15

Her heart was aflame.

She had not felt so happy for a long time. The simple idea that her symptoms might be caused by a psychological trauma, and not by physical deterioration, gave her new hope. After all, it might mean that her brain had not been altered, or attacked by necrosis which was spreading through her nervous system.

On the return cab journey she congratulated herself once more for having taken this initiative. She had turned her back on lesions, machines and biopsies and had opened her arms to understanding, language and Mathilde Wilcrau's smooth voice . . . She already missed her strange intonations.

When she reached rue de Faubourg-Saint-Honoré at about one in the afternoon, everything seemed clearer, more precise. She savoured every detail of her neighbourhood. They were like islands, an archipelago of specialities threading down the street.

At the junction of rue de Faubourg-Saint-Honoré and avenue Hoche, music was king: the dark lacquer of Hamm pianos answered to the dancers of the Salle Pleyel just opposite. Then it was Russia that dominated between rue de la Neva and rue Daru, with Moscovite restaurants and an Orthodox church. Finally, they reached the world of delicacies: the teas of Mariage Frères and the sweetness of the Maison du Chocolat: two brown mahogany façades, two varnished mirrors, like frames in a museum of delights.

Anna found Clothilde cleaning the shelves. She was busying herself with the ceramic vases, the wooden basins and the porcelain plates, which shared nothing with the chocolate apart from their familiar brownish tones, a copper gleam, or just an idea of happiness and well-being. A life of comfort that chinks and is drunk warm . . .

Clothilde turned round on her stool. "Ah, there you are! Can you give me an hour? I have to go to the supermarket."

It was fair enough. Anna had vanished all morning, so she could keep shop now during lunchtime. They handed over without exchanging a word, just a smile. Anna picked up the duster and took over the task at once, dusting, rubbing and polishing with all the vigour of her newly recovered good mood.

Then, suddenly, her energy faded, leaving a black hole in the middle of her breast. In a few seconds, she measured how false her joy was. What had been so positive about her consultation that morning? Whether it was a lesion or a trauma, what did that change about her state, her anxieties? What more could Mathilde Wilcrau do to cure her? How did that make her any the less mad?

She slumped down behind the main counter. The psychiatrist's idea was perhaps even worse than Ackermann's. The idea that an event, a psychological shock had sparked off her amnesia heightened her terror. What could be hiding behind such a zone of darkness?

Sentences echoed constantly in her mind, and above all the answer:

"Faces, and your husband." How could Laurent be linked with all this?

"Good afternoon."

The voice sounded above the tinkle of the bell. She did not need to look up to know who it was.

The man in the threadbare jacket advanced with his slow step. At that moment, she was absolutely *certain* that she knew him. It lasted only for a fraction of a second, but the impression was as powerful and piercing as an arrow. And yet her memory refused to give her the slightest clue.

Mister Corduroys continued to advance. He did not look at all embarrassed and paid no particular attention to Anna. His casual mauve, gilded gaze strayed over the rows of chocolates. Why did he not recognise her? Was he play-acting? A crazy idea stung her mind: what if he was a friend of Laurent, an accomplice whose job it was to spy on her and test her out? But why?

He smiled at her silence, and said in an off-handed voice: "As usual, please."

"Right away, sir."

Anna headed for the counter, feeling her hands trembling against her body. She had to make several attempts before she managed to pick up a bag and slip the chocolates inside. Finally, she laid the Jikolas on the scales.

"Two hundred grams. That will be ten euros fifty, please."

She glanced at him again. Already, she was not so sure . . . But the echo of the anxiety, the malaise, remained. The vague impression that this man, like Laurent, had altered his face using plastic surgery. It was the face in her memory, but it was not him . . .

The man smiled again, turning his mauve eyes to her. He paid, then left uttering a barely audible "good-bye".

Anna remained still for some time, petrified, in a stupor. Never before had an attack been so violent. It was as if it had eradicated all of that morning's hope. As if, after believing she would be cured, she had fallen even lower. Like prisoners who try to escape and, once they are caught, find themselves in a cell several feet underground.

The bell rang once more.

"Hi."

Clothilde crossed the shop, soaked to the skin, her arms full of carrier bags. She disappeared for a moment into the stockroom, then returned with an aura of freshness.

"What's up with you? You look like you've just seen a ghost."

Anna did not reply. The desire to vomit and the desire to cry were fighting for possession of her throat.

"Is something the matter?" Clothilde asked again.

Devastated, Anna looked at her. Then she got to her feet and said: "I'm going for a walk."

CHAPTER 16

Outside, it was raining even harder. Anna dived into the deluge. She let herself drift in the humid gusts of wind, in the twists of rain. With her dazed eyes, she looked at Paris as it swam and sank beneath the grey skies. Clouds were pushing in waves above the rooftops, the façades of the buildings were streaming, the sculpted heads on the balconies and windows looked like blue or green drowning faces, engulfed by the floods of heaven.

She went back up rue du Faubourg-Saint-Honoré, then avenue Hoche to her left, as far as parc Monceau. There, she passed by the black and gold railings of the gardens and took rue Murillo.

The traffic was heavy. Cars were splashing water and light. Hooded bikers were snaking away like little rubber Zorros. The pedestrians were struggling against the gusts, moulded and fashioned by the wind that wrapped their clothes like damp drapings around unfinished statues.

Everything was a dance of brown and black, with glimmers of dark oil mingled with silver and sickly light.

Anna went along avenue de Messine, between the bright buildings and huge trees. She did not know where her feet were taking her, nor did she care. She was wandering both physically and mentally.

Then she saw it.

On the opposite pavement, a shop window was exhibiting a coloured portrait. Anna crossed the road. It was a reproduction of a painting. A troubled, twisted, tormented face of violent colours. She approached, as though hypnotised. It exactly reminded her of her hallucinations.

She looked for the name of the painter. Francis Bacon. A self-portrait dating from 1956. An exhibition of the artist's work was being held on the first floor of the gallery. She found the entrance, a few doors to her right in rue de Téhéran, then went upstairs.

Red hangings separated the white rooms and gave the exhibition a solemn, almost religious atmosphere. A crowd was bustling around the paintings. But in total silence. A sort of icy respect, imposed by the images themselves, was filling the space.

In the first room, Anna found some canvases six feet high, all depicting the same subject: a holy man sitting on a throne. Dressed in purple robes, he was screaming as though on an electric chair. He was painted in red, then black, and then again in violet. But the same details recurred: the hands gripping the armrests, already burning, as though stuck to carbonised wood; the mouth screaming, opening to reveal a wound-like hole, while purplish-blue flames were rising all around . . .

Anna went through the first curtain.

In the next room, naked crouching men were trapped in pools of colour or primitive cages. Their bodies were twisted, deformed, like wild beasts. Or zoomorphic creatures, midway between several species. Their faces were mere scarlet splashes, bleeding maws, truncated features. Behind these monsters, the panels of paint were like the tiles of a butcher's shop or a slaughterhouse. A place of sacrifice, where bodies were reduced to carcasses, flayed masses, living carrion. Each time, the lines trembled, shifted, like a documentary filmed with a hand-held camera, shaking with urgency.

Anna felt her malaise mount, but she had not yet found what she was looking for: faces of suffering.

They were waiting for her in the last room.

A dozen smaller canvases protected by red velvet cordons. Savage, broken, fractured portraits; a chaos of lips, noses, bone, where eyes frantically searched for a direction.

These paintings came in groups of three. The first, entitled *Three Studies of the Human Head*, was dated 1953. Livid, blue, cadaverous faces bore traces of their first wounds. The second triptych seemed like a natural continuation, breaking through into a higher level of violence. *Study for Three Heads*, 1962. White faces shifted away from the viewer, the better to return and display their scars beneath a clown's make-up. Strangely, these wounds seemed to be trying to raise a laugh, like the children who were disfigured in the Middle Ages in order to turn them for ever into clowns and buffoons.

Anna moved on. She did not recognise her hallucinations. She was simply surrounded by masks of horror. Their mouths, cheekbones and stares spun around, twisting their deformities into unbearable spirals. The painter had clearly been relentless with these faces. He had attacked them, sliced them up with the sharpest weapons. Brushes, spatulas, knives . . . he had opened their wounds, flaying their skins, ripping into their cheeks . . .

Anna's head sank into her shoulders as she walked, doubled up with fear. She now only glanced at the portraits from beneath shivering eyelids. A series of studies, devoted to a certain "Isabel Rawsthorne", was an apotheosis of cruelty. The woman's features had been quite literally shattered. Anna retreated, desperately looking for a human expression in this swirl of flesh. But all she found were scattered fragments, tortured mouths, bulging eyes with circles like cuts.

Suddenly, she gave in to the panic, turned on her heels and rushed to the exit. She was crossing the gallery's entrance hall when she noticed a copy of the exhibition's catalogue, lying on a white counter. She stopped.

She had to see . . . to see his own face.

She feverishly flicked through the book, past photos of his workshop, reproductions of works, before finally coming across a portrait of Francis Bacon himself. A black-and-white photo, in which the artist's stare gleamed more brightly than the glossy paper.

Anna placed both her hands on the page in order to look him straight in the eye.

His eyes were blazing, avid, in a broad almost moonlike face, supported by powerful jaw. A short nose, scruffy hair and cliff-like brows completed the portrait of this man who seemed quite capable of standing up to the flayed masks of his paintings each morning.

Then a detail caught Anna's attention.

One of the painter's eyebrows was higher than the other. The hawkish, staring, astonished eye seemed to be fixed on some distant point. Anna grasped the unbelievable truth: Francis Bacon physically looked like his portraits. His appearance shared their madness and distortion. Had this asymmetric eye inspired the artist's deformed visions, or had his paintings finally disfigured their creator? In either case, the works merged with the artist's features . . .

This simple realisation produced a revelation.

If the deformities of Bacon's canvases had a real source, why shouldn't her own hallucinations have an underlying truth? Who could say that her own delusions did not arise from a sign, some detail that really existed?

Another suspicion froze her. What if, beneath her madness, she was fundamentally right? What if Laurent, and Mister Corduroys, had *really* changed their appearances?

She leaned on the wall and closed her eyes. Everything fitted together. Laurent, for some unknown reason, had taken advantage of her fits of amnesia in order to change his features. He had gone to see a plastic surgeon, so as to hide inside his own face. Mister Corduroys had done the same thing.

The two were accomplices. Together, they had committed some terrible crime and, for that reason, had altered their appearance. That was why she had a malaise when she looked at them.

With a shudder, she rejected how impossible or ridiculous such reasoning might seem. She quite simply sensed that she was getting near the truth, no matter how crazy it might sound.

It was her brain against the others.

Against all the others.

She ran to the door. On the landing, she noticed a painting she had not seen before, just above the banister.

A mass of scars was trying to smile at her.

CHAPTER 17

At the bottom of avenue de Messine, Anna spotted a café. She ordered a Perrier at the bar, then went straight downstairs in search of a phone book.

She had already lived out the same scene, that very morning, when on boulevard Saint-Germain she had looked for the number of a psychiatrist. It was perhaps a ritual, an act to be repeated, like crossing the circles of initiation, recurring ordeals, before reaching the truth . . .

Flicking through the dog-eared pages, she looked for "Plastic Surgery". She did not pay attention to the names, but to the addresses. She had to find a doctor in the immediate neighbourhood. Her finger stopped on the line: "Didier Laferrière, 12 rue Boissy-d'Anglas". So far as she recalled, this street was just by La Madeleine, about five hundred yards away.

Six rings, then a man's voice. She asked: "Dr Laferrière?"

"Speaking." Luck was on her side. She did not have to pass the obstacle of a receptionist.

"I'd like to make an appointment, please."

"My secretary's not here today, hang on . . ."

She heard the sound of a computer keyboard.

"When would suit you?"

The voice was strange, silky, lacking in tone. She answered: "At once. It's an emergency."

"An emergency?"

"If you let me see you, I'll explain."

There was a pause, a second's hesitation, as though full of mistrust. Then the cotton-wool voice asked: "How long will it take you to get here?"

"Half an hour."

Anna heard a slight smile in the voice. In the end, this urgency seemed to amuse him.

"I'll be expecting you."

CHAPTER 18

"I don't understand. What sort of operation are you interested in exactly?"

Didier Laferrière was a small man, with a neutral face and grey frizzy hair, which precisely matched his toneless voice. A discreet character, with furtive, imperceptible gestures. He spoke as though through a

86

screen of rice paper. Anna realised that she would have to penetrate this veil if she was going to obtain the information she wanted.

"I haven't really decided yet," she replied. "To start with, I'd like to know more about how operations can change a person's face."

"Change it in what way?"

"Completely."

The surgeon adopted a professorial tone: "In order to effect profound improvements, it is necessary to attack the bone structure. There are two main techniques. Grinding operations, which aim at reducing prominent features, and bone grafts which instead build up certain regions."

"How does it work exactly?"

He took a deep breath and paused for thought. His surgery was plunged in shadows. The windows were covered by shutters. A weak light caressed the Asian-style furniture. There was a confession-box atmosphere about the place.

"When it comes to grinding," he went on, "we reduce the height of the bones by passing beneath the skin. For grafts, we first remove the fragments, generally from the parietal bone, at the top of the skull, then we introduce them into the regions concerned. We sometimes also use prostheses."

He opened his hands, and his voice softened.

"Anything is possible. All that counts is your satisfaction."

"Such operations must leave traces, mustn't they?"

He smiled briefly.

"Not at all. We work using an endoscope. We slide optic tubes and micro-instruments beneath the tissue. Then we operate on the screen. The resulting incisions are minute."

"Can I see some photos of the scars?"

"Of course. But let's begin at the beginning. I want us to define together the sort of operation you are interested in."

Anna realised that he would at best show her toned-down pictures, with no visible marks. She tried a different approach.

"What about the nose? What can be done here?"

He furrowed his brow sceptically. Anna's nose was straight, narrow, slight. Nothing to be changed.

"It's a region you want to modify?"

"I'm looking at all the possibilities. What can you do with the nose?"

"A lot of progress has been made in this field. We can, quite literally, sculpt the nose of your dreams. We could draw the line together, if you like. I have some software that allows us to . . ."

"But what exactly happens during the operation?"

The doctor shifted about in his white jacket, which was standing in for his surgical coat.

"After we have made the area more supple . . ."

"How? By breaking the cartilage, is that it?"

The smile was still there, but the eyes were becoming inquisitive. Didier Laferrière was trying to work out Anna's intentions.

"We do indeed have to go through such a . . . radical step. But the whole thing is carried out under anaesthetic."

"Then what do you do?"

"Then we position the bones and cartilages according to the required line. I repeat. We can now offer you tailor-made work."

Anna pursued this direction.

"But that sort of operation must surely leave behind traces?"

"None. The instruments are introduced through the nostrils. We don't even touch the skin."

"And what about face-lifts?" she went on. "What technique do you use?"

"Endoscopy again. We pull the skin and muscles using minute tweezers."

"So no scars either?"

"Not a single one. We pass via the upper lobe of the ear. It's absolutely undetectable." He waved a hand. "Forget about scars, they're things of the past."

"And liposuction?" Didier Laferrière frowned.

"We were speaking about the face."

"But there's liposuction for the throat, isn't there?"

"True. It's even one of the easiest operations to perform."

"Does that leave scars?"

This was one question too many. The surgeon replied in a hostile tone. "I don't understand. What are you interested in, improvements or scars?"

Anna lost her composure. In a flash, she felt the panic she had experienced in the gallery come back. Heat was rising under her skin, from her throat up to her forehead. Her face was now presumably scarlet.

She murmured, hardly able to articulate: "Sorry. I'm very nervous. I'd . . . I'd like . . . In fact, before deciding, I'd like to see some photographs of operations."

Laferrière's voice softened; a touch of honey in dark tea.

"That's out of the question. Such pictures are extremely off-putting. All that we need concern ourselves about are the results, you follow me? As for the rest, that's my business."

Anna gripped the armrests of her chair. One way or another, she had to drag the truth out of this doctor.

"I'll never let you operate on me unless I see, with my own eyes, what you're going to do."

The doctor stood up, making an apologetic gesture.

"I'm sorry, but I don't think you're ready psychologically for such an operation."

Anna did not move.

"What have you got to hide?"

Laferrière froze.

"I beg you pardon?"

"I ask you about scars. You say they don't exist. I ask to see pictures of an operation. You refuse. So what have you got to hide?"

The surgeon leaned both of his fists on the desk.

"I carry out over twenty operations a day, young lady. I teach plastic surgery at Salpêtrière Hospital. I know my job. It consists in bringing people happiness by improving the way they look. Not in traumatising them by talking about scars and showing them pictures of broken bones. I don't know what you're looking for, but you won't find it here."

Anna returned his stare.

"You're an impostor."

He stood up, breaking into an incredulous laugh.

"What?"

"You refuse to show your work. You lie about the results. You try to pass yourself off as a magician, but you're nothing but a fraud. Just like all those other quacks."

The word "quack" produced the desired result. Laferrière's face started to go white until it was gleaming in the darkness. He swivelled round and opened a flexible slatted filing cabinet. From it, he removed a file of plastic-covered sheets and dumped it down on the desk in front of her.

"Is that what you want to see?"

He opened the file to reveal the first photograph. A face turned inside out like a glove, the skin stretched apart using haemostatic clamps.

"Or this?"

He showed a second picture: lips turned up, surgical scissors stuck in bleeding gums.

"How about this one?"

Third sheet: a hammer nailing a probe into a nostril. Her heart in her throat, Anna forced herself to look.

In the next photo, a lancet was slicing an eyelid, just above a bulging eye.

She raised her head. She had succeeded in fooling the doctor, all she had to do was continue.

"It's impossible that such operations never leave scars," she said.

Laferrière sighed. He rummaged through his cupboard again, then laid a second folder on the desk. With a weary voice, he commented on the first image: "Grinding of the forehead. By endoscopy. Four months after the operation."

Anna looked attentively at the transformed face. Three vertical lines, each measuring about five inches, crossed the forehead, along the roots of the hair. The surgeon turned the page.

"Removal of a piece of parietal bone for a graft. Two months after the operation."

The photograph showed a skull topped by spiky hair, under which could clearly be seen a pinkish S-shaped scar.

"The hair will soon cover the mark, which will in turn disappear," he added.

He flicked over the page, and continued: "A triple face-lift, by endoscopy. The stitches are intradermic and are absorbed. A month later, you see almost nothing."

Two shots of an ear, one frontal and one in profile, shared the page. On the upper crest of the lobe, Anna noticed a slight zigzag.

"Liposuction of the throat," Laferrière went on, revealing a further image. "The line you can see there will disappear. It's the operation that leaves the least trace."

He turned another page and emphasised, in an almost sadistic voice: "And if you want the lot, here's a scan of a face that has undergone a graft of the cheekbones. Beneath the skin, the traces of the operation remain for ever."

It was the most impressive picture. A bluish death's head, whose bone structure was covered with screws and fissures.

Anna closed the folder.

"Thank you, doctor. It was something I just had to see."

The doctor walked round his desk and stared at her intently, as though still trying to detect beneath her features the real reason for this consultation.

"But . . . sorry, I don't understand. What are you after?"

She stood up and put on her smooth black coat. For the first time, she smiled.

"I'm going to have to see for myself first."

CHAPTER 19

It was two in the morning.

It was still raining: a drum roll, a cadence, a slight hammering. With its different accents, beats and resonances on the windows, balconies, stone parapets.

Anna was standing in front of the living-room windows. In her sweat-shirt and tracksuit bottoms she was shivering with cold.

In the darkness, she stared through the windows at the form of the ancient plane tree. It was like a skeleton of bark, floating in the air. With charred bones, marked with scraps of lichen, looking almost silvery under the streetlamps. Bare claws awaiting their covering of flesh – spring leaves.

She looked down. On the table in front of her lay the objects she had bought that afternoon, after her visit to the surgeon: a Maglite electric torch and a special Polaroid camera for night shots.

For the last hour, Laurent had been asleep in the bedroom. She had stayed by his side, waiting for the moment. She had watched out for the slightest twitch as his body started to slumber. Then she had listened to his breathing as it became regular and unconscious.

First sleep.

The deepest.

She fetched her equipment. Mentally, she said farewell to the view outside, the large room with its glistening parquet and white settees. And to her routine now associated with this flat. If she was right, if what she had imagined was true, then she was going to have to flee. And then try to understand.

She walked up the corridor. She advanced so cautiously that she could hear the breathing of the building – the cracking of the parquet, the humming of the water heater, the rustling of the windows as the rain hit them . . .

Then she slid inside the bedroom.

Once beside the bed, she put her camera silently onto the table, then pointed her torch towards the floor. She covered it with her hand, so as to turn on its slender beam, which now heated her palm.

Only then did she hold her breath and lean over her husband.

In the light of the halogen, she could see his motionless profile, and his bodyline in the vague folds of the covers. Her throat tightened. She almost stopped, decided to drop it, but then she forced herself to continue.

She played the beam over his face.

No reaction. She could start.

Firstly, she raised his fringe slightly and looked at this brows. Nothing. There was no trace of the three scars on Laferrière's photo.

She moved the beam down to his temples. Nothing again. She played it over the lower part of his face, below his jaws and chin. Not the slightest hint of any anomaly.

She started trembling again. What if all this was just one more sign of her madness? She pulled herself together and continued her investigations.

She turned to his ears, pressing gently on the upper lobe so as to examine its top. No marks. She gingerly raised his eyelids slightly, looking for an incision. There was none. She scrutinised his nose and the inside of his nostrils. Nothing.

She was now covered in sweat. She tried once more to control the noise of her respiration, but her breaths were escaping through her lips and nose.

She remembered another possible scar. The stitched S on the scalp. She stood up, gently putting a hand into Laurent's hair, raising each lock of it, aiming her torch at the roots. There was nothing. No marks. No irregularities. Nothing. Nothing. Nothing.

Anna held back her tears. She was now rummaging recklessly around that head which had betrayed her, which had showed that she was mad, that she was . . .

A hand grabbed her wrist brutally.

"What the hell are you doing?"

Anna leapt back. Her torch rolled on to the floor. Laurent had already sat up. He turned on the lamp on the bedside table and repeated: "What the hell are you doing?"

Then he saw the Maglite on the ground and the Polaroid camera on the table.

"What's all this about?" he murmured, his lips tight.

Anna, prostrate against the wall, did not answer. Laurent pulled aside the covers and got up, picking up the electric torch. He examined it in disgust, then brandished it at her face.

"You were observing me, is that it? In the middle of the night? Jesus Christ, what were you looking for?"

Not a word.

Laurent wiped his brow and sighed wearily. He was dressed only in boxer shorts. He opened the door of the adjacent room, which served as a boudoir, and grabbed a sweater and a pairs of jeans, which he silently put on. Then he walked out of the bedroom, leaving Anna to her solitude and insanity.

She slid down the wall and curled up on the carpet. She thought of nothing, noticed nothing. Except for the beating inside her breast, which seemed to be getting louder and louder.

Laurent reappeared in the doorway, holding his mobile phone. He was smiling strangely, nodding with compassion, as if in the last few minutes he had calmed down and reasoned with himself.

He said softly, pointing at the phone: "Everything will be OK. I've called Eric. I'll take you to the institute tomorrow."

93

He bent down over her, then slowly drew her towards the bed. She put up no resistance. He sat her down cautiously, as though afraid he might break her – or else liberate some dangerous energy from her.

"You'll be all right now."

She nodded, staring at the torch which he had put on the bedside table, next to the camera. She stammered: "Not the biopsy. Not the probe. I don't want to be operated on."

"To begin with, Eric will just carry out some more tests. He'll do everything he can to avoid taking a sample. I promise you that." He kissed her. "Everything's going to be fine."

He offered her a sleeping pill. She refused.

"Please," he insisted.

She agreed to swallow it. Then he slid her between the sheets and lay down beside her, hugging her tenderly. He said not a word about his own concern. Not a single mention of his own disarray before his wife's utter insanity.

What did he really think?

Wasn't he relieved to be rid of her?

Soon, she felt his breathing slip into the regularity of sleep. How could he just doze off like that at such a moment? But maybe hours had already gone by . . . Anna had lost all notion of time. Her cheek against her husband's torso, she listened to his heart beat. The calm pulse of people who are not mad, who are not afraid.

She felt the effects of the tranquilliser gradually invade her.

A flower of sleep starting to bloom inside her body . . .

It seemed as if the bed was rising and leaving solid ground. She was slowly floating in the shadows. There was no point putting up any resistance, or trying to struggle against that current. She just had to let herself drift away along that running wave . . .

She snuggled up against Laurent, thought of the plane tree glistening in the rain in front of the living-room windows. Its bare boughs waiting to be covered with buds and leaves. A coming spring which she would not see.

She had just lived out her last season among the sane.

CHAPTER 20

"Anna? What are you doing? We're going to be late!"

In the scalding shower, Anna could barely hear Laurent's voice. She just stared at the droplets exploding on her feet, savouring the streams pouring around her neck, occasionally lifting her face up beneath those liquid tresses. Her entire body was limp, drowsy, overtaken by the water's fluidity. As perfectly docile as her mind.

Thanks to the tablet, she had managed to get a few hours' sleep. That morning she felt relaxed, neutral, indifferent to what might happen to her. Her despair had shifted into a strange calm. A sort of distant peace.

"Anna? Come on now!"

"OK, I'm coming."

She got out of the shower and jumped onto the floorboards in front of the basin. It was eight-thirty. Laurent, dressed and perfumed, was pacing up and down in front of the bathroom door. She quickly got ready, slipping on her underwear, then a black woollen dress by Kenzo, which evoked a stylised, futuristic mourning.

Quite appropriate.

She grabbed a brush and started to do her hair. Through the steam left by the shower, all she could see in the mirror was a misty reflection. She preferred it that way.

In a few days, maybe a few weeks, her daily reality would be her image in a dark glass. She would recognise nothing, see nothing, become totally alien to everything around her. She would not even bother about her own madness, letting it destroy what little remained of her sanity.

"Anna?"

"I'm coming!"

She smiled at Laurent's haste. Was he afraid of being late at the office, or in a hurry to offload his loony wife?

The mist started to fade from the mirror. She saw her face appear, red and puffy from the hot water. Mentally, she said good-bye to Anna Heymes. And also to Clothilde, the Maison du Chocolat, and to Mathilde Wilcrau, the poppy-lipped psychiatrist . . .

She imagined she was already at the Henri-Becquerel Institute. A locked, white room, without any contact with reality. That was what she needed. She was almost impatient to surrender herself to strange hands, to give herself up to the nurses.

She even started to come to terms with the idea of a biopsy, of a probe that would slowly descend into her brain and might locate the source of her illness. In fact, she could not care less about recovering. All she wanted to do was disappear, vanish, be of no more trouble to other people . . .

Anna was still brushing her hair when everything came to a halt.

In the mirror, beneath her fringe, she noticed three vertical scars. She could not believe it. With her left hand, she wiped away the last traces of steam, and breathlessly took a closer look. The marks were tiny, but definitely there, crossing her forehead.

Scars from plastic surgery.

The ones she had been looking for last night. She bit her fist to stop herself from screaming and doubled up, feeling her guts wrench up in spray of lava.

"Anna! What the hell are you doing?"

Laurent's cries seemed to be coming from another planet.

Trembling all over, Anna stood up and looked at her reflection once more. She turned her head and with a finger bent down her right ear. She found a white mark across the peak of the lobe. Then an identical one behind the other ear.

She drew back, trying to control her shaking body, both hands gripping the basin. Then she raised her chin, looking for further clues, the slight trace left by liposuction. She had no difficulty locating it.

An abyss was opening in front of her.

A freefall into the pit of her stomach.

She lowered her head, separating her hair in search of the final sign: an S-shaped scar, showing that some bone had been removed. Sure enough, that pink serpent was there waiting for her on her scalp, like a familiar revolting reptile.

She held on tighter to avoid collapsing as the truth exploded into her mind. She stared at herself, head down, hair flowing, measuring the depth of the pit into which she had fallen.

The only face that had changed was hers.

CHAPTER 21

"Anna! For heaven's sake, answer!"

Laurent's voice echoed in the bathroom, drifting through the last of the steam, joining the damp air outside through the open dormer window. His cries filled the courtyard of the building, pursuing Anna as far as the cornice she had now reached.

"Anna! Let me in!"

She was edging along sideways, back to the wall, balanced on the parapet. The cold stone stuck to her shoulder blades, the rain poured down her face as the wind blew her soaked hair into her eyes.

She avoided looking down at the courtyard, some sixty feet below, and stared straight ahead at the wall of the building opposite.

"LET ME IN!"

She heard the bathroom door crack. A second later, Laurent could be seen in the window frame she had just escaped through – his features ravaged, his eyes red.

At that very moment she reached the balustrade at the end of the balcony. She grabbed the stone rim, and pulled herself over it, falling onto her knees and hearing the black kimono she had pulled over her dress rip open.

"ANNA! COME BACK!"

Through the columns she could see her husband looking around for her. She got to her feet, ran along the terrace, scrambled over the farther balustrade and flattened herself against the wall in order to start along the next cornice.

At that instant, all hell broke loose.

A radio transmitter appeared in Laurent's hands. In a panicked voice, he yelled: "Calling all units! She's escaped. I repeat: she's running away!"

Seconds later, two men ran into the courtyard. They were dressed in civilian clothes, but wore the red armbands of policemen. They aimed their rifles at her.

Almost at once, a window opened on the third floor of the building opposite. A man appeared, holding a chrome-plated revolver in both hands. He glanced around until he found her, a perfect target.

More running could be heard on the ground. Three more men had joined the first two. One of them was their driver, Nicolas. They were all carrying the same automatic rifles with curved magazines.

She closed her eyes and put out her arms in order to balance. A profound silence inhabited her, wiping out any thoughts and bringing her a strange serenity.

She walked on, eyes tight shut, arms outstretched. She heard Laurent shout once more: "Don't shoot! For Christ's sake, we need her alive!"

She opened her eyes again. From an incomprehensible distance, she contemplated the perfect symmetry of the ballet. To her right, impeccably groomed Laurent was yelling into his radio and pointing at her. Opposite, the motionless sniper was gripping his gun – she could now see the mike close to his lips. Downstairs, five men in firing position were crouching, their faces raised.

And there she was, right in the middle of this army. A chalk-white shape dressed in black, posed like Christ.

She felt the curve of the gutter. She gathered herself, slid one hand over to the far side, and crossed over the obstacle. A few feet further on, a window stopped her. She remembered the layout of the building: this window led to the back staircase.

She raised her arm and elbowed it violently. The glass resisted. She tried again, swinging her arm with all her strength. The window shattered. She pressed down on her feet and leapt backwards.

The frame gave way. Laurent's cry accompanied her as she fell: "DON'T SHOOT!"

There was an endless moment, then she hit a hard surface. A black flame crossed her body. The shocks were multiple and violent. Her back, arms, heels crashed down on the sharp shards, while pain exploded in a thousand echoes through her limbs. Her legs shot up over her head. Her chin pressed down into her ribcage, taking her breath away.

Then darkness.

First the taste of dust. Then of blood. Anna came to. She was lying, curled up in the foetal position, at the bottom of the stairs. Looking up, she saw a grey ceiling and a globe of yellow light. She was where she had wanted to be: on the back staircase.

She grabbed the banister and pulled herself to her feet. Apparently, nothing was broken. All she found was a cut along her right arm – a shard of the window had torn her dress and stuck into her shoulder. Her gums had also been injured, her mouth was full of blood, but her teeth seemed to be still in place.

She slowly pulled out the piece of glass and then rapidly tore off a piece of her kimono to make an improvised tourniquet-cum-bandage.

She tried to assemble her thoughts. She had slid down one storey on her back, so this was the second floor. Her pursuers would soon appear on the ground floor. She leapt up the stairs four at a time, passing her own storey, then the fourth and the fifth.

Laurent's voice suddenly burst into the stairwell: "Hurry up! She's trying to get to the next building via the top floor!"

She speeded up and reached the seventh floor, mentally thanking Laurent for the tip.

She rushed down the corridor of what had been the servants' quarters, passing doors, a glass roof, basins, and then at last reached another staircase. She ran down several flights, then suddenly caught on – she was running into a trap. Her pursuers were communicating by radio. Some of them would be waiting for her at the bottom of this building, while the others were chasing her.

At that moment, to her left she heard the noise of a vacuum cleaner. She did not know which floor she was on, but that did not matter. This door must open on to a flat, which would in turn lead to another staircase.

She banged on it as hard as she could.

She felt nothing. Not the blows from her hand, nor the beating in her ribcage.

She knocked again. There was already a thundering of feet above her, approaching at high speed, and it seemed that she could also hear others coming up towards her. She pummelled on the door once more, using her fists like hammers, screaming for help.

At last, it opened.

A little woman in a pink pinafore appeared in the entrance. Anna shouldered her aside then closed the reinforced door. She turned the key twice in the lock then pocketed it.

She spun round to discover a huge, immaculately white kitchen. The stupefied cleaning lady was clinging on to her broom. Anna yelled into her face: "Don't open it again, got me?"

She grabbed her shoulders and repeated: "Don't open it, OK?"

There were already knocks from the other side.

"Police! Open up!"

Anna ran across the flat. She went down a corridor, past several bedrooms. It took a moment for her to realise that it was laid out in the same way as hers. She turned right to go into the living-room. Large paintings, furniture of red wood, oriental rugs, settees broader than mattresses. She now had to turn left to find the entrance hall.

She rushed onwards, tripping over a large placid dog, then bumped into a woman in a dressing-gown, with a towel over her hair.

"Who . . . who are you?" she yelled, holding her turban as though it was precious jar.

Anna nearly burst out laughing. That was not the right question to ask her today. She pushed the woman aside, reached the hall and opened the door. She was about to leave when she saw some keys and a remote control on a mahogany sideboard: the car-park. These buildings all led to the same one. She grabbed the bleeper and dived down the purple-carpeted staircase.

She could make it – she just knew she could.

She went straight down to the basement. Her chest was burning. She was breathing in short gasps. But her plan was coming together in her mind. The police trap was going to close in on the ground floor. Meanwhile, she would sneak out via the slope of the car-park, which led to the other side of the building, on rue Daru. There was a good chance that they had not thought of that exit yet . . .

When she reached the car-park, she ran across the concrete floor, without turning on the light, towards the swing door. She was just aiming the remote control, when it opened. Four armed men were running down the slope. She had underestimated the enemy. She just had time to hide behind a car, her two hands on the ground.

She saw them pass by, feeling the vibrations from their boots in her chest, and nearly burst into tears. They were now peering in between the cars, playing their torches across the floor.

She leaned back against the wall, and noticed that her arm was sticky with blood. The tourniquet had unravelled. She tightened it up again, pulling at the material with her teeth, while her mind raced in search of inspiration.

Her pursuers were slowly drawing away, searching, examining and combing every square inch of the basement. But they would also eventually retrace their steps and find her. She glanced round once more and, a few yards to her right, noticed a grey door. If her memory was right, this exit led to another building which also opened onto rue Daru.

Without another thought, she slid between the wall and the bumpers, reached the door and opened it just enough to be able to slip through it. A few seconds later, she burst into a bright, modern hallway. Nobody. She jumped down the stairs and leapt out.

She was running along the road, savouring the feel of the rain, when a screech of brakes brought her to a halt. A car had just come to a stop a few inches away from her, brushing against her kimono.

Scared and broken, she stepped back. The driver wound down his window and shouted: "You ought to look where you're going, darling!"

Anna paid no attention to him. She was peering left and right in search of police officers. It seemed to her that the air was charged with electricity and tension, as though a storm was brewing.

And the storm was her.

The driver slowly passed her.

"You should get your head examined, lady!"

"Piss off."

The man braked.

"What did you say?"

Anna threatened him with her bloodied finger.

"I told you to piss off!"

He hesitated, his lips trembling slightly. Then he seemed to understand that something was wrong, that this was not just any street slanging match. He shrugged and pulled away.

Another idea. She dashed towards the orthodox church, a few doors up the road. She went past the grating, across a gravel courtyard, then up the steps that led to the old varnished wooden door. She pushed it open and threw herself into the shadows.

The nave seemed to her to be plunged in utter darkness, but in reality it was the beating in her temples that was blinding her eyes. Little by little, she made out the brown tints of gold, the reddish icons, the coppery backs of chairs, like so many dampened flames.

She walked on cautiously, noticing other discreetly mild glimmers. Each object here was fighting for the few drops of light that were distilled by the stained-glass windows and the candles on their cast-iron chandeliers. Even the characters in the frescoes looked as if they wanted to extract themselves from their shadows to drink a little brightness. The entire space had an aura of a silvery glow – a gleaming play of shadows, containing a silent battle between light and dark.

Anna got her breath back. Her chest was burning up. Her skin and clothes were soaked in sweat. She stopped, leaned against a pillar and savoured the stone's coolness. Before long, her heart-beat started to slow down. Everything about the place seemed to have calming virtues: the candles swaying on their chandeliers, the long melting faces of Christ like bars of wax, the gleaming lamps hanging like lunar fruit.

"Is something the matter?"

She turned round to see Boris Godunov in person. A huge priest, dressed in black vestments, with a long white beard covering his chest. She could not help wondering which picture he had walked out of. In his deep voice, he said: "Are you all right?"

She glanced round at the doorway, then asked: "Do you have a crypt?"

"I beg your pardon?"

She forced herself to articulate each syllable: "A crypt. A place where funerals are held."

The priest thought he knew what she wanted. He adopted an appropriate expression and buried his hands in his sleeves.

"Who are you burying, my daughter?"

"Myself."

CHAPTER 22

When she got to emergency admissions at Saint-Antoine Hospital, she realised that she was in for another ordeal. A struggle against her madness and disease.

The strip-lights in the waiting-room reflected off the white tiles, wiping out any light from outside. It could as easily have been eight in the morning as eleven at night. The heat increased this stifling feeling. A suffocating, inert energy weighed down on her body like a lead casing drenched in antiseptic smells. Here, you entered the transit zone between life and death, which lay outside the succession of hours or days.

On the seats screwed to the walls sat a surrealistic sample of sick humanity. A man with a shaved scalp, his head between his hands, who was constantly scratching his forearm, leaving a deposit of yellow dust on the floor; his neighbour, a tramp strapped into a wheel-chair, who was swearing at the nurses in a throaty voice, while at the same time begging for them to put his guts back into place; just beside them, an old woman was standing dressed in just a paper coat, which she kept taking off, while mumbling unintelligibly, to reveal a grey body, with elephant wrinkles and a baby's nappy. Only one person looked normal. She could see him in profile sitting by the window. But when he turned round, the other half of his face was incrusted with shards of glass and scabs.

Anna was neither astonished nor scared by this chamber of horrors. On the contrary, it seemed like an excellent place to remain unnoticed.

Four hours before, she had dragged the priest down into the crypt. She had convinced him that she had Russian origins, was a fervent believer, had a terminal illness and wanted to be buried in holy ground. He had looked sceptical, but had still listened to her for half an hour. Thus he had unwittingly sheltered her while the men with red armbands had been combing the neighbourhood.

When she resurfaced, the coast was clear. The blood from her wound had clotted. She could walk the streets, with her arm in her kimono, without attracting too much attention. As she rushed on, she blessed the name of Kenzo and the extravagances of fashion, which meant that you could walk the streets in a dressing-gown while looking quite simply trendy.

For over two hours, she wandered aimlessly in the rain, mingling in among the crowds on the Champs-Elysées. She forced herself not to think, not to near the gulfs surrounding her consciousness.

She was free. Alive.

And that was already a lot.

At noon she was in Place de la Concorde, where she took the métro. Line number one, direction Château de Vincennes. Sitting at the rear of the compartment, she decided that she wanted confirmation, before even thinking about running away. She had mentally reviewed the hospitals on this line and had picked Saint-Antoine, just by the Bastille.

She had been waiting for twenty minutes when a doctor appeared carrying a large envelope of X-rays. He put it on an empty counter, then bent down to rummage through one of the drawers. She rushed over to him.

"I have to see you at once."

"Wait your turn," he said over his shoulder without even looking at her. "Nurse will call you."

Anna grabbed his arm.

"Please. I must have an X-ray."

The man turned round angrily, but his expression changed when he saw her.

"Have you checked in at reception?"

"No."

"Have you any health cover?"

"None."

The doctor looked her up and down. He was large, dark-haired and hearty, in a white robe and cork-heeled clogs. With his tanned skin, coat open in a V to reveal a hairy chest and gold medallion, he looked like a parody of a lady's man. He stared at her blatantly, a connoisseur's smile across his lips. Pointing at the ripped kimono and dried blood, he asked: "Is it for your arm?"

"No. My . . . my face hurts. I need an X-ray."

He frowned slightly, scratching his body hair – the harsh mane of a stallion.

"Was it a fall?"

"No, I've just got facial pain. I don't know."

"Or just sinusitis." He winked. "There's a lot of it about."

He looked round at the room and its occupants: the junky, the wino, the grandma . . . The usual suspects. He sighed, and suddenly seemed more inclined to take some time out with Anna.

He treated her to a broad Mediterranean grin, then whispered warmly: "I'll give you a good scanning, young lady. A full frontal."

He grabbed her arm.

"But first of all, let's strap you up."

An hour later, Anna was standing in the stone gallery that ran along the borders of the hospital garden. The doctor had showed her there, while she was waiting for the results of the tests.

The weather had changed. Darts of sunshine were melting into the downpour, transforming it into a silver mist of unreal clarity. Anna attentively observed the leaps and bounds of the rain on the leaves of the trees, the glinting puddles and the narrow streams sketched out between the gravel and roots of the thickets. This minor occupation allowed her to keep her mind empty and her latent panic at bay. Above all, no questions. Not yet.

The footfalls of clogs sounded to her right. The doctor was coming back, beneath the arcades of the gallery, holding the images. His smile had completely disappeared.

"You should have told me about your accident."

Anna jumped.

"What accident?"

"What happened to you? Was it a car crash?"

She stepped back in fear. He was shaking his head in disbelief.

"It's amazing what they can do now with plastic surgery. To look at you, I'd never have guessed . . ."

Anna seized the print-out from his hands.

It showed a skull that had been fractured, stitched and then totally stuck back together again. Black lines revealed grafts that had been performed on her brows and cheekbones. Marks around her nose showed that it had been completely re-sculpted. Screws in her jawbones and temples were keeping prostheses in place.

Anna broke into a nervous laughter, a laughing sob, before fleeing beneath the arcades.

The print-out waved in her hand like a blue flame.

IV

CHAPTER 23

For the past two days, they had been roaming around the Turkish quarter. Paul Nerteaux could not understand Schiffer's strategy. On Sunday evening, they should have gone straight round to see this Marek Ceziüs, alias Marius, the head of the Iskele, the main network of illegal Turkish immigrants. They should have shaken up this slave trader and got him to give them his files covering the three victims.

Instead of that, the Cipher had decided to regain contact with "his" neighbourhood, to find his feet again, as he put it. So for two days now he had been sniffing around, checking and observing his old manor, but without questioning anyone. Only the driving rain had allowed them to remain invisible in their car – to see without being seen.

Paul was champing at the bit, but he did have to admit that in forty-eight hours he had learned more about Little Turkey than he had during the three months of his inquiries.

Jean-Louis Schiffer had started by introducing him to the adjacent diasporas. They had gone to passage Brady, off boulevard de Strasbourg, the centre of the Indian world. Beneath a long glass roof, tiny brightly coloured shops and dark restaurants hung with blinds stretched into the distance. Waiters were calling out to the passers-by, while women in saris let their navels do the talking among the heavy fragrances of spices. In this rainy weather, with waves of humidity expanding and enlivening each odour, they could have been in a market in Bombay during the monsoon.

Schiffer had showed him the addresses that were used as meeting points for the Hindis, Bengalis and Pakistanis. He had drawn attention to the heads of each confession: Hindu, Muslim, Jain, Sikh and

Buddhist . . . Within a few doorways, he had summarised this concentrated exoticism which, he said, wanted nothing better than to dissolve.

"In a few years' time," he grinned, "the traffic cops round here will all be Sikhs."

Then they had taken up position on rue du Faubourg-Saint-Martin opposite the Chinese businesses. Groceries that looked like caverns, soaked with the smell of garlic and ginger; restaurants with drawn curtains that opened like velvet cases; the glistening windows and chrome counters of delicatessens, covered with salads and dumplings. At a distance, Schiffer had introduced him to the main community leaders, shopkeepers whose stores provided a mere five per cent of their total turnover.

"Never trust these buggers," he grimaced. "Not a single one of them's straight. Their heads are like their food. Full of things diced to pieces. Stuffed full of monosodium glutamate so as to put you to sleep."

Later they went back to boulevard de Strasbourg, where West Indian and African hairdressers shared the pavement with cosmetics wholesalers and joke shops. Under the copings, groups of Blacks sheltered from the rain, presenting a perfect ethnic kaleidoscope of all those who frequented the boulevard. Baoulés, Mbochis and Bétés from Ivory Coast, Laris from the Congo, Ba Congos and Baloubas from the former Zaire, Bamelekes and Ewondos from Cameroon . . .

Paul was intrigued by these ever-present yet perfectly idle Africans. He knew that most of them were drug dealers or conmen, but this did not stop him feeling a certain warmth towards them. Their lightness of mood, their humour and that tropical life, which they managed to transmit even to the asphalt, thrilled him. Above all, he found the women fascinating. Their smooth, dark stares seemed to have some hidden relationship with their lustrous hair, which had just been straightened at Afro 2000 or Royal Coiffure. Fairies of burnt wood, masks of satin with large dark eyes . . .

Schiffer gave him a more realistic, and detailed, description: "The Cameroonians are kings of forgery, from bank notes to credit cards. The Congolese specialise in threads: stolen clothes, fake labels and so on. The Ivorians are nicknamed "SOS Africa". Their speciality is false charities. They're always touching you for the starving Ethiopians or orphans of Angola. A lovely example of solidarity. But the most dangerous of all are the Zairians. Their empire is built on drugs. They reign over the entire neighbourhood. The Blacks are the worst of all," he concluded. "Pure parasites. Their only aim in life is to suck our blood."

Paul did not respond to any of these racist remarks. He had decided to remain oblivious to anything that did not directly concern their investigations. All he wanted was results. Nothing else mattered. Meanwhile, he was slowly progressing on other fronts. He had brought in two officers from the SARIJ, called Naubrel and Matkowska, so that they could follow up the lead about pressure tanks. The two lieutenants had already visited three hospitals, with negative results. They had now extended their inquiries to the contractors who work in the depths of Paris, under pressure so as to prevent the water table from leaking into their sites. Every evening, the workers used a decompression chamber. Darkness, underground . . . The lead sounded good to Paul. He was expecting a report later on that day. He had also asked a young recruit in the Brigade criminelle to collect other guidebooks and archaeological catalogues dealing with Turkey. The officer had made his first delivery the previous evening to his flat in rue du Chemin-Vert, in the eleventh *arrondissement*. A stack that he had not had time to go through yet, but which would soon be accompanying his insomnia.

On the second day, they entered the true Turkish area. This neighbourhood was bordered to the south by boulevards Bonne-Nouvelle and Saint-Denis; to the west by rue du Faubourg-Poissonnière and to the east by rue du Faubourg-Saint-Martin. To the north, the intersection of rue La Fayette and boulevard Magenta capped the district. Its spinal cord ran along boulevard de Strasbourg, which went up towards the Gare de l'Est. Its nerves spread out to each side: rue des Petites-Écuries, rue du Château-d'Eau . . . Its heart beat in the depths of Strasbourg-Saint-Denis métro station, irrigating this fragment of the East.

From an architectural point of view, the neighbourhood was unexceptional: some of its old grey buildings had been renovated, but many more were decrepit, as though they had lived a thousand lives. They all had the same layout: the ground and first floors were occupied by businesses: the second and third by sweatshops; then the upper storeys below the roof contained accommodation – overcrowded flats cut into two, or three, or four, covering the surface like little paper squares.

In the streets there was an atmosphere of impermanence, of passing through. Several of the businesses seemed devoted to movement, to the nomadic life, a precarious existence, always on the look-out. There were kiosks selling sandwiches to snack on while walking down the street; there were travel agents to prepare departures and arrivals; there were bureaux de change to acquire euros; there were photocopy stores to duplicate identity papers . . . Not to mention the numerous estate agents and signs marked "For Sale" . . .

In all of these details, Paul read the power of a permanent exodus, a human flood from a distant source, pouring endlessly and messily along the streets. But this quarter also had another purpose: the making of clothes. The Turks did not control this trade, which was run by the Jewish community of Sentier, but since the great migrations of the 1950s they had established themselves as a vital link in the chain. They supplied the wholesalers thanks to their hundreds of workshops and home workers. Thousands of hands working millions of hours which could – almost – compete with the Chinese. In any case, the Turks had the benefit of seniority and a slightly more legal social standing.

The two policemen had plunged into these crowded, agitated, ear-splitting streets. Among the delivery men, the open trucks, the bags and trolleys, the clothes passed from hand to hand. The Cipher acted as a guide once more. He knew their names, their owners and their specialities. He spoke of the Turks who had been his informers, the messengers he had had in his grip for various reasons, the restaurant owners who owed him favours. The list seemed endless. At the beginning Paul had tried to take notes, but he had soon given up. He let himself be carried onward by Schiffer's explanations, while observing the agitation all around them, picking up its cries, blaring horns, smell of pollution – everything that made the quarter what it was.

Finally, at noon on Tuesday, they crossed the final frontier and reached the kernel. The compact block known as "Little Turkey", covering rue des Petites-Écuries, the courtyard and passageway of the same name, rue d'Enghien, rue de l'Échiquier and rue du Faubourg-Saint-Denis. Only a few acres, but here all the buildings were inhabited by Turks from the basement to the attic.

This time Schiffer deciphered the scene for him, providing the access codes to this unique village. He revealed the purpose behind each doorway, each building, each window. This yard led to a goods depot which was in fact a mosque; that unfurnished room at the far end of a patio was the headquarters of an extreme left-wing group . . . Schiffer lit all the lanterns for Paul, clearing up mysteries that had been baffling him for weeks. Such as why there were always two fair-haired men dressed in black in the cour des Petites-Écuries.

"They're Lazes," the Cipher explained. "From the Black Sea, in the north-east of Turkey. They're fighters, warriors. Mustafa Kemal himself employed them as bodyguards. Their legend goes back a long way. In Greek mythology, they were the guardians of the Golden Fleece in Colchis."

Or the shadowy bar on rue des Petites-Écuries, which contained a photo of a large man with a moustache.

"It's the headquarters of the Kurds. And the picture's of Apo, or "uncle". Abdullah Oçalan, the head of the PKK, who's now in prison."

The Cipher then entered into a grandiose speech, which was almost a national anthem.

"The greatest nation without a state. Twenty-five million of them in all, twelve million in Turkey. Like the Turks, they're Muslims. Like the Turks, they wear moustaches. Like the Turks, they work in sweat-shops. The only problem is that they're not Turks, and nothing and nobody will ever make them change."

Schiffer then introduced him to the Alevis, who met on rue d'Enghien.

"They're called 'red-heads'. They're Shiite Muslims, who practise a secret rite. And they're hard nuts, take my word for it . . . Rebels, often leftists. And also an extremely close community based on initiation and friendship. They choose an 'oath brother' or 'initiate companion', and advance together towards God. They're a real force of resistance against traditional Islam."

When Schiffer spoke like that, he seemed to have a hidden respect for these peoples he at the same time constantly derided. In reality, he had a love/hate relationship with the Turkish world. Paul even remembered a rumour according to which he had almost married a girl from Anatolia. What had happened? How had the story ended? It was generally when he was beginning to imagine a superb romance between

Schiffer and the East that his partner came out with some terrible racist outburst. The two men were now sitting in their unmarked car, an ancient Golf which police headquarters had agreed to lend Paul at the outset of his inquiries. They were parked at the corner of rue des Petites-Écuries and rue du Faubourg-Saint-Denis, just in front of the Château d'Eau bar.

Night was falling and mingling with the rain to melt the scene into sludge, colourless mud. Paul looked at his watch. It was eight thirty.

"What the hell are we doing here, Schiffer? We should have gone for Marius today and . . ."

"Patience. The concert's about to start."

"What concert?"

Schiffer was fidgeting on his seat, flattening down the creases in his Barbour.

"I've already told you, Marius has a concert hall on boulevard de Strasbourg. It's an old porn cinema. There's a show on this evening. His bodyguards will be taking care of the door." He winked. "It's an ideal time to pay him a call."

He pointed at the street in front of them: "Start up and turn down rue du Château d'Eau."

Paul did so moodily. Mentally, he had given the Cipher just one chance. If he failed with Marius, then he would take him straight back to the home in Longères. But he was also impatient to see this monster at work.

"Park the other side of boulevard de Strasbourg," Schiffer ordered. "If we have problems, we can always leave via an emergency exit I know."

Paul drove across the street, up another block, then parked at the corner of rue Bouchardon.

"There won't be any problems, Schiffer."

"Give me the snaps."

He hesitated, then passed him the envelope containing the photos of the corpses. Schiffer smiled, then opened the car door.

"Just give me a free hand, and everything will be fine."

Paul then got out as well, thinking: "One chance, you old bugger. One and no more."

CHAPTER 24

In the concert hall, the beat was so strong that it obscured any other sensation. The shock wave hit you in the belly, stripping bare your nerves, then dived into your heels before surging back up your vertebrae, making them vibrate like the strips of a vibraphone.

Paul instinctively sank his head into his shoulders and bent double, as though dodging blows being rained on his stomach, chest and both sides of his head, where his eardrums were ablaze.

He blinked in order to get his bearings in the smoky atmosphere, while projectors on the stage were turning.

Finally, he made out the décor. Carved, gilded balustrades, stucco columns, fake crystal chandeliers, heavy crimson curtains . . . Schiffer had mentioned a former cinema, but instead it reminded him of the ancient kitsch of an old cabaret. A kind of music hall for operettas with frilly shirts, in which ghosts wearing brilliantine would have refused to yield their places to furious Neo-Metal groups.

On the stage, the musicians were writhing about, chanting their endless *fuckin'* and *killin'*. Bare-chested, gleaming with sweat and fever, they were wielding their guitars, mikes and drums as if they were assault rifles, raising the first rows in violent waves.

Paul left the bar and went down onto the floor. Diving in among the crowd, he felt suddenly nostalgic for the concerts of his youth: pogoing furiously, jumping like a spring to the heady riffs of the Clash; the four chords learnt on his second-hand guitar, which he ended up selling on when its strings started to remind him too much of the bloody zigzags in his father's car seat.

He realised that he had lost sight of Schiffer. He turned round, staring at the spectators who had remained at the top of the steps, by the bar. They were standing nonchalantly, glass in hand, deigning to respond to the frenzy on the stage by a mere slight swing of their hips. Paul looked among their shadowy faces, ringed with coloured beams. No Schiffer.

Suddenly, a voice burst into his ear: "Wanna score?"

Paul turned round to see a livid face, gleaming beneath its cap. "What?"

"I've got some great Black Bombays."

"You've got what?"

The man leaned over, hooking a hand over Paul's shoulder.

"Black Bombays. Dutch ones. Where've you been hiding?"

Paul pushed him away and produced his tri-colour card.

"That's where. Now piss off before I run you in."

He vanished like a blown-out flame. Paul stared for a moment at his card holder, with the stamp of the police, and measured the gulf between the concerts of back then and his present profile: an intransigent police officer, upholding law and order, implacably shaking up the dregs of society. Could he have imagined that twenty years back?

Someone tapped him in the back.

"Are you nuts?" Schiffer yelled. "Put that thing away!"

Paul was running with sweat. He tried to swallow, but could not. Everything trembled around him, the sparkling lights dislocated the faces, crumpling them up like sheets of aluminium foil.

The Cipher tapped him again, more amicably this time, on the arm.

"Come on. Marius is here. We'll catch him in his lair."

They headed off between the crush of shifting, waving bodies; a frenetic sea of shoulders and hips writhing in time, brutally, instinctively, with the rhythms being spat from off the stage. By elbowing their way through, the two cops managed to reach the front.

Schiffer then turned right, below the acute wailings of the guitars surging from the loudspeakers. Paul had a hard time keeping up with him. He noticed that he was talking with a bouncer, while the amplifier hummed furiously. The man nodded and opened a concealed door. Paul just had time to slip in through the gap.

It led into a narrow, ill-lit corridor. Posters gleamed on the walls. On most of them, the Turkish crescent and the communist hammer were joined into a political symbol. Schiffer explained: "Marius is head of an extreme left-wing group on rue Jarry. It was his pals who set fire to the Turkish prisons last year."

Paul vaguely remembered hearing about those riots, but he asked no questions. This was no time for geopolitics. The two men set off. The music continued to echo dully in their backs. Without stopping, Schiffer sneered: "Putting on concerts was a smart move. A real captive market."

"Sorry?"

"Marius also has a hand in dealing. Ecstasy. Uppers. Anything with speed in it."

Paul blinked.

"Or LSD. With these concerts, he can build up his own clientele. He's a winner every way."

It occurred to Paul to ask: "Do you know what Black Bombays are?"

"They're all the rage these days. It's Ecstasy cut with heroin."

How come a fifty-nine-year-old man, just out of a retirement home, knew the latest E trends? Another mystery.

"It's ideal when coming down," he went on. "After the excitement of speed, the heroin is calming. It's an easy passage from saucer eyes to pin-head pupils."

"Pin-head pupils?"

"Of course, heroin puts you to sleep. A junkie's always dozing off." He stopped. "I don't get it. You've never worked on a drug bust before?"

"I spent four years in the drug squad. But that doesn't make me a druggy."

The Cipher gave him his finest smile.

"How can you fight something you've never experienced? How can you understand the enemy if you don't know his strengths? You have to know what kids are looking for in that shit. And the strength of drugs, is that they're good. Jesus, if you don't know that, there's no point even trying to bust them."

Paul recalled his initial idea: Jean-Louis Schiffer, father of all cops, half-hero, half-demon, the best and the worst brought together in one man.

He swallowed his anger. His partner had set off again. A last bend, then two giants dressed in leather coats appeared on either side of a black-painted door.

The copper with the crew-cut produced his card. Paul shivered: where had this relic come from? This detail seemed to confirm their current situation. It was now the Cipher who was calling the shots. To make matters even worse, he started speaking in Turkish.

The bodyguard hesitated, then raised his hand to knock at the door. Schiffer stopped rapidly and opened the handle himself. On going in, he barked at Paul over his shoulder: "Not a word from you during the questioning."

Paul wanted to answer back appropriately, but he did not have time. This interview was going to be his initiation.

CHAPTER 25

"*Salaam aleikum*, Marius!"

The man slumped in his desk chair nearly toppled backwards.

"Schiffer . . . ? *Aleikum salaam*, my brother!"

Marek Ceziüs was already back in control. He stood up grinning broadly, and walked around his metal desk. He was wearing a red and gold football shirt, the colours of Galatasaray. His scrawny body floated in the satiny material like a banner on the terraces. It was impossible to guess how old he was. His reddish-grey hair looked like still-smouldering cinders. His features were frozen into an expression of cold joy, which gave him the sinister look of an ancient child. His coppery skin accentuated his robotic face and blended in with his rusty hair.

The two men embraced effusively. The windowless office, with its piles of papers, was saturated with smoke. Cigarette burns dotted the carpet. All the decorations seemed to date back to the 1970s: silvery cabinets and lava lamps, tom-tom stools, lamps suspended like mobiles, conical lampshades.

In a corner, Paul noticed a printing press, a photocopier, two binding machines and a guillotine. The perfect outfit for a political militant.

Marius's hearty laughter drowned out the distant din of the music.

"How long has it been?"

"At my age, you stop counting."

"We missed you, my brother. We really did."

The Turk spoke French without an accent. They embraced once more. Their play-acting had reached its peak.

"And the children?" Schiffer asked in a bantering tone.

"They grow up too quickly. I don't take my eyes off them for fear of missing something!"

"And my little Ali?"

Marius aimed a punch at Schiffer's belly, which stopped well before contact.

"He's the quickest of them all!"

Suddenly, he seemed to notice Paul. His eyes froze over, while his lips remained smiling.

"So you're back at work?" he asked the Cipher.

"Just for a simple consultation. Let me introduce you to Captain Paul Nerteaux."

Paul hesitated, then put out his hand, but no one took it. He contemplated his empty fingers in that over-bright room, full of fake smiles and the smell of cigarettes. Then, to keep up appearances, he took a look at a pile of handbills lying to his right.

"Still writing your Bolshevik stuff?" Schiffer asked.

"It's ideals that keep us alive."

The officer grabbed a sheet and translated out loud: ". . . *When the workers control the means of production . . .*" He laughed. "I thought you'd grown out of this sort of crap."

"Schiffer, my friend, it's the sort of crap which will outlive us."

"Only if someone keeps reading it."

Marius had recovered his complete smile, lips and eyes in unison.

"Some tea, my friends?"

Without waiting for an answer, he grabbed a large Thermos flask and filled three earthenware cups.

Applause was making the walls tremble.

"Aren't you fed up with those creeps?"

Marius sat back down behind his desk, blocking his desk-chair against the wall. He slowly raised his cup to his mouth.

"Music is the food of peace, my brother. Even this sort. In my country, the kids listen to the same bands as they do here. Rock will unite the future generations. It will wipe out what's left of our differences."

Schiffer pressed down the guillotine and raised his cup.

"To hard rock!"

The way Marius's form shifted oddly beneath his shirt seemed to express both amusement and weariness.

"Schiffer, you didn't come all this way, and bring this lad with you, to talk about music or our old ideals."

The Cipher sat down on the edge of the desk, sized up the Turk for a moment, then removed the horrifying photos from the envelope. Their disfigured faces scattered over the first drafts of posters. Marek Ceziüs drew back into his chair.

"What on earth are you showing me, my brother?"

"Three women. Three bodies discovered in your manor. Between November and now. My colleague thinks they're illegal immigrants. So I thought you might be able to tell us more."

The tone had changed. It sounded as if Schiffer had stitched each syllable with barbed wire.

"That's news to me," Marius said.

Schiffer smiled knowingly. "The whole neighbourhood must have been talking about little else ever since the first murder. So tell us what you know, and we'll all save a lot of time."

The dealer absent-mindedly picked up a packet of Karos, the local filter-less cigarettes, and took one out.

"My brother, I have no idea what you're talking about."

Schiffer stood back up and adopted the tone of a fair-ground barker: "Marek Ceziüs. Emperor of falsity and lies. King of smuggling and con tricks . . ."

He broke into a raucous laugh, which was also a roar, then stared down darkly at him.

"Talk, you piece of shit, before I lose my temper."

The Turk's face went as hard as glass. Sitting up straight in his chair, he lit his cigarette.

"You've got nothing, Schiffer. No warrant, no witnesses, no clues. You've just come here to ask for advice that I can't give you. I'm sorry."

He pointed at the door with a long flurry of grey smoke.

"Now, you'd better leave with your friend, and put an end to this misunderstanding."

Schiffer planted his heels in the scorched carpet and faced the desk.

"The only misunderstanding here is you. Everything's fake in this fucking office. These stupid handbills are fake. You don't give a shit about the last of the Commies rotting in prison in your country."

"You . . ."

"Your passion for music is fake. A Muslim like you thinks that rock is the work of the Devil. If you could burn down your own concert hall, you wouldn't hesitate for a moment."

Marius motioned to get up, but Schiffer pushed him back.

"Your cupboards are full of fake paperwork. You're no fucking workaholic. All this is run on smuggling and slavery!"

He went over to the guillotine and stroked its blade.

"You know as well as I do that this thing is just for cutting up your strips of acid into tabs."

He opened his arms, in a theatrical gesture, and addressed the grimy ceiling: "Oh my brother, tell me about these women before I turn your office over and find enough to pack you off to Fleury for years!"

Marek Ceziüs kept glancing at the door. The Cipher stood behind him, and leaned over his ear.

"Three women, Marius." He massaged his shoulders. "In less than four months. Tortured, disfigured, thrown onto the street. You brought them to France. Now give me their files and we'll go."

The distant pulses of the concert filled the silence. It sounded like the Turk's heart, beating inside his carcass. He murmured: "I don't have them any more."

"Why not?"

"I destroyed them. When the girls died, I threw away their records. No traces, no problems."

Paul was starting to get worried, but he appreciated this revelation. For the first time, the object of his inquiries had become real. The three victims had existed as women. They started to take form before his eyes. The corpses had become illegal immigrants.

Schiffer stood back in front of the desk.

"Watch the door," he said to Paul, without looking back at him.

"Wh . . . What?"

"The door."

Before Paul had time to react, Schiffer had leapt onto Marius and crushed his face against a corner of the desk. The nose bone snapped like a nut in a cracker. The cop lifted up his head in a shower of blood and pushed it against the wall.

"Give me the files, you cunt."

Paul rushed over, but Schiffer shoved him away. He was about to take out his gun when the dark maw of a Manhurin 44 Magnum

121

froze him. The Cipher had dropped the Turk and drawn at the same instant.

"Just watch the door."

Paul was horrified. Where had that gun sprung from? Marius was sliding off his chair and opening a drawer.

"Behind you!"

Schiffer swung and hit him full in the face with the barrel of his gun. Marius spun round full circle on his chair and landed amid the piles of handbills. The Cipher grabbed him by his shirt and stuck his gun under his throat.

"The files, you fucking Turk. Otherwise, I swear to you I won't leave you alive."

Marek was shaking. Blood was oozing out between his broken teeth, but his joyful expression remained in place. Schiffer put his gun away and dragged him to the guillotine.

Then Paul drew and yelled: "Stop it!"

Schiffer raised the guillotine and placed the man's hand beneath it.

"Give me the files, you shit heap."

"STOP OR I'LL SHOOT!"

The Cipher did not even look up. He slowly pressed down the blade. The skin of the phalanges started to give way under the edge. Black blood was bubbling up in places. Marius screamed, but not as loudly as Paul: "SCHIFFER!"

He crouched with both hands on the grip of his gun, aiming it at the Cipher. He had to shoot. He had to . . .

The door opened violently behind him. He was thrown forwards, rolled over and came to a stop at the foot of the metal desk, his neck at an unnatural angle.

The two bodyguards were drawing their guns when a spray of blood covered them. The screaming of a hyena filled the room. Paul realised that Schiffer had finished his work. He got up on to one knee, pointing his gun at the Turks.

"Back off!"

The men, hypnotised by the scene in front of them, did not move. Trembling from head to foot, Paul raised his 9 mm up to their faces.

"Back off, fuck you!"

He shoved the barrel into their chests and managed to force them back over the threshold. He closed the door with his back and could at last take a look at the nightmare.

Marius was on his knees, sobbing, his hand still trapped in the guillotine. His fingers had not been completely severed, but the phalanges had been exposed, the flesh cut from the bone. Schiffer was still holding the handle, his face deformed by a sardonic grin.

Paul put his gun away. He had to control this madman. He was about to charge, when the Turk pointed his good hand towards the silvery filing cabinets beside the photocopier.

"The keys!" Schiffer yelled.

Marius tried to take hold of the ring fixed to his belt. The Cipher grabbed it from him, and presented them one by one before his eyes. With a nod, the Turk indicated which of them would open the drawers.

The old copper started rummaging through the files. Paul took the opportunity to release the wounded man. He gingerly raised the blade, which was sticky with red stains. The Turk collapsed onto the floor, rolled up and groaned: "Hospital . . . hospital . . ."

Schiffer turned round, his eyes shining. He was holding a cardboard folder, tied up with a cloth strap. He flung it open to reveal the files and Polaroids of the three girls.

In a state of shock, Paul realised that they had won.

CHAPTER 26

They took the emergency exit and ran to the Golf. Paul shot off at once, nearly hitting a passing car.

He kept his foot down, swerving right into rue Lucien-Sampaix. He then suddenly realised that he was going the wrong way up a one-way street. He quickly took the next left onto boulevard Magenta.

Reality was dancing before his eyes. Tears added to the rain on the windscreen, blurring everything. He could just see the traffic lights which were bleeding like wounds in the downpour.

He crossed one junction without braking, then another, setting off a flurry of skidding cars and blaring horns. At the third light, he finally stopped. For a few seconds, his head spun, then he knew what he had to do.

Green.

He accelerated without releasing the clutch, stalled and swore.

He was turning the ignition key when Schiffer said: "Where are you going?"

"To the station," he panted. "I'm arresting you, you bastard."

From the far side of the square, the Gare de l'Est shone like a cruise ship. He was about to pull away, when the Cipher shifted his leg over to the other side and stamped on the accelerator.

"Fucking hell . . ."

Schiffer grabbed the wheel and turned it to the right. They shot down rue Sibour, a side road that ran beside the church of Saint-Laurent. Still using one hand, he turned again, forcing the Golf to bounce over the separations of the cycle path and come to a halt against the pavement.

Paul took the wheel in his ribs. He hiccuped, coughed, then melted into a burning sweat. He clenched his fist and turned towards his passenger, ready to smash his jaw.

The man's pallid face dissuaded him. Jean-Louis Schiffer looked twenty years older once more. His entire profile was melting into his flabby neck. His eyes were so glassy they looked transparent. A real death's head.

"You're a lunatic," Paul panted in disgust. "A fucking sicko. You can count on me to make the charge sheet look good. You're going to rot in prison, you fucking torturer!"

Without answering, Schiffer found an old map of Paris in the glove compartment and tore off a few pages to wipe the blood from his jacket. His blotchy hands were trembling, his words hissed from between his teeth: "There's no other way to deal with the fuckers."

"We're police officers."

"Marius is a shit. He manipulates whores over here by having their kids mutilated back home. An arm, a leg. It calms down the Turkish mothers."

"We represent the law."

Paul was getting his breath and his poise back. His eyesight was also returning with the flat black wall of the church, the gargoyles over their heads, standing like gallows, and the rain still assailing the night.

Schiffer threw away the reddened pages, opened the window and spat.

"It's too late to get rid of me."

"If you think I'm scared to answer for what I've done . . . then you've got another think coming. You're headed behind bars, even if I have to share your cell."

Schiffer raised a hand to switch on the roof light then opened the folder on his lap. He removed the papers concerning the three girls: they were loose laser-printed leaves, with a Polaroid stapled on each one. He tore off the photos and placed them on the dashboard, as if they were playing cards.

He cleared his throat again and asked: "What do you see?"

Paul did not move. The light from the streetlamps was making the pictures glisten above the steering wheel. For two months, he had been looking for these faces. He had pictured them, drawn them, wiped them out and started all over again a hundred times . . . Now they were in front of him, he felt as nervy as a virgin.

Schiffer took him by the scruff of the neck and forced him to look.

"What do you see?" he said huskily.

Paul opened his eyes wide. Three women with gentle features, slightly stunned by the flashlight, were staring at him. Their broad faces were rimmed by red hair.

"Do you notice anything?" the Cipher insisted.

Paul hesitated.

"They look alike, don't they?"

Schiffer burst out laughing and repeated: "They look alike? You mean they're carbon copies!"

Paul turned towards him. He was unsure if he had understood.

"And so?"

"So, you were right. The killer is after a particular face. A face which he both adores and detests, which obsesses him and provokes contradictory impulses. As for his motive, anything is possible. But we now know that he's pursuing an objective."

Paul's anger turned into a feeling of victory. So his intuitions had been right: they were illegal immigrants, with identical looks . . . Was he also right about the ancient statues?

Schiffer continued: "These photos are a huge step forward, take my word for it. Because they also provide us with a vital piece of information. The killer knows this neighbourhood like the back of his hand."

"That's nothing new."

"We figured that he's Turkish, not that he knows every sweatshop and cellar round here. Can you imagine the patience and perseverance you need to find girls who look that much alike? The bastard must have eyes everywhere."

Paul said, more calmly: "OK. I admit that I'd never have got hold of these photos without you. So I'll spare you the station. I'll just take you straight back to Longères without passing by the police."

He turned the ignition key, but Schiffer grabbed his arm.

"Don't be silly, kid. You need me now more than ever."

"It's all over for you."

The Cipher picked up one of the pieces of paper and held it under the light.

"We haven't just got their faces and identities. We've also got the addresses of their workshops. That's a solid lead."

Paul released the key.

"Maybe their colleagues saw something?"

"Remember what forensics said. Their stomachs were empty. They were going home after work. We'll have to question women who go the same way every evening. And also the bosses of the workshops. But to do that, you need me, my lad."

Schiffer did not have to press the point. For three months, Paul had been banging his head against the same wall. He imagined himself starting his inquiries again on his own, and obtaining an infinite series of zeros.

"I'll give you one day," he conceded. "We'll go round the workshops. We'll question their colleagues, neighbours and partners, if there are any. Then you go back to the home. And I'm warning you: the slightest fuck-up and I'll kill you. This time, I won't hesitate."

His partner forced a laugh, but Paul sensed that he was scared. Fear now gripped both of them. He was about to start up, when he paused once more – he wanted everything to be clear.

"Why were you so violent with that Marius?"

Schiffer looked up at the gargoyles, which rose into the darkness. Devils curled around their perches, incubuses with turned-up noses, demons with bat's wings. He remained silent for a while, then murmured: "There was no other way. They've decided not to speak."

"Who do you mean by *they*?"

"The Turks. The whole neighbourhood's gone dumb. We're going to have to rip out each scrap of the truth."

Paul's voice cracked, rising up a tone.

"But why are they doing that? Why don't they want to help us?"

The Cipher was still staring at those faces of stone. His pallor competed with that of the roof light.

"Don't you get it? They're protecting the killer."

V

CHAPTER 27

Between his arms, she had been a river.

A fluid, supple, open energy. She had breezed through the nights and days like a ripple touches underwater greenery, without ever altering its languid pace. She had flowed between his hands, crossing shadowy forests, beds of moss, dark rocks. She had risen up in the clearings that burst into her eyes when pleasure came. Then she had abandoned herself once more, in a slow shift, translucent beneath his palms . . .

Over the years, there had been distinct seasons. Light, laughing rivulets of water. Manes of foam shaken by anger. Fords, too, truces during which their physical contact ceased. But such pauses were sweet. They had the lightness of reeds, the smoothness of bare pebbles.

When the current picked up again, pushing them again to the farthest shores, beyond sighs, their lips apart, it was to reach at last the ultimate pleasure, where everything was one – and the other was all.

"You understand, doctor?"

Mathilde Wilcrau jumped. She looked at the Knoll couch, just two yards away – the only piece of furniture in the room that did not date to the eighteenth century. A man was lying there. A patient. Lost in a daydream, she had completely forgotten about him and had not listened to a word he had said.

She concealed her embarrassment by saying: "No, I'm afraid I don't. You're not being very clear. Can you try and put it another way, please?"

The man launched into a new explanation, his nose facing the ceiling, hands crossed on his chest. Mathilde discreetly took a moisturising cream from a drawer. The freshness of the product on her hands brought her back to herself. Such moments of abstraction were becoming increasingly frequent and profound. She was now pushing the neutrality of the analyst to its extreme: she was quite literally no longer there. In the past, she used to listen to her patients' every word. She observed every slip of the tongue, hesitation and excess. They formed a thread that allowed her to find a path back through their neuroses and traumas . . . But now?

She put the pot away and continued to rub the cream into her hands. Nourish. Hydrate. Soothe. The man's voice was now just a murmur, rocking her profound melancholy.

Yes, between his arms she had been a river. But the fords had multiplied, the truces grown longer. At first, she had refused to worry, to see in these pauses a sign of a falling away. She had been blind with hope and faith in love. Then a taste of dust settled on her tongue, a sharp pain had gripped her limbs. Soon, even her veins seemed to have dried up, like lifeless mineral deposits. She felt empty. Even before their hearts had put a name to the situation, their bodies had spoken.

Then the split broke through into their minds, and their words finished off the motion: their separation became official. The period of formalities began. They had to see a magistrate, calculate the alimony, organise the move. Mathilde had been irreproachable. Ever alert. Ever responsible. But her mind was already elsewhere. As soon as she could, she tried to remember, to travel within herself, in her own story, amazed to find so few traces in her memory, so few instants from the past. Her entire being was like a burnt desert, an ancient site where only some meagre ridges among the overly white stones still gave a sign of what had been.

She reassured herself by thinking of her children. They incarnated her destiny, were her last source of life. She devoted herself to them. She abandoned herself completely during the final years of their education. But they, too, had ended up leaving her. Her son had vanished into a strange town, both tiny and huge, made up entirely of chips and microprocessors, while her daughter had found her path in travelling and ethnology. Or so she claimed. All that she was sure of was that her path lay far away from her parents.

So now she had to take an interest in the only person she had left: herself. She denied herself nothing – clothes, furniture, lovers. She went on cruises and trips to places that had always fascinated her. In vain. Such extravagance seemed merely to hasten her downfall into old age.

Desertification was continuing its ravages. Lifeless sand spread ever farther inside her. Not only in her body, but in her heart. She became harder, harsher towards others. Her judgements were abrupt, her opinions strong and final. Her generosity, understanding and compassion deserted her. The slightest indulgent gesture cost her an effort. Her feelings became paralysed, making her hostile to other people.

She ended up arguing with her closest friends, and found herself alone, really alone. Having run out of enemies, she took up sport so as to confront herself. Her achievements included mountain climbing, rowing, hang-gliding, shooting . . . Training became a permanent challenge for her, an obsession that drained way her anxieties.

Now, she had got over such excesses, but her life was still dotted by frequent exertions. A hang-gliding course in the Cévennes, the yearly climbing of the "Dalles" near Chamonix, the triathlon event in the Val d'Aoste. At the age of fifty-two, she was fit enough to make any teenager green with envy. And, every day, with a hint of vanity, she looked at the trophies that shone on her authentic Oppenordt school chest-of-drawers.

In reality, what delighted her was a different sort of victory: an intimate, secret triumph. During all those years of solitude, she had never once resorted to drugs. She had never taken the slightest anxiolytic or antidepressant.

Every morning she looked at herself in the mirror and recalled this achievement. The jewel in her crown. A personal certificate of endurance which proved that she had not exhausted her reserves of courage and willpower.

Most people live in hope of the best.

All that Mathilde Wilcrau feared was the worst.

Of course, in the middle of that desert, there was her work. Her consultations at Sainte-Anne Hospital and appointments at her private practice. The hard style and the soft style, as they say in the martial arts, which she had also practised. Psychiatric care and psychoanalytic attention. But, after a time, these two poles had ended up merging into the same routine.

Her timetable was now marked by several strict, compulsory rituals. Once a week, when possible, she had lunch with her children, who spoke only of success for themselves, and the failure of her and their father. Every weekend, she visited antique shops, between two training sessions. Then, on Tuesday evening, she attended the seminars at the Society of Psychoanalysis, where she would still see a few familiar faces. Particularly former lovers, whose names she had even forgotten and who had always seemed bland to her. But perhaps she was the one who had lost the taste for love. As when you burn your tongue, and can no longer taste your food . . .

She glanced at the clock. Only five more minutes before the end of the session. The man was still talking. She wriggled on her chair. Her body was already prickling with the sensations to come – the dryness in her throat when she pronounced the concluding words after a long silence; the smoothness of her fountain-pen on her diary, when she jotted down the next appointment; the rustling of leather when she got up . . .

A little later, in the hallway, the patient turned round and asked her anxiously: "I didn't go too far, did I, doctor?"

Mathilde shook her head with a smile, and opened the door. So what had he revealed this time that was so important? It did not matter. He was sure to do even better next time. She went out onto the landing and switched on the light.

She screamed when she saw her.

The woman was hunched up against the wall, clutching her black kimono. Mathilde recognised her at once: Anna something. The one who needed a good pair of glasses. She was white and shaking from head to foot. What was this all about?

Mathilde pushed the man downstairs and turned angrily towards this little brunette. She did not tolerate her patients just showing up like that, without warning, without making an appointment. A good psychiatrist should always be a good bouncer.

She was about to give her a piece of her mind, when the woman beat her to it, holding a face scan up to her nose: "They've wiped away my memory and my face."

CHAPTER 28

Paranoid psychosis.

The diagnosis was clear. Anna Heymes claimed that she had been manipulated by her husband and Eric Ackermann, as well as by some other men who were members of the French police force. Against her will, she was supposed to have been brainwashed and part of her memory removed. Her face had been altered using plastic surgery. She did not know why or how, but she had been the victim of a plot, or an experiment, which had damaged her personality.

She explained all this in hurried tones, brandishing her cigarette like a conductor's baton. Mathilde listened to her patiently, noting as she did how thin she was – anorexia could be another symptom of her paranoia.

Anna Heymes then came to the end of her unbelievable yarn. She had uncovered the plot that very morning, in the bathroom, when she discovered the scars on her face, while her husband was about to take her to Ackermann's clinic.

She had escaped through the window and had been chased by policemen in civilian dress who were armed to the teeth and equipped with radio transmitters. She had hidden in an Orthodox church, then had had her face X-rayed at Saint-Antoine Hospital in order to obtain tangible proof of her operation. Then she had wandered around till nightfall, waiting to take refuge with the only person she now trusted – Mathilde Wilcrau. There we are.

Paranoid psychosis.

Mathilde had treated hundreds of similar cases at Sainte-Anne Hospital. The first thing to do was to calm the patient down. After a deal of comforting words, she had managed to give her an intra-muscular injection of fifty milligrams of Tranxene.

Anna Heymes was now sleeping on her couch. Mathilde was sitting behind her desk, in her usual position.

All she had to do now was to phone up Laurent Heymes. She could even see to it that Anna was sectioned, or else contact Eric Ackermann, who was treating her. In a few minutes, everything would be sorted out. It was just routine.

So why hadn't she called? For the last hour, she had been sitting there, without picking up the phone. She stared round at the furniture, which glinted in places, reflecting the light from the window. For years, she had been surrounded by these rococo-style furnishings, most of which had been bought by her husband. She had fought hard to retain possession of them during their divorce. Firstly to piss him off, then, she realised, to keep something of him. She had never made up her mind to sell them. She was now living in a sanctuary. A mausoleum of varnished antiques that reminded her of the only years that had really counted.

Paranoid psychosis. A textbook case.

Except that there were the scars. The traces she herself had observed on the young woman's forehead, ears and chin. She could even feel the screws and implants under her skin that were holding up her face's bone structure. That terrifying print-out then gave her the details of the operations.

During her years of practice, Mathilde had encountered many paranoiacs, but very few of them went around with concrete proof of their delusions written into their faces. Anna Heymes was wearing a sort of mask that had been stitched onto her flesh. A rind of skin that had been fashioned and moulded to dissimulate her smashed bones and atrophied muscles.

Was she quite simply telling the truth? Had these men – policemen with it – made her undergo such treatment? Had they shattered the bones of her face? Had they interfered with her memory?

There was another disturbing element in this business: the presence of Eric Ackermann. She remembered a tall red-head with a face pitted with acne. One of her countless suitors at university, but above all a man of extraordinary intelligence, which verged on the sublime.

At the time, what fascinated him was the human brain and "inner travel". He had followed the experiments conducted by Timothy Leary on LSD at Harvard and, via this approach, he claimed to be exploring uncharted regions of consciousness. He took all sorts of psychotropic drugs while analysing his own altered states. He sometimes even spiked fellow students' coffee with LSD, "just to see". Mathilde smiled as she remembered his weirdness. It had been a crazy period, with psychedelic rock, protest movements, the hippies . . .

Ackermann had predicted that, one day, machines would allow us to travel inside the brain and observe its activity in real time. And time had proved him to be right. He had become one of the best-qualified neurologists in this field, thanks to new technologies such as the positron camera and the encephalogram.

Was it possible that he was conducting an experiment on this young woman?

She looked in her address book for the phone number of a student who had taken her courses at Sainte-Anne in 1995. On the fourth ring, she answered.

"Valérie Rannan?"

"Speaking."

"This is Mathilde Wilcrau."

"Professor Wilcrau?"

It was past eleven, and her tone of voice was suddenly alert.

"What I am going to ask you will probably sound rather odd, especially at this time of night . . ."

"What do you want?"

"I just want to ask you a few questions about your doctoral thesis. It was about mental manipulation and sensory isolation, if I remember correctly."

"It didn't seem to interest you very much at the time."

Mathilde noticed a slightly aggressive tone in her answer. She had in fact refused to direct her work. She had not believed in this line of research. For her, brainwashing was more part of a collective fantasy, or an urban legend. She soothed out her voice with a smile: "Yes, I know. I was rather sceptical. But right now I need some information for an article I have to write on a short deadline."

"You can always ask."

Mathilde did not know where to start. She was not even sure what she wanted to find out. She started, at random: "In the synopsis of your thesis, you wrote that it is possible to efface someone's memory. Is it . . . is it true?"

"The techniques were developed in the 1950s."

"By the Soviets, is that right?"

"The Russians, the Chinese, the Americans, just about everybody. It was a major element in the Cold War. Destroying the memory. Removing convictions. Modelling personalities."

"What methods were used?"

"Always the same ones: electroshocks, drugs, sensory deprivation."

There was silence.

"Which drugs?" Mathilde asked.

"I worked mostly on the CIA's programme, MK-Ultra. The Americans used sedatives. Phenotrazine. Sodium amytal. Chlopromazine."

Mathilde knew the names. They were the heavy artillery of psychiatry. In hospitals, these products were grouped together under the generic name "chemical straitjacket". But in reality, they were more like a grinder, a machine to mould the mind.

"What about sensory isolation?"

Valérie Rannan sneered.

"The most advanced experiments were conducted in Canada, from 1954 onwards, in a clinic in Montreal. First, the psychiatrists interviewed some of their female patients, who were depressives. They forced them to confess their faults, and any fantasies they were ashamed of. Then, they locked them in completely dark rooms, in which they could no longer see the floor, walls or ceiling. After that, they placed footballer's helmets on their heads, in which extracts from their confessions were played on a loop. The women constantly heard the same words, the same sentences, which were the most painful parts of their confessions. The only respite was the sessions of electroshock therapy and sleep cures under sedation."

Mathilde glanced over at Anna, asleep on the couch. Her chest rose and fell slightly as she breathed.

The student went on: "When the patients could no longer remember their names or their pasts, when they had no willpower left, the real treatment began. The therapists changed the tapes in the helmets, which now played out orders and commands, which were supposed to forge their new personalities."

Like all psychiatrists, Mathilde had heard of such aberrations, but she could not convince herself of either their reality, or their effectiveness.

"What were the results?" she asked in a neutral voice.

"All the Americans managed to produce were zombies. The Russians and Chinese seem to have obtained better results, using more or less identical methods. After the Korean War, over seven thousand American prisoners of war returned to their country, absolutely convinced by communist values. Their personalities had been conditioned."

Mathilde rubbed her shoulders. A tomblike chill was rising up her limbs.

"And do you think that laboratories have continued to work in this field since then?"

"Of course."

"What sort of labs?"

Valérie laughed sarcastically.

"You're really on another planet, aren't you? We're talking about military research centres. All armies work on manipulating brains."

"In France too?"

"In France, in Germany, in Japan, in the USA. Everywhere that has the technological means. New products are constantly coming out. Right now, there's a lot of talk about a chemical compound called GHB, which wipes out what you have experienced during the previous twelve hours. It's called the 'rapist's drug', because a drugged victim won't remember a thing. I'm sure the army is still working on that kind of product. The brain is the most dangerous weapon in the world."

"Thank you, Valérie."

She sounded surprised.

"You don't want any precise sources? A bibliography?"

"That's all right. I'll call you back if necessary."

CHAPTER 29

Mathilde went over to Anna, who was still asleep. She examined her arm in search of traces of injections. Nothing. She looked at her hair. Repeated absorption of sedatives provoked an electrostatic inflammation of the scalp. No particular sign.

She stood up in amazement at having almost believed the woman's story. No, really, she must be out of her mind as well . . . At that moment, she once again noticed the scars on the forehead – three tiny vertical lines barely an inch apart. She could not resist touching the temples and jaw. The prostheses shifted around beneath the skin.

Who had done that? How could Anna have forgotten such an operation?

Right from her first visit, she had mentioned the institute where the tomographic tests had been carried out. *It's in Orsay. A hospital full of soldiers.* Mathilde had written the name down somewhere in her notes.

She looked quickly through her pad and came across a page full of her usual doodling. In the top right-hand corner, she had written "Henri-Becquerel".

Mathilde fetched a bottle of water from the closet next to her consulting room then, after taking a long swig from it, she picked up the phone and dialled a number.

"René? It's Mathilde. Mathilde Wilcrau." A slight hesitation. The time. The years gone by. The surprise . . . Then a deep voice finally said: "How are things?"

"I'm not disturbing you?"

"Of course not. It's always a pleasure to hear your voice."

René Le Garrec had been her teacher and professor when she was studying at Val-de-Grâce Hospital. A military psychiatrist and specialist in the traumas of war, he had set up the first medico-psychiatric emergency units open to victims of terrorism, war or natural disasters. He was a pioneer who had proved to Mathilde that you can wear a uniform without necessarily being an idiot.

"I just wanted to ask you something. Do you know the Henri-Becquerel Institute?"

She noticed a slight hesitation.

"Yes, I do. It's a military hospital."

"What do they work on there?"

"They used to work on nuclear medicine."

"And now?"

Another hesitation. Mathilde was sure of one thing: she was venturing into forbidden territory.

"I don't know exactly," the doctor replied. "They treat certain forms of trauma."

"From war?"

"I think so. I'd have to ask."

Mathilde had worked for three years in Le Garrec's department. No mention had ever been made of this institute. As though trying to cover the clumsiness of his lie, the soldier went on the attack.

"Why are you asking me this?"

She made no attempt to duck and dive.

"I have a patient who's had tests done there."

"What sort of tests?"

"Tomographic ones."

"I didn't know they had a Petscan."

"It was Ackermann who carried them out."

"The cartographer?"

Eric Ackermann had written a book about the techniques for exploring the brain, bringing together the work of various teams from around the world. It had since become the standard reference book. Since its publication, the neurologist had the reputation of being one of the greatest topographers of the human brain. A traveller who voyaged around this region of the anatomy as though it were the sixth continent.

Mathilde confirmed. Le Garrec observed: "It's odd he's working with us."

The "us" amused her. The army was more than just a corporation, it was a family.

"You're right," she said. "I knew Ackermann at university. He was a real rebel. A conscientious objector, drugged up to his eyeballs. I find it hard to picture him working with soldiers. I think he was even condemned for illegal production of narcotics."

Le Garrec could not help laughing.

"But that could be the reason. Do you want me to contact them?"

"No thanks. I just wanted to know if you had heard about their work, that's all."

"What's your patient called?"

Mathilde now realised that she had gone a step too far. Le Garrec was going to start asking questions himself or, even worse, refer the matter to his superiors. Suddenly, the world Valérie Rannan had described seem more probable. A universe of secret, impenetrable experiments, conducted in the name of a higher reason.

She tried to deflate the tension.

"Don't worry, it was only a detail."

"What's the patient's name?" the officer insisted.

Mathilde felt the chill riser higher in her body.

"Thanks," she replied. "I'll . . . I'll call Ackermann myself."

"As you like."

Le Garrec was retreating too. They both adopted their usual roles, their usual casual tone. But they knew that, during this brief conversation, they had crossed the same minefield. She hung up after promising to ring him back for lunch some time.

So, it was certain that the Henri-Becquerel Institute had its secrets. And Eric Ackermann's presence in this business deepened the mystery even more. Anna Heymes's "delusions" were now seeming less and less psychotic . . .

Mathilde went into the private part of her flat. She had a particular gait: shoulders up, arms along her body, fists raised and, above all, hips slightly swaying. When she was young, she had spent a long time perfecting this oblique step, which she thought suited her figure. It had now become second nature to her.

When she reached her bedroom, she opened a varnished writing desk, decorated with palm leaves and bunches of reeds. A Meissonnier, 1740. She used a miniature key, which she always kept on her, and pulled open a drawer.

She opened a box made of woven bamboo, incrusted with mother-of-pearl. At the bottom, there was a piece of chamois leather. With her thumb and forefinger, she pulled aside rolls of cloth and revealed the glittering presence of a forbidden object.

A Glock 9 mm automatic pistol.

An extremely light weapon, with a mechanical lock and a Safe-Action catch. Before, this pistol had been used as a piece of sports equipment, and had been authorised by an official licence. But now this gun, loaded with sixteen armour-plated bullets, was no longer authorised. It had become an instrument of death, forgotten by the labyrinthine French bureaucracy . . .

Mathilde weighed the gun in her palm, thinking over her current situation. A divorced psychiatrist, with a lousy sex life, hiding an automatic pistol in her writing desk. She smiled and murmured: "How symbolic can you get . . ."

When she returned to her consulting room she made another phone call, then went over to the couch. She had to shake Anna extremely hard before she obtained any signs of waking up.

Finally, the young woman rolled over slowly. She stared at her hostess, showing no surprise, her head to one side. In a low voice, Mathilde asked: "You didn't tell anyone that you'd come to see me?"

She shook her head.

"No one knows that we know each other?"

Same answer. It occurred to Mathilde that she might have been followed. It was now double or quits.

Anna was rubbing her eyes with the palms of her hands, making herself look even more strange, with her lazy eyelids, that languidness about her temples, above her cheekbones. She still had the marks from the blanket on her cheek.

Mathilde thought of her own daughter, the one who had left home and had tattooed on her shoulder the Chinese ideogram for "the Truth".

"Come on," she whispered. "We're going."

CHAPTER 30

"What did they do to me?"

The two women were speeding along boulevard Saint-Germain towards the Seine. The rain had stopped, but left its presence everywhere in the glints, glitters and blue splashes of the night's vibrato.

To conceal her doubts, Mathilde adopted a professorial tone.

"A treatment," she said.

"What sort of treatment?"

"Clearly something new, which has allowed them to alter parts of your memory."

"Is that possible?"

"Normally speaking, no. But Ackermann must have come up with something . . . revolutionary. A technique connected with tomography and the brain's regions."

While driving, she constantly peered round at Anna, who was slumped on the seat, staring forwards, her two hands clenched between her thighs.

"A shock can cause partial amnesia," she went on. "I treated a footballer after a collision during a match. He could remember part of his existence, but not all of it. Maybe Ackermann has found a way to do the same thing using drugs, irradiation, or some other technique. A sort of screen that has been pulled across your memory."

"But why?"

"In my opinion, the answer lies in Laurent's work. You must have seen something that you shouldn't have, or else you have some information connected with his activities, or maybe you're just a guinea-pig . . . Anything is possible. We're in a world of madmen."

At the end of boulevard Saint-Germain, the Institut du Monde Arabe appeared to their right. Clouds were drifting across its glassy sides.

Mathilde was amazed at how calm she felt. She was driving at over sixty miles an hour, an automatic pistol in her bag, with this death's head by her side, and she did not feel at all afraid. Instead, she had a sensation of a certain distance, mingled with child-like excitement.

"And can my memory be restored?"

Anna spoke awkwardly. Mathilde recognised this tone. She had heard it a thousand times during consultations at the hospital. It was the voice of obsession, of madness. Except that this time, her delusions corresponded to reality.

She chose her words carefully: "I can't answer that until I know what technique was used. If it was a chemical substance, then maybe there's an antidote. If surgery was used then . . . I'd be more pessimistic."

The little Mercedes was gliding past the zoo in the Jardin des Plantes. The sleep of the animals and stillness of the park seemed to unite in the darkness to dig out an abyss of silence.

Mathilde saw that Anna was crying, in the small staccato sobs of a little girl. After a while, she recovered her voice, which was mixed with tears: "But why change my face?"

"That's a mystery. Maybe you were in the wrong place at the wrong time. But that wouldn't mean having to change your appearance. Unless the situation's even crazier, and they've altered your entire identity."

"You mean, I was someone else before?"

"That's what the plastic surgery could lead us to suppose."

"I'm . . . I'm not Laurent Heymes's wife?"

Mathilde did not reply. Anna went further: "But what about my . . . feelings. My . . . intimacy with him?"

Anger gripped Mathilde. In the midst of this horror, Anna was still thinking about love. There was nothing to be done about it. When a woman was shipwrecked, it was always "desire and feelings first".

"All my memories of being with him . . . I can't have just invented them!"

Mathilde shrugged, as though to alleviate the seriousness of what she was about to say.

"Maybe your memories were implanted. You told me yourself that they're fading away, that they seem unreal . . . Normally speaking, such a thing is impossible. But someone like Ackermann is capable of anything. And the police must have given him unlimited means."

"The police?"

"Wake up, Anna. The Henri-Becquerel Institute. The soldiers. Laurent's job. Except for the Maison du Chocolat, your universe was entirely made up of policemen and uniforms. They were the ones who did this to you. And now they're looking for you."

They had reached the perimeter of the Gare d'Austerlitz, which was being renovated. One of its façades revealed its own inner void, like a cinema set. The windows gaping below the sky looked like the left-overs of a bombing. On the left, in the background, the Seine ran on. Dark silt drifting slowly . . .

After a long pause, Anna said: "There's someone in this story who isn't a policeman."

"Who?"

"The customer in the shop. The one I recognise. My colleague and I call him 'Mister Corduroys'. I don't know how to explain this, but I sense that he's not part of all this. That he belongs to the part of my life that they've wiped out."

"But why has he crossed your path?"

"Maybe it's a coincidence."

Mathilde shook her head.

"Look, one thing I'm sure of is that there aren't any coincidences in this business. You can be certain that he's working with the others. If his face rings a bell, it's probably because you saw him with Laurent."

"Or because he likes Jikolas."

145

"Sorry?"

"Chocolates with a marzipan filling. It's one of the shop's specialities." She laughed breathlessly, then wiped her tears. "In any case, it's logical enough if he doesn't recognise me, given that my face has completely changed."

Then she added, in despair: "We must find it. We must uncover something about my past!"

Mathilde refrained from commenting. She was now driving up boulevard de l'Hôpital, under the iron arches of the overhead métro line.

"Where are we going?" Anna cried out.

Mathilde crossed over the street diagonally, then parked in the wrong direction beside the campus of La Pitié-Salpêtrière Hospital. She switched off the ignition, then turned towards the little Cleopatra.

"The only way we can understand your story is to find out who you were 'before'. To judge by your scars, the surgery was carried out about six months ago. Somehow or other, we're going to have to go back beyond that point." She pressed her finger against her forehead. "You must remember what happened before that date."

Anna glanced up at the signpost of the teaching hospital.

"You want . . . you want to question me under hypnosis?"

"We don't have time for that."

"So what are you going to do?"

Mathilde pushed a black lock of hair back behind Anna's ear.

"If your memory can't tell us anything, and your face has been obliterated, there's still one thing that remembers who you are."

"What?"

"Your body."

CHAPTER 31

The biological research unit of La Pitié-Salpêtrière was lodged in the faculty of medicine. A long six-storey block, it was dotted with hundreds of windows, giving a dizzying idea of the number of laboratories it must contain.

This typically 1960s architecture reminded Mathilde of the universities and hospitals she had studied in. She had a particular feeling for such places and, to her mind, their style was forever associated with knowledge, authority and learning.

They walked towards the gate, their feet clacking on the silvery pavement. Mathilde entered the security code. Inside, cold and darkness welcomed them. They crossed a huge hall to an iron lift to the left, which looked like a safe.

Its interior smelt of grease. It felt to Mathilde that she was ascending a tower of knowledge, alongside the superstructures of science. Despite her age and experience, she felt crushed by this place, which evoked a temple for her. It was sacred territory.

The lift continued to rise. Anna lit a cigarette. Mathilde's senses were so acute that it was as though she could hear the crackling of the burning paper. She had dressed her protégée in some of her daughter's clothes, which had been left in her flat after a New Year's party. The two women were the same size, and also wore the same shade: black.

Anna was now wearing a slim-fitting velvet coat, with long narrow sleeves, silk bell-bottoms and highly polished shoes. These party clothes made her look like a little girl in mourning.

At last, on the fifth floor, the doors opened. They went up a corridor covered with red tiles, punctuated by doors with frosted glass windows. A soft light was coming from the far end. They approached it.

Mathilde opened the door without knocking. Professor Alain Veynerdi was expecting them, standing beside a white bench.

This small vigorous sixty-year-old had the dark skin of a Hindu and the dryness of papyrus. Beneath his impeccable white coat, he was clearly wearing even more impeccable evening dress. His hands had been manicured, his nails looked lighter than his skin, like little mother-of-pearl lozenges at the tips of his fingers. His grey Brylcreemed hair was carefully combed back. He looked like a painted figure straight out of a Tintin comic. His bowtie gleamed like the key of some secret mechanism, waiting to be wound up.

Mathilde took care of the introductions and once more went through the main points of the lie she had told the biologist over the phone. Anna had had a car accident eight months before. Her vehicle had burnt, her identity papers were inside, and her memory had been obliterated. The injuries to her face had required extensive surgery. Her identity was therefore a total mystery.

The story was barely believable, but Veynerdi did not live in a rational world. All that mattered to him was the scientific challenge that Anna represented.

He pointed at the stainless-steel table.

"Shall we start straight away?"

"Hang on," Anna protested. "Maybe you'd better tell me what you're going to do first."

Mathilde turned to Veynerdi.

"Can you explain, Professor?"

He looked at the young woman.

"I'm afraid we'll have to give you a little anatomy lesson . . ."

"Don't put on your airs and graces with me."

He smiled briefly, as bitterly as a lemon.

"The elements that make up the human body regenerate according to specific cycles. The red corpuscles are reproduced every hundred and twenty days. The skin sloughs completely in five days. The lining of the intestines is renewed in just forty-eight hours. However, within this constant reconstruction, the immune system contains cells which conserve traces of contact they have had with foreign bodies for long periods of time. They are called memory cells."

He had a smoker's voice, deep and husky, which did not fit with his immaculate looks.

"When confronted with a disease, the cells produce molecules for defence or recognition, which carry the mark of the attack. When they are reproduced, they transmit this defensive information. It's a sort of biological record, if you will. The entire principle of vaccination is based on this system. It is enough to put the human body in contact with a pathogen just once for cells to produce protective molecules for years. What applies to illness also applies to any other external element. We always keep traces of our past life, of our countless contacts with the world. It is possible to study these marks and give them a date and origin."

He bowed slightly.

"This as yet little-known field is my speciality."

Mathilde remembered when she had first met Veynerdi, during a seminar on memory in Majorca in 1997. Most of the guests were neurologists, psychiatrists and psychoanalysts. They had discussed synapses, networks, the subconscious, and had all mentioned the complexity of memory. Then, on the fourth day, a biologist in a bowtie had spoken, and their horizons had completely changed. Behind his reading desk, Alain Veynerdi was talking about physical not mental memory.

The specialist presented a study he had conducted on perfumes. The constant impregnation of alcoholised substances in the skin ends up "engraving" certain cells, thus forming an identifiable marker, even after the subject has stopped using the fragrance. He cited the example of a woman who had used Chanel Number 5 for ten years, and whose skin still bore its chemical signature four years later.

That day, the audience left the lecture hall in rapture. Suddenly, memory had become something physical, which could be analysed chemically, under the microscope . . . Suddenly, that abstract entity, which constantly evaded the instruments of modern technology, had turned out to be material, tangible, observable. A human science had become an exact one.

Anna's face was lit up by the low lamp. Despite her weariness, her eyes were sparkling brightly. She was beginning to understand.

"In my case, what sort of things can you find out?"

"Trust me," the biologist replied. "In the secret of your cells, your body has kept marks of your past. We are going to reveal traces of the physical environment in which you lived before your accident. The air you breathed. The sort of food you ate. The signature of the perfume you wore. One way or another, I am sure you are the same woman as before."

CHAPTER 32

Veynerdi switched on various machines. Their glittering lights and computer screens revealed the true dimensions of the laboratory: a large room cluttered with analytical equipment, whose walls were divided between bay windows and cork lining. The bench and stainless-steel table reflected each light source, stretching them into green, yellow, pink and red filaments.

The biologist pointed to a door on the left.

"Get undressed in the changing-room, please."

Anna disappeared. Veynerdi put on some latex gloves, laid sterile sachets on the tiles of the counter, then stood behind a long line of test-tubes. He looked like a musician preparing to play a glass xylophone.

When Anna returned, she was wearing just a pair of black knickers. Her body was thin and scrawny. Every time she moved, her bones seemed to be about to tear through her skin.

"Lie down please."

Anna climbed up onto the table. Whenever she made an effort, she seemed more robust. Her dry muscles swelled her flesh, giving a strange impression of strength and power. This woman was concealing a mystery, a latent energy. Mathilde thought of the shell of an egg, transparently revealing the form of a tyrannosaurus.

Veynerdi removed a needle and a syringe from their sterile packs.

"We'll start with a blood test."

He stuck the needle into Anna's left arm, without causing the slightest reaction. He frowned, and asked Mathilde: "Have you given her a sedative?"

"Yes, an intramuscular dose of Tranxene. She was highly agitated this evening, so . . ."

"How much?"

"Fifty milligrams."

The biologist grimaced. This injection was going to interfere with his tests. He removed the needle, placed a dressing in the crook of Anna's arm, then slipped behind the bench.

Mathilde followed his every move. He mixed the blood he had collected with a hypotonic solution, in order to destroy the red corpuscles and leave only the white ones. He placed the sample in the black cylinder of a centrifuge, which looked like a little oven. Turning at a thousand rotations per second, the machine separated the white corpuscles from the final residue. A few moments later, Veynerdi extracted a translucent deposit from it.

"Your immune cells," he commented for Anna's benefit. "These are the ones that contain the information we're interested in. We'll now take a closer look . . ."

He diluted the concentrate with some saline solution, then poured it into a flow cytometer – a grey block in which each corpuscle was isolated and subjected to a laser beam. Mathilde knew the procedure: the machine was going to locate the defensive molecules and identify them, thanks to a catalogue of markers which Veynerdi had compiled.

"Nothing very important," he said after a few minutes. "All I've found is contact with quite ordinary illnesses and pathogenic agents. Bacteria, viruses . . . Though fewer than average. You led an extremely healthy existence, madam. Nor have I found traces of any exogenic agents. No perfume. No particular impregnations. A real blank slate."

Anna sat motionless on the table, her arms crossed over her knees. Her diaphanous skin reflected the colours of the security lights, like a piece of glass; it was so white it was nearly blue. Veynerdi approached, holding a far longer needle.

"We're now going to perform a biopsy."

Anna stiffened.

"Don't worry," he murmured. "It's painless. I'm simply going to remove a little lymph from a ganglion in the armpit. Lift your arm, please."

Anna raised her elbow above the table. He introduced the needle, while mumbling in his smoker's voice: "These ganglions are in contact with the pulmonary region. If you have breathed in any particular particles, a gas, pollen, or anything significant, these white globules will remember."

Still drowsy from the anxiolytic, Anna did not jump in the slightest. The biologist went back behind his counter and proceeded to carry out some more operations.

Several minutes passed, then he said: "I've found nicotine, and tar. You used to smoke in your past life."

Mathilde butted in: "She still does."

The biologist nodded in reply, but added: "As for the rest, there is no significant trace of any particular atmosphere or surroundings."

He picked up a small flask and went over to Anna once more.

"Your globules have not retained the sort of memories I was hoping for, madam. So we shall now try a different sort of analysis. Some parts of the body do not conserve the print of external agents, but their actual traces. We are now going to explore these microstocks."

He brandished a jar.

"I'm going to ask you to urinate in this flask."

Anna got slowly up and returned to the changing-room. A real zombie. Mathilde observed: "I don't see what you'll find in her urine. We're looking for traces going back over a year and . . ."

The expert cut her short with a smile.

"Urine is produced by the kidneys, which act as filters. And crystals build up inside them. I can detect traces of these concretions. Some date from several years ago, and can tell us much about the subject's diet, for example."

Anna returned to the room, holding the bottle. She seemed increasingly absent and alien to the work being performed on her.

Veynerdi used the centrifuge once again to separate the elements, then turned to a new machine: a mass spectrometer. He deposited the golden liquid inside, then started the process of analysis.

Greenish waves came up on the computer screen. The scientist clicked his tongue in exasperation.

"Nothing. This young lady is decidedly difficult to read . . ."

He changed tack, concentrating even harder, taking more samples, running more tests, plunging within Anna's body.

Mathilde followed each motion and listened to his commentaries.

First, he removed some dentine, living tissue inside teeth in which certain products, such as antibiotics, can build up in the blood. Then he looked at the melatonin produced by the brain. According to him, the level of this hormone, which is mostly produced at night, could reveal Anna's old round of sleeping and waking.

Then he carefully removed a few drops of humour from her eyes, which could contain minuscule residues of certain foods. Finally, he cut off some hair, which retained the memory of exogenic substances and then secreted them in turn. The phenomenon was well known. The body of a person poisoned with arsenic will continued to exude the substance after death, through the hair roots.

After three hours of tests, the scientist had almost admitted defeat. He had found nothing, or nearly nothing. The portrait he could offer of the previous Anna was insignificant. A woman who smoked, otherwise leading a very healthy life; who probably suffered from insomnia, to judge from the irregular levels of melatonin; who had eaten olive oil since her childhood – he had found greasy traces of it in her eyes. The final point was that she dyed her hair black. In reality she had lighter hair, which was almost red.

Alain Veynerdi took off his gloves and washed his hands in the sink cut into the bench. Tiny beads of sweat were glistening on his forehead. He looked exhausted and disappointed.

One last time, he went over to Anna, who had gone back to sleep. He walked around her, apparently still searching, seeking for a sign, a hint that would allow him to decipher that diaphanous body.

Suddenly, he bent down over her hands. He took hold of her fingers and looked at them attentively. He then woke her up. As soon as she opened her eyes, he asked her with barely contained excitement: "I can see a brown stain on your fingernail. Do you know where it came from?"

Anna stared round in confusion. Then she looked at her hand and raised her eyebrows.

"I don't know," she mumbled. "It's a nicotine stain, isn't it?"

Mathilde joined them. She too could now see a tiny ochre mark on the tip of the nail.

"How often do you cut your nails?" the biologist asked.

"I don't know . . . About every three weeks."

"Do you have the impression that they grow quickly?"

Anna yawned without answering. Veynerdi went back to his bench, murmuring: "How could I have missed that?" He picked up a tiny pair of scissors and a transparent box, then returned to cut off the piece of Anna's fingernail which seemed to interest him so.

"If they grow normally," he said softly, "these extremities date back to the period before your accident. This stain is part of your past life."

He switched the machines back on. While their motors purred again, he diluted the sample in a tube containing a solvent.

"That was a close call," he smiled. "In another few days, you would have cut your nails and we would have lost this precious remnant."

He placed the sterile tube in the centrifuge and turned it on.

"If it's nicotine," Mathilde commented, "I don't see what you can . . ."

Veynerdi placed the liquid in a spectrometer.

"I may be able to work out which brand of cigarettes she smoked before her accident."

Mathilde did not understand why he was so enthusiastic. Such information would not reveal anything important. On the screen of the machine, Veynerdi observed the luminous diagrams. Minutes passed by.

"Professor," Mathilde was losing patience. "I don't understand. This is nothing to get worked up about. I . . ."

"It's extraordinary."

The light of the monitor was illuminating a fixed look of wonder on the scientist's face.

"It isn't nicotine."

Mathilde went over to the spectrometer. Anna sat up on the metal table. Veynerdi turned on his seat towards the two women.

"It's henna."

A wave of silence engulfed them.

The researcher tore off the square-ruled paper which the machine had just printed out, then he typed the data into his computer keyboard. It at once flashed up a list of chemical components.

"According to my catalogue of substances, this stain comes from a specific vegetal composition. A very rare sort of henna, cultivated on the plains of Anatolia."

Alain Veynerdi stared triumphantly at Anna. He seemed to have waited all his life for this moment.

"Madam, in your previous existence, you were Turkish."

VI

CHAPTER 33

One hell of a night.

Paul Nerteaux had dreamed of a stone monster, a malignant titan prowling through the tenth *arrondissement*. A Moloch who dominated the Turkish quarter, demanding human sacrifices.

In his dream, the monster wore a half-human, half-bestial mask, of Greek and Persian style. Its mineral lips were white hot, its penis stuck with blades. Every one of its steps made the earth quake, dust rise and cracks appear in the buildings.

He had finally woken up at three o'clock, covered in sweat. Shivering in his little three-room flat, he had made some coffee, then examined the fresh batch of archaeological documents that the boys from the Brigade criminelle had left in front of his door the previous evening.

Until dawn, he browsed through the museum catalogues, tourist brochures and scientific studies, observing and scrutinising each sculpture, comparing it with the autopsy photos – and unconsciously with the mask in his dreams. Sarcophagi from Antalya. Frescoes from Cilicia. Bas-reliefs from Karatepe. Busts from Ephesus . . .

He had crossed over ages and civilisations without obtaining the slightest clue.

Paul Nerteaux then went to the Trois Obus café by porte de Saint-Cloud. He confronted the smell of coffee and tobacco, forcing himself to ignore his senses and pushing down his nausea. His lousy mood was not just because of his nightmares. It was Wednesday and, like every Wednesday, he had had to call Reyna at daybreak to tell her that he could not look after Céline.

He spotted Jean-Louis Schiffer standing at the end of the bar. Closely shaven, wrapped up in a Burberry raincoat, he was looking decidedly better as he dunked his croissant in his coffee.

When he saw Paul, he grinned broadly.

"Slept well?"

"Great."

Schiffer stared at his rumpled appearance, but made no comment. "Coffee?"

Paul nodded. A black concentrate rimmed with brown foam immediately appeared on the bar. The Cipher picked up the cup and nodded towards a free table beside the window.

"Let's sit down. You're not looking too good."

At the table, he handed him the basket of croissants. Paul refused. The very idea of swallowing something brought acid up to his nostrils. But he had to admit that Schiffer was playing at being buddies that morning. He asked: "And you, did you sleep well?"

"Like a log."

Paul pictured once more the sliced fingers and bloody guillotine. After the carnage, he had accompanied the Cipher to porte de Saint-Cloud, where he had a flat on rue Gudin. Ever since that moment, a question had been bugging him.

"If you've got this flat," he pointed through the window at the grey square, "what the hell were you doing at Longères?"

"The herding instinct. The desire to be around coppers. I was bored to death all on my own."

The explanation rang false. Paul remembered that Schiffer was registered at the home under a pseudonym, his mother's maiden name. Someone in the Special Branch had tipped him off. Another mystery. Was he hiding? If so, who from?

"Show me the files," the Cipher said.

Paul opened the folder and placed the documents on the table. They were not the originals. He had dropped into his office early that morning to make photocopies. Clutching a Turkish dictionary, he had studied each file and had managed to work out each victim's name and personal details.

The first one was called Zeynep Tütengil. She used to be employed in a workshop beside La Porte Bleue Turkish baths, which belonged to a certain Talat Gürdilek. She was twenty-seven, childless, but married to Burba Tütengil. They lived at 34 rue de la Fidélité. She came from some village with an unpronounceable name near the town of Gaziantep, in the south-east of Turkey and had been living in Paris since September 2001.

The second's name was Ruya Berkes. She was twenty-six and single. She worked from home, at 58 rue d'Enghien, for a certain Gozar Halman – a name Paul had already seen on several police reports – a sweatshop owner who specialised in leather and furs. Ruya Berkes came from Adana, a city in the south of Turkey. She had been in Paris for just eight months.

The third was Roukiye Tanyol. She was thirty, single, and was a seamstress for a company called Sürelik, based in passage de l'Industrie. She had been living incognito in a woman's home at 22 rue des Petites-Écuries. Like the first victim, she was born in the province of Gaziantep.

This information provided no common points. There was not the slightest indication, for example, of how the murderer spotted them or approached them. But above all, it did not give these women the slightest presence or sensation of reality. Their Turkish names even increased their inscrutability. To convince himself that they were flesh and blood, Paul had had to turn back to the Polaroids. Their broad, rather smooth features suggested generously rounded bodies. He had read somewhere that the ideal of Turkish beauty corresponded to just such a physique, with moonlike faces . . .

Schiffer continued studying the data, his glasses on the tip of his nose. Still feeling nauseous, Paul hesitated before drinking his coffee. The din of voices and the chinking of glass and metal were getting on his nerves. Above all, the drunken conversations at the bar needled him. He just could not stand such wasters, killing themselves with one arm on the counter and the other constantly raised . . .

How many times had he gone to fetch one or both of his parents from a zinc bar? How many times had he picked them up from the sawdust and cigarette butts, while he was struggling against the desire to puke over them?

The Cipher removed his glasses and concluded: "We'll start with the third workshop. The most recent victim. While memories are still fresh. Then we'll work back to the first one. After that, we'll go round to their homes, their neighbours, and retrace their journeys to work. He must have jumped them somewhere, and no one's invisible."

Paul downed his coffee in one. Over his burning bile, he said: "Don't forget, Schiffer, the slightest fuck-up and . . ."

"You whack me. I haven't forgotten. Anyway, this morning we're changing tactics."

He waggled his fingers as though manipulating a puppet.

"We're now playing it softly softly."

With the light flashing, they took the bypass. The greyness of the Seine, added to the granite of the sky and the riverbanks, made for a smoothly monotonous world. Paul liked this crushingly dull and depressing weather. Another hurdle for this energetically wilful officer to cross.

On the way, he listened to the messages on his mobile. Bomarzo the magistrate wanted an up-date. His voice was tense. Paul now had just two days before he was going to put more officers from the Brigade criminelle on to the case. Naubrel and Matkowska were pursuing their investigations. They had spent the previous day with the "moles", workmen who dig into the depths of Paris and who decompress every evening in specially built chambers. They had questioned the managers of eight different companies and drawn a blank. They had also paid a call on the main manufacturer of these chambers, in Arcueil. According to the boss, the idea that a decompression chamber had been used by someone who was not a qualified engineer was absolutely ridiculous. Did this mean that the killer had such knowledge, or was it a false lead? The officers were now continuing their investigations in other sectors of industry.

When they reached place du Châtelet, Paul spotted a patrol car which was turning up boulevard de Strasbourg. He caught up with it by rue des Lombards, and motioned to the driver to stop.

"Just a second," he told Schiffer.

From the glove compartment, he took the Kinder Surprises and chewy sweets he had bought an hour before. In his hurry, the bag tore and its contents fell onto the floor. Blushing with embarrassment, Paul picked them up and got out of the car.

The uniformed officers had stopped and were waiting beside their car, thumbs hooked over their belts. Paul rapidly explained what he wanted them to do, then spun round. When he sat back down behind the wheel, the Cipher waved a sweet in the air.

"Wednesday, no school for the kids."

Paul pulled off without responding.

"I used to use patrol cars as messengers too. To take my girlfriends presents . . ."

"Your employees you mean . . ."

"That's right, kid, that's right . . ."

Schiffer unwrapped the bar of caramel and folded it into his mouth.

"How many kids have you got?"

"One daughter."

"How old is she?"

"Seven."

"What's her name?"

"Céline."

"A bit posh for a copper's kid."

Paul thought so too. He had never understood why Reyna, the Marxist idealist, had given their child such a precious name.

Schiffer was chewing away.

"And the mother?"

"Divorced."

Paul drove through a red light and past rue Réaumur.

The fiasco of his marriage was the last thing he wanted to discuss with Schiffer. With relief, he spotted the red and yellow McDonald's sign that stood at the beginning of boulevard de Strasbourg.

He speeded up, not giving his partner the chance to ask any more questions.

Their hunting ground was in sight.

CHAPTER 34

At ten o'clock, boulevard de Strasbourg looked like a battlefield in full fury. The pavements and carriageways dissolved into a single frenetic mass of passers-by, slipping in between a maze of trapped, hooting vehicles. Above them, the sky was colourless, as taut as a tarpaulin full of water, about to split at any moment.

Paul decided to park at the corner of rue des Petites-Écuries and follow Schiffer, who was already making his way through the cardboard boxes being carried on men's backs, the arms hung with clothing and the loads wobbling on the trolleys. They turned down passage de l'Industrie and found themselves beneath an arch of stone, leading to an alleyway.

Sürelik's workshop was a block of bricks, propped up by a framework of riveted metal. The façade was gabled, with a Gothic arch, glazed tympanums and sculpted terracotta friezes. The bright red edifice oozed a sort of enthusiasm, a cheerful faith in the future of industry, as though someone inside had just invented the wheel behind these very walls.

A few yards from the door, Paul grabbed Schiffer by the lapels of his coat and pushed him under the porch. He then searched him thoroughly to check he was not armed.

The old copper tutted reprovingly.

"You're wasting your time, kid. Softly softly, like I said."

Paul turned round without a word and headed towards the workshop.

Together, they pushed open the metal door and entered a large square space, with white walls and a painted cement floor. Everything was spick and span. The light-green metal structures, bulging with rivets, reinforced the overall sensation of solidity. Large windows let in oblique rays of light, while galleries ran along each wall, like the bridges of an ocean-going liner.

Paul had been expecting a pit; what he found was an artist's studio. About forty workers, all of them men, were neatly spaced out and labouring behind their sewing machines, surrounded by cloth and open boxes. In their overalls, they looked like special agents stitching up coded messages during the war. A cassette recorder was playing some Turkish music. A coffee pot was sizzling on a gas ring. A craftsman's paradise.

Schiffer stamped on the floor with his heel.

"What you were imagining is downstairs. In the cellars. Hundreds of female workers crammed together like sardines. Illegal immigrants the lot of them. We're inside now, but this is only the respectable front."

He pulled Paul towards the machines, walking between the workers, who forced themselves not to look up.

"Lovely, aren't they? Model workers, my lad. Industrious, obedient, disciplined."

"Why be so sarcastic?"

"The Turks aren't hard-working at all. They're spongers. They aren't obedient. They're indifferent. They aren't disciplined. They follow their own rules. They're a load of fucking vampires. Pillagers who can't even be bothered to learn our language . . . What's the point? They're just here to earn as much as they can, then piss off back home. Their motto is 'take it all, leave nothing'."

Schiffer grabbed Paul by the arm.

"They're a plague, my boy."

Paul pushed him away violently.

"Never call me that again."

He looked up as if Paul had just threatened him with a gun. He stared at him quizzically. Paul wanted to tear that expression off his face, but then a voice sounded behind them.

"What can I do for you, gentlemen?"

A squat man, dressed in spotless blue overalls, was coming towards them, an oily smile glued onto his moustache.

"Ah, Inspector!" he said in astonishment. "It's been so long since I've had the pleasure of seeing you!"

Schiffer burst out laughing. The music had stopped. The activity of the machines had ceased. A deathly silence reigned.

"Aren't we on first name terms any more?"

Instead of replying, the workshop's boss looked round distrustfully at Paul.

"This is Paul Nerteaux," the cop continued. "He's a police captain. And my immediate boss. But he's above all a pal."

He slapped Paul on the back and grinned.

"You can trust him like you can trust me."

Then he went over to the Turk and put his arm round his shoulders. The ballet was choreographed down to the slightest movement.

"Let me introduce you to Ahmid Zoltanoi," he said to Paul. "The best workshop manager in all of Little Turkey. As starchy as his overalls, but with a heart of gold, deep down. People round here call him Tanoi."

The Turk bowed slightly. Beneath his coal-black eyebrows, he seemed to be weighing up this newcomer. Friend or foe? He turned back to Schiffer, with his oily voice: "I heard you had retired."

"Force of circumstances. When there's an emergency, who do they call up? Uncle Schiffer, that's who."

"What emergency are you talking about, Inspector?"

The Cipher swept the pieces of cloth off a table and placed the picture of Roukiye Tanyol on it.

"Recognise her?"

The man bent down, hands in his pockets, thumbs out like gun triggers. He seemed to be balancing on the starchy folds of his overalls.

"Never seen her before."

Schiffer turned over the Polaroid. On the white edge, written in indelible marker, could distinctly be seen the victim's name and the address of the Sürelik workshop.

"Marius has coughed up. And the rest of you will follow. Believe me."

The Turk's face fell. He gingerly picked up the photo, put on his glasses and stared at it.

"Yes, her face does ring a bell."

"And the chimes must be pretty loud. She'd been here since 2001, hadn't she?"

Tanoi put down the photo.

"Yes."

"What was her job?"

"Sewing-woman."

"She worked downstairs, I suppose?"

The manager raised his eyebrows while putting away his glasses. The workers had now started sewing again. They seemed to realise that the policemen were not after them, and it was their boss who had problems.

"Downstairs?" he asked.

"In the cellars," Schiffer was getting annoyed. "Now wake up, Tanoi, or I'll lose my temper."

The Turk swayed slightly on his heels. Despite his age, he looked like a contrite schoolboy.

"Yes, she worked in the lower workshop."

"Where was she from, Gaziantep?"

"Not exactly, a nearby village. She spoke a southern dialect."

"Who's got her passport?"

"She had no passport."

Schiffer sighed, as though saddened by this fresh lie.

"Tell me about her disappearance."

"There's nothing to tell. She left the workshop on Thursday morning. She never made it home."

"Thursday morning?"

"Yes, at six. She was on the night shift."

The two officers glanced at each other. So she had indeed been on her way home when she was jumped, but this had been at dawn. They had been right, except for the time of day.

"You say she never made it home," the Cipher continued. "Who told you that?"

"Her fiancé."

"They went home together?"

"No, he's on the day shift."

"Where can I find him?"

"Nowhere. He went back home."

Tanoi's answers were as stiff as the stitches in his overalls.

"He didn't try to recover the body?"

"He had no papers. He couldn't speak French. So he fled in grief. A Turkish destiny. An exile's destiny."

"Spare me the violins. Where are her colleagues?"

"What colleagues?"

"The ones who go home at the same time. I want to question them."

"That's impossible. Gone, all of them, vanished."

"Why?"

"They're scared."

"Of the killer?"

"No, of you. Of the police. No one wants to get caught up in this affair."

The Cipher stood squarely in front of the Turk, hands behind his back.

"I think you know far more than you're letting on, fat man. So, let's take a stroll down into the cellars. It might refresh your memory."

The Turk did not budge. The sewing machines continued to rattle. Music was twisting beneath the steel girders. He hesitated another second, then headed towards an iron door under one of the galleries.

The officers followed him. At the bottom of the stairs, they dived down a dark corridor, went through a metal door, then took a second corridor with a clay floor. They had to bend their heads to walk. Bare light bulbs, hanging from the pipes on the ceiling, lit the way. Two rows of doors made of planks of wood, numbered with chalk figures, faced each other. A humming rose up from the depths.

When they reached a turning, their guide stopped and picked up a metal bar concealed behind the springs of an old wire mattress. Advancing cautiously, he started knocking on the pipes across the ceiling, setting off a series of deep echoes.

Suddenly, invisible enemies appeared. Rats gathered together on a cast-iron arch above their heads. Paul remembered the forensic scientist's v ords: *With the second one, it was different. I think he used something . . . that was alive.*

The manager swore in Turkish and banged as hard as he could in their direction. The rodents vanished. The entire corridor was now vibrating. Every door was trembling on its hinges. Finally, Tanoi stopped in front of number 34.

He forced the door open with his shoulder. A thundering noise exploded outwards.

Light spread into the tiny workshop. About thirty women were sitting behind sewing machines, which were going at full speed, as though propelled by their own momentum. Bent double beneath the strip-lights, the seamstresses were pushing pieces of cloth underneath the needles, without paying the slightest attention to the visitors.

The room measured no more than twenty square yards and had no means of ventilation. The air was so heavy – with smells of dyes, particles of cloth, the stench of solvents – that it was barely breathable. Some of the women wore scarves over their mouths. Others had babies on their laps, wrapped in shawls. Children were also working, grouped together on the piles of fabric, folding them and packing them in boxes. Paul was suffocating. He was like a character in a film who wakes up in the middle of the night only to find out that his nightmare is real.

Schiffer adopted his most sincere delivery:

"This is the real face of Sürelik Limited! Twelve or fifteen hours' work, several thousand garments produced per day, per worker. The

Turkish version of our three eight-hour shifts reduced to just two, or even one. And the same applies in all the other cellars, my lad."

He seemed almost delighted by the cruelty of the scene.

"But don't forget, all this has the state's blessing. Everyone closes their eyes. The clothing industry is based on slavery."

The Turk was trying to look ashamed, but a flame of pride was burning in his pupils. Paul looked around at the women. A few eyes rose in response, but their hands continued their flurry, as though nothing and nobody could stop them.

He then pictured among them the matt faces, long wounds and bloody crevices of the victims. How did the killer get to these underground women? How had he noticed that they looked alike?

The Cipher launched into another round of questions, his voice raised above the din: "When there's a change of shift, that's when the delivery boys take away the finished products, isn't it?"

"That's right."

"If you include all the workers coming out of the shops, that means there's quite a crowd on the streets at six in the morning. And no one saw anything?"

"I swear to you."

The cop leaned against the wall of breeze-blocks.

"Don't swear. Your God is less merciful than mine. Have you spoken to the bosses of the other victims?"

"No."

"You're lying, but never mind. What do you know about this series of murders?"

"They say that the women are tortured, their faces destroyed. That's all I know."

"And the police have never been round to see you?"

"No."

"So what's your private police force doing?"

Paul trembled . . . It was the first time he had heard of such a thing. So the neighbourhood had its own force of order. Tanoi yelled over the machines: "I don't know. They found nothing."

Schiffer pointed at the women.

"And what do they think?"

"They daren't go out. They're scared. Allah cannot allow this. The neighbourhood is accursed! Azrael, the Angel of Death, is upon us!"

The Cipher smiled, gave the man a friendly tap on the back and pointed at the door.

"Steady on now . . . You're finally starting to sound human . . ."

They went out into the corridor. Paul followed them, closing the planks over the machine hell. He had only just done so, when he heard a stifled groan. Schiffer had just rammed Tanoi up against the piping.

"Who's killing the girls?"

"I . . . I dunno."

"Who are you covering, you fucker?"

Paul did not intervene. He sensed that Schiffer would not go any further. Just a final burst of rage, to save his honour. Tanoi did not answer, his eyes popping out of their orbits.

The Cipher released his grip, letting him get his breath back beneath the bare bulb which was swinging like a hypnotist's pendulum. Then he murmured: "You keep all this under your hat, Tanoi. Not a word about our little visit to anyone."

The sweatshop manager looked up at Schiffer. He had already recovered his servile expression.

"My hat has always been in place, Inspector."

CHAPTER 35

The second victim, Ruya Berkes, had not worked in a sweatshop, but from her home at 58 rue d'Enghien. She used to hand-stitch the linings of coats, which she then delivered to the Gozar Halman fur warehouse, at 77 rue Sainte-Cécile, a road perpendicular to rue du Faubourg-Poissonnière. They could have started with the woman's flat, but Schiffer decided to go straight to see her employer, whom he had apparently known for some time.

As he drove in silence, Paul savoured his return to fresh air. But he was also dreading fresh revelations. He saw the shop windows begin to darken, weighed down with brown materials and languid folds as the car moved away from rue du Faubourg-Saint-Denis and rue du Faubourg-Saint-Martin. In each store, fabrics and cloths were being replaced by skins and furs.

He turned right into rue Sainte-Cécile.

Schiffer pulled at his arm. They had arrived at number 77.

This time, Paul was expecting a sewer full of flayed skin, cages clotted with blood, the stench of dead meat. What he found was a little courtyard, full of light and flowers, whose paving stones looked as if they had been polished by the morning mist. The two officers crossed to the far side, to a building dotted with barred windows, which was the only edifice resembling an industrial warehouse.

"I'm warning you," Schiffer said, as he went through the door. "Gozar Halman is a Tansu Ciller fanatic."

"Who's that? A footballer?"

The policeman sniggered. They went up a staircase of grey wood.

"Tansu Ciller is the former prime minister of Turkey. A degree at Harvard, international diplomacy, minister of foreign affairs, and then head of the government. A model career."

Paul's response was blasé.

"A typical career for a politician."

"Except that Tansu Ciller is a woman."

They reached the second floor. Each landing was as vast and dark as a chapel. Paul remarked: "There can't be that many Turkish men who take a woman as their role model."

The Cipher burst out laughing.

"Really, if you didn't exist, then someone would have to invent you. Gozar *is* a woman! She's a *teyze*, a fairy godmother in every sense of the term. She watches over her brothers, her nephews, her cousins and her workers. She takes care of getting them work permits. She sends round people to renovate their hovels. She sends their parcels and money orders for them. And then she gives out backhanders to the cops so that they will leave them alone. She's a slave-driver, but a benevolent one."

Third floor. Halman's warehouse was a large room with a parquet that had been painted grey, scattered with pieces of polystyrene and crumpled papers. In the middle, planks laid on trestles acted as counters. On them lay piles of cardboard boxes, acrylic shopping bags, pink plastic bags from the penny market, protective bags for suits, from which some men were removing coats, jackets and stoles, examining then smoothing them out, checking their linings, and finally putting them on hangers suspended from gantries. In front of them, women dressed in head-scarves and long skirts, with dark rugged faces, seemed to be wearily awaiting their verdict.

A glazed mezzanine, veiled by a white curtain, overlooked the area: an ideal position to supervise the workplace. Without hesitating, or saying a word to anyone, Schiffer seized the banister and started climbing the steep stairs that led to the platform.

At the top, they had to confront a barrier of plants before entering an attic room, which was almost as large as the space beneath it. Windows edged with curtains looked out over a landscape of slate and zinc – the rooftops of Paris.

Despite its dimensions, the workshop's décor made it look more like a boudoir from the 1900s. Paul went inside, drinking in every detail. Doilies protected the modern equipment – computer, hi-fi, television – or else decked the framed photos, glass knick-knacks and huge dolls drowned in acres of lace. The walls were decorated with tourist posters singing the praises of Istanbul. Small, brightly coloured rugs were hung up like tapestries. Paper Turkish flags, dotted around all over the place, echoed the postcards that were pinned up in groups on the wooden pillars that supported the roof.

A solid oak desk, covered with a leather blotter, took up the right of the room, leaving the centre to a green velvet divan standing on a huge rug. Nobody was there.

Schiffer headed towards an opening hidden behind a bead curtain and cooed: "My princess, it's me, Schiffer. There's no need to doll yourself up."

The only reply was silence. Paul advanced and took a closer look at the photos. In each of them, a short-haired quite attractive red-head was smiling in the company of a famous president: Bill Clinton, Boris Yeltsin, François Mitterrand. This was presumably Tansu Ciller . . .

A rustling sound made him turn his head. The bead curtain opened to reveal the double of the woman in the photos, in person, but even larger than life.

Gozar Halman had accentuated her resemblance to the politician, no doubt to give herself additional authority. Her black tunic and trousers, set off by just a few pieces of jewellery, were rather sober. The way she moved and walked was in the same register, expressing the haughty distance of a businesswoman. Her look seemed to draw an invisible line around her. The message was clear: any attempt at seduction was doomed from the start.

But at the same time, her face told a different story. It was as broad and white as Pierrot Lunaire, framed by red hair, with violently sparkling eyes. Gozar's eyelids were painted orange, and dotted with spangles.

"Schiffer," she said in a hoarse voice. "I know why you're here."

"At last, someone with their wits about them!"

Looking distracted, she tidied away some papers on her desk.

"I knew that they'd resurrect you sooner or later."

She did not really have an accent – more of a light lilt that ran through each sentence, which she seemed to cultivate for its charm.

Schiffer introduced them, temporarily abandoning his sneering tone. Paul sensed that he was going to play it straight with this woman.

"What do you know about it all?" he asked at once.

"Nothing. Less than nothing."

She leaned over her desk for a few more seconds, then went to sit on the settee, slowly crossing her legs.

"The neighbourhood's scared," she whispered. "All sorts of rumours are flying round."

"For example?"

"Stories that contradict one another. I even heard that the killer was one of your men."

"Our men?"

"Yes, a policeman."

Schiffer waved the idea away with the back of his hand.

"Tell me about Ruya Berkes."

Gozar was caressing the lace cloth covering the armrest of the settee.

"She brought round her articles every two days. She came here on 6 January 2002, but not on the 8th. That's all I can tell you."

Schiffer took out his notepad and pretended to read it. Paul sensed that he was just trying to keep his countenance. This woman was clearly a match for him.

"Ruya was the killer's second victim," he went on, eyes still on his notes. "The body was found on 10 January."

"God save her soul."

Her fingers were fidgeting with the lace.

"But it's none of my business."

"It's everyone's business now. And I need information."

The tone was mounting, but Paul detected a strange familiarity in their exchange. A complicity between fire and ice, which had nothing to do with this investigation.

"I have nothing to say," she repeated. "The neighbourhood will close in around this affair. As it always does."

Her words, voice and tone made Paul observe her more closely. She was fixing her dark eyes, topped with red gilt, straight on the Cipher. They made him think of strips of chocolate filled with orange rind. But, more importantly, he suddenly understood the truth of the situation: Gozar Halman was the Turkish woman whom Schiffer had almost married. What had happened? Why had it fallen through?

The fur seller lit a cigarette. A long languid drag of blue smoke.

"What do you want to know?"

"When did she deliver her coats?"

"At the end of the day."

"Alone?"

"Yes, always alone."

"Do you know which way she came?"

"Via rue du Faubourg-Poissonnière. At that time, the streets are crowded, if that's your next question."

Schiffer turned to generalities.

"When did Ruya Berkes arrive in Paris?"

"May 2001. Haven't you seen Marius?"

He ignored the question.

"What sort of woman was she?"

"A peasant. But she had also lived in the city."

"Adana?"

"First Gaziantep, then Adana."

Schiffer leaned over. He seemed interested by this detail.

"She came from Gaziantep?"

"Yes, I think so."

He was pacing round the room, his fingers idling over the knick-knacks.

"Was she literate?"

"No, but she was modern. Not a slave of tradition."

"Did she go out in Paris? Go for walks? Go out to night clubs?"

"I said modern, not loose. She was a Muslim. You know as well as I do what that means. Anyway, she didn't speak a word of French."

"How did she dress?"

"As a Westerner," the tone mounted again. "Schiffer, what are you after?"

"I'm trying to work out how the killer jumped her. It isn't easy to approach a girl who never goes out, never speaks to anyone and has no leisure activities."

His questions were leading nowhere. They were the same as an hour before, and were receiving the same inevitable answers. Paul stood in front of the bay window, looking over the courtyard and drew aside the curtain. The Turks were still working away, money was changing hands, above furs that were curled up like sleeping animals.

Behind him, Schiffer's voice pressed on: "What was Ruya's state of mind?"

"Like all the others: 'my body is here, my heart is back there'. All she wanted to do was to go home, get married and have children. She was here in transit. The daily round of a worker ant, stuck in front of her sewing machine, sharing a two-room flat with two other women."

"I want to question her flatmates . . ."

Paul stopped listening and observed the comings and goings downstairs. These exchanges were like bartering, an ancestral ritual. The Cipher's voice broke into his mind once more:

"And what do you think about the murderer?"

There was a long enough silence to make Paul turn back towards the room.

Gozar had stood up, and was now staring out of the window at the rooftops. Without moving, she murmured: "I think it is more . . . political."

Schiffer went over to her.

"What do you mean?"

She spun round.

"This affair could go above and beyond the interests of a single killer."

"Gozar, explain yourself!"

"I have nothing to explain. The whole neighbourhood's scared, and I'm no exception. No one will help you."

Paul shivered. The Moloch in his nightmare, with the quarter in his clutches, seemed more real than ever. A god of stone looking for its prey in the cellars and hovels of Little Turkey.

The *teyze* concluded: "This conversation's over, Schiffer."

The cop pocketed his notepad and, without trying to insist, walked away. Paul took a last look at the negotiations downstairs.

It was then that he spotted him.

A delivery man – black moustache and blue Adidas jacket – had just arrived in the warehouse, his arms laden with a box. He automatically looked up at the mezzanine. When he saw Paul, his face froze.

He put down his load, said something to one of the labourers by the coat hangers, then withdrew towards the door. His final glance up at the platform confirmed what Paul had sensed. He was frightened.

The two officers went down to the lower floor. Schiffer spat: "That stubborn bitch really pisses me off with her subtle hints. Fucking Turks. Warped the lot of them . . ."

Paul speeded up and leapt out of the door. He peered down the stairwell. A brown hand was skidding along the banister. The man was legging it.

He muttered to Schiffer, as he arrived on the landing: "Come on. Quick."

CHAPTER 36

Paul ran as far as the car. He got in and turned the ignition key in one movement. Schiffer just had time to sit beside him.

"What's going on?" he grumbled.

Without answering, Paul pulled away. The figure had just turned right at the end of rue Sainte-Cécile. He accelerated and turned into rue du Faubourg-Poissonière, once again coming up against the crowds and chaos.

The man was walking quickly, slipping between the delivery men, the passers-by, the smoke of the pancake and pitta sellers, glancing round nervously over his shoulder. He was heading towards boulevard Bonne-Nouvelle. Schiffer said moodily: "Are you going to explain yourself, or what?"

Paul changed up to third and murmured: "There was a man at Gozar's place. When he spotted us, he ran away."

"So what?"

"He smelt us out. He's afraid of being questioned. Maybe he knows something about our business."

Their customer now turned left, into rue d'Enghien. Luckily for them, he was walking in the direction of the traffic.

"Or he doesn't have a work permit," Schiffer muttered.

"At Gozar's? Who does? No, this guy's got a special reason to be afraid. I can just sense it."

The Cipher stuck his knees up against the dashboard. He asked gloomily: "Where is he?"

"Left pavement. The Adidas jacket."

The Turk was still heading up the street. Paul tried to follow him as discreetly as possible. A red light. The silvery blue form grew more distant. Paul felt that Schiffer's stare was following him too. The silence in the car was marked by a particular depth: they had understood each other, they now shared the same calm, the same attention, concentrating on their target.

Green.

Paul pulled away, gently pressing on the pedals, feeling an intense heat rising up his legs. He accelerated, just in time to see the Turk swerve right, into rue du Faubourg-Saint-Denis, still in the direction of the traffic.

Paul followed, but the street was jammed, blocked, suffocating in a mass which was casting its din of cries and hooting horns up into the grey air.

He bent his neck and squinted. Above the bodywork and the heads were rows of shop signs – wholesale, retail, retail-wholesale . . . The Adidas jacket had disappeared. He looked further. The façades of the buildings were fading away in the mist of pollution. At the far end, the arch of porte Saint-Denis was glimmering in the smoky light.

"I can't see him any more."

Schiffer opened his window. The din burst into the car. He pushed his head outside. "Further up," he said. "To the right."

The traffic started moving. The blue patch stood out against a group of pedestrians. Another stop. Paul said to himself that the jam was playing into their hands, by letting them drive at walking pace and so keep tabs on him . . .

The Turk vanished again, then reappeared between two delivery trucks, just in front of the café Sully. He kept glancing round. Had he spotted them?

"He's shitting himself," Paul commented. "He knows something."

"That doesn't mean a thing. There's not a snowball's chance in hell . . ."

"Trust me. Just this once."

Paul changed to first again. His neck was burning and the collar of his parka was damp with sweat. He accelerated and caught up with the Turk at the end of rue du Faubourg-Saint-Denis.

Suddenly, at the foot of the arch, the man crossed the road, practically in front of them, but without noticing them. He started heading down boulevard Saint-Denis.

"Shit," Paul said. "It's one-way."

Schiffer sat up. "Park. We'll continue on . . . Fuck it, he's taking the métro!"

The figure had trotted across the boulevard, then disappeared down the steps of Strasbourg-Saint-Denis station. Paul swerved violently and came to a halt just in front of a bar called L'Arcade, in the slip-road alongside the arch.

Schiffer was already out.

Paul lowered the sun visor marked POLICE and leapt out of the Golf.

The Cipher's raincoat was flapping between the cars like a banner. Paul felt a surge of fever. In a second, he drank it all in, the excitement in the air, Schiffer's rapidity, the determination that united them for once.

He too zigzagged through the traffic on the boulevard and caught up with his partner just as he was heading downstairs.

The two officers rushed into the entrance of the station. A crowd was hurrying along beneath the orange vault. Paul stared round: to the left, the glass fronts of the ticket offices; to the right the blue métro map; in front, the automatic doors.

No Turk.

Schiffer dived into the mass, performing an extraordinary slalom in the direction of the doors. Paul stood up on tiptoe and caught sight of the man, who was turning right.

"Line 4!" he yelled to his partner, who was now invisible among the passengers.

Already, at the end of the ceramic corridor, the swishing sound of opening métro doors could be heard. A wave of panic ran through the crowd. What was happening? Who was shouting? Who was shoving? Suddenly, a roar broke through the din.

"Open the fucking gates!"

It was Schiffer's voice.

Paul dashed towards the ticket office, just to his left. He leaned over to the window and yelled: "Open the gates!"

The métro employee froze.

"What?"

Far off, the siren marked the departure of the train. Paul shoved his warrant card up against the glass.

"Fucking hurry up and open the fucking gates!"

The doors opened.

Paul elbowed his way though, stumbled, then managed to force himself past. Schiffer was running beneath the red vault, which now seemed to be palpitating like a living organ.

He caught up with him by the stairs. He took them four at a time. They had not even covered half the distance when the train doors clicked shut.

Schiffer bellowed as he ran. He was about to reach the platform when Paul grabbed his collar, forcing him to stay back. The Cipher was speechless. The lights of the train passed before his staring eyes. He looked like a madman.

"He mustn't see us!" Paul shouted into his face.

Schiffer kept staring at him, stunned, unable to get his breath back. Paul then added, more softly, as the whistling of the métro drew away: "We've got forty seconds to get to the next station. We'll bag him at Château-d'Eau."

They glanced at each other in mutual understanding, then ran back up the stairs, dodged through the traffic and leapt into the car.

Twenty seconds had already gone by.

Paul drove around the arch and swerved right, while lowering his window. He stuck the magnetic light on the roof and shot off down boulevard de Strasbourg with his siren blaring.

They covered the five hundred yards in seven seconds. When they reached the junction with rue du Château-d'Eau, Schiffer motioned to get out. Once again, Paul held him back.

"We'll wait for him on the surface. There are only two exits, on either side of the boulevard."

"What makes you think he'll get out here?"

"We'll let twenty seconds go by. If he stays in the train, then we'll have another twenty seconds to grab him at Gare de l'Est."

"And what if he doesn't get out there?"

"He won't leave the Turkish quarter. Either he'll hide somewhere, or else he'll go and warn someone. Either way, it will be *here* on our turf. We'll have to follow him all the way. To see where he goes."

The Cipher looked at his watch.

"Let's go."

Paul peered round one last time, right, left, then shot off again. In his veins, he could feel the vibrations of the métro as it passed beneath his wheels.

Seventeen seconds later, he stopped in front of the grating of the courtyard of the Gare de l'Est, stopped the siren and the flashing light. Once more, Schiffer went to leap out, but Paul said: "We're staying here. We can see just about all the exits. The main one's on the courtyard. There's another to the right on rue du Faubourg-Saint-Martin. Then to the left on rue du 8-Mai-1945. That gives us three chances out of five."

"Where are the other two?"

"On either side of the train station. In rue du Faubourg-Saint-Martin and rue d'Alsace."

"What if he takes one of them?"

"They're further away from the platform. It'll take him over a minute to get there. We'll wait for thirty seconds. If he doesn't materialise, I'll drop you off in rue d'Alsace, and I'll take Saint-Martin. We can stay in contact using our mobiles. He can't escape us."

Schiffer remained silent. Wrinkles of thought were furrowing his brow.

"How do you know where all the exits are?"

Despite his fever, Paul grinned.

"I learned them by heart, in case of pursuit."

The face of grey scales smiled back at him.

"If chummy doesn't reappear, I'll have your balls for breakfast."

Ten, twelve, fifteen seconds.

The longest in his existence. Paul observed the figures emerging from each métro exit, shaken by the wind. No Adidas jacket.

Twenty, twenty-two seconds.

The flow of passengers became more staccato, beating to the rhythm of his heart.

Thirty seconds.

He changed up to first and said: "I'll drop you in rue d'Alsace."

He screeched away, turned left down rue du 8-Mai-1945 and let the Cipher out at the beginning of rue d'Alsace without giving him a moment to say anything. He then spun round and, with his foot flat down, reached rue du Faubourg-Saint-Martin.

Ten more seconds had ticked by.

This part of rue du Faubourg-Saint-Martin was very different from its lower reaches, in the Turkish quarter. All that could be seen here were empty pavements, warehouses and administrative buildings. An ideal exit route.

Paul watched the second hand on his watch. Each click dug into his flesh. The anonymous crowd broke up, scattering into this excessively large street. He stared towards the interior of the train station. He saw its huge glass roof, which made him think of a greenhouse, full of noxious shoots and carnivorous plants.

Ten seconds.

The chances of seeing the Adidas jacket reappear were now practically nil. He thought of the métro trains passing beneath the earth, of the departures of mainline and suburban trains, dispersing beneath the open sky, of the thousands of faces and minds dashing below the grey girders.

He could not have been mistaken. It just was not possible.

Thirty seconds.

Still nothing.

His mobile rang. He heard Schiffer's guttural voice: "Useless fucker."

Paul joined him at the foot of the staircase that cut rue d'Alsace in the middle, thus raising it above the immense gulf of rail lines. The policeman climbed into the car and repeated: "Dickhead."

"We can always try Gare du Nord. You never know. We . . ."

"Shut it. We've lost him. It's over."

Paul nevertheless accelerated towards the Gare du Nord.

"I should never have listened to you," Schiffer went on. "You've got no experience. You know nothing. You . . ."

"There he is."

To the right, at the end of rue des Deux-Gares, Paul had just spotted the Adidas jacket. The man was now trotting along the upper part of rue d'Alsace, just over the railway.

"The bugger," the Cipher said. "He used the outside staircase in the mainline station. He went out via the platforms."

He pointed up.

"Drive straight on. No siren. No speeding. We'll grab him in the next street. Nice and easy."

Paul changed down to second and kept to the 20 k.p.h. speed limit, with his hands trembling. They were crossing rue La Fayette, when the Turk suddenly surged out a hundred yards further on. He stared round, then froze.

"Shit!" Paul yelled, remembering that he had left the magnetic light on the roof of the car.

The man started to run as though the pavement was on fire. Paul stepped on the accelerator. The massive bridge that appeared in front of them seemed to him like a symbol. A stone giant opening its black arms beneath a stormy sky.

He accelerated again and passed the Turk half-way along the bridge. Schiffer leapt out before the car had stopped. Paul braked and in his rear-view mirror saw Schiffer's figure tackling the Turk like a rugby scrum-half.

He swore, turned off the ignition and got out of the Golf. The copper had already grabbed the runaway by his hair and was ramming him against the railings of the bridge. In a flash, Paul pictured Marius's hand in the guillotine. Never again. He took out his Glock as he ran towards the two men.

"Stop!"

Schiffer was now pushing his victim over the edge. His strength and speed were astonishing. The man in the jacket was stuck between two metal spikes, feebly kicking his legs.

Paul felt certain that he was going to throw him into mid-air. But the Cipher clambered up beside him, grabbed the first stone cross-beam then immediately yanked the Turk up there with him.

This manoeuvre had taken just a few seconds, and the physical feat added even more to Schiffer's diabolical standing. When Paul arrived, the two men were already out of reach, perched in the crook of those concrete arms. The runaway was screaming while his torturer, back to the void, was raining blows on him and yelling at him in Turkish.

Paul clambered up the metal spikes, then froze half-way up.

"BOZKURT! BOZKURT! BOZKURT!"

The Turk's cries echoed in the damp air. He first thought that it was a call for help, but he saw Schiffer release his victim, then push him towards the pavement, as though he had now obtained what he wanted.

By the time Paul had grabbed his handcuffs, the man was limping away hastily.

"Let him go!"

"Wh-what?"

Schiffer dropped down in turn onto the pavement. He fell on his left side, grimaced, then pulled himself up onto his knee.

"He told me what he knew," he spat between coughs.

"What? What did he say?"

Schiffer stood up. Out of breath, he was clutching the top of his left thigh. His skin was purplish, marked with white spots.

"He lives in the same building as Ruya. He saw them take the girl away, on the stairs. On 8 January, at eight p.m."

"Them?"

"The Bozkurt."

Paul did not understand. He stared back into Schiffer's chrome blue eyes and thought of his second nickname: Mister Steel.

"The Grey Wolves."

"The what?"

"The Grey Wolves. An extreme right-wing group. The killers of the Turkish mafia. We got it all wrong. They're the ones who are killing the girls."

CHAPTER 37

The tracks spread out, unbroken, into the distance. It was a hard, frozen network, imprisoning the mind and senses. Lines of steel that engraved the eyes like barbed wire, points designating new directions without ever becoming free from their rivets or iron. Turnings that disappeared over the horizon, but still evoked the same feeling of ineluctable rigidity. And the bridges of filthy stone or dark metal, with their ladders, gantries and turrets, topped off the whole.

Schiffer had taken an unauthorised route down to the tracks. Paul had then caught up with him, twisting his ankle on the sleepers.

"Who are the Grey Wolves?"

Schiffer walked on without replying, breathing in short gasps. The black stones rolled beneath his feet.

"It would take too long to explain," he said at last. "It's all part of Turkish history."

"Tell me, for Christ's sake! You owe me an explanation!"

The Cipher kept walking, still holding his left side. Then, in a hollow voice, he began: "It was during the 1970s. There was the same over-heated atmosphere in Turkey as in Europe. Leftist ideas were universally accepted. There was about to be a sort of May '68 . . . But, over there, tradition always wins. A resistance group was set up. Men of the extreme right, led by a real Nazi called Alpaslan Turkes. They started out by forming little units in the universities, then they recruited young peasants in the countryside. These recruits called themselves the 'Grey Wolves' or 'Bozkurt'. Or else 'Ülkü Ocaklari', the 'Young Idealists'. Right from the start, their main argument was violence."

Despite the heat of his body, Paul's teeth were chattering so hard that the noise echoed around his skull.

"At the end of the 1970s," Schiffer went on, "the extreme right-wingers and the extreme left-wingers took up arms. There were bomb-ings, pillage and murder. At the time, about thirty people were killed a day. It was a real civil war. The Grey Wolves were trained in special camps. The recruits became younger and younger. They were indoc-trinated and transformed into killing machines."

Schiffer was still swaying along the rails. His breathing became more regular. He kept his eyes on the gleaming lines as though they were dictating the direction of his thoughts.

"Finally, in 1980, the Turkish army seized power. Everything returned to order. The fighters on both sides were arrested. But the Grey Wolves were soon released. Their ideas were the same as the soldiers'. But now they had become idle. As for those kids, who had been trained in camps, all they knew how to do was to kill. So, logically enough, they were employed by people who needed hit men. Firstly the government, always pleased to find boys ready to discreetly top Armenian leaders or Kurdish terrorists. Then the mafia, which was beginning to control the opium market of the Golden Crescent. For the mafiosi, the Grey Wolves were a god-send. A force that was strong, armed, experienced and above all with links with the powers that be. Ever since, the Grey Wolves have been carrying out their contracts. Ali Agça, the man who shot the Pope in 1981, was a Bozkurt. Today, most of them have become mercenaries and have left their political ideals behind them. But the most dangerous ones still remain fanatics, terrorists who are capable of anything. Lunatics who believe in the supremacy of the Turkish race, and the return of the Ottoman Empire."

Dazed, Paul listened. He could see no connection between this ancient history and his investigation. He finally asked: "And you're telling me that it's these men who are killing the women?"

"The Adidas jacket saw them taking Ruya Berkes away."

"He saw their faces?"

"They were wearing balaclavas, in commando kit."

"Commando kit?"

The Cipher sneered.

"They're warriors, lad. Soldiers. They drove off in a black station wagon. The Turk couldn't remember its registration number, or even its make. Or doesn't want to remember."

"Why is he sure that it was the Grey Wolves?"

"They shouted slogans. They have their own distinctive signs. There's no doubt about it. What's more, it fits in with the rest of the situation. The silence of the community. The fact that Gozar mentioned 'something political'. The Grey Wolves are in Paris. The Turkish quarter is bricking it."

Paul could not accept such a different, unexpected direction, which

183

broke entirely with his own intuitions. He had worked too long on the idea of an isolated killer. He insisted: "But why such violence?"

Schiffer continued up the tracks, which were gleaming in the mist.

"They come from distant lands. The plains, deserts and mountains where such torture is standard. You were working on the hypothesis of a serial killer. With Scarbon, you thought you could recognise a quest for suffering in the wounds of the victims, or the traces of some trauma or something . . . But you overlooked an extremely simple solution. These women were tortured by professionals. Experts trained in the camps of Anatolia."

"What about the mutilations after death? The cuts on their faces?"

The Cipher's weary gesture seemed to accept all forms of cruelty.

"One of them is maybe even nuttier than the rest. Or else, perhaps they don't want their victims to be recognised, for the face they're looking for to be identified."

"That they're looking for?"

The copper stopped and turned round towards Paul.

"You still don't understand what's going on, lad? The Grey Wolves have a contract. They're looking for a woman."

He rummaged through his blood-stained raincoat and then showed him the Polaroids.

"A woman with this face, answering this description: a red-head, a seamstress, illegal alien, originally from Gaziantep."

Paul silently looked at the photos in that wrinkled hand.

Everything was taking shape. Burning up.

"A woman who knows something that they need to drag out of her. On three occasions, they thought they'd got her. And they were wrong each time."

"Why are you so sure? How can we be certain that they haven't found her?"

"Because if one of them had been their target, then she would have talked, you can be sure of that, and they would have gone."

"So . . . so you think the hunt's still on?"

"For sure."

Schiffer's irises were glistening below his lowered eyelids. Paul thought of silver bullets which, alone, can kill werewolves.

"You got the wrong lead, lad. You were looking for a killer. You were grieving the dead. But it's a living woman who you need to find. Someone very much alive, who is being hunted by the Grey Wolves."

He gestured round at the buildings alongside the rail tracks.

"She's there, somewhere, in this neighbourhood. In the cellars. In the attics. In the depths of a squat or home. She's being pursued by the worst killers imaginable and you alone can save her. But you're going to have to act quickly. Very, very quickly. Because those bastards are highly trained, and every door in the quarter is open to them."

The Cipher grabbed Paul by his shoulders and stared intensely at him.

"As they say, it never rains but it pours. I've got another piece of good news for you: if you want to pull it off, I'm the only chance you've got."

VII

CHAPTER 38

The telephone bell exploded into his ears.

"Yes?"

No answer. Eric Ackermann slowly hung up, then looked at his watch. Three p.m. The twelfth anonymous call since yesterday. The last time he had heard a human voice was the previous morning when Laurent Heymes had called to tell him that Anna had escaped. When he attempted to phone him back later that afternoon, there was no answer on any of his numbers. Was it already too late for Laurent?

He had tried other contacts. In vain.

That evening, he had received the first anonymous call. At once, he checked through his window. Two police officers were posted in front of his building, on avenue Trudaine. So the situation was now clear. He was no longer someone to be contacted, or a partner to be kept informed. He was now someone to be watched, an enemy to be controlled. In the space of a few hours, a boundary had shifted beneath his feet. He was now on the wrong side of it, on the side of those responsible for the disaster.

He stood up and went to his bedroom window. The two policemen were still stationed outside Lycée Jacques-Decourt. He stared at the grass borders which ran along the middle of the entire avenue, the plane trees swaying, still bare, in the sunlight, the grey structures of the kiosk on square d'Anvers. Not a single car passed, and the street looked, as usual, like a forgotten by-way.

A quotation came to his mind: "Distress is physical if the danger is concrete, psychological if it is instinctual." Who had written that? Freud? Jung? How was danger going to manifest itself in his case? Were they going to shoot him down in the street? Jump him as he slept? Or just lock him up in a military prison? Torture him in order to obtain all the documents concerning the programme?

Wait. He had to wait till nightfall before he could put his plan into action.

Still standing by the window, he mentally went over the career that had brought him here, to death's antechamber.

Fear had been at the beginning.

And fear would be at the end.

His odyssey had started in June 1985, when he had joined Professor Wayne C. Drevets's team at Washington University in Saint Louis, Missouri. The scientists had given themselves an ambitious objective: to localise the zone in the brain that caused fear, using positron emission tomography. To do so, they had drawn up a very strict protocol of experiments, which aimed at creating terror in their voluntary guinea-pigs. The appearance of snakes, the promise of an electric shock, which would seem all the worse the longer the wait . . .

After several series of tests, they had located this mysterious area. It was in the temporal lobe, at the edge of the limbic circuit, in a little region called the amygdala, a kind of niche that corresponds to our "basic brain". It is the oldest part of the organism – the one humankind shares with the reptiles – which also houses sexual instinct and aggression.

Ackermann remembered those thrilling days. For the first time, he was observing on a computer screen cerebral zones just as they were being activated. He knew that he had now found his career and his path forward. The positron camera would be his ship allowing him to voyage through the human cortex.

He became a pioneer, a cartographer of the brain.

When he returned to France, he had applied for funding from such public bodies as INSERM, the CNRS, the École des Hautes Études en Sciences Sociales, as well as various universities and hospitals in Paris, thus increasing his chances of receiving a budget.

A year went by without any answers. He went into exile in Great Britain, where he joined Professor Anthony Jones's department at the University of Manchester. With this fresh team, they set out for a different neuronal region – the one governing pain.

Once again, he took part in a series of tests on subjects willing to undergo painful stimuli. And once again, he saw a new region lighting up on the screens: the land of suffering. It was not a concentrated region, but a set of points that were activated simultaneously. A sort of spider's web running all through the cortex.

A year later, Professor Jones wrote in the journal *Science*: "Once registered by the thalamus, the sensation of pain is orientated by the cingulum and the frontal cortex towards the more or less negative. Only then does it became a sensation of suffering."

This fact was of primordial importance. It confirmed the major role of thought in the perception of pain. In so far as the cingulum acts as a selector of associations, feelings of suffering could be reduced thanks to a series of purely psychological exercises, thus diminishing and channelling its "resonance" in the brain. For example, in the case of burns, it was enough to think about the sun, instead of the burnt flesh, for the pain to recede. Suffering could be fought by the mind. The very topography of the brain proved it.

Ackermann had returned to France in a state of exaltation. He could already picture himself at the head of a multi-disciplinary research team, a superstructure bringing together cartographers, neurologists, psychiatrists, psychologists . . . Now that the brain was revealing its physiological keys, collaboration between all these disciplines became possible. The days of rivalry were over. They now just had to *look at the map*, and unite their forces!

But his requests for funding remained unanswered. Disgusted and in despair, he ended up in a tiny laboratory in Maisons-Alfort, where he started using amphetamines to get over his depression. Soon, full to the gills with Benzedrine, he convinced himself that his requests had been overlooked through simple ignorance. The powers of the Petscan were not sufficiently well known.

He decided to bring together all the international studies of the brain's cartography into one definitive work of reference. He started travelling again, to Tokyo, Copenhagen, Boston . . . He met with neurologists, biologists, radiologists, he read their articles and drew up summaries of them. In 1992, he published a work of six hundred pages: *Functional Imagery and Cerebral Geography*, an atlas revealing a new world, a strange new geography containing continents, seas, archipelagos . . .

Despite the success of his book within the scientific community, French institutions still remained silent. Even worse, two positron cameras had been bought in Orsay and Lyons, and never once had his name been mentioned. Never once was he consulted. As a ship-less explorer, Ackermann had plunged even deeper into his universe of designer drugs. If he could remember certain soaring voyages on Ecstasy at this time, which had taken him beyond himself, he could also recall the abysses that opened in his mind after bad trips.

He was at the bottom of one of these pits when he received a letter from the Atomic Energy Commission.

At first he thought that he was still hallucinating. Then the news sank in. A positive answer. Given that use of a positron camera involves injecting a radioactive marker, the commission was interested in his work. A special board even wanted to meet him in order to discuss how the commission might participate in funding his programme.

The following week, Eric Ackermann went to its headquarters in Fontenay-aux-Roses. He was in for a surprise. The committee was made up essentially of soldiers. This had brought a smile to his lips. These uniforms reminded him of the good old days, when he was a Maoist and had attacked the riot police on the barricades of rue Gay-Lussac in 1968. It was a vision that inspired him. He had also swallowed a handful of Benzedrine to ward off nerves. So if he had to convince these johnnies, then he would talk the hind leg off a donkey . . .

His presentation lasted several hours. He started by explaining how use of the Petscan had allowed the zone of fear to be identified as early as 1985, and how this discovery meant that specific drugs could now be developed to lessen its grip on the human mind.

That is what he told the army.

Then he described Professor Jones's work and how he had localised the neuronal circuit of pain. He pointed out that, by associating these locations with psychological training, it was possible to limit suffering.

That's what he told a committee of generals and army psychiatrists.

He then spoke of other research – into schizophrenia, the memory, the imagination . . .

Gesticulating wildly, rattling off statistics and references, he made them glimpse extraordinary possibilities: thanks to cerebral cartography, they were now going to be able to observe, control and fashion the human brain!

A month later, he received a second invitation. They agreed to finance his project, on condition that it was carried out in the Henri-Becquerel Institute, a military hospital in Orsay. He would thus have to work with military colleagues, in perfect transparency.

Ackermann burst out laughing. He was going to work for the Ministry of Defence! Him! A pure product of the counter-culture of the 1970s, a crazed trick-cyclist high on speed . . . He convinced himself that he would be smarter than his paymasters, and would manipulate them, without being manipulated himself.

He was completely wrong.

The phone echoed once more in his room.

He did not even bother to answer. He drew his curtains and stood openly in the window. The sentinels were still there.

Avenue Trudaine was a delicate mingling of brown tones – shades of dried mud, old gold, ancient metals. When looking at it, he always thought, without knowing why, of a Chinese or Tibetan temple, with peeling red or yellow paint revealing the bark of another reality.

It was four p.m. and the sun was still high in the sly.

Suddenly, he decided not to wait for nightfall.

He was too impatient to get away.

He crossed the living-room, grabbed his bag and opened the door.

Fear had been at the beginning.

And fear would be at the end.

CHAPTER 39

He went down to the building's car-park via the emergency staircase. From the doorway, he peered around the dark space. No one. He crossed the floor then unlocked a black iron door, hidden behind a pillar. At the end of the corridor, he emerged in Anvers métro station. He glanced back. Nobody was following him. The crowd of passengers bustling around made him panic for an instant. Then he reasoned with himself: they would actually help him escape. Without slowing down, he made his way through them, his eyes fixed on another door at the far side of that ceramic area.

When he reached the photo booth, he pretended to be waiting for his pictures, while facing the narrow entrance and rummaging through the set of keys he had procured. After a while he found the right one, and discreetly opened the door marked PERSONNEL ONLY.

Sighing with relief, he was alone again. A pungent odour hung in the corridor: a bitter, heavy smell which he could not identify, but which seemed to be inching all over him. He advanced, tripping over mouldy cardboard boxes, forgotten cables and metallic containers. At no time did he look for the light. He fumbled with his keys, opening padlocks, gratings and reinforced doors. He did not bother to lock them again, but found their presence behind his back reassuring, like so many layers of protection.

Finally, he reached a second car-park, below square d'Anvers. It was exactly like the first one, except that the floor and walls were painted light green. Everything was deserted. He headed onward. He was pouring with sweat, trembling all over, feeling either boiling hot or chilled in turn. Apart from his anxiety, he realised that he was starting to get withdrawal symptoms.

Finally, at number 2033, he spotted the five-door Volvo. Its imposing appearance, metal grey bodywork and registration plate bearing a number from the Haut-Rhin department, in the east of France, reassured him. His entire organism seemed to stabilise and relocate its centre of balance.

As soon as the problems had started with Anna, he realised that they were going to get worse. More than anyone else, he knew that her breakdowns were going to multiply, and that sooner or later the project would turn into a catastrophe. So he had thought of an escape plan. First move: go back to Alsace, where he was born. Since he could not change his name, he would conceal himself among all the other Ackermanns on the planet – over three hundred of them just in the departments of the Bas and Haut-Rhin. He could then organise the real departure: Brazil, New Zealand, Malaysia . . .

He removed a remote control from his pocket. He was about to use it, when a voice hit him in the back: "Sure you haven't forgotten anything?"

He turned round and saw a black-and-white creature, wrapped up in a velvet coat, just a few yards away.

Anna Heymes.

His first reaction was a burst of anger. He thought of a bird of ill omen, a curse following his every step. Then he changed his mind. "Hand her over," he thought. "Hand her over, it's the only way."

He dropped his bag and adopted a comforting tone: "Anna, where on earth were you? Everyone's been looking for you."

He walked towards her, opening his arms.

"You did the right thing coming to see me. You . . ."

"Don't move."

He stopped dead still then slowly, very slowly, turned towards the second voice. Another figure was standing in front of a pillar, to his right. He was so amazed that a mist passed over his eyes. Confused memories were drifting up to the surface of his mind. He knew this woman.

"Mathilde?"

Without answering, she approached. He said again, in a dazed tone: "Mathilde Wilcrau?"

She stood in front of him, pointing an automatic pistol at him in her gloved hand. Looking from one of them to the other, he stammered: "You . . . you know each other?"

"When you no longer trust your neurologist, where do you go? To a psychiatrist."

As before, she lengthened her syllables into deep undulations. Nobody could forget such a voice. A flood of saliva filled his mouth. A sludge which tasted just like the stench in the corridor. He knew what it was now: the bitter, profound, malevolent taste of fear. He was its sole source. It was exuding from every pore of his body.

"Have you been following me? What do you want?"

Anna went over to him. Her indigo eyes glittered in the greenish light of the car-park. Eyes like a dark ocean, slightly slanted, almost Asian. She smiled and said: "What do you think I want?"

CHAPTER 40

In the field of the neurosciences, in neuropsychology and cognitive psychology, I'm the best, or at least one of the best, in the entire world. This isn't vanity. It's quite simply a recognised fact in the scientific community. At the age of fifty-two, I have become what is called a reference.

But I only really became important in these fields when I deserted the scientific world, when I left the beaten track and took a forbidden path. A path that no one had taken before me. It was only then that I became a major researcher, a pioneer who will mark his epoch.

The trouble is, it's already too late for me . . .

March 1994

After sixteen months of tomographic experiments on the memory – the third season of the "Personal Memory and Cultural Memory" programme – the repetition of certain anomalies led me to contact those laboratories which were using in their experiments the same radioactive labelled water as my team: Oxygen-15.

The answer was unanimous. They hadn't noticed a thing.

This didn't mean I was wrong. It just meant that I was using higher doses on the subjects of my experiments and that my unusual results could be explained by this fact. I sensed something important had happened. I had crossed a threshold and this threshold revealed the true power of this substance.

It was too early to publish. I just wrote a report for the Atomic Energy Commission, which was funding my work, summarising that season's results. On the last page, I appended a note mentioning the repetition of certain unusual events during the tests. These events concerned the indirect influence of Oxygen-15 on the human brain, and they undoubtedly ought to be studied during a specific research programme.

Their reaction was instantaneous. I was called in to AEC headquarters in May. In a huge conference hall, a dozen specialists were waiting for me. With their short-cropped hair and rigid turn of phrase, I recognised them at once. They were the same soldiers who had interviewed me two years before, when I'd made my initial presentation of my research programme.

I started at the beginning: "The principle of PET (positron emission tomography) involves injecting radioactive labelled water into the subject's blood. Once made radioactive itself, it emits positrons which a camera then captures in real time, thus allowing cerebral activity to be localised. Personally, I selected a classic radioactive isotope, Oxygen-15, and . . ."

A voice interrupted me: "In your note, you mention some anomalies. What do you mean exactly? What happened?"

"I noticed that, after the tests, some subjects confused their own memories with the stories they had been told during the sessions."

"Can you be more precise?"

"Several exercises in my protocol consisted of communicating imaginary stories, short fictions which the subject then had to summarise orally. After the tests, the subjects repeated these stories as if they were true. They were absolutely convinced that they had really experienced these inventions."

"And you think it was the use of Oxygen-15 that sparked off this phenomenon?"

"I suppose so. A positron camera cannot have any effect on the consciousness. It's a non-invasive technique. Oxygen-15 was the only product administered to the subjects."

"How do you explain its influence?"

"I can't. Maybe it's the impact of radioactivity on the neurons. Or an effect of the molecule itself on the neuro-transmitters. It's as if the experiment excites the cognitive system, thus making it permeable to information given during the test. The brain can no longer tell the difference between imaginary data and personal experiences."

"Do you think that, using this substance, it might be possible to implant in a subject's consciousness memories that are . . . shall we say, artificial?"

"It's far more complex than that, I . . ."

"Do you think it's possible, yes or no?"

"We could certainly explore this possibility."

Silence. Another voice said: "During your career, you've worked on brainwashing techniques, haven't you?"

I burst out laughing in a vain attempt to defuse this inquisitorial atmosphere.

"Over twenty years ago. In my PhD thesis!"

"Have you followed the progress that has been made in the field?"

"More or less. But there's a lot of unpublished research on the subject. Work that has been classified top secret. I don't know if . . ."

"Can substances be used to act as an effective chemical screen to block out a subject's memory?"

"Yes, there are several such products."

"Which ones?"

"We're talking here about manipulations that are . . ."

"Which ones?"

I answered grudgingly: "There's much talk these days about substances like GHB, or gamma-hydroxybutyrate. But to achieve this kind of objective, it's better to use a more common product. Like Valium, for instance."

"Why?"

"Because, at certain doses, Valium not only provokes partial amnesia, it also introduces automatisms. Patients become open to suggestion. What is more, we also have an antidote, so the subject can recover his memory afterwards."

Silence. The first voice: "Supposing that a subject had been given such a treatment. Would it be possible to inject new memories, using Oxygen-15?"

"If you're expecting me to . . ."

"Yes or no?"

"Yes."

Another silence. All their eyes were fixed on me.

"The subject would remember nothing?"

"No."

"Neither the Valium treatment, nor the use of Oxygen-15?"

"No, but it's too early to . . ."

"Apart from you, who else knows about this?"

"Nobody. I contacted some other laboratories that use the isotope, but no one had noticed anything and . . ."

"We know who you've contacted."

"You're spying on me?"

"Did you speak about it to the heads of the laboratories?"

"No, it was via email. I . . ."

"Thank you, professor."

At the end of 1994, a new budget was voted through for a programme entirely devoted to the effects of Oxygen-15. Such are the ironies of fate. After encountering so many difficulties getting funding for a programme that I had planned, presented and defended, I was now being given financing for a project I hadn't even envisaged.

April 1995

The nightmare began. I was visited by a policeman, escorted by two goons dressed in black. He was a giant with a grey moustache, dressed in a woollen gabardine. He introduced himself as Commissioner Philippe Charlier. He seemed jovial, smiling and relaxed, but my old hippy instincts whispered to me that he was dangerous. I saw in him a violent breaker of rebellion, a bastard sure that what he was doing was right.

"I've come to tell you a story," he announced. "A personal memory. About a wave of terrorist attacks that spread panic throughout France from December 1985 to September 1986. The rue de Rennes, and so on. Remember? In all thirteen dead and two hundred and fifty wounded.

"At the time, I was working for the DST, or Direction de la Surveillance du Territoire. We had been given unlimited means. Thousands of men, surveillance systems, unrestricted powers of detention. We dug around in the Islamist groups, the Palestinian supporters, the Lebanese networks and Iranian communists. Paris was completely under our control. We even offered a reward of a million francs to anyone providing information. All that for nothing. We couldn't find a single lead, or clue. Zero. And the attacks were continuing, killing, wounding and demolishing property. We were powerless to stop them.

"One day, in March 1986, we had a 'breakthrough' and netted all the members of the group: Fouad Ali Salah and his accomplices. They were storing their guns and explosives in a flat on rue de la Voûte, in the twelfth *arrondissement*. Their meeting point was a Tunisian restaurant on rue de Chartres, in the Goutte d'Or quarter. I was the one who led the operation. Within a few hours, we arrested the lot of them. Nice, clean work, and no foul-ups. From one day to the next, the bombings stopped. The city was calm once more.

"And do you know what brought this miracle about? What the 'breakthrough' was that changed everything? One of the members of the group, Lotfi ben Kallak, had quite simply decided to change sides. He contacted us, and handed in his accomplices in exchange for the reward. He even agreed to organise the ambush from within.

"Lotfi was crazy. No one gives up their life for a few hundred thousand francs. No one accepts to live like a hunted beast, to run away to the ends of the earth knowing that, sooner or later, they would catch up with him. But I could measure the impact of his betrayal. For the first time, we were inside the group. At the heart of the system, you see? From that moment, everything became easy, clear and effective. And that's the moral of my story. Terrorists have just one strength – secrecy. They strike wherever and whenever they want. There's only one way to stop them. You have to infiltrate their network. Infiltrate their brains. And then, you can do what you want. Like with Lotfi. And thanks to you, we're going to do just that with all the others."

Charlier's idea was simple: turn round people close to terrorist networks using Oxygen-15, then inject them with artificial memories – for example, a motive for revenge – so as to convince them to co-operate and hand over their brothers in arms.

"The programme will be called Morpho," he explained. "Because we're going to change the psychic morphology of these Arabs. We're going to modify their personalities and their cerebral make-up. Then we'll release them into the world they came from. Like rabid dogs in the pack."

In a voice that chilled my blood, he concluded: "You've got a straight-forward choice. Either you enjoy unlimited funding, as many subjects as you want, the chance to direct a scientific revolution in complete confidentiality. Or else you return to the shitty life of a petty researcher, running around after money, labs going broke, publishing obscure articles. And don't forget that we're going to run the programme anyway, with you, or with others who will be given all your results and notes. You can count on other scientists to exploit the influence of Oxygen-15, and then claim it as their discovery."

During the next few days, I asked around. Philippe Charlier was one of the five commissioners of the Sixth Division of the Direction centrale de la Police judiciaire (the DCPJ). He was one of the leaders of the war against international terrorism, under the orders of Jean-Paul Magnard, the head of the division.

His colleagues had nicknamed him the "Green Giant", and he was well-known for his obsession with infiltration, and the violence of his methods. He had even been sidelined on several occasions by Magnard, who was just as intransigent, but who had remained faithful to the traditional methods and distrusted any experimentation.

However, this was in spring 1995, and Charlier's ideas were of topical importance. France was under threat from a terrorist network. On 25 July, a bomb exploded in Saint-Michel RER station, killing ten people. The GIA was suspected, but there was not the slightest lead to help stop this wave of attacks.

The Minister of Defence, in association with the Minister of the Interior, decided to fund the Morpho project. Even if this operation could not be effective about any particular case – the timeline being too short – the moment had now come to use new weapons against terrorism.

At the end of summer 1995, Philippe Charlier came to see me again, and already spoke of a guinea-pig chosen from among the hundreds of Islamists who had been arrested during their investigations.

It was then that Magnard won a decisive battle. A bottle of gas had been found on a high-speed train line, and the police from Lyons were about to destroy it. But Magnard demanded that they examine it first. On it, they discovered the fingerprints of a suspect, Khaled Kelkal, who turned out to be one of those behind the attacks. The rest is history. Kelkal was tracked like a beast through the forests around Lyons, then shot down on 29 September. His network was dismantled.

It was a triumph for Magnard, and his good old-fashioned methods.

No more Morpho.

Exit Philippe Charlier.

And yet, the budget was still there. The ministries in charge of the country's security gave me plentiful funds to continue my research. During the very first year, my results proved that I was right. It really was Oxygen-15, when injected in large doses, which made neurons permeable to artificial memories. Under its influence, the memory became porous, letting in elements of fiction and incorporating them as real experiences.

My protocol grew more precise. I was working on dozens of different subjects, all provided by the army, or else volunteers from the ranks. At this stage, the conditioning was extremely light. Only one artificial memory at a time. I then waited several days to check if the 'graft' was holding.

But we still had to carry out the ultimate experiment: conceal a subject's memory and implant a new one. I was in no hurry to attempt such brainwashing. What's more, the police and the army had apparently forgotten about me. At the time, Charlier had been relegated to fieldwork, and was excluded from the circles of power. Magnard was the undisputed boss, with his traditional ideas. I was hoping that they'd leave me alone for good. I dreamed of going back to civilian life, of officially publishing my results, of a beneficial use for my discoveries . . .

All of which might have been possible without September 11, 2001.

The attacks on the Twin Towers and the Pentagon.

The wave of those explosions blew away all of the police's certitudes, all their investigative and surveillance techniques, on a global scale. The secret services, information agencies, police forces and armies of all the countries threatened by al-Qaeda were on tenterhooks. The politicians were panicking. Once more, terrorism had shown that its greatest strength was secrecy.

There was talk of holy war, of chemical attacks, atomic bombs . . .

Philippe Charlier was back in the front line. He was the man to deal with such persistence and obsession. A figure of power, with methods that were obscure, violent and . . . effective. The Morpho project was resurrected. Terrible words were on everyone's lips – conditioning, brainwashing, infiltration . . .

In mid-November, Charlier turned up at the Henri-Becquerel Institute. With a broad smile, he announced: "The A-rabs are back."

He invited me to lunch in a restaurant specialising in Lyons cuisine: hot sausage and Burgundy wine. The nightmare started up again in the stench of fat and cooked blood.

"Do you know the annual budget of the CIA and FBI?" he asked.

I shook my head.

"Thirty billion dollars. The two agencies have spy satellites and submarines, automatic reconnaissance equipment and mobile phone tapping systems. The most cutting-edge technology in the field of surveillance. Not to mention the National Security Agency and its know-how. The Americans can listen in and spy anywhere. There are no more secrets on earth. Or so everyone thought. The entire world felt concerned. People were even talking about Big Brother . . . But then there was September 11th. A few men, armed with plastic knives, destroyed the Twin Towers of the World Trade Center and took a good lump out of the Pentagon, while notching up a score of a good three thousand dead. The Americans listen to everything, receive everything, except when it's coming from people who are really dangerous."

The Green Giant was not smiling any more. He slowly turned his palms to face the ceiling, above his plate.

"Can you imagine the two sides of the scales? On the one hand, thirty billion dollars. On the other, some plastic knives. What do you think makes the difference? What made the fucking scale tip?"

He hit the table violently.

"Willpower. Faith. Madness. Confronted with an armada of technology, and thousands of American agents, a handful of determined men managed to slip through all their surveillance. Because no machine will ever be as powerful as the human mind. Because servants of the state, leading ordinary lives with normal ambitions, will never be able to catch fanatics who don't give a damn about their own lives, who are completely given over to a higher cause."

He paused, got his breath back, then went on: "The kamikaze pilots of September 11th had removed all their body hair. Do you know why? So as to be perfectly pure at the moment they entered paradise. What can you do against loonies like that? You can't spy on them, bribe them or understand them."

His eyes were glittered with a strange light, as if he had warned everyone of the imminent catastrophe.

"I'll repeat: there's just one way to round up fanatics. Turn one of them against the others. Get a convert so as to be able to read the depths of their madness. Then, and only then, will we beat them."

The Green Giant laid his elbows on the tablecloth, put his rounded lips to his wine glass, then raised his moustache with a smile.

"I've got some good news for you. As of today, the Morpho project is back on. I've even found you a guinea-pig."

The wicked grin widened.

"A young lady."

CHAPTER 41

"Me."

Anna's voice hit the concrete like a table-tennis ball. Eric Ackermann smiled weakly, almost apologetically, at her. He had now been talking non-stop for almost an hour, sitting in his five-door Volvo, the door open, legs stretched outside. His throat was dry and he would have given anything for a glass of water.

Leaning against the pillar, Anna Heymes remained still, as slender as a graffito in Indian ink. Mathilde Wilcrau continually paced up and down, putting on the lights when the time switch turned them off.

While speaking, he observed them both: the slight, pale and dark one who, despite her youth, seemed struck with a very ancient, even mineral, rigidity; and the large one who, on the contrary, was vegetal and vibrant with lingering freshness. Still that over-red mouth, that over-black hair, that clash of brute colours, like a market stall.

How could he be having such ideas at a time like this? Charlier's men must be searching the neighbourhood, escorted by the local police officers, all out to get him. Battalions of armed men set on gunning him down. And that need for drugs which was mounting, along with his thirst, irritating every inch of his body . . .

Anna repeated, a few tones lower: "Me . . ."

She took a packet of cigarettes from her pocket. Ackermann risked asking: "I couldn't have one, could I?"

She lit her Marlboro first, hesitated for a moment, then offered him one. At the moment she lit her lighter, darkness fell again. The flame pierced the night, making a negative print of the scene.

Mathilde turned the lights back on.

"What then, Ackermann? We're still missing the main point. Who is Anna?"

Her tone was still threatening, but void of any anger or hatred. He now knew that these women would not kill him. No one turns into a murderer just like that. His confession was voluntary and also a relief. He waited for the taste of burning tobacco to fill his throat before answering.

"I don't know everything. Far from it. But according to what I was told, your name is Sema Gökalp. You're an illegal Turkish immigrant. You come from the Gaziantep region, in the south of Anatolia. You used to work in the tenth *arrondissement*. They took you to the Henri-Becquerel Institute on 16 November 2001, after a short stay in Sainte-Anne Hospital."

Anna remained impassive, leaning against the pillar. His words seemed to pass through her, with no apparent impact, like a bombardment of invisible, but lethal, particles.

"I was kidnapped?"

"Found, more like. I don't know what happened exactly. A clash between Turks. The pillaging of a sweatshop around Strasbourg-Saint-Denis. Some kind of racket. I'm not sure. All I know is that when the cops arrived, you were the only person left in the workshop. You were hiding in a stockroom . . ."

He took a drag. Despite the nicotine, the smell of fear lingered.

"Charlier heard about the case. He immediately realised that he had a perfect guinea-pig for his Morpho project."

"What do you mean 'perfect'?"

"No ID papers, no family, no friends. And, even better, in a state of shock."

Ackermann glanced at Mathilde knowingly. Then he returned to Anna.

"I don't know what you saw that night, but it must have been something terrible. You were completely traumatised. Three days later, your limbs were still paralysed by a cataleptic fit. You jumped at the slightest noise. But the most interesting thing is that the trauma had disturbed your memory. You seemed incapable of remembering your name, your identity, the few scraps of information in your passport. You kept muttering incoherently. This amnesia had prepared the ground for me.

I was going to be able to implant new memories even more quickly. You were ideal."

Anna yelled: "You fucking bastard!"

He closed his eyes and nodded, then he seemed to pull himself back together, and added cynically: "What's more, you spoke perfect French. It was that fact which gave Charlier the idea."

"What idea?"

"To start with, all we wanted to do was to inject artificial fragments into the head of a foreigner, with a different culture. We wanted to see what would happen if we tried, for example, to alter the religious convictions of a Muslim. Or give her a reason for resentment. But you offered other possibilities. You spoke our language perfectly. Physically, you could easily pass for a European. So Charlier placed the bar even higher. Total conditioning. We would totally wipe out your personality and culture, and replace them with Western ones."

He paused. The two women remained silent. A tacit invitation to continue.

"Firstly, I increased your amnesia by injecting an overdose of Valium. Then I started working on conditioning you. Constructing a new personality. Using Oxygen-15."

Intrigued, Mathilde asked: "How did you proceed?"

Another drag, then he answered, incapable of taking his eyes off Anna.

"Mainly by exposure to information. In every form. Words. Films. Sounds. Before each session, I injected a radioactive substance into you. The results were incredible. Each piece of information turned into a real memory in your brain. Every day, you were becoming more and more like the real Anna Heymes."

The slender woman stood up from the pillar.

"You mean, *she really exists*?"

The smell in the car-park was stronger and stronger, as though of rotten flesh. He was starting to decay as he sat there, while the craving for amphetamine raised a slope of panic in his mind.

"We had to fill your mind with a coherent set of memories. The best way was to choose a real person and use her life story, photos and video films. That's why we chose Anna Heymes. We had all the necessary material."

"Who is she? Where is the real Anna Heymes?"

He pushed his glasses up his nose, before saying: "Several feet underground. She's dead. Heymes's wife committed suicide six months ago. So the place was vacant, so to speak. All your memories are part of her story. The dead parents. The family in the South-West. The wedding in Saint-Paul-de-Vence. The law degree."

At that moment, the light went out. Mathilde turned it on again. The return of her voice coincided with the return of light.

"And you would have let such a woman loose again in the Turkish community?"

"No, that would have been senseless. This was a trial run. An attempt at . . . total conditioning. To see how far we could go."

"In the end," Anna asked, "what would you have done to me?"

"No idea. That was out of my hands."

Another lie. Of course he knew what was awaiting her. What was to be done with such an embarrassing guinea-pig? Lobotomy or elimination, that's what. When Anna next spoke, she seemed to have understood that dark reality. Her voice was as cold as a blade: "Who is Laurent Heymes?"

"Exactly who he claims to be. The research director of the Ministry of the Interior."

"Why did he participate in this farce?"

"It's all because of his wife. She was depressive, uncontrollable. Towards the end, Laurent got a job for her. A special mission for the Ministry of Defence concerning Syria. Anna stole some documents. She wanted to sell them to the authorities in Damascus before running away somewhere or other. She was nuts. The affair leaked out. Anna panicked and committed suicide."

Mathilde did not understand: "And this was a way of putting pressure on Laurent Heymes, even after her death?"

"He was always afraid of a scandal. His career would have been in ruins. A top civil servant married to a spy . . . Charlier has a complete dossier on the subject. He has a hold over Laurent, like he does over everyone else."

"Everyone else?"

"Alain Lacroux. Pierre Caracilli. Jean-François Gaudemer." He turned towards Anna. "All those supposedly high-ranking officials you had dinner with."

"Who are they?"

"Puppets, crooks, bent coppers, who Charlier has information on, and who were forced to attend the carnival."

"Why those dinners?"

"That was my idea. I wanted to confront your mind with the outside world and observe your reactions. Everything was filmed. The conversations recorded. You must understand that your entire existence was fake: the building on avenue Hoche, the janitor, the neighbours . . . Everything was under our control."

"A laboratory rat."

Ackermann stood up and tried to take a few steps, but he immediately found himself stuck between the car door and the wall. He slumped back down onto his seat.

"This programme was a scientific revolution," he replied hoarsely. "Moral considerations were irrelevant."

Anna offered him another cigarette over the car door. She seemed ready to forgive him, so long as he told her all.

"What about the Maison du Chocolat?"

When he lit the Marlboro, he noticed that he was shaking. A shock wave was on its way. The craving was soon going to start screaming beneath his skin.

"That was one of our problems," he said through a cloud of smoke. "Your job took us by surprise. We had to tighten our surveillance. Cops were constantly watching you. The doorman of a restaurant, I think . . ."

"La Marée."

"Yes, that's it."

"When I was working in the Maison du Chocolat, there was a regular customer. A man I had the impression I recognised. Was he a policeman?"

"Maybe. I don't know all the details. All I do know is that you were escaping from us."

Again, night fell and Mathilde woke up the strip-lights.

"The real problem was your fits," he went on. "I immediately sensed that there was a fault line, and that things were going to go from bad to worse. Your trouble with faces was just a precursor. Your real memory was beginning to resurface."

"Why faces?"

"No idea. This was pure experimentation."

His hands were trembling more and more. He concentrated on what he had to say.

"When Laurent caught you observing him at night, we realised that the problem was worsening. We had to section you."

"Why did you want to conduct a biopsy?"

"To be sure what was going on. Maybe the huge jab of Oxygen-15 had caused a lesion. I just had to understand!"

He broke off, sorry that he had shouted. It felt as if short-circuits were sizzling in his skin. He threw away his cigarette and stuck his hands between his thighs. How long could he hold out?

Mathilde Wilcrau then asked the crucial question: "Where are Charlier's men looking? How many of them are there?"

"I don't know. I've been sidelined. Laurent too. I'm not even in touch with him any more . . . As for Charlier, the programme's over. The vital thing now is to catch you and put you out of circulation. You read the papers. You know what they're saying in the media and how outraged public opinion is about a little bit of phone tapping. Imagine what would happen if this story got out."

"So there's a price on my head, is there?" Anna asked.

"More like a desperate need for treatment. You don't know what you've got in your mind. You must give yourself up to Charlier. To us. It's your only chance to recover, and save all of our skins!"

He looked up over the curve of his glasses. The two of them now appeared out of focus, and it was better that way. He added: "Jesus, you don't know Charlier! I'm sure all of this was perfectly illegal. So now he'll be sweeping up. Right now, I don't even know if Laurent is still alive. It's a total fiasco. Unless we can treat you again . . ."

His voice was dying in his throat. What was the point of going on? Even he no longer believed in the possibility. Mathilde then said, in her deep voice: "All of which does not explain why you altered her face."

Ackermann felt a smile rise to his lips. He had been expecting this question right from the start. He stared straight into Anna's eyes.

"You were like that when we found you. When I did the first scan, I discovered the scars, implants and screws. It was incredible. A complete surgical overhaul. It must have cost a fortune. Not the sort of operation an illegal immigrant worker could pay for."

"What do you mean?"

"I mean you're not a simple worker. Charlier and the others got it wrong. They thought they were kidnapping some faceless Turk. But you're much more than that. Crazy as it might seem, I reckon you were hiding out in the Turkish quarter when they discovered you."

Anna burst into tears. "It's not possible . . . It's not possible . . . When's all this going to stop?"

"In a way," he went on bitterly to the end, "this fact explains the success of the treatment. I'm no magician. I could never have transformed a simple working girl from Anatolia to this extent. And definitely not in a few weeks. Only Charlier could swallow such nonsense."

Mathilde returned to the point: "What did he say when you told him that her face had been altered?"

"Nothing because I didn't tell him. I kept this crazy secret to myself."

He looked at Anna.

"Even last Saturday, when you came to Becquerel I switched the X-rays. The marks appear on all of the images."

Anna dried her tears.

"Why did you do that?"

"I wanted to finish the experiment. It was such a golden opportunity . . . Your psychic state was ideal. All that mattered was the programme . . ."

Anna and Mathilde remained speechless.

When the little Cleopatra spoke again, her voice was as dry as a leaf of incense.

"If I'm not Anna Heymes, and I'm not Sema Gökalp. Then who am I?"

"I don't have the slightest idea. An intellectual maybe, a political refugee . . . Or a terrorist . . . I . . ."

The neon lights went out once more. Mathilde stuck out her hand. The darkness seemed to be deepening, like a flood of tar. For a moment he thought to himself: "I was wrong, they are going to kill me." But then Anna's voice echoed through the shadows.

"There's only one way to find out."

No one turned the lights back on. Eric Ackermann guessed what she was going to say. Just beside him, Anna murmured: "You're going to give me back what you stole. My memory."

VIII

CHAPTER 42

He had got rid of the kid, which was already something.

After the chase at the station and the revelations, Jean-Louis Schiffer had taken Paul Nerteaux to a bar called La Strasbourgeoise, just in front of the Gare de l'Est. He had then analysed once more what was really at stake in this investigation, how it was now a 'woman hunt'. For the moment, that was all that mattered. Forget the other victims and the killers. They just had to unmask the Grey Wolves' target, the girl they had been looking for in the Turkish quarter for the past five months and had so far failed to find.

Finally, after an hour's heated conversation, Paul Nerteaux had admitted defeat and decided to do a U-turn. His intelligence and ability to adapt never ceased to amaze Schiffer. The kid had then defined their new strategy himself.

First point: have an identikit portrait of the target done, based on photographs of the three corpses, then distribute it in the Turkish quarter.

Second point: reinforce their patrols, increase the identity controls and searches throughout Little Turkey. Such a tactic might seem derisory, but Nerteaux reckoned that they stood a chance of finding her by sheer good fortune. Things like that happened: after twenty-five years on the run, Toto Riina, the Godfather of Cosa Nostra, had been arrested in central Palermo during a routine inspection of ID cards.

Third point: go back to see Marius, the head of the Iskele, and study his files to see if other working girls matched the description. Schiffer liked this idea, but he could hardly return there in person after what he had done to that slave-driver.

So he kept the fourth point for himself: go and see Talat Gürdilek, for whom the first victim had worked. They had to finish questioning the murdered women's employers, and he was up for the job.

The fifth and final point was the only one aimed at the killers themselves: launch an investigation in Immigration and Visas to see if any Turkish residents known for their links with the extreme right or the mafia had arrived in France since November 2001. This meant sifting though all of the arrivals from Anatolia over the past five months, comparing them with Interpol records and also applying to the Turkish police.

Schiffer did not see the point of such an approach. He knew too well the close relationship that existed between his Turkish colleagues and the Grey Wolves, but he had let the enthusiastic youngster rattle on.

In reality, he did not see the point in a single one of these methods. But he had been patient, because another idea had occurred to him . . .

While they were on their way to Ile de la Cité, where Nerteaux intended to explain his new plan to Bomarzo, the investigating magistrate, he decided to chance his arm. He explained that the best way to advance now would be for them to split up. While Paul was distributing copies of the identikit portrait and briefing the men in the commissariats of the tenth *arrondissement*, he would drop round to see Gürdilek . . .

The young captain had kept his answer to himself until he had seen the magistrate. He had kept him waiting in a bar over the road from the Palais de Justice for two hours, and had even set an orderly to watch over him. Then he reappeared from his appointment as pleased as Punch. Bomarzo was giving him a free hand to carry out his plan. Apparently, this thrilled him so much that he now agreed to all Schiffer's requests.

He had dropped him off at six p.m. on boulevard de Magenta, near the Gare de l'Est, and had arranged to meet up at eight p.m. at the café Sancak, on rue du Faubourg-Saint-Denis in order to report.

Schiffer was now walking along rue de Paradis. Alone at last! Free at last . . . To breath the acidic air of the neighbourhood, to feel the magnetic force of "his" patch. The end of the day was like a pale, drowsy fever. On each windowpane, the sun placed its particles of light, a sort of gilded talc, which had the macabre grace of an embalmer's make-up.

He strode along, psyching himself up for his confrontation with Talat Gürdilek, one of the major mafia bosses of the quarter. He had arrived in Paris during the 1960s, aged seventeen, penniless, unqualified, and now he owned twenty sweatshops and factories in France and Germany, as well as a good dozen dry cleaners and launderettes. A godfather who ruled over every level of the Turkish quarter, official or unofficial, legal or illegal. When Gürdilek sneezed, the entire ghetto caught a cold.

At number 58 Schiffer pushed open a gateway. He entered a dark cul-de-sac, crossed by a central gutter, with noisy workshops and printers' studios on either side. At the end of the alley there was a rectangular courtyard, with rhomboid paving stones. On the right, a tiny staircase led down into a long ditch, overhung with small, half-deserted gardens.

He loved this hidden place, which was unknown even to most of the inhabitants of the building. A heart within the heart, a trench that disturbed all of the usual vertical or horizontal reference points. An iron door barred the way. He touched the handle. It was warm.

He smiled and knocked vigorously.

After some time a man opened it, liberating a cloud of steam. Schiffer muttered a few words of explanation in Turkish. The doorman stood to one side to let him in. The copper noticed that he was bare-footed. Another smile. Nothing had changed. He dived into the suffocating heat.

The white light revealed a familiar scene: the tiled corridor, the large heating pipes hanging from the ceiling, wrapped in pale green surgical cloth; the streams of tears on the floor tiles; the warped metal doors that punctuated each section and which looked like the sides of boilers, whitened with quicklime.

They walked on like this for some minutes. Schiffer felt his shoes slapping in the puddles. His body was already damp with sweat. They turned down another row of white tiles, full of mist. To the right, an opening revealed a workshop which sounded like a giant breathing.

Schiffer paused to contemplate the scene.

Beneath the ceiling of pipes and ducts, splashed with light, about thirty women with bare feet and white masks were slaving away over tubs and ironing boards. Jets of steam were shooting up in a regular rhythm. The smell of detergent and alcohol saturated the atmosphere.

Schiffer knew that the pumping station of the Turkish baths was nearby, under their feet, drawing water from a depth of two hundred and fifty feet, circulating through the ducts, its iron removed, chlorine added, heated, then directed either towards the Turkish baths themselves, or towards this underground laundry. Gürdilek had had the idea of placing them together in order to exploit a single system of plumbing for two distinct activities. It was an economical strategy: not a drop of water was wasted. As he passed, the copper had a good look, observing the masked women, their foreheads beaded with sweat. Their soaking coats stretched around their breasts and buttocks, which were large and sagging, just as he liked. He noticed that he had an erection. He took this as a good sign.

They walked on.

The heat and humidity continued to grow. A particular fragrance sometimes broke through, then vanished, so that Schiffer thought he had dreamt it. But a few paces further on, it reappeared and grew clearer.

This time, Schiffer was sure of it.

He started breathing more shallowly. Acrid itching started up in his nose and throat. Contradictory sensations filled his respiratory system. He had the impression of sucking on ice, yet his mouth was aflame. That odour was refreshing and scalding at the same time, aggressive and purifying in the same breath.

Mint.

They continued onward. The smell became a stream, a sea in which Schiffer was drowning. It was even worse than he remembered. At each step, he was turning more and more into a tea-bag at the bottom of a cup. The chill of an iceberg froze his lungs, while his face felt like a mask of burning wax.

When he reached the end of the corridor, he was almost suffocating, breathing in short gasps. He seemed to be advancing through a gigantic inhaler. Knowing that this was not far from the truth, he entered the throne room.

It was an empty rather shallow swimming-pool, surrounded by thin white columns which stood out against the hazy background of steam. Prussian blue tiles marked the sides, like in old Parisian métro stations.

Wooden screens covered the far wall, decked with Ottoman ornamentation: moons, crosses and stars.

In the centre of the pool, a man was sitting on a ceramic slab.

Heavy and burly, he had a white towel knotted around his waist. His face was drowned in shadows.

In the stifling fumigation, his laughter pealed out.

The laughter of Talat Gürdilek, the mint-man, the man with the scorched voice.

CHAPTER 43

Everyone in the Turkish quarter knew his story.

He arrived in Europe in 1961, taking the classic route, beneath the false bottom of a tanker. In Anatolia, he and his companions had been closed in behind a sheet of iron, which had then been bolted into place. The illegal immigrants thus had to lie there, without light or fresh air, during the forty-eight-hour journey.

The heat and lack of air was oppressive. Then, when crossing the mountain passes of Bulgaria, the cold had seeped in through the metal and pierced them to the core. But the real torture started when they were approaching Yugoslavia, when the tanker, which contained cadmiumic acid, began to leak.

Slowly, the coffin of metal filled with toxic gases. The Turks yelled, shook and banged at the plate that was weighing down on them, but the lorry continued on its way. Talat realised that no one was going to free them before their arrival point, and screaming or moving would only worsen the effects of the acid.

He remained still, breathing as little as possible.

At the Italian frontier, the travellers joined hands and prayed. At the German border, most of them were dead. At Nancy, where the first drop-off had been planned, the driver discovered a row of thirty corpses, covered with urine and excrement, mouths open in their last gasps.

Only one teenager had survived. But his respiratory system had been

219

destroyed. His trachea, larynx and nasal fossae had been permanently burnt – his sense of smell had been irredeemably destroyed. His vocal cords had been eroded – his voice would now be nothing but the rubbing of sandpaper. As for his breathing, chronic inflammations would mean that he regularly had to inhale steamy fumigations.

At the hospital, the doctor had called in an interpreter to give the young immigrant this devastating diagnosis and inform him that he would be sent back to Istanbul by plane in ten days' time. Three days later, Talat Gürdilek escaped, his face bandaged like a mummy, and walked to Paris.

Schiffer had always known him with his inhaler. When he was still just a young sweatshop manager, he carried it with him all the time, and spoke to you between two blasts. Later, he adopted a translucent mask that imprisoned his hoarse voice. Then his problems worsened, but his financial means had increased. At the end of the 1980s, Gürdilek purchased La Porte Bleue Turkish baths on rue du Faubourg-Saint-Denis and took over a room for his own personal use. It was a sort of huge lung, a tiled refuge full of steam laden with mentholated Balsofumine.

"*Salaam aleikum*, Talat. I'm sorry to disturb you at bath time."

Wrapped in a cloud of steam, the man laughed again.

"*Aleikum salaam*, Schiffer. So you're back from the dead."

The Turk's voice was like the crackling of flaming branches.

"It's more the dead that have brought me back."

"I've been expecting you."

Schiffer took off his coat – he was soaked to the bone – then went down the steps into the pool.

"Apparently everyone's been expecting me. So what can you tell me about the murders?"

The Turk sighed deeply, with a scraping of metal.

"When I left my country, my mother poured water after my steps. She traced out a path of chance, which was supposed to make me return. I never went back, my brother. I stayed in Paris and watched the situation deteriorate. Things have never been worse."

The cop was now just two yards from the boss, but he still could not make out his face.

"*Exile is a hard labour*, as the poet said. And I would say that it's getting even harder. In the past, they used to treat us like dogs. They exploited us, robbed us, arrested us. Now they're killing our women. Where will it all end?"

Schiffer was in no mood for such cracker-barrel philosophy.

"You're the one who sets the limits," he replied. "Now three working girls have been killed on your territory, one of them from your own workshop. That's rather a lot."

Gürdilek agreed with an idle gesture. His shadowy shoulders were like a scorched mountain.

"We're on French territory here. It's up to your police to protect us."

"Don't make me laugh. The Wolves are here and you know it. What do they want?"

"I don't know."

"You don't want to know."

There was a silence. The Turk breathed deeply.

"I'm the master of this quarter," he said at last. "But not of my country. This business started in Turkey."

"Who sent them?" Schiffer asked more loudly. "The clans of Istanbul? The families of Antep? The Lazes? Who?"

"I swear to you I don't know, Schiffer."

The cop stepped forward. At once, a rustling sound broke through the fog beside the pool. His bodyguards. He stopped immediately, trying to make out Gürdilek's appearance. But all he could see were fragments of shoulders, hands and torso. A dark, matt skin, wrinkled by water like crêpe paper.

"So you're just going to let the massacre go on?"

"It will stop when they have sorted their business out, when they have found the girl."

"Or when I've found her."

The dark shoulders quaked.

"Now it's my turn to laugh. You're no match for them."

"Who can help me find her?"

"Nobody. If anyone knew anything, they would have talked already. And not to you, to *them*. All that our people want is peace."

Schiffer thought for a moment. It was true what Gürdilek said. It was one of the aspects of the mystery that baffled him. How could this woman have survived so long with an entire community ready to betray her? And why were the Wolves still looking for her in the same neighbourhood? Why were they so sure that she was still there?

He changed tack: "What happened exactly in your workshop?"

"I was in Munich at the time and I . . ."

"Cut the crap, Talat. I want all the details."

The Turk sighed in resignation.

"They burst into the workshop on the night of 13 November."

"What time?"

"At two a.m."

"How many of them were there?"

"Four."

"Did anyone see their faces?"

"They were wearing balaclavas. According to the girls, they were armed to the teeth. Rifles, hand guns. The works."

The Adidas jacket had described the same scene. Warriors in commando kit, at work in the middle of Paris. In his forty years on the force, he had never heard of such a thing. What had this woman done to deserve such treatment?

"And then?" he murmured.

"They grabbed the girl and left. That's all. It was over in three minutes."

"How did they identify her in the workshop?"

"They had a photo."

Schiffer took a step back and recited: "She was called Zeynep Tütengil. She was twenty-seven. Married to Burba Tütengil. No children. She lived at 34 rue de la Fidélité. Originally from the Gaziantep area. Here since September 2001."

"You've done your homework, my brother. But this time, it won't get you anywhere."

"Where's her husband?"

"Back home."

"The other workers?"

"Forget this business. You're too square-headed for this kind of dung heap."

"Stop talking in riddles."

"In the good old days, everything was clear-cut. There were frontiers between the various camps. But now they no longer exist."

"What the hell are you talking about?"

Talat Gürdilek paused. Wisps of steam were still concealing his face. He finally said: "If you want to know more, ask the police."

Schiffer started.

"The police? What police?"

"I've already told all this to the boys at Louis-Blanc station."

The burning of the mint suddenly seemed more intense.

"When?"

Gürdilek leaned over his tiled block.

"Listen good, Schiffer, because I won't repeat myself. The night the Wolves left here, they ran into a patrol car. They were pursued but managed to lose your men. So they came round here asking questions."

Schiffer listened to this revelation in total amazement. For a fleeting moment, he thought that Nerteaux must have hidden this report from him. But there was no reason for him to have done so. The kid quite simply did not know about it.

The crater-like voice went on: "In the meantime, my girls had made themselves scarce. The cops just noted the break-in and the damage. The workshop manager didn't say a thing about the kidnapping or the commandos. In fact, he wouldn't have said anything at all if there hadn't been the girl."

Schiffer leapt to his feet.

"What girl?"

"The cops discovered a worker, hidden away in the machine room in the baths."

Schiffer could not believe his ears. Since the beginning of the affair, someone had seen the Grey Wolves. And she had been questioned by the boys of the tenth *arrondissement*! How come Nerteaux had never heard about that? One thing was sure, the cops at the station had covered up their discovery. *Jesus fucking Christ.*

"And what was this girl called?"

"Sema Gökalp."

"How old is she?"

"Thirtyish."

"Married?"

"No, single. A strange girl. A loner."

"Where's she from?"

"Gaziantep."

"Like Zeynep Tütengil?"

"Like all the girls in this workshop. She'd been working here for a few weeks. Since October."

"Did she see the kidnapping?"

"She had a front-row seat. The two of them were checking the temperature in the conduits. The Wolves took Zeynep while Sema hid in the back room. When the cops found her, she was in a state of shock. Half dead with fear."

"And then?"

"Never saw her again."

"They sent her back to Turkey?"

"No idea."

"Answer me, Talat. You must have asked around."

"Sema Gökalp has disappeared. The next day, she wasn't at the police station any more. She vanished into thin air. *Yemim ederim.* I swear it!"

"Schiffer was still sweating profusely. He forced himself to control his voice. "Who was leading the patrol that night?"

"Beauvanier."

Christophe Beauvanier was one of the captains at Louis-Blanc. A budding Mr Universe, who spent all his spare time in the sports club. Not the sort who would keep a story like this under his hat. Word must have come from higher up ... Frissons of excitement were shaking his drenched rags.

The boss seemed to be following his thoughts.

"They're covering for the Wolves, Schiffer."

"Don't talk rubbish."

"I'm telling the truth and you know it. They removed the witness. A woman who must have seen everything. Maybe even the face of one of the killers. Maybe a detail which would allow them to identify them. They're covering for the Wolves, that's all there is to it. The other murders were committed with their blessing. So you can drop your airs and graces of upholding law and order. You're no better than us."

Schiffer avoided swallowing his spit so as not to worsen the burning in his throat. Gürdilek was wrong. The Turks' influence could not possibly rise that high in the ranks of the French police. He was well placed to know that. For twenty years, he had liaised between the two worlds.

So there must be another explanation.

And yet, he could not get one detail out of his mind. A version that could corroborate the hypothesis of a plot in high places. The fact that an inquiry into three murders had been entrusted to Paul Nerteaux, an inexperienced captain just off the last banana boat. Only the kid himself believed that they trusted him that much. It was starting to smell of a set-up . . .

Thoughts surged through his burning temples. If this shit-heap was true, if this business really was part of a French-Turkish alliance, if the politicians of both countries really were working for their own interests, at the expense of those poor girls and the hopes of a young copper, then Schiffer would help him all the way.

Two men against the rest. That was the sort of language he liked.

He turned round in the steam, waved to the old pasha, then without a word went back up the steps.

Gürdilek gargled a last laugh: "It's time to put your own house in order, my brother."

CHAPTER 44

Schiffer shoved the door of the commissariat open with his shoulder.

Everyone's eyes focused on him. Soaked to the skin, he stared back, savouring their panicked expressions. Two patrols wearing oilskins were on their way out. Some lieutenants in leather jackets were slipping on their red armbands. The great manoeuvres had begun.

Schiffer noticed a pile of identikit portraits on the counter. He thought of Paul Nerteaux, who was handing out these posters in every police station in the tenth *arrondissement*, as if they were political handbills, without suspecting in the slightest that he had been set up. Another wave of fury gripped him.

Without a word, he climbed up to the first floor. He dived down a corridor dotted with plywood doors and went straight to the third one.

Beauvanier had not changed. Puffed-up build, black leather jacket and Nike trainers with massive soles. This cop was suffering from an affliction that was becoming rife among his fellows: yoof culture. He was nearing fifty, but was still trying to look like a trendy rapper.

He was putting on his belt, before his nocturnal expedition.

"Schiffer?" he choked. "What the hell are you doing here?"

"How are things, sweetheart?"

Before he had time to answer, Schiffer grabbed him by the lapels of his jacket and rammed him against the wall. Some colleagues were already arriving in rescue. Beauvanier waved to them over his aggressor in a sign of peace.

"It's OK, lads. We're mates."

Schiffer murmured into his ear: "Sema Gökalp. Last 13 November. Gürdilek's Turkish baths."

His eyes widened. His mouth trembled. Schiffer banged his head against the wall. The cops rushed at him. He could already feel them seizing his shoulders. But Beauvanier waved his hand again, forcing himself to laugh.

"I've told you, he's a friend. Everything's fine!"

The grip loosened. Footfalls receded. Finally, the door closed, slowly, almost regretfully. In turn, Schiffer relaxed his hold and asked, more calmly: "What did you do with the witness? How did you make her disappear?"

"It just happened like that, man. I didn't make anyone disappear . . ."

Schiffer stepped back to get a better look at him. His face was strangely sweet. The features of a young girl, ringed with extremely black hair, and with very blue eyes. He reminded him of an Irish girl-friend he had had in his youth. An "Irish Black" full of contrasts, instead of the classic red-head.

The cop-rapper was wearing a baseball cap, visor pointing at the nape of his neck, presumably to look even more like a bad boy.

Schiffer pulled over a chair and sat him down on it forcibly.

"I'm all ears. I want it down to the last detail."

Beauvanier tried to smile, in vain.

"That night, a patrol car ran into a BMW. There were these guys coming out of La Porte Bleue baths and . . ."

"I know all that. When did you come in?"

"Half an hour later. The boys called me up. I joined them round at Gürdilek's place. With a unit of technical officers."

"Was it you who found the girl?"

"No, they'd already found her. She was soaking. You know how those girls work there, it's . . ."

"Describe her to me."

"Small. Brunette. As thin as a rake. Her teeth were chattering. She was mumbling incoherently. In Turkish."

"Did she tell you what she'd seen?"

"Not a thing. She couldn't even see we were there. The lass was completely traumatised."

Beauvanier was not lying. His voice rang true. Schiffer was pacing up and down the room, constantly peering at him.

"What do you reckon happened round there?"

"I dunno. Some racketeering maybe. Some lads putting the scares on."

"Racketeering at Gürdilek's place? No one would try that one on him."

The officer adjusted his leather jacket, as though his neck was itching.

"You never know with these Turks. There's maybe a new clan in the neighbourhood. Or else it might be the Kurds. That's their business, man. Gürdilek didn't even want to press charges. So we just went through the motions . . ."

Another thought struck Schiffer. Nobody at La Porte Bleue had mentioned the kidnapping of Zeynep or the Grey Wolves. So Beauvanier *really* believed in this business about racketeering. No one had ever established the link between this little "visit" and the discovery of the first body, two days later.

"So what did you do with Sema Gökalp?"

"At the station, we gave her a tracksuit and some covers. She was trembling all over. We found her passport sewn into her skirt. She didn't have a visa or anything. So straight to Immigration. I faxed them a report. Then I sent another fax to headquarters, place Beauvau, just to cover myself. So all I had to do then was wait."

"And?"

Beauvanier sighed, sliding his finger under his collar.

"She just kept on trembling. It was getting worrying. Her teeth were chattering. She couldn't eat or drink. At five a.m. I decided to take her to Sainte-Anne's."

"Why you and not a constable?"

"Because they wanted to put her in a straitjacket. And then . . . I dunno, there was something about her . . . So I filled out a 32–13 and took her along . . ."

His voice was fading. He was now constantly scratching his neck. Schiffer noticed deep acne scars. "A druggy," he thought to himself.

"The next morning, I called up the boys at Immigration and told them to go to the hospital. At lunchtime they phoned back. They hadn't found the girl."

"She'd run away?"

"No. Some policemen came round and took her away at ten in the morning."

"What policemen?"

"You're not going to believe this."

"Try me."

"According to the doctor on duty, they were from the DNAT."

"The anti-terrorist division?"

"I checked myself. They had a transfer order. Everything was above board."

For a return to his manor, Schiffer could not have hoped for a better fireworks display. He sat on a corner of the desk. Every time he moved, he gave off a whiff of mint.

"Did you contact them?"

"I tried to. But they weren't very forthcoming. From what I understood, they'd picked up my report at place Beauvau. Then Charlier issued his orders."

"Philippe Charlier?"

The captain nodded. The entire story seemed to be right over his head. Charlier was one of the five commissioners of the anti-terrorist division. An ambitious officer, whom Schiffer had known since joining the anti-gang squad in 1977. A real bastard. Maybe smarter than he was, but just as brutal.

"And then?"

"And then, nothing. Not another word."

"Don't take the piss out of me."

Beauvanier hesitated. There were beads of sweat on his forehead. He lowered his eyes.

"The next day, Charlier called in person. He asked me loads of questions about the case. Where we'd found her, in what circumstances, and so on."

"What did you tell him?"

"What I knew."

"In other words nothing, dickhead," thought Schiffer. The baseball-capped copper concluded: "Charlier told me that he'd now be dealing with the case. Seeing the magistrate, going to Immigration Control, the usual procedure. He hinted that I'd do well to keep quiet about it."

"Do you still have your report?"

A smile slipped over that panicked face.

"What do you think? They came round and picked it up that very day."

"What about the daybook?"

The smile turned to laughter.

"What daybook? Listen, man, they wiped out every trace. Even the recording of the radio message. They made the witness vanish. Just like that."

"Why?"

"How the hell should I know? That girl couldn't tell them anything. She was completely out to lunch."

"And you, why didn't you say anything?"

The cop lowered his voice.

"Charlier's got a hold on me. An old story . . ."

Schiffer punched him on the arm, in a friendly manner, then stood up. Pacing around the room once more, he digested this information. Amazing as it might seem, the removal of Sema Gökalp by the DNAT belonged to another affair, which had nothing to do with the series of murders committed by the Grey Wolves. But that did not reduce the importance of this witness in his case. He had to find her – because she had seen it all happen.

"Are you back on service?" Beauvanier hazarded.

Schiffer adjusted his drenched clothes and ignored the question. He noticed one of Nerteaux's identikit pictures on the desk. He picked it up, like a bounty hunter, and asked: "Do you remember the name of the doctor who took charge of Sema at Sainte-Anne?"

"Of course. Jean-François Hirsch. We have a little arrangement about prescriptions and . . ."

Schiffer was no longer listening. His stare came to rest on the portrait. It was a skilful synthesis of the three victims. Smooth, broad features, shyly beaming out from under red hair. A fragment of Turkish poetry suddenly crossed his mind: *The padishah had a daughter / Like the moon of the fourteenth day* . . .

Beauvanier asked again: "Does that business at La Porte Bleue have anything to do with this girl?"

Schiffer pocketed the picture. He grabbed the officer's cap and turned it round the right way.

"If anyone asks, you can always give them some rap, *man.*"

CHAPTER 45

Sainte-Anne's Hospital. 21.00 hours.

He knew the place well. The long wall of the enclosure, with its serried stones; the small doorway at 17 rue Broussais, as discreet as an artistes' entrance; then the vast, undulating, intricate mass of buildings mingling different centuries and styles of architecture. A fortress, enclosing a universe of madness.

But that evening, the citadel did not seem as well guarded as all that. Banners hung up on the first façades announced the situation: "SECURITY ON STRIKE!", "JOB CREATION OR DEATH!" Further on, others added: "NO TO OVERTIME!", "MAKE-UP DAYS = FIDDLE", "BANK HOLIDAYS STOLEN!" . . .

The idea of Paris's largest psychiatric hospital being left to its own devices, with its patients running around in complete freedom, amused Schiffer. He could just picture such a bedlam, in which the lunatics had taken over the asylum and replaced the doctors on night duty. But, as he entered, all he found was a completely deserted ghost town.

He followed the red signposts directing him to neurosurgical and neurological emergency admissions, looking at the names of the various alleyways as he went. He had just taken allée Guy de Maupassant, and was now in Sentier Edgar Allan Poe. He wondered if this was a symptom of the hospital planners' sense of humour. Maupassant had lost his reason before dying and the alcoholic author of *The Black Cat* cannot have had all his wits about him by the end either. In communist neighbourhoods, the streets were named after Karl Marx or Pablo Neruda. Here they commemorated the great lunatics.

Schiffer sniggered to himself, trying to keep up his usual appearance of a hard-nut copper. But he already felt panic biting into him. There were too many memories, too much agony behind these walls . . .

It was in one of these buildings that he had ended up on returning from Algeria, when he was only just twenty. Traumatised by what he had seen and done, he had remained as an in-patient for several months, dogged by hallucinations and suicidal tendencies. Others, who had fought by his side in the Détachements Opérationnels de Protection, did not hesitate. He remembered one lad from Lille who had hanged himself as soon as he got home. And another from Brittany who had cut off his right hand with an axe on his father's farm – the hand he had used to plug in the electrodes, and pressed heads down in bathtubs . . .

Emergency admissions was deserted.

A large, empty space, covered with scarlet tiles. The pulp of a blood orange. Schiffer pressed the bell, then saw a traditionally dressed nurse arrive, with her white coat done up at the waist with a belt, hair in a bun and bifocals.

The woman looked ill at ease when she saw his gaunt appearance, but he quickly flashed his card at her and explained the reason for his visit. Without a word, she set off in search of Dr Jean-François Hirsch.

He sat down on one of the seats that were attached to the wall. The ceramic tiles seemed to be growing darker. Despite all his efforts, he just could not chase away the memories that were surging up from the depths of his skull.

1960

When he had arrived in Algeria, as an 'intelligence officer', he had not attempted to evade the brutality of his work, or escape from it by using alcohol or pills from the infirmary. On the contrary, he had gone at it hammer and tongs, day and night, convinced that he was still master of his own destiny. War had forced him to make the big decision, the only choice that mattered: which side he was on. He could no longer change his mind or turn his coat. And he had to be in the right. It was that or blow your brains out.

He tortured people twenty-four hours a day. He dragged confessions out of the local populace. First by using the traditional methods of beatings, electrocution and drowning. Then he had come up with his own techniques. He had organised fake executions, dragging hooded prisoners out of the town, watching them shit themselves as he pressed his gun against their heads. He had devised cocktails of acid, which he had forced them to drink, by pushing funnels down their throats. He had stolen medical instruments from hospitals, in order to vary the treatment, for example the stomach pump which he used to inject water into their nostrils . . .

He shaped and sculpted fear, always giving it new forms. When he decided to bleed his prisoners, both to weaken them and give their blood to victims of terrorist attacks, he felt strangely light-headed. It was as if he was becoming a god, holding the right to give life or death to mankind. Sometimes, in the interrogation room, he would laugh out of context, blinded by his power, staring with wonder at the blood covering his fingers.

A month later he had become completely mute and had been repatriated. His jaw was paralysed. He was incapable of pronouncing the slightest word. He had been admitted to Sainte-Anne, in a unit entirely devoted to traumatised combatants. The sort of place where the walls echoed with groans, where it was impossible to finish your breakfast before one of your neighbours had vomited over it.

Enclosed in silence, Schiffer lived a life of pure terror. In the gardens, he lost his sense of direction, no longer knowing where he was, asking himself if the other patients were the detainees he had tortured. When he walked in the galleries of the main building, he inched along the walls, so that his "victims wouldn't see him".

When he slept, nightmares took over from his hallucinations. Naked men writhing on chairs, testicles sparking below the electrodes, jaws cracking against enamel sinks, bleeding nostrils blocked with syringes . . . In fact, they were not visions, but memories. Above all, he pictured the man hung upside down, whose skull he had smashed with a kick. Then he woke up, covered in sweat, feeling those brains splash out over him once more. He looked round the interior of his room, and saw the smooth walls of a cellar, the bathtub that had been taken down there and, on the table in the middle, the generator and ANGRC 9 radio . . .

Doctors explained to him that it was impossible to repress such memories. Instead, they advised him to confront them, to allot a moment of close attention to them every day. Such a strategy fitted with his personality. He had not drawn back when out in the field, and he was not going to fall to pieces now, in these gardens full of ghosts.

He had signed himself out and returned to civil existence.

He applied to become a policeman, concealing his psychiatric problems, and emphasising his rank of sergeant and his military decorations. The political context played in his favour. There were more and more terrorist attacks by the OAS in Paris. They needed more men to track down those responsible. They needed experienced field operatives . . . And there, he was in his element. His street savvy had astonished his superiors. His methods, too. He worked alone, without anyone's help. All that mattered to him were the results, no matter how they were obtained.

His existence would henceforth be in this image. He would rely on himself and only on himself. He would be above the law, above human considerations. He would be a law unto himself, drawing from his own willpower the right to deliver justice. It was a sort of cosmic pact: his word against the shit-heap of the world.

"What can I do for you?"

The voice made him jump. He stood up and took in the new arrival.

Jean-François Hirsch was tall – over six feet – and slim. His long arms ended in massive hands. To Schiffer, they looked like two counterweights to balance his slender frame. His head also was large, rimmed with brown curly hair. Another counterweight . . . He was not wearing a white coat, but a heavy green one. Apparently he was on his way home.

Schiffer introduced himself, without producing his card.

"Chief Lieutenant Jean-Louis Schiffer. I have a few questions to ask you. It will only take a few minutes."

"I was on my way out. And I'm late. Can't it wait till tomorrow?"

The voice was yet another counterweight. Deep. Stable. Solid.

"Sorry," Schiffer said. "It's important."

The doctor looked him up and down. The smell of mint drifted between them like a barrier of freshness. Hirsch sighed and sat down on one of the bolted seats.

"OK, so what's the problem?"

Schiffer remained standing.

"It's about a young Turkish woman you examined on the morning of 14 November 2001. She had been brought in by Lieutenant Christophe Beauvanier."

"What about her?"

"It would seem that there were some procedural irregularities."

"What department are you from?"

The cop played double or quits.

"It's an internal inquiry. I'm from the Inspection Générale des Services."

"I warn you right from the start that I'll tell you nothing about Beauvanier. Ever heard of professional ethics?"

The quack had misunderstood the point of the inquiry. Obviously he must have helped Mr Universe get over one of his drug problems. Schiffer got on his high horse.

"My inquiry does not concern Christophe Beauvanier, even though you put him on a course of methadone."

The doctor raised an eyebrow – Schiffer had guessed right – then adopted a lighter tone: "So what do you want to know exactly?"

"What interests me about the Turkish girl are the policemen who took her in *the next day*."

The psychiatrist crossed his legs and smoothed down his trousers.

"They arrived about four hours after she had been admitted. They had a transfer order and an expulsion certificate. Everything was in order. Almost too much so, I'd say."

"Why?"

"The forms were stamped and signed. They had come directly from the Minister of the Interior. And this was only ten in the morning. It was the first time I'd seen so much red tape pulled over an anonymous asylum seeker."

"Tell me about her."

Hirsch stared at the tips of his shoes. He was getting his thoughts together.

"When she arrived, I thought she was suffering from hypothermia. She was trembling and breathless. But when I examined her, I found that her temperature was normal. Nor had her respiratory system been damaged. Her symptoms were caused by hysteria."

"What do you mean?"

He smiled in superiority.

"I mean that she had the physical symptoms, but none of the physiological causes. It all came from here," he pointed a finger at his temple. "The head. That woman had received a psychological shock. And her body was reacting as a result."

"What sort of shock do you think it was?"

"Terrible fear. She had all the signs of exogenic anxiety. A blood test confirmed it. We detected traces of a high discharge of hormones. There was also a particularly sharp rise of cortisol. But all this is getting a little technical for you . . ."

The smile widened.

The airs and graces were starting to piss Schiffer off. The doctor seemed to sense this, adding in a more natural tone: "That woman had suffered enormous stress. So much so, you could say she had been traumatised. She reminded me of cases you sometimes see after battles, on the front. Inexplicable paralysis, sudden asphyxia, stuttering, that kind of . . ."

"I know. Describe her to me. I mean, physically."

"Brown hair. Very pale. Very thin, almost anorexic. With a Cleopatra hair-cut. A very harsh look, but which didn't detract from her beauty. On the contrary. In that respect, she was rather . . . impressive."

Schiffer was beginning to picture her. Instinctively, he sensed that she could not have been just a plain working girl.

"And you treated her?"

"I started by injecting an anxiolytic. Her muscles then relaxed. She began to laugh and chatter incoherently. It was a fit of delirium. What she said was meaningless."

"But she was speaking in Turkish, wasn't she?"

"No, in French, like you and me."

A completely crazy idea crossed his mind. But he decided to push it into the distance, so as to keep a cool head.

"Did she tell you what she'd seen? What had happened at the Turkish baths?"

"No. She just came out with unfinished sentences, senseless words."

"For example?"

"She said that the wolves had got it wrong. Yes, that's it . . . She talked about wolves. She kept saying that they'd taken away the wrong girl. It was incomprehensible."

The idea flashed back forcefully into his consciousness. How had that working girl known that the kidnappers were Grey Wolves? How did she know that they had hit the wrong target? There was only one answer. Their real prey was her.

Sema Gökalp was the woman to be hit.

Schiffer fitted the pieces of puzzle together with ease. The killers had a lead: their target worked at night, in Talat Gürdilek's sweatshop. They had arrived in the laundry and taken away the first woman who looked like the photo in their possession: Zeynep Tütengil. But they had made a mistake. The real red-head had taken the precaution of dying her hair brown.

Another idea occurred to him. He took the identikit portrait from his pocket.

"Did she look at all like this?"

The man leaned over.

"No. Why the question?"

Schiffer pocketed the poster without answering.

A second flash. Another confirmation. Sema Gökalp – or the woman who was hiding behind that name – had taken her metamorphosis even further. She had altered her face. She had resorted to plastic surgery. A classic technique for those who burn their bridges thoroughly. Especially in the world of crime. Then she had adopted the identity of simple working girl, in the steam of La Porte Bleue. But why had she stayed in Paris?

For a few seconds, he tried to think his way under the skin of that Turk. On the night of 13 November 2001, when she saw the hooded Wolves arrive, she had thought that it was all over for her. But the killers had grabbed the girl next to her. A red-head who looked like her previous self. *That woman had suffered enormous stress.* It was putting it mildly.

"What else did she say?" he asked. "Please, try to remember."

"I think . . ." he stretched his legs and stared again at his shoelaces. "I think she said something about a strange night. A special night, when there were four moons. She also mentioned a man in a black coat."

If there had been further proof, this was it. Four moons. There could only be a handful of Turks who knew the meaning of this symbol. The truth surpassed fiction.

Because now he knew who the prey was.

And why the Turkish mafia had sent its Wolves after her.

"What about the police officers who came the next day?" he said, trying to control his excitement. "What did they say when they took her away?"

"Nothing. They just showed their papers."

"What did they look like?"

"Giants. In pricey suits. Like bodyguards."

Philippe Charlier's men. Where had they taken her? To an official detention centre? Had they sent her back to her country? Did the anti-terrorist unit know who Sema Gökalp really was? No, there was zero chance of that. Another reason lay behind this mysterious kidnapping.

He saluted the doctor, crossed the red room, then turned round when he reached the door.

"Supposing that Sema was still in Paris, where would you look for her?"

"In a lunatic asylum."

"She's had enough time to recover her spirits, hasn't she?"

The tall man stretched.

"I didn't express myself clearly enough. She wasn't just afraid. She had met Terror in person. She had gone past the threshold of what a human being can stand."

CHAPTER 46

Philippe Charlier's office was at 133 rue du Faubourg-Saint-Honoré, not far from the Ministry of the Interior.

Just off the Champs-Elysées, these luxury blocks with their sleepy façades were in reality bunkers placed under high surveillance. They were the powerhouses of the Paris police.

Jean-Louis Schiffer went through the gate and into the garden. The park formed a large square of grey pebbles, as clean and neat as a Zen landscape, with closely cut privet hedges forming the external barriers, and trees stretching out their pruned, stump-like branches. This was no place of combat, Schiffer thought as he crossed the enclosure. It was a place of deception.

At the rear, the large town house had a slate roof, and a glazed veranda supported by structures of black metal. Its white façade was decked with cornices, balconies and other forms engraved in the stone. "Empire period," Schiffer thought to himself when he spotted the crossed laurel leaves on the round amphorae in their niches. In fact, that was how he described all architecture that came after the era of fortifications and keeps.

On the steps, two uniformed officers were advancing towards him.

Schiffer asked for Charlier. It was ten p.m., but he was sure that this white-collar cop was still weaving his plots, in the light of his desk lamp.

Without taking his eyes off him, one of the officers called on his phone. While he listened to the answer, he scrutinised the visitor even more closely. Then the men made him go through a metal detector, before searching him thoroughly.

Finally, he was allowed to cross the veranda into a large stone room.

"On the first floor," he was told.

Schiffer headed towards the stairs. His footfalls echoed like in a church. Between two cast-iron torches the worn granite steps, topped with marble banisters, led up to the next storey.

Schiffer smiled. Terrorist hunters were clearly not short of a penny or two when it came to the décor.

The first floor appeared more modest: panels of polished wood, mahogany lamps, brown carpet. At the end of the corridor, there was a final barrier to be crossed: the checkpoint which revealed the true status of Commissioner Philippe Charlier.

Behind bullet-proof glass, four men were on duty, dressed in black Kevlar outfits. They were wearing combat jackets containing several hand guns, magazines, grenades and other such delights. Each of them was holding a short-barrelled automatic H & K rifle.

Schiffer was searched once more. They informed Charlier, this time by radio. At last he was allowed through to a double door of light-coloured wood, with a copper plaque. Given the atmosphere, there was no need to knock.

The Green Giant was sitting in shirt sleeves behind a solid oak desk. He stood up, grinning broadly.

"Schiffer, my old chap . . ."

There was a silent handshake, during which the two men sized each other up. Charlier was immutable. A good six feet tall. Weighing over two hundred and thirty pounds. An affable mountain, with a broken nose, a teddy bear's moustache and still, despite his great responsibilities, a gun on his belt.

Schiffer noticed the quality of the shirt – sky blue with a white collar, the famous Charvet design. But despite his efforts to appear elegant, there was still something terrible in the officer's appearance – a physical power that placed him on another level from the rest of humanity. On the Day of the Apocalypse, when men had only their hands to defend themselves, Charlier would be one of the last to die . . .

"What can I do for you?" he asked, slumping down once more onto the leather of his desk chair, and looking with disdain at his scruffy visitor. He tapped his fingers on the stacks of files on his desk. "I've got a lot of work to do."

Schiffer sensed that his relaxed attitude was false. Charlier was tense. Without even looking at the chair the commissioner offered him, he launched into the attack: "On 14 November 2001 you had a witness to a break-in at a private business transferred. It happened in La Porte Bleue, some Turkish baths in the tenth *arrondissement*. The witness's name was Sema Gökalp. The head of the investigation was Christophe Beauvanier. The problem is that no one knows where the woman was transferred to. You wiped out every trace of her. You made her vanish. I don't care why. All I want to know is where she is now."

Without answering, Charlier yawned. It was a good imitation, but Schiffer knew how to interpret the signs. The ogre was horrified. A bombshell had just dropped on to his desk.

"I don't know what you're talking about," he said at last. "Why are you looking for this woman?"

"She's linked to a case I'm investigating."

The commissioner adopted a calm tone.

"But Schiffer, you've retired."

"I'm back on the job."

"What job? Which case?"

Schiffer knew that he was going to have to give certain things away if he was going to get the slightest piece of information.

"I'm investigating the three murders in the tenth *arrondissement*."

The knobbly face stiffened.

"But the local boys are taking care of that. Who called you in?"

"Captain Paul Nerteaux, who's in charge of the case."

"So what's that got to do with your Sema something?"

"It's the same case."

Charlier started fiddling with a paperknife, a sort of oriental dagger. Each movement gave away how increasingly nervous he was.

"Well, I did see some report about that business at the baths," he admitted at last. "A problem of racketeering, if I remember . . ."

Thanks to all those years spent questioning suspects, Schiffer was able to recognise the slightest nuance, the merest shift in a voice's intonation. Charlier was basically telling the truth. As far as he was concerned, the attack on La Porte Bleue meant nothing. It was time to add some more bait and hook him for good.

"It wasn't about racketeering."

"Oh no?"

"No, the Grey Wolves are back, Charlier. They were the ones who raided the baths. That night, they kidnapped a girl. The corpse that we discovered two days later."

Charlier's bushy eyebrows seemed to form two question marks.

"Why would they bother slicing up a working girl like that?"

"They have a contract. They are looking for a woman in the Turkish quarter. You can trust me on that score. And they've got the wrong one three times now."

"What connection is there with Sema Gökalp?"

It was now time to lie a little.

"That night at the baths, she saw everything. She's a vital witness."

A twitch passed across Charlier's eyes. He had not been expecting that. Not at all.

"So what do you think it's all about? What's at stake?"

"I don't know," Schiffer lied once more. "But I'm looking for the killers, and Sema could put me on the right track."

Charlier leaned back into his chair.

"Give me just one reason to help you."

The copper finally sat down. The negotiation had begun.

"I'm feeling generous," he smiled. "So I'll give you two. The first is that I could reveal to your superiors that you spirit away witnesses in a murder case. That's not bad for a start."

Charlier smiled back at him.

"I've got all the paperwork. I can provide her expulsion order and her plane ticket. Everything's in order."

"Your arm is long, Charlier, but it doesn't stretch as far as Turkey. With just one phone call, I could prove that Sema Gökalp never arrived there."

The commissioner seemed to weigh less heavily on his chair.

"Who'd believe a bent copper? Ever since your days in the anti-gang you've been collecting skeletons in your cupboard," he opened his hands, indicating the room. "And I'm at the top of the pyramid."

"That's the advantage of my position. I have nothing to lose."

"Give me the second reason."

Schiffer leaned his elbows on the desk. He knew now that he had won.

"The stiffening of security measures in 1995. When you let yourself go on those North African suspects in Louis-Blanc station."

"Are you blackmailing a commissioner?"

"Or else getting it off my conscience. I'm retired. I might feel like making a clean breast of it. Of my memories of Abdel Saraoui, who you beat to death. If I open the way, the boys at Louis-Blanc will all follow. Believe me, they still haven't digested the howls that came from his cell that night."

Charlier was staring at the paperknife in his huge hands. When he next spoke, his voice had changed: "Sema Gökalp can't help you any more."

"You mean, you . . ."

"No, she underwent an experiment."

"What kind of experiment?"

Silence. Schiffer repeated: "What kind of experiment?"

"Psychic conditioning. A new technique."

So that was it. Psychic manipulation had always fascinated Charlier. Infiltrating terrorists' minds, conditioning consciousnesses, that kind of crap . . . Sema Gökalp was a guinea-pig, the subject of some crazy experimentation.

Schiffer thought over the absurdity of the situation. Charlier had not chosen Sema Gökalp, she had quite simply fallen into his hands. He did not know that she had altered her appearance. Nor did he know who she really was.

He stood back up, charged with electricity from head to foot.

"Why her?"

"Because of her mental state. Sema was suffering from partial amnesia, which made her all the more suitable to undergo the experiment."

Schiffer leaned forwards, as though he had problems hearing.

"Are you telling me that you brainwashed her?"

"Yes, the programme did contain such treatment."

He banged his fists on the table.

"Fucking idiots. That was the last memory you should have wiped out! She had things to tell me!"

Charlier raised an eyebrow.

"I don't understand what you're on about. How could that girl have anything of importance to reveal? She just saw a few Turks making off with a woman, that's all."

Onwards again.

"She's got some information about the killers," Schiffer said at last, while prowling around the room like a caged beast. "I also think she knows the identity of the target."

"The target?"

"The woman the Wolves are looking for. And have not yet found."

"Does it really matter?"

"Three murders, Charlier. They're starting to mount up, aren't they? And they'll go on killing until they find her."

"And you want to hand her over?"

Schiffer smiled without replying.

The movement of Charlier's shoulders almost split the stitches in his shirt. Finally, he said: "Anyway, I can no longer help you."

"Why?"

"She's escaped."

"You're kidding!"

"Does it look as if I am?"

Schiffer did not know whether to laugh or scream. He sat back down, grabbing the paperknife which Charlier had just dropped.

"Bloody incompetent as usual. What happened?"

"The aim of our experiment was to alter a personality completely. Something never attempted before. We managed to transform her into a middle-class Frenchwoman, married to a top civil servant. A simple Turkish lass, can you imagine that? There's now no limit to conditioning, we're going to . . ."

"I don't give a shit about your experiment," Schiffer butted in. "Just tell me how she ran away."

The commissioner frowned.

"Over the past few weeks, she'd been having attacks of forgetfulness, or hallucinations. The new personality we had given her was starting to break up. We were about to hospitalise her, when she split."

"When was that?"

"Yesterday. Tuesday morning."

Unbelievable. The target of the Grey Wolves was back on the streets. Neither Turkish nor French. With a mind like a sieve. From the bottom of this darkness, a light shone.

"So her original memory is coming back?"

"We don't know. But she certainly didn't trust us any more."

"Where are your men at?"

"Nowhere. They're searching Paris. And still haven't found her."

It was the moment to play his ace. He stuck the paperknife into the wooden desk.

"If her memory's returning, then she'll react like a Turk. And that's my area. I stand the best chance of copping her."

The commissioner's expression changed. Schiffer pressed his point: "She's a Turk, Charlier. A special sort of game. You need someone who knows that universe and who will act discreetly."

He could follow the idea that was making its way through the giant's brain. He stepped back, as though taking aim.

"Here's the deal. You give me twenty-four hours. If I find her, then I'll hand her over to you. But I get to question her first."

Another, pregnant silence. Finally, Charlier opened a drawer and produced a pile of documents.

"Her file. She's now called Anna Heymes and . . ."

In a single bound, Schiffer grabbed the cardboard folder and opened it. He flicked through the typed pages, the medical reports, and found the target's new face. Exactly as Hirsch had described her. There was not a single feature in common with the red-head the killers were tracking. From that point of view, Sema Gökalp had nothing more to fear.

The anti-terrorist warrior went on: "The neurologist treating her is called Eric Ackermann and . . ."

"I couldn't care less about her new personality, or who did what to her. She's going to return to her origins. That's what matters. What do you know about Sema Gökalp? About the Turk she used to be?"

Charlier wriggled in his chair. Veins were beating at the base of his neck, just above his shirt collar.

"Nothing at all! She was just a working girl with amnesia . . ."

"Did you keep her clothes, her papers, her personal effects?"

He swept the question away with his hand.

"We destroyed everything. At least, I think we did."

"Check."

"They were just scruffy rags. Nothing of any interest for . . ."

"Just pick up your fucking phone and check."

Charlier grabbed the receiver. After two calls, he groaned: "I don't believe it. Those useless buggers forgot to destroy her clothes."

"Where are they?"

"In a deposit box at headquarters. Beauvanier had given her new threads. And the boys of Louis-Blanc sent the old ones to the prefecture. No one thought of going to fetch them. So much for an elite brigade . . ."

"What name were they registered under?"

"Sema Gökalp, of course. When we fuck up, we don't do things by halves."

He picked up another, blank form, which he started to fill in. An open sesame to the prefecture. "Like two predators sharing the same prey," Schiffer thought.

The commissioner signed the paper then slid it across the desk.

"You've got all night. If you fuck up, I'll call in the Special Branch."

Schiffer pocketed the pass and stood up.

"You won't saw off the branch. We're sitting on the same one."

CHAPTER 47

It was time to come clean with the kid.

Jean-Louis Schiffer went back up rue du Faubourg-Saint-Honoré and turned into avenue Matignon, where he spotted a phone box just by the roundabout on the Champs-Elysées. The battery of his mobile was flat again.

As soon as Paul Nerteaux recognised his voice, he yelled: "Jesus Christ, Schiffer. Where the hell are you?" The voice was trembling with rage.

"In the eighth *arrondissement*, with the bigwigs."

"It's nearly midnight. What on earth have you been doing? I waited for hours at Sancak's and . . ."

"A crazy story, but I've got plenty of news."

"Are you in a phone box? I'll find another one and call you back. My battery's dead."

Schiffer hung up, wondering if the police might one day miss the arrest of the century because of a lack of lithium. He half-opened the door of the booth – he was stifling himself with his own stench of mint.

The night was mild, with no rain or breeze. He observed the passers-by, the shopping malls, the ashlar buildings. An existence of luxury, of comfort which had eluded him, but was perhaps now back in his reach . . .

The phone rang. He did not give Nerteaux time to speak: "Where are you at with your patrols?"

"I've got two vans and three cars," he replied proudly. "Seventy patrolmen and officers from the BAC are combing the area. I've declared the entire neighbourhood as an emergency zone. I've given the identikit portraits to all the commissariats and police units in the tenth. All the homes, bars and associations have been searched. There isn't a single person in Little Turkey who hasn't seen the picture. I'm about to go to the police station in the second and . . ."

"Forget all that."

"What?"

"This is no time to play at soldiers. We've got the wrong face."

"WHAT?"

Schiffer took a deep breath.

"The woman we're looking for has had plastic surgery. That's why the Grey Wolves can't find her."

"Do you . . . do you have proof?"

"I've even got her new face. Everything fits. She splashed out on an operation costing several hundred million francs in order to wipe out her previous identity. She completely changed her physical appearance. She dyed her hair brown and lost twenty kilos. Then she hid out in the Turkish quarter six months ago."

Silence. When Nerteaux next spoke, his voice had lost several decibels.

"Who . . . who is she? How did she get the money for the operation?"

"No idea," he lied. "But she's no simple working girl."

"What else have you found out?"

Schiffer thought for a few seconds. Then he told it all. The raid by the Grey Wolves, who had got the wrong target. Sema Gökalp in a state of shock. Her detention at Louis-Blanc, then admission to Sainte-Anne's. The kidnapping organised by Charlier and the grotesque treatment.

Finally, the woman's new identity: Anna Heymes.

When he stopped talking, Schiffer could almost hear the cogs turning at full speed in the young officer's brain. He imagined him, completely stunned in a phone box, lost somewhere in the tenth *arrondissement*. Like him. Two coral fishermen suspended in their lonely cages, in the middle of the ocean's depths . . .

Finally, Paul asked sceptically: "Who told you all this?"

"Charlier in person."

"He confessed?"

"We're old pals."

"Bullshit."

Schiffer burst out laughing.

"I see that you're starting to understand what sort of world we're in. In 1995, after the explosion in Saint-Michel RER station, the DNAT –

which was still called the Sixth Division – was decidedly nervy. A new law allowed them to detain people longer, without charge. It was real hell. I know, because I was there. There were round-ups all over town, in Islamist groups, and especially in the tenth. One night, Charlier turned up at Louis-Blanc. He was sure that he had the right suspect – a certain Abdel Saraoui. He went at him with his bare fists. I was in the office next door. The next morning, the guy died of a ruptured liver in Saint-Louis Hospital. So this evening, I reminded him of the good old days."

"You're so corrupt that you're almost coherent."

"Who cares, so long as we get a result?"

"I had a different idea of my crusade, that's all."

Schiffer opened the door of the booth again and took a breath of fresh air.

"So now," Paul asked. "Where's Sema?"

"That's the icing on the cake, lad. She's just scarpered. She lost them yesterday morning. She must have found out what they were up to. Her original memory must be coming back."

"Shit . . ."

"Quite. There's a woman wandering around Paris right now with two identities, with two groups of bastards chasing her, and with us in the middle. In my opinion, she must be investigating her own past. She's trying to find out who she really is."

Another pause from the other end of the line.

"So what do we do now?"

"I've made a deal with Charlier. I convinced him that I was the best placed to find the girl. Turks are my speciality. So he's handed me the case, for one night. He's on a knife's edge. His project was illegal. And it could blow up in his face. I've got his file on the new Sema, and two leads. The first one's for you, if you're still in the race."

He could hear the sound of pages turning. Nerteaux was taking out his notepad.

"Go on."

"Plastic surgery. Sema splashed out on one of the best surgeons in Paris. We have to find him, because he was in contact with the *real* target, before her operation, before she was brainwashed. He must be the only person in town who can tell us anything about the woman the Grey Wolves are looking for. Are you up for it?"

Nerteaux did not reply at once, he was presumably writing this down.

"There must be hundreds of names to go through."

"Not at all. You have to go and see the best, the real virtuosi. And among them, the ones who lack scruples. Having your face completely redone is never innocent. You've got all night. At the speed things are going, we won't be alone on this lead for long."

"Charlier's men?"

"No. Charlier doesn't even know that she's altered her appearance. I'm talking about the Grey Wolves. They've been held in check for three months now. So they're eventually going to twig that they're not looking for the right face. Plastic surgery will occur to them, and they'll look for the quack. We're going to end up on the same track. I can just feel it. I'll leave you the girl's file at rue de Nancy, with the photo of her new face. Go round and fetch it, then start working."

"Shall I give the portrait to the patrols?"

Schiffer broke into a sweat.

"That's the last thing you should do. Just show it to the doctors at the same time as the identikit. Got me?"

Silence once again saturated the line.

They were, more than ever, like a pair of divers lost in the deep.

"What about you?" Nerteaux asked.

"I'll take care of the second lead. Luckily enough, the boys from the DNAT forgot to destroy Sema's old clothes. They might contain a clue, an indication, something to lead us back to her former identity."

He looked at his watch. Midnight. They did not have much time left, but he still wanted to make a final check. "So, nothing new your end?"

"The Turkish quarter is being put to the sword, but now . . ."

"And Naubrel and Matkowska still haven't come up with anything?"

"No, nothing."

Nerteaux sounded astonished by the question. The lad must have thought that the investigation into the high-pressure chambers did not interest him. On the contrary, this business of nitrogen bubbles intrigued him.

When Scarbon had mentioned it, he had added "I'm no diver". But Schiffer was. In his youth he had spent years exploring the Red Sea and the coast of China. He had even considered the idea of dropping everything and opening a diving school in the Pacific.

So, he knew that high pressure does not just create a problem of gas in the blood, it also leads to hallucinations, a state of drunkenness that divers call rapture of the depths.

At the beginning of their inquiries, when they thought they were tracking a serial killer, this detail puzzled Schiffer. He did not see why a murderer capable of slicing up women's vaginas with razor blades would be bothered to create nitrogen bubbles in his victims' veins. It did not fit. However, in the context of a grilling, then this rapture of the depths had a point.

One of the bases of torture was the nice and nasty technique. A good beating, then offer a cigarette. A few electroshocks, then a sandwich. It is in fact during these moments of respite that the person generally cracks.

By using a chamber, the Wolves had quite simply applied this alternation while bringing it to its ultimate state. After the most terrible torments, they had suddenly submitted their subjects to an abrupt feeling of relaxation and euphoria brought on by the high pressures. They were presumably hoping that the violence of this contrast would make them speak, or that the drunkenness would act as a truth serum . . .

Behind this nightmarish technique, Schiffer sensed the implacable presence of a master of ceremonies. A genius of torture.

Who?

He chased away his own panic and murmured: "There can't be that many pressure chambers in Paris."

"My men haven't found anything. They've been to the sites where such equipment is found. They've questioned the industrial engineers who conduct tests on resistance. It's a blind alley."

Schiffer sensed a strange note in Nerteaux's voice. Was he hiding something? But he did not have time to press the point.

"What about the ancient masks?" he went on.

"Does that interest you too?"

Paul was increasingly sceptical.

"In a situation like this," Schiffer replied, "everything interests me. One of the Wolves might have an obsession, a particular kink. Where are you at now?"

"Nowhere. And I haven't had the time to progress. I don't even know if my boys have found any more sites and . . ."

In conclusion, he broke off.

"Report back in two hours. And find a way to recharge your battery."

He hung up. In a flash, Nerteaux's figure passed before his eyes. His Indian hair, his eyes like grilled almonds. A cop whose features were too fine, who did not shave and who dressed in black to make himself look tough. But also a born policeman, despite his naivety.

He realised that he liked the kid. He even wondered if he was not starting to go soft, if he had been right to include him in what had now become "his" investigation. Had he told him too much?

He left the phone booth and hailed a cab.

No. He had kept back his trump card.

He had not told Nerteaux the most important point.

He climbed into the car and gave the address of police headquarters, Quai des Orfèvres.

He now knew who the target was, and why the Grey Wolves were looking for her.

Because he had spent the last ten months looking for her too.

CHAPTER 48

A rectangular box of white wood, seventy centimetres long by thirty deep, stamped with the red wax seal of the French Republic. Schiffer blew the dust off the lid and said to himself that the only remaining proof of Sema Gölkalp's existence lay in this baby's coffin.

He took out his Swiss army knife, slid its finest blade beneath the seal, snapped the red blotch and lifted the top. A musty smell rose to his nostrils. As soon as he saw the garments, he just knew that they would contain something for him.

Instinctively, he glanced over his shoulder. He was in the basement of the Palais de Justice, in the booth with a filthy curtain where freed prisoners could discreetly check that all their personal effects had been returned to them.

The ideal place to dig up a corpse.

First he found a white coat and a mob cap of creased paper – the standard uniform of Gürdilek's workers. Then her day clothes: a long pale green skirt, a crocheted raspberry-red cardigan, a slate-blue blouse with a rounded collar. Cheap rags from the cheapest of stores.

The clothes were Western, but their cut, colours and above all context gave them the look of Turkish peasant girls, who still wore baggy mauve trousers and bright yellow or green blouses. He felt sinister desire rising inside him, excited by the idea of stripping, humiliation and servile poverty. The pale body he pictured beneath these clothes bit into his nerves.

He looked at the underwear. A small, flesh-coloured bra and a pair of fluffy, black, threadbare panties, whose shiny appearance had been caused by wear. They suggested the figure of an adolescent. He thought of the three corpses: wide hips, heavy breasts. This woman had not just altered her face, she had sculpted her body down to the bone.

He continued his search. Worn-out shoes, laddered tights, a shabby fleece coat. The pockets had been emptied. He felt the bottom of the box in the hope that their contents had been placed there together. A plastic bag confirmed his hopes. It contained a set of keys, a book of métro tickets, beauty products imported from Istanbul . . .

He examined the keys. They always fascinated him. He knew each and every type: flat ones, cross-cut ones, lever keys or those with active branches. He was also an expert when it came to locks. Their mechanisms reminded him of the cogs inside the human body, which he loved to violate, torture, control.

He looked at the two keys on the ring. One opened a grooved lock – probably of some home, hotel room or derelict flat, long occupied by the Turkish community. The second was flat, and presumably was for the upper lock on the same door.

No interest.

Schiffer stifled a curse. His find had turned up nothing. These objects and garments simply sketched the portrait of an anonymous working girl. Too anonymous, for that matter. It stank of fancy dress, of a caricature.

He was sure that Sema Gökalp had a hiding place somewhere. When you are capable of changing your face, losing twenty kilos, voluntarily adopting the underground existence of a slave, then you must have a place to fall back on.

Schiffer remember what Beauvanier had said: *we found her passport sewn into her skirt*. With his fingers, he felt each garment. He lingered over the lining of the coat. Along the lower hem they came to rest on a lump. A hard, long, jagged obtrusion.

He tore open the material and shook it.

A key dropped into his hand.

A piped key stamped with the number 4C 32.

He thought: it must be a left-luggage locker.

CHAPTER 49

"No, not left-luggage. They use codes now."

Cyril Brouillard was a brilliant locksmith. Jean-Louis Schiffer had found his wallet on the site of a break-in, where a supposedly impregnable safe had been opened with the skill of a virtuoso. He had then gone to the address of the owner of the ID papers, and come across a young short-sighted lad with shaggy fair hair. When he gave him back his documents, he told him that he ought to learn to be less absent-minded. He had then covered up the break-in in exchange for an original Bellmer lithograph.

"So what is it?"

"A self-storehouse."

"A what?"

"A furniture warehouse."

Since that night, Brouillard did whatever Schiffer asked. Opening doors for unauthorised searches, turning locks to catch crooks red-handed, safe-breaking to obtain compromising documents. This thief was a perfect alternative to having a warrant.

He lived above his shop on rue de Lancry – a locksmith's workshop which he had bought thanks to his nocturnal activities.

"Can you tell me more?"

Brouillard examined the key beneath his desk lamp. He was unlike any other burglar. As soon as he approached a lock, a miracle happened. A vibration. A touch. A mystery that unfolded. Schiffer never wearied of watching him at work. It was like observing some hidden force of nature. The very essence of an inexplicable gift.

"Surger's," the crook whispered. "You can see the letters engraved on the side."

"Do you know the place?"

"Of course. I've got several cubby holes there myself. It's open day and night."

"Where?"

"Château-Landon. On rue Girard."

Schiffer swallowed his spit. It seemed on fire.

"Do you have the entry code?"

"AB 756. Your key is numbered 4C 32. On level four. The floor with the mini-boxes."

Cyril Brouillard looked up, pushing back his glasses. His voice waxed lyrical.

"The storey with the little treasure troves . . ."

CHAPTER 50

The building looked out over the tracks of the Gare de l'Est, as imposing and solitary as a cargo ship coming into port. With its four floors, it looked as though it had been renovated and freshly painted. An island of cleanliness harbouring goods in transit.

Schiffer went through the first gate and crossed the car-park.

It was two a.m., and he was expecting to see a night watchman appear, wearing a black outfit marked SURGER, flanked by an aggressive dog and carrying an electric prod.

But no one came.

He entered the code and opened the glass door. At the far end of the hall, which was plunged in a strange red glow, he saw a concrete corridor, punctuated by a series of metal doors. Every twenty yards, perpendicular alleyways crossed the main axis, creating the impression of a labyrinth of compartments.

He walked straight on, beneath the safety lights, until he reached a staircase at the far end. Each of his steps made an almost imperceptible dull thud on the pearl-grey cement. Schiffer savoured this silence, this solitude, this mingled tension of power and intrusion.

He reached the fourth floor and stopped. Another corridor opened up, containing apparently smaller compartments. *The storey with the little treasure troves.* Schiffer searched in his pocket and removed the key. He read the numbers on the doors, got lost, then finally found 4C 32.

Before opening it, he stood still. He could almost sense the presence of the Other, there behind the barrier – of this woman who still did not have a name.

He knelt down, turned the key in the lock, then swiftly raised the metal screen.

A box measuring three feet by three appeared in the gloom. Empty. He kept cool. He had not been expecting to find a compartment full of furniture and hi-fi equipment.

From his pocket, he took out the torch he had pinched from Brouillard. Crouching at the threshold, he slowly played the beam around the concrete cube, lighting up the slightest cranny, each breeze-block, until he discovered a cardboard box at the back.

The Other was closer and closer.

He dived into the darkness, stopping in front of the box. He stuck his torch between his teeth and started to search.

There were clothes, all of dark colours, and all by famous designers: Issey Miyake, Helmut Lang, Fendi, Prada . . . His fingers ran up against some underwear. A clear darkness. That was what came to mind. The material was of an almost indecent softness and sensuality. The watered silk seemed to retain its own reflections. The lace fluttered from the contact of his hands . . . This time no desire, no erection. The pretentiousness of such lingerie, the haughty pride that could be seen in it, cut away any such thoughts.

He went on searching and, wrapped in a silk scarf, found a second key.

A strange, rudimentary, flat key.

More work for Monsieur Brouillard.

All that was missing now was the final proof.

He looked further, rummaging, scattering.

Suddenly, a golden brooch, depicting poppy leaves, caught the beam of his torch like a magic scarab. He dropped his light, which was dripping with sweat, spat, then murmured into the darkness: "*Allaha sükü!*[1] You're back."

[1] God be praised!

IX

CHAPTER 51

Mathilde Wilcrau had never been so near to a positron camera.

From the outside, it looked just like a traditional scanner: a wide, white wheel with a stainless steel stretcher inside, equipped with various analytical and measuring instruments; nearby, a stand supporting a drip; a small trolley covered with vacuum-packed syringes and plastic bottles. In the half-light of the room, it made for a strange construction. A sort of massive hieroglyph.

In order to get access to such a machine, the fugitives had had to go as far as the University Hospital in Reims, some sixty miles from Paris. Eric Ackermann knew the head of its radiology department and had telephoned him at his home. The doctor had immediately dashed out to welcome the neurologist effusively. He looked like a frontier officer, receiving the visit of a famous general.

For six hours, Ackermann had been slaving feverishly around the machine. In the control room, Mathilde Wilcrau watched him at work. Leaning over Anna, who was lying with her head inside the machine, he was giving her injections, checking the drip and projecting images onto a tilted mirror inside the upper reaches of the cylinder. And, most of all, he was talking.

As she watched him through the window, running around like a mad thing, Mathilde could not resist succumbing to a certain fascination. This lanky, immature creature, to whom she would not have lent her car, had pulled off a unique scientific experiment in a vicious political context. He had made a huge step forwards in the understanding and control of the brain.

In other circumstances, this advance could have led to major therapeutic developments. It would have inscribed his name in the history books of neurology and psychiatry. Would the Ackermann method get a second chance?

The tall red-head was still busying himself and twitching nervously. Mathilde read between his gestures. Apart from the tension caused by this special session, Ackermann was drugged up to the eyeballs. He was hooked on speed or other uppers. In fact, as soon as they had arrived in the hospital, he had made a shopping trip to the pharmacy. Such synthetic drugs suited him perfectly. He was a thing possessed, living by and for chemical substances . . .

Six hours.

Rocked by the purring of the computers, Mathilde had nodded off on several occasions. Then she had woken up and tried to gather her thoughts. In vain. One idea blinded her, like a light blinds a moth.

Anna's metamorphosis.

The day before, she had picked up a vulnerable creature with amnesia, as fragile as a baby. Then the discovery of that henna had changed everything. The woman had crystallised around that revelation, like quartz. At that moment she seemed to understand that the worst was no longer to be feared, it was to be sought – and confronted. It was she who had decided to take the enemy by surprise and trap Eric Ackermann, despite the risks involved.

It was she who was now in command.

Then, during the questioning in the car-park, Sema Gökalp had appeared. The mysterious working girl, with all her contradictions. The asylum seeker from Anatolia, who spoke perfect French. The prisoner in a state of shock, whose silence and altered face concealed a different past . . .

Who hid behind this new name? Who was this person who was capable of transforming herself utterly into someone else?

The answer would come back with her memory. Anna Heymes. Sema Gökalp . . . She was like a Russian doll, with layered identities, with each name, each appearance containing another secret.

Eric Ackermann got up from his chair. He removed the catheter from Anna's arm, pushed away the drip and tilted up the mirror in the machine. The experiment was over. Mathilde stretched, then tried one more time to put her thoughts in order. She just couldn't. Another image chased that hope away.

Henna.

Those red lines on the hands of Muslim women seemed to trace out an unbridgeable frontier between her Parisian world and the distant life of Sema Gökalp. A culture of deserts, arranged marriages and ancestral rites. A savage, terrifying universe born of scorched winds, predators and rock.

Mathilde closed her eyes.

Tattooed hands; the brown whirls curling around the palms of calloused hands, about dark wrists and knotty fingers; not an inch of virgin flesh; this red line was unbroken, it stretched out, unravelling, turning back on itself, in loops and curls, giving birth to an hypnotic geography . . .

"She's asleep."

Mathilde jumped. Ackermann was standing in front of her. His white coat was loose around his shoulders, like a flag. Beads of sweat winked on his forehead. Twitches and shakes racked his body, but a strange solidity also emanated from his figure – the confidence of know-how beneath the nerves of the addict.

"How did it go?"

He took a cigarette from the computer desk and lit up. He inhaled deeply, then replied through a tunnel of blue smoke.

"I started by giving her an injection of Flumazenil, the antidote to Valium. Then I wiped out the conditioning I had given her, by activating each zone of her memory using Oxygen-15. I retraced my steps precisely."

He sketched a vertical axis with his cigarette.

"With the same words, and same symbols. It's a shame I don't have Heymes's photos or videos any more. But I think most of the work has been done. For the moment, her ideas are rather muddled. Her real memories are coming back, little by little. Anna Heymes is going to disappear and leave her place to the initial personality. But watch out!" he said waving his cigarette. "This is purely experimental!"

A real loony, Mathilde thought. A mix of coldness and exaltation. She was going to say something, but another flash stopped her. Henna, once again. *The lines on the hand come alive; the hooks, whirls and twists slither along the veins, curling up around the phalanges; until they reach the nails stained with pigments . . .*

"Right now, this won't be much fun for her," Ackermann went on, taking another drag. "The various levels of her consciousness are going to telescope. Sometimes she won't be able to tell the difference between what is true and what is false. But her original memory will slowly begin to dominate. With Flumazenil, there are also risks of convulsions, but I've given her a little something to reduce the side-effects . . ."

Mathilde pushed back her hair. She must look like a ghost.

"What about the faces?"

He chased away the smoke with a vague gesture.

"That should sort itself out too. Her reference points are going to become more fixed. When her memory returns, her reactions should become more stable. But, I repeat, all of this is extremely new and . . ."

Mathilde noticed a movement behind the window. She rushed at once into the room. Anna was already sitting on the table of the Petscan, her legs dangling down, leaning back on her hands.

"How do you feel?"

A smile flickered over her face. Her pale lips barely stood out from her skin.

Ackermann came back and turned off the last of the machines.

"How do you feel?" she repeated.

Anna glanced at her in hesitation. Mathilde understood at once. This was no longer the same person. Those indigo eyes were smiling at her from inside a different consciousness.

"Got a cigarette?" she asked in reply, in a voice that was seeking its tonality.

Mathilde handed her a Marlboro. She looked at the slender hand which took it. It was almost as if she could see that henna as a filigree. *Flowers, spikes and snakes curling around a clenched fist. A tattooed fist, holding an automatic pistol . . .*

Behind the mist of smoke, the woman with the dark fringe murmured: "I would rather have been Anna Heymes."

CHAPTER 52

Falmières railway station, six miles west of Reims, was a solitary block, dropped alongside the tracks in the middle of the countryside. A millstone building stuck between the black horizon and the silence of the night. Yet, with its small yellow lantern and laminated glass umbrella roof, it had a reassuring look about it. Its slates, its walls divided into two blue and white bands, and its wooden fences gave it the appearance of a shiny toy from an electric train set.

Mathilde braked in the car-park.

Eric Ackermann had asked them to drop him off at a station. "Any one will do, I'll manage."

Since they had left the hospital, no one had said a word. But the quality of the silence had changed. The hatred, anger and defiance had melted away and a strange sort of complicity had even started up among the three fugitives.

Mathilde turned off the engine. In her rear-view mirror she could see the neurologist's pale face, like a shard of nickel on the back seat. They got out together.

Outside, the wind had risen. Violent gusts were slapping against the asphalt. In the distance, jagged clouds were drifting away like a battalion armed with assegais, revealing an extremely pure moon – a large fruit with blue pulp.

Mathilde did up her coat. She would have given anything for a tube of moisturising cream. It felt as if each squall were drying her skin, digging deeper into the wrinkles on her face.

They walked as far as the flowered fence, still without a word. It made her think of an exchange of hostages during the Cold War, on a bridge in old Berlin – there was no way to say goodbye.

Anna suddenly asked: "What about Laurent?"

She had already asked that question in the car-park under place d'Anvers. It was another aspect of her story: the revelation of a love that persisted despite such betrayal, lies and cruelty.

Ackermann seemed too tired to lie.

"To be honest, there's little chance he's still alive. Charlier won't leave any traces. And Heymes was unreliable. He would have cracked as soon as anyone questioned him. He might even have gone so far as to hand himself in. Since the death of his wife, he . . ."

The neurologist paused. For a moment, Anna seemed to be standing up to the wind, then her shoulders slumped. She turned around silently and returned to the car.

Mathilde took a final look at the lanky frame, topped with a flaming red mane, awash in its raincoat.

"And you?" she asked, almost in pity.

"I'm going to Alsace, to lose myself amid all the other Ackermanns."

A sardonic laugh shook his frame. Then he added, in a lyrical gush: "And then I shall find another destination. The roving life for me!"

Mathilde did not respond. He swayed, hugging his bag against his chest. Just as he used to be at university. He half opened his mouth, hesitated, then murmured: "Anyway, thanks . . ."

He flicked his index finger in a cowboy salute, and turned round towards the isolated station, holding his arms up against the wind. Where on earth could he go? "And then I shall find another destination. The roving life for me!"

Was he talking about a place on earth, or a fresh region of the brain?

CHAPTER 53

"Drugs."

Mathilde was focusing on the white lines of the motorway, which were shooting past rapidly. They flashed in front of her eyes, as some sorts of plankton shine at night in the wakes of ships. A few seconds later, she glanced round at her passenger. Her face was like chalk, smooth, inscrutable.

"I'm a drug runner," Anna went on in a neutral tone. "A smuggler. A supplier for the big dealers. A go-between."

Mathilde nodded, as though she had been expecting this revelation. In fact, she was ready for anything. There were no limits to the truth. That night, each new step revealed dizzying gulfs.

She turned her attention back to the road. Several long seconds passed before she asked: "What kind of drugs? Heroin? Cocaine? Amphetamines? What?"

By the time she had finished, she was almost yelling. She gripped the steering wheel. Calm down. At once.

"Heroin. Only heroin. Several kilos on each trip. Never more. From Turkey to Europe. On me. In my luggage. Or by other means. There are the tricks of the trade. My job was to know them. All of them."

Mathilde's throat was so dry that each breath was agony.

"Who . . . who were you working for?"

"The rules have changed, Mathilde. The less you know, the better."

Anna's tone was now strange, almost condescending.

"What's your real name?"

"I have no real name. That's part of the job."

"How did you work? Give me some details."

Anna remained silent for a long time, as dense as marble. Then, after an extended pause, she went on: "It wasn't really an exciting life. Growing old in airports. Knowing the best stopovers. The least well guarded borders. The simplest, or else the most complicated connecting flights. The towns where your bags are left on the runway. The customs posts where you're searched, and the ones where you aren't. The structure of holds. Places of transit."

Mathilde listened, but paid attention mostly to the timbre of her voice. Never had it rung so true.

"A schizophrenic lifestyle. Constantly speaking different languages, answering to different names, having several nationalities. And your only home the standard comfort of VIP lounges in airports. And always, everywhere, fear."

Mathilde blinked away the sleep. Her eyesight was getting hazy. The lines on the road were floating, drifting apart . . . She asked again: "Where are you from exactly?"

"I can't remember yet. But it will come back, I'm sure of it. For the moment, I'm concentrating on the present."

"So what happened? Why were you in Paris posing as a working girl? Why did you alter your appearance?"

"It's a classic story. I wanted to hold on to my last consignment. To rob my employers."

She paused. Each memory seemed to cost her an effort.

"It was in June, last year. I had a delivery to make in Paris. A special load. Extremely precious. I had a contact here, but I chose a different route. I hid the heroin and went to see a plastic surgeon. I think . . . yes, I think at the time I had a good chance. But during my convalescence, something unexpected happened. Something no one expected: the attacks on September 11th. From one day to the next, borders turned into solid walls. So there was no way I was going to leave with the dope, as planned. Nor could I leave Paris. I had to stay there and wait for the situation to calm down, while knowing that my bosses would do everything to find me . . . So I hid where, normally speaking, no one would look for a Turk who was hiding out: among the Turks. With the illegal immigrant workers in the tenth *arrondissement.* I had a new face, and a new identity. No one would spot me."

The voice faded away, as though exhausted. Mathilde tried to revive the flame.

"What happened then? How did the police find you? Did they know about the drugs?"

"That's not how things turned out. It's still vague, but I can just about picture the scene . . . in November, I was working in a laundry. A kind of underground dry cleaner's in some Turkish baths. A place you just couldn't imagine. At least, not under a mile from where you live. One night, they came."

"The police?"

"No. Turks sent by my employers. They knew I was hiding there. Someone must have given me away. I don't know . . . What is sure is that they didn't know that I'd altered my appearance. Right in front of me, they jumped a girl who looked like I used to be. Zeynep something . . . God save me, when I saw those killers arrive . . . All I can remember is a flash of fear . . ."

Mathilde tried to complete the story, to fill in the gaps.

"How did you end up with Charlier?"

"I have no precise memories about that. I was in a state of shock. The cops must have found me at the baths. I can see a police station, then a hospital . . . Somehow or other, Charlier heard about me. An amnesic immigrant. With no work permit in France. The perfect guinea-pig."

Anna seemed to be weighing up her own hypothesis, then she

266

murmured: "There's an incredible irony in all this. Because the cops never realised who I really was. Without meaning to, they protected me from the Turks."

Mathilde's guts were beginning to ache – with fear, worsened by fatigue. Her eyes were failing. The white lines on the road were turning into gulls, vague birds fluttering convulsively.

At that moment, the signpost for the Paris ring-road appeared. They were nearly back. She concentrated on the marks on the asphalt and continued: "Who are these men who are looking for you?"

"Forget about that. As I said, the less you know, the safer you'll be."

"I helped you," she replied, with gritted teeth. "I protected you. So come on! Tell me the truth."

Anna hesitated again. It was her world – a world she had surely never spoken about before.

"There's something special about the Turkish mafia," she said at last. "For their dirty work, they use political activists. They're called the Grey Wolves. They're nationalists. Extreme right-wing fanatics who believe in the return of Greater Turkey. Terrorists trained in camps when they're still children. Compared with them, Charlier's goons are just like scouts with Swiss army knives."

The blue signs were growing larger. PORTE DE CLIGNANCOURT. PORTE DE LA CHAPELLE. All Mathilde wanted to do now was to drop this living bomb off at the first taxi rank. To go back home, to comfort and security. What she wanted was to sleep for twenty hours, to wake up and say "it was only a nightmare".

She took the turning into Paris and said: "I'm staying with you."

"No, that's impossible. I've got something important to do."

"What?"

"Pick up my load."

"I'll come with you."

"No."

A knot tightened in her belly. More of pride than courage.

"Where is it? Where are the drugs?"

"In Père-Lachaise cemetery."

Mathilde looked round at Anna. She seemed wizened, but also harder, denser – a quartz crystal compressed amid layers of the truth . . .

"Why there?"

"I had twenty kilos. I had to find some safe storage."

"I don't see any connection with a cemetery."

Anna smiled to herself dreamily.

"A little white powder amid all the grey powder . . ."

A red light brought them to a halt. After the crossroads, rue de La Chapelle turned into rue Marx-Dormoy. Mathilde repeated more loudly: "What's the link with a cemetery?"

"It's green now. Place de la Chapelle, then turn towards place de Stalingrad."

CHAPTER 54

The city of the dead.

Broad, straight alleyways, lined with imposing trees which certainly looked the part. Huge blocks, raised monuments, dark smooth tombs.

In the moonlight, this part of the cemetery was decked with generous flower-beds – a luxurious, opulent distribution of space.

A hint of Christmas floated in the air. Everything seemed crystallised, enveloped by the dome of night, like in those small globes that have to be shaken to make the snow scatter across the landscape.

They had attacked the fortress via the gate on rue du Père-Lachaise, near place Gambetta. Anna had guided Mathilde along the gutter that bordered the entrance, then between the iron spikes on the wall. The descent on the other side had been even easier – electric cables followed the course of the stones at this point.

They were now going up avenue des Combattants-Étrangers. Beneath the moon, the tombs and epitaphs stood out clearly. A bunker had been dedicated to Czechoslovaks who had died in the First World War. A white monolith stood in memory of the Belgian troops. A colossal spike with multiple edges, like a Vasarely painting, paid homage to the dead Armenians . . .

When Mathilde spotted the large building, topped by two chimneys, at the end of the slope, she understood. *A little white powder amid all the grey powder.* The columbarium. With a strange cynicism,

Anna the smuggler had hidden her stock of heroin among the funeral urns.

Against the night sky, the building looked like a cream and gold mosque, topped with a broad cupola, dominated by its chimneys like minarets. Four long edifices surrounded it, laid out in a quincunx.

Once inside the surrounding wall, they crossed the neat gardens with their thick, square hedges. Further on, Mathilde could see galleries full of racks and flowers. They made her think of marble pages, incrusted with coloured writing and seals.

The place was deserted.

Not a night watchman to be seen.

Anna reached the end of the park, where the stairs of a crypt plunged down beneath the shrubbery. At the bottom of the steps, the cast-iron gate was padlocked. For a few seconds, they looked for a way inside. As though providing inspiration, a fluttering of wings made them look up: some pigeons were shuffling about in front of the grating of a small window, at a height of six feet.

Anna stepped back to gauge the size of the niche. Then she braced her feet on the door's metal ornaments and clambered up. A few seconds later, Mathilde heard the scrape of the grating being pulled away, then the short slap of broken glass.

Without a second's thought, she followed.

When she reached the top, she slipped in through the gap. She had just reached the ground when Anna put on the light.

The sanctuary was huge. Its straight galleries, arranged around a square shaft, were dug out in granite, stretching away into the darkness. At regular intervals, lamps diffused a glimmer of light.

They went over to the balustrade of the shaft. Three further levels lay beneath them, multiplying their tunnels. The ceramic basin at the bottom of this gulf looked tiny. It was as if they were at the heart of a subterranean city, built around a sacred spring.

Anna took one of the staircases. Mathilde followed her. As they went down, the humming of a ventilation system could be heard. At each landing, the feeling of being in a temple, or a giant tomb, became ever more crushing.

On the second level, Anna took an alley to her right, punctuated with hundreds of compartments with black and white tiles. They walked on for some time. Mathilde observed the scene with curious detachment. Sometimes she noticed a detail among the openings. A bouquet of fresh flowers on the ground, enveloped in aluminium foil. An ornament or decoration standing out in a niche. Such as the silk-screened face of a black woman, her frizzy hair spilling across the marble surface. The epitaph read: YOU WERE ALWAYS THERE. YOU WILL BE ALWAYS THERE. Or, further on, a photograph of a child with grey rings under its eyes, stuck on a plain plaster plaque. Beneath it, someone had written in felt-tip pen: SHE IS NOT DEAD BUT SLEEPETH. SAINT MATTHEW.

"Here," Anna said.

A larger niche stood at the end of the corridor.

"The crowbar," she ordered.

Mathilde opened the bag she had slung over her shoulder and took it out. At once, Anna stuck it between the marble and the wall and pressed down as hard as she could. A crack started to snake across the surface. At the base of the block, she applied the crowbar once more. The plaque crashed to the floor, in two pieces.

Anna picked up the tool and used it as a hammer against the plaster wall at the back of the niche. Particles flew up, sticking in her black hair. She continued to bang stubbornly, without paying heed to the noise she was making.

Mathilde could no longer breathe. It felt to her as though these bangs were resonating as far as place Gambetta. How long would it be before the watchmen showed up?

Silence fell once more. In a white cloud, Anna dived into the niche and removed the rubble. Large sweepings of dust hit the wall.

Suddenly, a tinkling sound was heard behind their backs.

The two women turned round.

At their feet, a metal key was shining amid the plaster debris.

"Try using that. You'll save time."

A man with short-cropped hair was standing at the entrance of the gallery, his figure reflected on the floor tiles. It looked as if he was standing on water.

Lifting up his shotgun, he asked: "Where is it?"

He was dressed in a rumpled raincoat, twisted across his body, but this in no way lessened the impression of power that he radiated.

Especially his face, lit to one side by the rays of a lamp, gave off a look of quite startling cruelty.

"Where is it?" he repeated, taking a step forwards.

Mathilde felt like death. A stabbing pain was digging into her guts, her legs were giving way. She had to grab hold of the niche to stop herself from falling. This was no longer a game. This was not shooting practice, the triathlon, or any sort of calculated risk.

They were quite simply going to die.

The intruder kept coming. With a precise gesture, he armed his gun.

"For fuck's sake! Where's the fucking smack?"

CHAPTER 55

The man in the raincoat caught fire.

Mathilde dived to the ground. At the moment when she hit the floor, she realised that the flame had burst out of his gun. She rolled over the plaster rubble. At that instant, a second fact became clear to her. Anna had fired first. She must have hidden an automatic pistol in the niche.

More shots followed. Mathilde curled up, her fists clenched over her head. Niches were exploding above her, freeing their urns and their contents. When the ash started to fall on her, she screamed. Grey clouds rose up, as the bullets whistled and ricocheted. In a fog of dust, she saw sparks flying from the marble angels, filaments of fire springing up across the debris, vases rolling onto the floor, then bouncing up with silvery glints. The corridor was like a starry hell, mingled with gold and iron . . .

She curled up tighter. The shots were smashing apart the niches, ripping up the flowers. The urns broke open, spilling their ash as the bullets crashed through space. She started to crawl, closing her eyes, jumping at each explosion.

Suddenly, silence returned.

Mathilde stopped at once, waiting a few seconds before opening her eyes.

She could not see anything.

The gallery was completely full of ash, as though after a volcanic eruption. The stink of cordite mingled with the cinders, thus worsening the sensation of asphyxia.

Mathilde dared not move. She almost called out Anna's name, but stopped herself.

She should not let the killer spot her.

While analysing the situation, she examined her body. She was unwounded. She closed her eyes again and concentrated. Not a breath, not a sound anywhere near her, with the exception of a few pieces of rubble, which continued to fall with dull thuds.

Where was Anna?

Where was the man?

Were they both dead?

She squinted in the attempt to see something. Finally, two or three yards further on, she noticed a lamp which was giving off a vague light. She remembered how they punctuated the alleyway about every ten yards. But which one was it? The one by the entrance to the corridor? Which way was the exit? To her right, or to her left?

She fought back a cough, swallowed her saliva, then silently picked herself up on to an elbow. She started crawling towards the left, avoiding the rubble, the shells, the spillage from the urns . . .

Suddenly, the fog materialised in front of her.

A completely grey figure: the killer.

Her lips opened, but his hand pressed hard over her mouth. In the blood-red eyes which were staring at her, Mathilde could read: *One sound, and you're dead.* The barrel of a revolver was rammed into her throat. She rapidly fluttered her eyelashes as a sign of assent. Slowly, the man removed his fingers. She gave him another imploring look, guaranteeing her total submission.

At that moment, a ghastly sensation hit her. Something had happened that made her feel even more awful than the idea of dying: she had dirtied herself.

Her sphincters had loosened.

Urine and excrement oozed between her thighs, soaking her tights.

The man grabbed her by the hair, and dragged her across the floor. Mathilde bit her lips to stop herself from screaming. They passed through the clouds of mist, between the vases, flowers and human ash.

They prowled around the galleries several times. Still being pulled brutally, Mathilde slipped along in the dust, making a soft rustling sound. She kicked her legs, but the movement made no noise. She opened her mouth, but nothing came out of it. She was sobbing, groaning, whistling between her teeth, but the dust absorbed everything. Through her pain, she realised that this silence was her best ally. At the slightest sound, the man would kill her.

The advance slowed. She felt his grip loosen. Then the man grabbed her again, and started going up stairs. Mathilde braced herself. A wave of agony ran from her skull to the base of her spine. It felt as if deadly clamps were pulling the skin of her face. Her legs were still kicking, heavy, wet, filthy with shame. She smelt the ghastly waste that was staining her legs.

Then everything came to a halt again.

It only lasted a second, but that was enough.

Mathilde twisted around to see what was happening. Anna's form was standing out against the fog, while the killer soundlessly aimed his gun.

With a wrench, she lifted herself up on a knee to warn her.

Too late. He pressed the trigger, causing a deafening crash.

But nothing happened as expected. The figure exploded in a thousand shards, the cinders changed into a lethal hail. The man yelled. Mathilde freed herself and rolled backwards, down to the bottom of the steps.

As she fell, she realised what had happened. He had not fired at Anna, but at a glass door, stained with dust, which was sending back his own reflection. Mathilde landed on her back and witnessed the impossible truth. Just as the back of her head hit the floor, she saw the real Anna, like a grey statue, crouching in the gutted window. She had been awaiting them there, as though floating above the dead.

At that moment, Anna leapt down. Hanging with her left hand from a niche, she swung her body as fast as she could. In her other hand, she held a spike of broken glass. Its sharp end stuck into the man's face.

By the time he had aimed his gun, Anna had pulled out the blade. The bullet flew through the dust. The next second, she attacked once more. The shard slid across his temple and sliced into his flesh. Another bullet went astray through the air. Anna was already crouched against the wall.

Forehead, temples, mouth. Back she came again and again. The man's face was being torn apart in bloody slices. Staggering, he dropped his gun, clumsily flapping his arms, as though pestered by killer bees.

At last, Anna went in for the kill. With all her weight, she leapt on him. They rolled onto the ground. The spike stuck into his right cheek. Anna kept up the pressure, literally slicing apart the flesh and exposing the gums.

Mathilde eased herself up the stairs on her back, pressing on her elbows. She was yelling, without managing to take her eyes off that savage combat.

Anna at last dropped her weapon and stood up. The man, gesticulating in a heap of ashes, was trying to pull the glass out of one of his eyes. Anna picked up the gun, and pushed his hands aside. She grabbed the shard, twisting it around and pulling it out of the socket, with the red eye stuck on it. Mathilde tried again to look away, but failed. Anna rammed the barrel into the gaping hole and pulled the trigger.

CHAPTER 56

Silence again.

The acrid smell of ash again.

The overturned urns, with their sculpted lids.

The scattered colours of the plastic flowers.

The body slumped down a few inches from Mathilde, spraying her with blood, brains and pieces of bone. One of its arms was touching her thigh, but she did not have the strength to push it away. The beating of her heart was so feeble that each interval seemed to her to be the final one.

"We've got to go. The watchmen will be here soon."

Mathilde raised her eyes.

What she saw tore into her heart.

274

Anna's face had turned to stone. The dust of the dead had gathered in the hollows of her features, changing them into cracked furrows, wrinkled gulches. In contrast, her eyes were blood-shot and raw.

Mathilde thought of the eye stuck on the point of glass. She wanted to vomit.

Anna was holding a sports bag, which she had presumably removed from the niche.

"The heroin's fucked," she said. "So let's not waste any more time here."

"Who are you? For heaven's sake, who are you?"

Anna put the bag down and opened it.

"He wouldn't have pulled his punches either, believe me."

She picked up the wads of dollars and euros, counted them rapidly then put them back in the bag.

"He was my contact in Paris. The person who was supposed to take care of the heroin in Europe. To handle the distribution networks."

Mathilde looked down at the corpse. She saw a brownish grimace, from which a single eye was staring up at the ceiling. As an epitaph, she wanted his name.

"What was he called?"

"Jean-Louis Schiffer. He was a cop."

"Your contact was a cop?"

Anna did not reply. From the bottom of the bag she produced a passport and flicked over its pages quickly. Mathilde returned to the body.

"You were . . . partners?"

"He'd never seen me, but I knew his face. We had a sign of recognition. A brooch shaped like a poppy. And also a kind of password: four moons."

"What does that mean?"

"Forget it."

Kneeling on the ground, she continued her search. She came across several magazines for an automatic pistol. Mathilde observed her in disbelief. Her face looked like a mask of dry mud, a ritualistic figure, frozen in the earth. There was nothing human left about Anna.

"What are you going to do now?" Mathilde asked.

The woman stood up and removed a hand gun from her belt – no doubt the automatic she had found in the niche. She released the spring in the handle, thus removing the empty clip. Her confident gestures revealed the reflexes born of training.

"Leave. There's nothing for me now in Paris."

"Where to?"

She slipped a fresh magazine into the gun.

"Turkey."

"Turkey? But why? If you go there, they'll find you."

"Wherever I go, they'll find me. I have to cut out the source."

"The source?"

"The source of this hatred. The origin of this vengeance. I have to go back to Istanbul. Take them by surprise. They won't be expecting me there."

"Who do you mean, *they*?"

"The Grey Wolves. Sooner or later, they'll discover my new face."

"So what? There are thousands of places you could hide."

"No. When they find out what I now look like, they'll know where to find me."

"Why?"

"Because their leader has seen me, in a completely different context."

"I don't get it."

"I repeat: forget it! They'll chase me till they find me and kill me. For them, this is no normal contract. It's a question of honour. I betrayed them. I broke my oath."

"What oath? What are you talking about?"

She slipped down the safety catch and put the gun behind her back.

"I'm one of them. I am a Wolf."

Mathilde's breathing stopped, her blood seemed to slow. Anna knelt down and took her by her shoulders. Her face was now colourless, but when she spoke her pink, almost fluorescent tongue could be seen between her lips.

A mouth of raw meat.

"You're alive and that's a miracle," she said gently. "When it's all over, I'll write to you. I'll give you the names, the circumstances, everything. I want you to know the truth, but later. When I'm ready to put an end to this story, and when you're in safety."

Haggard, Mathilde did not answer. For a few hours – an eternity –

she had protected this woman as though she were her own flesh and blood. She had made her into a daughter, her baby.

And in fact, she was a killer.

A being of violence and cruelty.

An unbearable sensation started up in her innards. A shifting of slime in a decaying pond. The ghastly dampness of her open, slack entrails.

At that moment, the idea of being pregnant took her breath away.

Yes, that night she had given birth to a monster.

Grabbing the sports bag, Anna stood up.

"I'll write to you. I promise. I'll explain everything."

She vanished into a screen of ash.

Mathilde remained still, staring into the empty gallery.

In the distance, the sirens of the cemetery were blaring.

X

CHAPTER 57

"It's Paul."

A breath at the other end of the line.

"Do you know what time it is?"

He looked at his watch. Only just six a.m.

"Sorry. I haven't slept."

The breath changed into a weary sigh.

"What do you want?"

"I just want to know if Céline got her sweets."

Reyna's voice hardened.

"You're sick."

"Did she get them, yes or no?"

"And that's why you're calling me at six in the morning?"

Paul banged on the window of the phone box. The battery of his mobile was flat again.

"Just tell me if she was pleased. I haven't seen her for ten days!"

"What really made her pleased were the men in uniforms who brought them round. She talked about that all day. For fuck's sake. All that ideological effort to end up with pigs as baby-sitters . . ."

Paul pictured his daughter looking admiringly at the silver buttons, her eyes glistening at the candy the patrolmen had given her. It warmed his heart. Suddenly, with a cheerful tone, he promised: "I'll call back in a couple of hours. Before she leaves for school."

Without a word, Reyna hung up.

He left the booth and took a deep breath of night air. He was on place du Trocadéro, between the Musée de l'Homme, the Musée de la Marine and Théâtre de Chaillot. It was drizzling on the central square, which was surrounded by fences, and was clearly being renovated.

He followed the planks, which formed a corridor and crossed the esplanade. The drizzle was putting a greasy film on his face. It was far too warm for the season, making him sweat in his parka. This humid weather matched his mood. He felt dirty, worn-out, empty. There was a taste of papier mâché in his mouth.

Since Schiffer's phone call, just before midnight, he had been following up the plastic surgery lead. After taking on board this new twist in his investigation – a woman with an altered face, being chased by both Charlier's men and the Grey Wolves – he went to the headquarters of the French Medical Association on avenue de Friedland, in the eighth *arrondissement*, in search of doctors who might have had some dealings with justice. As Schiffer had put it: "Having your face completely redone is never innocent." So he had to find a surgeon with no scruples. His initial idea was to look for those who had police records.

He had immersed himself in the archives, and had made no bones about calling the departmental head to help him, even in the middle of the night. The search had turned up over six hundred files, just for the Paris region over the past five years. How to wade through such a list? At two a.m., he had phoned Jean-Philippe Arnaud, the president of the Association of Plastic Surgeons, to ask his advice. In reply, the sleepy voice had provided three names of virtuosi with iffy reputations, who might have accepted to carry out such an operation without asking too many questions.

Before hanging up, Paul had questioned him about other scalpels among the "respectable" surgeons. After some prompting, Jean-Philippe Arnaud had added seven more names, while insisting that they were recognised practitioners and would never have got involved in such a business. Paul cut short his comments and thanked him. So at three in the morning he had had a list of ten names. For him, the night was still young . . .

He stopped at the far side of the Trocadéro, between the two museums, looking over the Seine. Sitting on the steps, he let himself be seduced by the beauty of the view. The gardens were laid out in different levels, with fountains and statues forming a dreamlike landscape. The Pont d'Iéna added touches of light to the river, as far as the Eiffel Tower on the opposite bank, looking like a huge cast-iron paperweight. All around, the dark buildings of the Champ-de-Mars slept in religious silence. Overall, the scene was reminiscent of a hidden Tibetan kingdom, a marvellous Xanadu, at the end of the known world.

Paul went through what he had learned over the previous few hours.

To begin with, he had tried phoning up the surgeons. But his very first call proved to him that he would not find out anything that way: the man had hung up in his face. In any case, the vital point was to show them the pictures of the victims and the one of Anna Heymes that Schiffer had left for him at Louis-Blanc station.

So he called round to see the first of the "shifty" surgeons on rue Clément-Marot.

According to Jean-Philippe Arnaud, this millionaire from Colombia was suspected of having operated on the godfathers of Medellin and Cali. He was extremely renowned for his skill. It was said that he could operate using either his right or his left hand.

Despite the late hour, the artist in question had not gone to bed – or rather, was not asleep. Paul had disturbed him in full action, in the scented shadows of a vast penthouse. He had not seen his features clearly, but had grasped that these faces rung no bells.

The second address was of a clinic on rue Washington, on the other side of the Champs-Elysées.

Paul had grabbed the surgeon just before an emergency operation on a victim of first-degree burns. He had played his part, producing his card, sketching out details of the case, placing the pictures on the table. The man had not even lowered his surgical mask. He had just shaken his head before leaving to take care of that charred flesh. Paul remembered what Arnaud had said: this character artificially cultivated human skin. It was said that, after burning, he could modify people's fingerprints, thus completing a new identity for criminals on the run . . .

Paul had gone once more into the night.

He had found the third surgeon fast asleep in his flat on avenue d'Eylau, near the Trocadéro. He was another celebrity, who was supposed to have operated on the greatest stars of show-business. But no one knew "who" or "what on". It was also rumoured that he had altered his own appearance after some problems with the police in his native South Africa.

He had received Paul warily, his hands jammed in his dressing-gown pockets like revolvers. After looking at the photos in disgust, he had uttered a categorical "never seen them before".

Paul had emerged from these three visits as though he had been swimming underwater. At six in the morning, he had suddenly felt in need of something familiar, something he knew. So he called up the only family that he had – or what was left of it. But the call had not comforted him. Reyna was still on another planet. And Céline, still fast asleep, was light years away from his world. A world in which killers put living rodents in women's vaginas, and where cops cut off people's fingers to get information . . .

Paul raised his eyes. Dawn was stretching up in the sky, like the curve of a distant star. A broad mauve strip was gradually turning pink and, at the top of its arc, was distilling a hint of sulphur, already dotted with white, sparkling particles. The mica of day . . .

He stood up and retraced his steps. When he reached place du Trocadéro, the cafés were opening their doors. He spotted the lights of Le Malakoff, where he had arranged to meet his two assistants, Naubrel and Matkowska.

The previous day, he had told them to drop the business about high-pressure chambers and instead obtain as much information as they could about the Grey Wolves and their political history. While Paul was focusing on the "target", he also wanted to know something about the hunters.

In the doorway of the café, he paused for a moment and considered another problem that was bugging him – the disappearance of Jean-Louis Schiffer. He had heard nothing from him since that phone call at eleven last night. Paul had tried contacting him several times, in vain. Instead of fearing for the worst, or for his life, he sensed that the bastard had doublecrossed him. Now that he was free again, Schiffer had presumably found a hot lead and was following it up all on his own.

Controlling his anger, Paul mentally gave him one more chance. He had until ten o'clock to show a sign of life. After that, he would put out an arrest warrant. He had nothing more to lose.

He pushed open the door of the bar, feeling his mood grow ever darker.

CHAPTER 58

The two lieutenants were already ensconced in a recess. Before joining them, Paul rubbed his face with his hands and tried to flatten out his parka. He wanted to look like what he in fact was – their superior – and not some tramp blown in from the night.

He crossed the over-bright, over-renovated room, where everything looked fake, from the chandeliers to the backs of the chairs. A trashy bar, used to the vapours of alcohol and drunken chatter, but at this hour still empty.

Paul sat down in front of the officers, pleased to see their jovial faces once more. Naubrel and Matkowska were not great investigators, but they still had the enthusiasm of youth. They made Paul think of the carefree, light existence that he had never had.

They started by assailing him with details of their nocturnal quest. After ordering a coffee, Paul interrupted them: "All right, lads. Get to the point."

They exchanged a knowing glance, then Naubrel opened a thick file of photocopies.

"The Grey Wolves are basically a political organisation. From what we've found out, lefty ideas were dominant in Turkey in the 1960s. Just like in France. So the extreme right wing rose up in reaction. A man called Alpaslan Türkes, an army colonel who used to have links with the Nazis, set up a party: the Nationalist Action Party. He and his men stood as a bastion against the red peril."

Matkowska took over: "As well as the official group, ideological clubs were started for the young. First in the universities, then in the country-side. The kids that joined them called themselves 'Idealists' or else 'Grey Wolves.'" He glanced at his notes. "Or Bozkurt in Turkish."

This all corresponded to what Schiffer had told him.

"In the 1970s," Naubrel went on, "the communist versus fascist war increased in tension. The Grey Wolves armed themselves. In some parts of Anatolia, training camps were opened. The young Idealists were indoctrinated there, trained in the martial arts, and taught how to use guns. Illiterate peasants were transformed into armed, trained fanatical killers."

Matkowska took out another wad of photocopies.

"In 1977, the Grey Wolves went into action: planting bombs, machine-gunning public edifices, assassinations of public figures . . . The communists hit back. A real civil war broke out. At the end of the 1970s, between fifteen and twenty people were being killed every day in Turkey. It was pure and simple terror."

Paul butted in: "But what about the government? The police? The army?"

Naubrel smiled.

"That's just the point. The army let things go to pot so that they could clear up the mess later on. In 1980, they organised a coup d'état. A neat job, with no messing. The terrorists on both sides were arrested. The Grey Wolves felt betrayed. They had fought against communism, and now a right-wing government was putting them in jail . . . At the time, Türkes wrote: 'I am in prison, but my ideas are in power.' In fact, the Grey Wolves were soon freed. Türkes gradually started up his political activities once more. In his wake, other Grey Wolves went straight. They became politicians and members of parliament. But there were still the hit men left, the peasants who had been trained in camps. All they knew was violence and fanaticism."

"Yeah," Matkowska went on. "And now they were orphans. The right wing was in power, and didn't need them any more. Türkes was too busy becoming respectable to want to have anything to do with them. When they were released from prison, what could they do?"

Naubrel put down his coffee cup and answered the question. They had their double-act off to a tee.

"They became mercenaries. They were armed and experienced. So they worked for the highest bidder, the state or the mafia. According to the Turkish journalists we contacted, it's an open secret that the Grey Wolves were used by the MIT, the Turkish secret service, to assassinate Armenian and Kurdish leaders. They formed a militia, or death squads. But most of all, it was the mafia that employed them as debt collectors, racketeers, bodyguards . . . In the mid-1980s, they oversaw the development of the drugs trade in Turkey. Sometimes they even replaced the mafia clans and took over the reins. They have a vital advantage over classic crooks: they have kept their links with the powers that be and especially with the police. Over the past few years, a series of scandals has revealed the close links between the mafia, the state and nationalism."

Paul thought this over. It all seemed like vague, ancient history to him. The word "mafia" was a catch-all term. Still the same images of an octopus, plots and invisible networks . . . What did it all really mean? Nothing in this brought him any nearer to the killers he was chasing, nor to their female target. He had no faces, no names to go on.

As though following his train of thought, Naubrel laughed proudly: "And now for some pictures!"

He pushed aside the papers and stuck his hands in an envelope.

"We took a look at the photo archives of the *Milliyet* newspaper on the Net. It's one of Istanbul's biggest dailies. And we found this."

Paul picked up the image.

"What is it?"

"The funeral of Alpaslan Türkes. The 'Old Wolf' died in April 1997. He was eighty. It was a real national event."

Paul could not believe his eyes. The funeral had drawn thousands of Turks. The caption on the photo even read: "A funeral procession of four kilometres, escorted by ten thousand policemen."

It was a solemn, magnificent scene. As black as the crowd gathered around the procession, in front of Ankara's Grand Mosque. As white as the snow that was falling that day in large flakes. As red as the Turkish flags, floating all around among the "faithful" . . .

The next pictures showed the head of the main group. He recognised Tansu Ciller, the former prime minister, and supposed that other Turkish dignitaries must have been there too. He even noted the presence of emissaries from neighbouring countries, wearing the traditional costumes of Central Asia, with their fur hats and gold embroidered greatcoats.

Suddenly, Paul had another idea. Mafia godfathers must also have taken part in the procession . . . The heads of the families of Istanbul and other regions of Anatolia must have come to pay a final homage to their political ally. Among them, there might even be the people behind the very case he was working on. The man who had set the killers on the track of Sema Gökalp . . .

He examined the other photos, which revealed interesting details about the crowd. For example, most of the red flags did not have just one crescent – the symbol of Turkey – but three arranged in a triangle. This was echoed by other posters featuring a wolf howling beneath three moons.

It seemed to Paul that he was looking at an army on the march, stone warriors with primitive values and esoteric symbols. More than just a political party, the Grey Wolves were a sort of sect, a mystical clan with ancestral traditions.

In the final reproductions, another detail surprised him: the militants were not lifting clenched fists when the coffin passed, as he had thought. Their salute was more original, with two raised fingers. He focused on a woman, in tears in the snow, who was making this strange gesture.

When he looked more closely, he saw that she was raising her index and little fingers, while her other two fingers were bent beneath her thumb, as though forming a pincer. He asked, out loud: "What does that gesture mean?"

"I dunno," Matkowska replied. "They're all doing it. It must be a sign of recognition. They look completely nuts to me!"

That sign was the key. Two fingers up, pointing to the sky, like ears . . .

Suddenly, the penny dropped.

Facing Naubrel and Matkowska, he made the gesture.

"Jesus," he whispered. "Can't you see what it represents?"

Paul moved his hand till it was in profile, pointed like a snout towards the window.

"Look carefully."

"Shit," Naubrel murmured. "It's a wolf. The head of a wolf."

CHAPTER 59

On the way out of the bar, Paul announced: "We'll split up."

The two cops took the blow. After a sleepless night, they had obviously hoped to go home. He ignored their desperate stares.

"Naubrel, you get back onto the decompression chambers."

"What? But I . . ."

"I want a complete list of sites containing that sort of equipment in the entire Paris region."

The officer opened his hands in a gesture of impotence.

"It's a blind alley, Captain. Matkowska and I have been through the lot. From masonry to heating, from sanitation to glaziers. We've visited test sites, we've . . ."

Paul stopped him. If he had followed his own opinion, then he would have dropped the matter too. But Schiffer had asked him about the lead during their phone call, which meant that he had good reason to take an interest in it. And more than ever, Paul was beginning to trust the old man's instincts . . .

"I want a list," he said firmly. "With all the places where there's a chance the killers might have used a chamber . . ."

"What about me?" Matkowska asked.

Paul handed him the keys to his flat.

"You go to my place, rue du Chemin-Vert. From the letter box, you get all the catalogues, guide books and documents about ancient masks and busts. There's someone on the Murder Squad collecting them for me."

"Then what do I do with them?"

He did not really believe in this lead either. But he could hear Schiffer asking: *What about the ancient masks?* Maybe Paul's hypothesis was not that bad after all . . .

"You sit down comfortably in my flat," he went on firmly. "Then you compare all the images with the faces of the victims."

"Why?"

"To look for similarities. I'm sure the way the killer disfigures them is based on some archaeological remains."

The incredulous officer stared at the keys, glittering in his palm. Paul made no further explanations. Walking towards his car, he concluded: "Report at noon. But if you find anything solid before, call me at once."

It was now time to deal with a fresh idea which was bugging him. Ali Ajik, a cultural attaché at the Turkish embassy, lived a few blocks away. It might be worth contacting him. He had always been co-operative during this case and Paul now needed to talk to a Turkish citizen.

In his car, he picked up his mobile, which was at last fully recharged. Ajik was not asleep – or at least so he said.

A few minutes later, Paul was clambering up the diplomat's stairs. He was shaking slightly, from the lack of sleep, hunger and excitement . . .

He was welcomed into a small, modern flat, which had been transformed into Ali Baba's cave. Varnished furniture sparkled with copper glints. Medallions, frames and lanterns took the walls by storm with gold and bronze beams. The floor vanished beneath superimposed rugs, vibrant with the same ochre shades. This Thousand and One Nights décor did not fit the man himself. Ajik was a modern Turkish polyglot, aged about forty.

"Before me," he explained apologetically, "the flat was occupied by a diplomat of the old school."

He smiled, his hands stuck in the pockets of a pearl-grey tracksuit.

"So what's the panic?"

"I want to show you some photos."

"Some photos? No problem. Come on in. I'm making some tea."

Paul wanted to refuse, but he had to play the game. This visit was informal, not to say illegal – he was stepping beyond the limits of diplomatic immunity.

He sat down on the floor, among the rugs and embroidered cushions, while Ajik, cross-legged, poured tea into small bulbous glasses.

Paul observed him. He had regular features with short-cropped black hair that fitted over his skull like a balaclava. A clear face, drawn by a Rotring. Only his stare was disturbing, with asymmetric eyes. The left pupil never moved, remaining forever fixed on you, while the other was fully mobile.

Without touching his scalding glass, Paul went straight to the point: "Firstly, I want to talk about the Grey Wolves."

"Is this a new case?"

Paul ducked the question.

"What do you know about them?"

"It was all a long time ago. They were really powerful in the 1970s. Extremely violent people . . ." He slowly took a sip. "Have you noticed my eye?"

Paul tried to look astonished, as if to say "now that you mention it . . ."

"Yes, of course you'd noticed it," Ajik smiled. "It was the Idealists who struck it out. On the university campus, when I was a left-wing militant. Their methods were rather . . . harsh."

"And now?"

Ajik gestured wearily.

"They no longer exist. Or not as terrorists, anyway. They don't need to use force any more. They're in power in Turkey."

"I'm not talking about politicians. I'm talking about hard men. The people who work in organised crime."

Ajik's expression became more ironic.

"All those stories . . . In Turkey, it's hard to tell fact from fiction."

"Some of them work for mafia families, yes or no?"

"They certainly did in the past. But now . . ." he wrinkled his brows. "Why are you asking me this? Has it got something to do with all those murders?"

Paul decided to press on: "From what I understand, even though they work for the mafia, these men remain loyal to their cause."

"That's right. In fact, they look down on the gangsters who employ them. They are convinced that they are serving a higher ideal."

"Tell me about it."

Ajik took a deep breath, exaggerating the swelling of his chest; as though puffing himself up with patriotism.

"The return of the Turkish Empire. The illusory Turan."

"What's that?"

"I'd need an entire day to explain that."

"Please," Paul said more abruptly. "I have to understand what drives these people."

Ali Ajik leaned on an elbow.

"The origins of the Turkish people lie in the steppes of Central Asia. Our ancestors had slanted eyes and lived in the same regions as the Mongols. To take an example, the Huns were Turks. These nomads crossed all of Central Asia before reaching Anatolia in about the tenth century of the Christian era."

"But what's the Turan?"

"A primordial empire, which is supposed to have existed long ago, uniting all of Central Asia's Turkish speakers. A sort of Atlantis, which historians often mention, but without offering any real proof of its existence. The Grey Wolves dream of this lost continent. Their hope is to unite the Uzbeks, the Tatars, the Uigurs, the Turkmen and thus form a mighty empire stretching from the Balkans to Baikal."

"Is that feasible?"

"No, of course not. But there is a hint of reality in such a fantasy. Today, nationalists are promoting economic alliances, a sharing of natural resources between the Turkish-speaking peoples. Such as oil."

Paul remembered those men with slanting eyes and embroidered coats at the funeral of Türkes. He had been right: the world of the Grey Wolves was a state within a state. An underground nation, beyond the laws and boundaries of other countries. He took out the photos of the funeral. His Buddha position was starting to give him cramp.

"Do these pictures mean anything to you?"

Ajik picked up the first one, and murmured: "Türkes's burial . . . I wasn't in Istanbul at the time."

"Do you recognise any important people?"

"But the entire ruling class was there! Members of the government. Representatives of right-wing parties. Candidates for Türkes's succession . . ."

"Are there any active Grey Wolves? I mean, known villains?"

The diplomat looked through the snaps. He seemed more ill at ease, as though the very sight of these men raised an ancient terror in him. He pointed: "This one. Oral Celik."

"Who's he?"

"The accomplice of Ali Agça. One of the two men who tried to assassinate the Pope in 1981."

"And he's at large?"

"That's Turkey for you. Don't forget the close links between the Grey Wolves and the police. Or how corrupt our judicial system is . . ."

"Do you recognise any others?"

Ajik appeared more reticent.

"I'm no specialist."

"I'm talking about celebrities. Heads of the families."

"Babas, you mean?"

Paul made a mental note of the term, which was presumably the Turkish equivalent of "godfather". Ajik spent some time on each photo.

"Some faces ring a bell," he said at last, "but I can't put a name to them. People who appeared regularly in the press, during trials for gun-running, kidnapping, illegal casinos . . ."

Paul took a felt-tip pen from his pocket.

"Put a ring round each face you recognise. And jot the name down beside, if it comes back to you."

The Turk drew several circles, but wrote no names. Suddenly, he stopped.

"This one's a real star. A national figure."

He pointed at a large man, aged about seventy, who was walking with a stick. His high forehead, grey hair brushed back and jutting jaw gave him the profile of a stag. He oozed power.

"His name's Ismail Kudseyi. He's undoubtedly the most powerful *büyük-baba* in Istanbul. I read an article about him recently . . . Apparently, he's still in business today. One of Turkey's major drug runners. Photos of him are a rarity. It's said that he had the eyes torn out of a photographer who had managed to take a surreptitious series of portraits of him."

"And his criminal activities are well known?"

Ajik burst out laughing.

"Of course! In Istanbul, people say that all Kudseyi has to fear is an earthquake."

"And is he linked to the Grey Wolves?"

"In a big way. He's one of their historic leaders. Most of today's police officers were trained in his camps. He's also famous as a philanthropist. His foundation provides grants for underprivileged children. All this with a background of fervent patriotism."

Paul noticed a detail.

"What's he got on his hands?"

"Scars caused by acid. It's said that he started out as a hit man in the 1960s. He used to get rid of his victims in caustic soda. Another rumour."

Paul felt a strange tingling in his veins. Such a man could well have ordered the execution of Sema Gökalp. But why? And why him rather than the next man in the procession? How could he run an investigation at a distance of over a thousand miles?

He looked at the other ringed faces. Harsh rigid stares, moustaches whitened by the snow . . .

He could not help feeling a certain respect for these lords of crime. Among them, he noticed a young man with a thick head of hair.

"And him?"

"The new generation. He's Azer Akarsa. One of Kudseyi's protégés. Thanks to the backing of his foundation, this young peasant has become a big businessman. He's made a fortune on the fruit market. Today, Akarsa owns huge orchards in his native region, near Gaziantep. And he isn't even forty yet. A real young Turk in every sense of the term."

The name Gaziantep set off a spark in Paul's mind. All of the victims came from that area. Was it just a coincidence? He gazed at the young man in his corduroy jacket, done up to the neck. He looked less like a business prodigy and more like a dreamy, Bohemian student.

"And is he in politics too?"

Ajik nodded in confirmation.

"A modern leader. He has set up his own clubs. Their members listen to rap, talk about Europe, drink alcohol. It all seems very liberal."

"So he's a moderate, then?"

"Only in appearance. In my opinion, Akarsa is a pure fanatic. Maybe the worst of them all. He believes in a radical return to the roots. He's obsessed by Turkey's prestigious past. He, too, has his own foundation, which finances archaeological work."

Paul thought of those ancient masks, faces carved like stone. But it was not a lead. Nor even a theory. It was a crazy idea totally lacking in support.

"Any criminal activities?" he asked.

"No, I don't think so. Akarsa doesn't need any money. And I'm sure that he looks down on those Grey Wolves who have compromised themselves with the mafia. To his mind, they are unworthy of the 'cause.'"

Paul glanced at his watch. Nine thirty. He still had plenty of time to see a few more surgeons. He put away the photos and got to his feet.

"Thanks, Ali. I'm sure all this information's going to be useful, one way or another."

The man showed him out. In the doorway, he asked: "You still haven't answered my question. Do the Grey Wolves have anything to do with that series of murders?"

"Yes, there is a possibility that they're involved."

"But . . . how?"

"I can't tell you."

"Do you . . . do you think they're in Paris?"

Without answering, Paul walked down the corridor. He stopped by the stairs.

"One last thing, Ali. Why are they called the Grey Wolves?"

"Because of our foundation myth."

"What myth?"

"It's said that, a long time ago, the Turks were a mere starving horde, wandering homelessly in the heartlands of Central Asia. When they were on their last legs, some wolves fed them and protected them. Grey wolves, who gave birth to the real Turkish people."

Paul noticed that he was gripping the rail so tightly that his knuckles were white. He pictured a pack roaring across the infinite steppes, mingling with the grey gleam of the sun. Ajik concluded: "They protect the Turkish race, Captain. They are the guardians of our origins, of our initial purity. Some of them even think that they're the distant descendants of a white she-wolf, called Asena. I hope you're wrong, and that these people aren't in Paris. Because they're not ordinary criminals. They're unlike anything or anybody you've ever seen before."

CHAPTER 60

Paul was getting into his Golf when his phone rang.

"Maybe I've found something, Captain."

It was Naubrel.

"What?"

"I questioned a heating engineer, and I discovered that they use pressure chambers in a field we haven't explored yet."

His head was still full of wolves and steppes. He could not really see what the officer was talking about. He asked: "What field do you mean?"

"The preservation of food. It's a Japanese technique that's just been adopted. Instead of heating products, you put them under high pressure. It's more expensive, but it means you conserve their vitamins and . . ."

"For Christ's sake get to the point. Have you got a lead or not?"

Naubrel's voice darkened.

"In the Paris region, there are several factories which use this method. Suppliers of luxury goods, like organic food or stuff for up-market delis. There's a site which looks particularly interesting, in the Bièvre valley."

"Why?"

"It belongs to a Turkish company."

Paul felt the roots of his hair tingle.

"What's its name?"

"Matak Limited."

Two syllables that obviously meant nothing to him.

"What sort of things do they produce?"

"Fruit juices and luxury jams. According to my information, it's more of a laboratory than an industrial site. It's a pilot project."

The tingling turned into electric waves. Azer Akarsa, the nationalist golden boy, had made his money from fruit trees. Could the country lad from Gaziantep have a connection here?

Paul's voice rose.

"Right. So now you're going to give the place a visit."

"Now?"

"When do you think? I want you to search through their pressurised chambers with a fine-tooth comb. But watch out. No question of having a warrant, or flashing your police card."

"So how do you expect me to . . . ?"

"Find something. I also want you to identify the Turkish owners of the factory."

"But that must be a holding, or some private company!"

"Ask the managers at the plant. Then contact the French Chamber of Commerce. The Turkish one too, if necessary. I want a list of the main shareholders."

Naubrel apparently guessed that his boss had a precise idea in mind.

"What are we after?"

"Maybe a name. Azer Akarsa."

"Jesus, these names . . . Can you spell that?"

Paul did so. He was about to hang up when the officer asked: "Have you been listening to your radio?"

"Why?"

"Last night, a body was found in Père-Lachaise. It's been mutilated."

A stab of ice in his side.

"A woman?"

"No. A man. A cop who used to work in the tenth. Jean-Louis Schiffer. He specialised in Turks and . . ."

The major damage caused by a bullet in a human body is not made by the bullet itself, but by its wake, creating a disastrous vacuum, the trail of a comet through the flesh, tissue and bone.

In the same way, Paul felt these words rip through him, amplifying inside him, drawing out a line of pain that made him scream. But he did not hear his own cry, because he had already placed his flashing light on the roof and turned on the siren.

CHAPTER 61

They were all there.

He could rank them by their clothes. The bigwigs from place Beauvau, in black coats and shiny shoes, wearing mourning like a second skin. The commissioners and brigade chiefs, in camouflage green or autumnal hound's tooth, like lurking huntsmen. The inspectors in leather jackets and red armbands, looking like pimps recruited for a militia. Most of them, whatever their rank or duties, had a moustache. It was a sign of unity. A label that transcended their differences. As inevitable as the official stamps on their cards.

Paul went past the row of vans and patrol cars, with their silently turning lights, at the foot of the columbarium. Then he discreetly slipped under the security cordon which blocked the entrance to the buildings.

Once inside, he turned left beneath the arcades and leaned back against a pillar. He had no time to admire the place – the long galleries whose walls were covered by names and flowers, that atmosphere of holy respect, hovering above the marble, where the memory of the dead drifted like a mist above the waters. He concentrated on the group of officers standing in the gardens, in the hope of spotting some familiar faces.

The first one he saw was Philippe Charlier. Draped in his loden coat, the Green Giant more than ever lived up to his nickname. Beside him, there was Christophe Beauvanier, in his baseball cap and leather jacket. The two officers Schiffer had quizzed last night, who seemed to have dashed there like jackals to check if his corpse really was cold. A little further on, Paul made out Jean-Pierre Guichard, the Public Prosecutor, Claude Monestier, the chief commissioner at Louis-Blanc, and also Thierry Bomarzo, the magistrate, one of the few people present who knew what part Schiffer had played in this fuck-up. Paul realised what this scene meant for him: his career was finished.

But the most amazing thing was the presence of Morencko, the head of OCRTIS, and of Pollet, chief of the Drug Squad. This was all rather excessive for the death of an ordinary retired inspector. It made Paul think of a bomb, whose true power is revealed only after it has exploded.

He approached, still covered by the pillars. His head should have been teeming with questions. Instead, what struck him was the way this procession of dark figures, beneath the arches of the sanctuary, looked strangely like the funeral of Alpaslan Türkes. There was the same ceremony, same solemnity, same moustaches. In his own way, Jean-Louis Schiffer had also managed to get a state funeral.

He noticed an ambulance at the far end of the lawn, parked beside an underground entrance. Some male nurses in white coats were smoking cigarettes and talking with some uniformed officers. They were presumably waiting for forensics to have finished their job so that they could take the body away. That meant Schiffer was still inside.

Paul left his hiding place and headed for the entrance, sheltered by the privet hedges. He was going down the stairs when a voice hailed him:

"Oi! You can't go down there!"

He turned round and brandished his card. The orderly froze, almost standing to attention. Without a word, Paul abandoned him to his surprise and went down as far as the cast-iron gate.

At first, it felt as if he was entering the maze of a mine, with its tunnels and landings. Then his eyes got used to the darkness and he made out the nature of the place. White and black alleyways punctuated with thousands of niches, names, wreathes suspended in glass cases. A troglodyte city dug out of the rock.

He leaned over a shaft that revealed the lower floors. A white halo was shining up from the second level down: the men from the forensic department were there. He found another staircase and took it. As he approached the light, the atmosphere seemed to get even darker and heavier. A peculiar smell of something dry, sharp and stony itched into his nose.

When he reached the floor, he turned right. He was now following the smell more than the light source. At the first turning he saw some technicians dressed in white overalls, their heads covered by paper hats. They had set up their base camp at the intersection of several galleries. Their chrome-plated cases, lying on plastic sheets, were open to reveal test-tubes, phials and sprays . . . Paul approached silently – the two figures had their backs to him.

He did not need to force a cough. The space was saturated with dust. The cosmonauts turned round. They were wearing masks shaped like an inverted Y. Once again, Paul flashed his card. One of them shook its insect-like head, while raising its gloved hands.

A muffled voice was heard – impossible to tell which one was speaking.

"Sorry, but we've started looking for fingerprints."

"Just a second. He was my partner. Jesus, you can understand that, can't you?"

The two Ys looked at each other. A few seconds passed. One of the technicians then grabbed a mask from his case.

"Third row," he said. "Follow the projectors. And stay on the planks. Not a single step on the floor."

Ignoring the mask, Paul set off. The man stopped him.

"Take it. You won't be able to breathe."

Paul cursed as he slipped the white shell over his head. He went along the first alley on the left, across the raised planks, stepping over the cables of the projectors that had been set up at each intersection. The walls seemed never-ending, repeating a litany of niches and commemorative inscriptions, while the air particles gained in density.

Finally, after a last turning, he understood the reason for such precautions.

Beneath the halogen lights everything was grey: the floor, walls and ceiling. The ashes of the dead had escaped from their urns, which had been blown apart by bullets. Dozens of them had rolled onto the ground, mingling their contents with the plaster and rubble.

On the walls, Paul managed to identify impacts coming from two different guns – a large calibre, like a shotgun, and a small semi-automatic pistol, probably a 9 or 45 mm.

He went on, fascinated by this lunar scene. He had seen photos of towns in the Philippines that had been shrouded over after a volcanic eruption. Their streets frozen by the cooling lava. Haggard survivors, with faces like statues, carrying stone children in their arms. The same picture was now in front of him.

He crossed another yellow band then, suddenly, at the end of a row, he saw him.

Schiffer had lived like a dog.

Now he had died like a dog – in a final burst of violence.

His totally grey body was arched up, side-on, with one leg bent back beneath his raincoat, his right hand raised, curled up like a cockerel's foot. Behind, a pool of blood ran out of what was left of his skull, as though one of his darkest dreams had exploded in his brains.

But the worst part was his face. The cinders covering him did not quite conceal the horror of the wounds. An eyeball had been torn out – excised more like, with all of its socket. Lacerations dug into his throat, forehead and cheeks. One of them, which was longer and deeper, revealed the jaw bone then rose up to the torn socket. It drew his mouth out into a ghastly grin, overflowing with silvery pink slime.

Doubled up with a sudden fit of nausea, Paul pulled off his mask. But his guts were totally empty. In his convulsions, the only questions that came to mind were the obvious ones: why had Schiffer come to this place? Who had killed him? Who could have attained such a degree of barbarity?

At that moment, he dropped to the ground and burst into tears. Within seconds, they were running down his cheeks, with him not even thinking of trying to hold them back, or wipe away the mud that was building up on his face.

He was not crying for Schiffer.

Nor was he crying for the murdered women.

He was crying for himself.

For his loneliness and the blind alley he was now in.

"It's time we had a word, no?"

Paul turned round at once.

A man he had never seen before, in glasses, without a mask, and whose long dust-covered face looked like a stalactite, was smiling at him.

CHAPTER 62

"So it was you who put Schiffer back into circulation, was it?"

The voice was clear, strong, almost merry, matching the blueness of the sky.

Paul shook the ash from his parka and sniffed – he had recovered a semblance of composure.

"That's right. I needed some advice."

"What sort of advice?"

"I'm working on a series of murders, in the Turkish quarter in Paris."

"Was your idea approved by your superiors?"

"You know the answer to that already."

The bespectacled man nodded. He was not just tall. His entire bearing seemed to surge up, with his haughty head, raised chin, and high brows set off by grey curls. A top investigator in the prime of life, with the prying look of a greyhound.

Paul probed a little: "Is this an internal investigation?"

"No, I'm Olivier Amien. From the Geopolitical Drugs Observatory."

Paul had often heard this name during his time at OCRTIS. Amien was supposed to be the king of France's anti-drug war. A man in charge of both the national and international squads.

They turned their backs on the columbarium and headed down an alleyway, which was reminiscent of a paved nineteenth-century side road. Paul saw some grave-diggers smoking cigarettes, leaning on a tomb. They were presumably discussing that morning's incredible find.

In a voice laden with innuendo, Amien went on: "You worked for some time on the drug squad, I believe . . ."

"Yes, for a few years."

"In what field?"

"Petty dealers. Cannabis mostly. The North African networks."

"You never had anything to do with the Golden Crescent?"

Paul wiped his nose with the back of his hand.

"If you got straight to the point, then we'd both save a lot of time . . ."

Amien beamed.

"I hope you don't mind if I give you a little lesson in modern history . . ."

Paul thought of all the names and dates he had absorbed so far that day.

"Go on. I'm making up for lost time."

The top cop pushed his glasses up his nose and began: "I suppose you remember the Taliban? Since September 11th, you can't escape from fundamentalists. The media has been full of stories about their lives and works . . . blowing up the Buddhas, their hospitality for Bin Laden, and their despicable attitude to women, to culture and to any form of tolerance. But there's one side of them which is less well known, and which was the only good point about their regime. Those monsters fought effectively against the production of opium. In their very first year in power, they practically eradicated poppy growing in Afghanistan. From three thousand three hundred tons of opium-based products in 2000, the total fell to just one hundred and eighty five tons in 2001. In their eyes, such activities are contrary to the Qur'an . . . But of course, as soon as Mullah Omar was deposed, cultivation started up all over again. Even as we speak, the peasants of Ningarhar are watching the flowers bloom on plants they sowed last November. They'll soon start harvesting, at the end of April."

Paul's attention came and went, as though carried on an inner tide. His tears had softened his feelings. He was in a hyper-sensitive state, liable to burst into laughter or start sobbing again at the slightest thing.

"But before the attacks of September 11th," Amien went on, "no one expected their regime to fall so soon. So the drug smugglers were already looking for new suppliers. In particular, the Turkish *büyük-babas*, the 'grandfathers' in charge of exporting heroin to Europe, had made contact with other producers such as Uzbekistan and Tadjikistan. I don't know if you're aware of the fact, but such countries have the same linguistic roots."

Paul sniffed again.

"Yes, I'm starting to be aware now."

Amien nodded curtly.

"In the past, the Turks had always bought their opium from Afghanistan and Pakistan. They had the morphine refined in Iran, then produced the heroin in their laboratories in Anatolia. With their Turkic cousins, they had to change their methods. They refined the gum in the Caucasus, then produced their powder in the far east of Anatolia. It took some time to set up these new networks and, so far as we know, it was still a makeshift job as late as last year. Then, in the winter of 2000–2001, we heard talk of a possible alliance. A triangular agreement between the Uzbek mafia, who control vast fields of production, the Russian clans, who are the heirs of the Red Army, which for years supervised the routes through the Caucasus and the refineries in that region, and the Turkish families who would then produce the actual heroin. But we had no names, no facts, just some interesting details suggesting that a high-level allegiance was being prepared."

They were now in a darker part of the cemetery. Black vaults, side by side, with grim doors and sloping roofs. It was like a mining village crouching under a coal-black sky.

Amien clicked his tongue before continuing: "These three criminal groups decided to inaugurate their joint venture with a pilot consignment. A small quantity of dope which would be exported as a test and stand as a symbol. It would be an open door on the future . . . For this special occasion, each partner wanted to display their particular abilities. The Uzbeks supplied a top-quality gum. The Russians called in their best chemists to refine the base-morphine and, at the other end of the line, the Turks produced some practically pure heroin. A special Number Four. Nectar. We suppose that they also dealt with exporting the dope and transferring it to Europe. They had to prove their reliability in this field. They were now up against considerable competition from the Albanians and Kosovans, who had become masters of the routes through the Balkans."

Paul did not see what this story had to do with him.

"All this occurred at the end of the winter of 2001. We were expecting to see this famous consignment arrive at our frontier in the spring. It was a unique opportunity to nip this new network in the bud . . ."

Paul gazed round at the tombs. This time it was a bright area, sculpted and varied as a music made of stone that was whispering in his ears.

"As early as the month of March, the customs men in Germany, France and Holland went on high alert. The ports, airports and border roads were watched round the clock. In each of our countries, members of the Turkish communities were questioned. We shook up our informers, bugged dealers' phones . . . By the end of May, we still hadn't found anything. Not a single clue or piece of information. In France, we started to get worried. So we decided to dig a little deeper into the Turkish community. To call in a specialist. A man who knew the Anatolian networks like the back of his hand, and who could become a real mine-sweeper."

These last words dragged Paul back to reality. He now grasped the connection between the two cases.

"Jean-Louis Schiffer," he said without thinking.

"Exactly. The Cipher. Or Mister Steel. As you prefer."

"But he was retired."

"So we had to ask him to re-enlist."

Everything fell into place. The cover-up of April 2001. The Paris appeal court dropping charges against Schiffer for the murder of Gazil Hemet. Paul deduced, out loud: "Jean-Louis Schiffer did a deal. He insisted that you drop the Hemet affair."

"I can see that you know this business well."

"I'm part of it myself. And I'm beginning to see how deals are done in the police. The life of a little dealer isn't worth shit compared to the ambitions of a big boss."

"You're forgetting our main motivation: to stop a huge network from being set up, to destroy . . ."

"Stop. I know the music already."

Amien raised his long hands, as though giving up any argument on the subject.

"In any case, our problem was quite different."

"What do you mean?"

"Schiffer doublecrossed us. When he found out which clan was involved in the alliance, and how the convoy was being sent, he didn't tell us. We think he offered his services to the cartel. He must have suggested taking charge of the dope in Paris and then distributing it around the best dealers. Who better than him knew the drug scene in France?"

Amien smiled cynically.

"Our intuition failed us in this case. What we wanted was Mister Steel. What we got was the Cipher . . . We gave him the chance to pull off the stunt that he'd been waiting for for years. This business would be his crowning triumph."

Paul remained silent. He tried to put the pieces of the puzzle together, but there were too many gaps. After a minute, he asked: "If Schiffer had rounded off his career with a caper like that, what was he doing rotting away in the Longères home?"

"It was because, once more, nothing went to plan."

"Meaning?"

"The runner sent by the Turks never showed up. In the end, it was he who tricked everyone by making off with the consignment. Schiffer must have been scared that they'd suspect him. So he decided to lie low by locking himself away in Longères until things blew over. Even a man like him feared the Turks. You can imagine the fate in store for traitors . . ."

Another memory: the Cipher hiding under an assumed name in Longères, his hunted look in the home . . . Yes, he was afraid of the reprisals of the Turkish clans. The pieces were coming together, but Paul was still unconvinced. The overall pattern seemed too weak, too vague.

"That's just a load of guesswork," he replied. "You haven't got the slightest proof. To begin with, why are you so sure that this dope never arrived in Europe?"

"There are two points which make that clear. First off, heroin of that quality would have made its mark on the market. There would have been an upsurge in overdoses, for instance. And that didn't happen."

"And the second point?"

"We found the dope."

"When?"

"Today," Amien glanced over his shoulder. "In the columbarium."

"Here?"

"If you'd gone a little further into the crypt, you'd have seen it for yourself, scattered among the ashes of the dead. It must have been stashed in one of the niches that were blown apart during the shoot-out. It's unusable now," he smiled again. "I must admit that the symbolism is rather powerful – white death ending up among the grey dead . . . It was that heroin which Schiffer came to fetch last night. It was his investigations that led him to it."

"What investigations?"

"Yours."

The wires still refused to make their connection. Paul mumbled: "I don't get it."

"But it's perfectly obvious. For some months, we have been thinking that the runner used by the Turks was a woman. In Turkey, women can become doctors, engineers and ministers. So why not drug smugglers?"

This time, the connection clicked into place. Sema Gökalp. Anna Heymes. The woman with two faces. The Turkish mafia had sent its Wolves to track down the girl who had betrayed them.

The target was the runner.

A thought flashed across Paul's mind. That night, Schiffer had jumped Sema just as she was picking up her stash.

There had been a fight.

There had been a murder.

And the prey was still on the run . . .

Olivier Amien was no longer in a laughing mood.

"Your investigations interest us, Nerteaux. We have established a link between the three victims in your case, and the woman we're looking for. The heads of the Turkish cartel have sent over their hit men to smoke her out, and so far they've failed. Where is she, Nerteaux? Have you got the slightest idea where to find her?"

Paul did not reply. He was mentally going back along the track that had passed right under his nose. The Grey Wolves were torturing women in their search for some dope. Schiffer, with his usual flair, gradually sniffing out that they were looking for the very person who had doublecrossed him by making off with the precious load . . . Suddenly, he made up his mind. Without a word of introduction, he told Olivier Amien the whole story. The kidnapping of Zeynep Tütengil in November 2001. The discovery of Sema Gökalp in the baths. The intervention of Philippe Charlier and the brainwashing. The programme of mental conditioning. The creation of Anna Heymes. Her escape and rediscovery of her own story as she gradually got her memory back . . . until she became a drug runner once more and returned to the cemetery.

When Paul fell silent, the officer looked completely baffled. After a long pause, he asked: "That's why Charlier's here?"

"Beauvanier, too. They're up to their ears in this story. They wanted to see for themselves that Schiffer's really dead. But there's still Anna Heymes. And Charlier has to find her before she talks. He'll eliminate her as soon as he locates her. You're coursing the same hare."

Amien stood in front of Paul and froze. His expression was as hard as stone.

"I'll deal with Charlier. What have you got to localise the woman?"

Paul looked at the tombs around them. An ancient portrait in an oval frame. A placid Virgin, head leaning to one side, draped in a languid cape. A silent Christ, in a bronze-like mood . . . There must be one salient detail in all this, but which one?

Amien grabbed his arm.

"Have you got a lead? Schiffer's death is going to land on your plate. Your career in the police is over. Unless we lay our hands on the girl and the whole affair is made public. With you as the hero. So I'll ask again. Have you got a lead?"

"I want to continue the investigation myself," Paul declared.

"Give me the information, then we'll see."

"I want your word."

Amien lost his patience.

"Out with it!"

Paul stared round one more time at the monuments: Mary's eroded face, Jesus's long features, the cameo with its sepia tint . . . At last he caught on. Faces. That was the only lead he had on her.

"She's altered her appearance," he murmured. "By plastic surgery. I have a list of ten surgeons capable of performing such an operation in Paris. I've already seen three of them. Give me one day to question the others."

Amien was clearly disappointed.

"And . . . and that's all you've got?"

Paul thought of the fruit conserve plant and his vague suspicions about Azer Akarsa. But if that bastard was involved in the murders, he wanted him just for himself.

"Yes," he lied. "That's all. But it's far from nothing. Schiffer was convinced that the surgeon would help us find her. Let me prove to you that he was right."

Amien clenched his jaw. He now looked like a predator. He pointed at a gate behind Paul's back.

"Alexandre-Dumas métro station is just there. Now vanish. I'll give you till noon to find her."

Paul realised that the officer had led him here intentionally. That he had always intended to suggest this sort of deal. He slipped a visiting card into his pocket.

"My mobile number. Find her, Nerteaux. It's your only chance. Otherwise, in a few hours' time, you'll be the target."

CHAPTER 63

Paul did not take the métro. No self-respecting policeman takes the métro.

He sprinted as far as place Gambetta, past the cemetery wall, until he found his car in rue Emile-Landrin. He grabbed his old map of Paris, which was still stained with blood, and re-read the list of remaining medics.

Seven surgeons.

Spread out in four parts of Paris and in two suburban towns.

He marked their addresses with circles on his map, and worked out the quickest itinerary from one to the other, starting from the twentieth *arrondissement*.

When he was sure which route to take, he placed his flashing light on the roof and put his foot down, concentrating on the first name.

Dr Jérôme Chéret.

18 rue du Rocher, in the eighth *arrondissement*.

He headed due west, going up boulevard Rochechouart, then boulevard de Clichy. He took the protected bus lanes, lapping up the cycle routes and gliding up on to the pavements. He even took two one-way streets in the wrong direction.

When he had reached boulevard des Batignolles, he slowed down and called up Naubrel.

"Where are you at?"

"I'm on my way out of Matak Limited. I managed to wangle my way in with the Hygiene Department. A surprise inspection."

"And?"

"An immaculately white, clean plant. A real laboratory. I saw the high-pressure chamber. It's spotless. Nothing to be hoped for in that direction. I also spoke to the engineers . . ."

Paul had imagined a half-abandoned industrial site, full of rust, where somebody's screams would never have been heard. But suddenly, the idea of a spick-and-span lab seemed even more appropriate.

"Did you speak to the manager?"

"Yeah. Discreetly. He's French. Sounded squeaky clean to me."

"And further up? Have you identified the Turkish owners?"

"The site belongs to a public company called YALIN AS, which is in turn part of a holding group registered in Ankara. I've contacted the Chamber of Commerce and . . ."

"Hurry up. Pinpoint the shareholders. And don't forget the name of Azer Akarsa."

He hung up and looked at his watch. Twenty minutes since he had left the cemetery.

At Villiers crossroads, he swerved rapidly left into rue du Rocher. He turned off the siren and lights, to arrive in a more discreet fashion.

At 11.20 he rang at Jérôme Chéret's door. He was invited to go through a side entrance, so as not to scare the clientele. The surgeon received him in the hush of an antechamber, leading to the operating theatre.

"Just a quick glance," Paul told him after a few words of explanation.

This time, he showed just two documents: the identikit of Sema and Anna's new face.

"She's the same woman?" the surgeon said in admiration. "Lovely work."

"Do you know her or not?"

"Neither one, nor the other. Sorry."

Paul ran down the stairs across the red carpets, past the white plaster mouldings. A cross on his map, and off he went.

It was 11.40.

Dr Thierry Dewaele.

22 rue de Phalsbourg, seventeenth *arrondissement*.

Same kind of building, same questions, same answers.

At 12.15, he was turning the ignition key, when his phone rang in his pocket. A message from Matkowska. He had called during his brief interview with the doctor. The signal had failed to penetrate behind those thick, swanky walls. He phoned back at once.

"I've got something new about those ancient sculptures," Matkowska said. "There's an archaeological site which contains giant heads. I've got some photos of them. These statues have fissures . . . just like the mutilations . . ."

Paul closed his eyes. He did not know what thrilled him the most: getting close to a crazy murderer, or having been correct right from the start.

Matkowska went on, in a trembling voice: "They're the heads of half-Greek, half-Persian gods, that go back to the beginning of the Christian era. The sanctuary of a king, at the top of a mountain, in eastern Turkey . . ."

"Where exactly?"

"In the south-east. Near the border with Syria."

"Give me the names of the main towns."

"Hang on."

He heard the sound of pages turning, and muffled curses. He looked at his hands. They were not shaking. He felt ready, wrapped up in a casing of ice.

"There we are. There's a map. The Nimrud Dağ site is near Adiyaman and Gaziantep."

Gaziantep. Another lead pointing towards Azer Akarsa. *He owns huge orchards in his native region, near Gaziantep*, Ali Ajik had said. Were these orchards at the foot of the mountain where the statues were found? Had Azer Akarsa grown up in the shadow of those colossal heads?

Paul went back to the crux of the matter. He needed to hear confirmation for himself.

"And these heads really look like the victims' faces?"

"It's amazing, Captain. The same cracks, the same mutilations. There's one statue, of a fertility goddess called Commagene, which is identical to the third victim. No nose, the chin rubbed down . . . I've superimposed the two pictures. They're identical down to the last detail. I don't know what it all means, but it really puts the shits up you, I . . ."

Paul knew by experience that, after long inquiries, the vital clues could sometimes fall together in the space of a few hours. He could hear Ajik's voice once more: *He's obsessed by Turkey's prestigious past. He, too, has his own foundation, which finances archaeological work.*

Was this golden boy financing restoration work on this very site? Did these ancestral faces fascinate him for some personal reason?

Paul paused, breathed deeply, then asked himself the vital question: was Azer Akarsa the main killer? The leader of the commando? Could his passion for ancient stone go as far as to express itself in acts of torture and mutilation? It was too early to go any further. Paul closed his mind to this theory and ordered: "Concentrate on these monuments. Try to find out if there's been any recent restoration work. And if so, who's financing it."

"Do you have an idea?"

"Maybe a foundation, but I don't know what it's called. If you find one, look at the names of its organisers and its main financiers. Look out for a certain Azer Akarsa."

Once again, he spelled the name. Sparks of fire now seemed to be bursting out between these letters, like shards of flint.

"Is that all?" the officer asked.

"No," Paul said breathlessly. "Also check up the visas given to Turkish nationals since last November. See if Akarsa was one of them."

"But that'll take hours!"

"No it won't. Everything's computerised. I've already put someone on the visa lead at the Immigration Office. Contact him and give him the name. And be quick about it."

"But . . ."

"Move it."

CHAPTER 64

Didier Laferrière.

12 rue Boissy-d'Anglas, eighth *arrondissement.*

When he walked through the door, Paul had a feeling – a cop's hunch, an almost paranormal sensation. There was something for him here.

The surgery was plunged in darkness. The doctor, a little man with grey frizzy hair, was sitting behind his desk. In a neutral voice, he asked: "The police is it? What can I do for you?"

Paul explained the situation and produced his photos. The medic seemed to shrink even further. He switched on his desk light and leaned over the pictures.

Without a moment's hesitation, he pointed at the portrait of Anna Heymes and said: "I haven't operated on her, but I know this woman."

Paul clenched his fists. Sweet Jesus, he had hit lucky.

"She came to see me a few days ago," the surgeon went on.

"Can you be more precise?"

"Last Monday. If you want, I can check my diary . . ."

"What did she want?"

"She behaved rather oddly."

"In what way?" The surgeon shook his head.

"She asked me a series of questions about the scars left by certain operations."

"What's so odd about that?"

"Nothing. It's just . . . Either she was play-acting, or she's suffering from amnesia."

"Why?"

The doctor tapped his finger on the portrait of Anna Heymes.

"Because she has *already* had surgery. At the end of the consultation, I noticed her scars. I have no idea what she wanted from me. Maybe she was thinking of suing the person who operated on her," he looked at the picture. "But whoever it was did a splendid job."

Another mark for Schiffer. *In my opinion, she must be investigating her own past.*

And that was exactly what had happened. Anna Heymes was tracking

Sema Gökalp. Paul was drenched in sweat. It felt as though he was walking a path of fire. The target was there, in front of him, at hand's reach.

"Is that all she said?" he asked. "She didn't leave an address, a phone number?"

"No. She just said *I'm going to have to see for myself*. I've no idea what she meant. Who on earth is this woman?"

Without a word, Paul stood up. He grabbed a wad of Post-Its from the desk and wrote down his mobile number.

"If she ever gets back in touch with you, do your best to locate her. Talk to her about her operation. About possible side-effects. Make something up. Just pinpoint her then call me. OK?"

"Are you sure you're all right?"

Paul stopped, his fist on the door handle.

"Why's that?"

"I don't know. You're all red."

CHAPTER 65

Pierre Laroque.
    24 rue Maspero, sixteenth *arrondissement*.
    Nothing.

Jean-François Skenderi.
    Clinique Massener, 58 avenue Paul-Doumer, sixteenth *arrondissement*.
    Nothing.

At two o'clock, Paul was crossing the Seine once more.

Towards the Left Bank.

He had stopped using his flashing light and siren – too much of a headache – and was looking for some snatches of peace among the faces of the pedestrians, the colours of the shop fronts and the gleam of sunlight. He was amazed by all these city dwellers living out a normal day, amid a normal existence.

He called his lieutenants several times. Naubrel was still battling it out with the Chamber of Commerce in Ankara, while Matkowska was trawling through the museums, archaeological institutes, tourist offices and even UNESCO in search of the bodies which were funding work at Nimrud Dağ. At the same time, he was keeping an eye on the list of visas which the search progamme had thrown up, but Akarsa's name stubbornly refused to appear.

Paul was sweltering inside his own body. Fiery rashes were burning his face. A migraine was pulsating down into the nape of his neck. His heart beats had grown so loud he could count them. He needed to stop at a chemist's, but he kept putting that off until after the next crossroads.

Bruno Simonnet.

139 avenue de Ségur, seventh *arrondissement*.

Nothing.

The surgeon was a huge man, holding a bulky tom cat in his arms. Seeing them together like that, in perfect harmony, it was impossible to say who was stroking whom. Paul was putting away his pictures when the doctor remarked: "You're not the first person to show me that face."

"Which one?" Paul started.

"This one."

Simonnet pointed at the identikit portrait of Sema Gökalp.

"Who showed it to you? A policeman?"

He nodded, his fingers still tickling his cat's neck. Paul thought of Schiffer.

"Was he middle-aged, tough looking, with silvery hair?"

"No. He was young. With scruffy hair. Like a student. He had a slight accent."

Paul took each blow like a boxer on the ropes. He had to lean against the marble mantelpiece.

"Was his accent Turkish?"

"How should I know? But oriental, probably, yes."

"When did he come?"

"Yesterday morning."

"What name did he give?"

"He didn't."

"Any means of contact?"

"No. Which was strange. In the films you always leave your calling card, don't you?"

"I'll be back."

Paul ran to his car. He grabbed one of the photos of Türkeş's funeral in which Akarsa could be seen. When he returned, he asked: "Can you see the same man in this picture?"

The surgeon pointed at the man in the corduroy jacket.

"That's him. No doubt about it."

He looked up.

"So he's not one of your colleagues?"

Paul fished up a few scraps of cool from the depths of his soul and showed him the portrait of the red-head once again.

"You told me that he asked you to identify this woman. Was it the same picture? An identikit like this one?"

"No. It was a black-and-white photo. Of a group, in fact. On a university campus, or something like that. The quality was rather poor, but she's the same woman as in your picture, I'm sure about that."

The image of Sema Gökalp, young and valiant, amid other Turkish students, flashed before his eyes.

The only photo the Grey Wolves had.

A blurred image that had cost the lives of three innocent women.

Paul drove off leaving tyre marks on the asphalt.

He put his flashing light back on the roof and switched it on. Its gleam and the siren pierced through this bell-jar of a day.

Deductions poured through his mind.

His heart beat in unison.

The Grey Wolves were now following the same lead as he was. After three corpses, they had understood their mistake. They were now looking for the surgeon who had transformed their target.

Another posthumous victory for Schiffer.

We're going to end up on the same track. I can just feel it.

Paul looked at his watch. Two thirty.

And only two names left on his list.

He had to get to the surgeon before the killers did.

He had to find the woman before they did.

Paul Nerteaux versus Azer Akarsa.

The son of nobody versus the son of Asena, the White Wolf.

CHAPTER 66

Frédéric Gruss lived in the heights of Saint-Cloud. While Paul was driving along the fast lane towards the Bois de Boulogne, he phoned Naubrel once more.

"Still nothing from the Turks?"

"Sorry, Captain. I'm . . ."

"Forget it."

"What?"

"Have you still got your copies of the photos of Türkes's funeral?"

"Yes, on my computer."

"There's one where you can see the coffin right in the foreground."

"Just a second. I'll get a pen."

"In that photo, the third person to the left is a young man in a corduroy jacket. I want you to make a blow-up of his portrait and put out a wanted notice in the name of . . ."

"Azer Akarsa?"

"Spot on."

"Is he the killer?"

Paul's throat muscles were so tense, he found it difficult to speak.

"Just put out the notice."

"OK. Is that all?"

"No. Go and see Bomarzo, the magistrate in charge of murder investigations. Ask him for a warrant to search the premises of Matak Limited."

"Me? But it'd be better if it was you who . . ."

"Tell him I sent you. Tell him I've got some hard evidence."

"Evidence?"

"An eye-witness. Then call Matkowska and ask him for the pictures of Nimrud Dağ."

"Of what?"

Once again, he spelled out the name and explained his thinking.

"And check with him if Akarsa's name appears on the list of visa holders. Get all that together then head round to see the magistrate."

"What if he asks me where you are?"

Paul hesitated.

"Then give him this number."

He read out Olivier Amien's mobile number. They can sort this shit out between themselves, he thought as he hung up. Saint-Cloud bridge was in sight.

Three thirty.

Boulevard de la République was quite literally glittering in the sunlight, snaking up the hill that led to Saint-Cloud. A fresh blooming of springtime, already bringing out naked shoulders and languid poses along the café terraces. What a shame. For the final act, Paul would have preferred a sky laden with menace. An apocalyptic firmament, torn by lightning and darkness.

As he drove along the boulevard, he remembered his visit to the morgue with Schiffer. How many centuries had gone by since then?

In the heights of the town, the roads were quiet and empty. The crème de la crème of leafy suburbs. A concentrated dot of vanity and wealth looking down over the Seine valley and the "lower quarters".

Paul shivered with fever, exhaustion and excitement. Brief absences punctuated his vision. Dark stars hit the back of his eyes. He was unable to fight off sleep. It was one of his weaknesses. Something he had never been able to do, even when he was little and petrified, waiting for his father to come home.

His father. The image of the old man was started to meld into that of Schiffer, the lacerations in the car seat with the wounds on that body covered with ash . . .

The sound of a horn woke him up. The light had gone green. He had fallen asleep. In a fury, he pulled off and finally reached rue des Chênes.

He turned down it, looking for number 37. The buildings were invisible, hidden behind stone walls or rows of pine trees. Insects were humming. All of nature seemed drenched with spring sun.

He found a parking space just in front of the right building: a black gate, stuck between whitewashed ramparts.

He was about to ring when he noticed that the gate was ajar. An alarm bell started ringing in his head. This did not fit with the general atmosphere of vigilance in the neighbourhood. Instinctively, Paul pulled back the Velcro strip that was keeping his gun in place.

The garden in the property was a typical one: a strip of lawn, grey trees and a gravel path. At the far end, a huge mansion rose up with white walls and black shutters. A two or three place garage, with a closed swing door, stood next to it. No dog, no servants came to meet him. Apparently, there was not the slightest movement within.

The alarm bell in his head started ringing louder.

He went up the three steps that led to the front door and noticed something else that was wrong. A broken window. He swallowed his saliva then, very slowly, took out his 9 mm. He pushed back the pane and clambered over the sill, being careful not to crush the shards of glass on the floor. Three feet to his right, there was a hall. Silence enfolded his every move. He turned his back to the door and walked down the corridor.

To his left, a half-open door was labelled WAITING ROOM. Further on, to his right, another door was wide open. It was presumably the surgeon's consulting room. First he noticed its walls, covered with soundproofing made of a mix of plaster and straw. Then its floor. Photographs were scattered across it. Faces of women that were bandaged, swollen, stitched. The final confirmation of his suspicions. Someone had searched the place.

A crack sounded from the other side of the wall.

Paul froze, his fingers gripping his gun. In a split second, he realised that he had lived only for this moment. The length of his existence did not matter. Nor did life's pleasures, hopes and disappointments. All that counted was heroic courage. He knew that the next minute would give his stay on earth its meaning. A few ounces of bravery and honour in the scales of his soul . . .

He was leaping towards the door, when the wall exploded.

Paul was thrown to the far side of the corridor. Fire and smoke were filling it. By the time he noticed a hole no bigger than a plate, two more shots ripped through the soundproofing. The straw in the plasterboard caught fire, turning the corridor into a tunnel of flame.

Paul curled up on the floor, his neck singed by the blaze, pieces of plaster and straw tumbling down onto him.

Almost at once, silence fell. Paul looked up. In front of him, there was nothing but a heap of rubble, revealing a clear view of the surgery.

They were there.

Three men dressed in black commando kits, strapped with cartridge belts and wearing balaclavas. Each of them was holding a SG 5040 grenade launcher. Paul had never seen one except in a catalogue, but he recognised the model at once.

At their feet lay a corpse in a dressing-gown. Frédéric Gruss had paid the final price for the risks of his trade.

Automatically, Paul felt for his gun. But it was too late. His stomach was frothing with blood, seeping red streams into the folds of his jacket. He felt no pain – he supposed this meant that he had been fatally wounded.

Sharp crunching sounds could be heard to his left. Despite his deafened ears, Paul heard with unreal clarity the feet treading down across the rubble.

A fourth man appeared in the doorway. The same black figure, hooded, gloved, but with no grenade launcher.

He walked over and looked at Paul's wound. Then he pulled off his balaclava. His face was painted all over. The brown curves and whirls on his skin depicted the maw of a wolf. His moustache, brows and eyes were all lined with black. This had presumably been done using henna, but it looked like the make-up of a Maori warrior.

Paul recognised the man in the photograph. Azer Akarsa. He was holding a Polaroid photo: a pale oval surrounded by black hair. Anna Heymes just after her operation.

So the Wolves were now going to be able to find their prey.

The hunt would go on. But without him.

The Turk knelt down.

He looked straight into Paul's eyes, then softly said: "The high pressure drives them mad. Pressure wipes out pain. The last one was singing when her nose was cut off."

Paul closed his eyes. He did not really understand what was being said, but he was sure of one thing: this man knew who he was, and had been informed about Naubrel's visit to his laboratory.

In flashes, he glimpsed the wounds of the victims, the cuts on their faces. A homage to ancient stone, signed Azer Akarsa.

He felt the bubbles rise up to his lips. It was blood. When he opened his eyes again, the Wolf Man was pointing a .45 at his forehead.

His last thought was for Céline.

And the fact that he had not had time to call her before she left for school.

XI

CHAPTER 67

Roissy-Charles-de-Gaulle airport.

Thursday 21 March, four p.m.

There is only one way to conceal a gun in an airport.

Firearm enthusiasts generally think that a Glock automatic pistol, essentially made of polymers, can slip through X-rays and metal detectors. Wrong. The barrel, recuperator, firing pin, trigger, clip spring and a few other parts are still made of metal. Not to mention the bullets.

There is only one way to conceal a gun in an airport.

And Sema knew it.

She remembered how as she stood in front of the windows in the airport's shopping mall, while waiting to board Turkish Airlines flight TK 4067 to Istanbul.

First she bought a few clothes and a travel bag – there's nothing more suspicious than a passenger with no luggage – then some photographic equipment. An F2 Nikon camera, two lenses, one 35–70 mm the other 200 mm, then a small box of tools specially for this make, plus two lead-lined bags to protect films during security checks. She carefully put them all away in her professional Promax bag, then went to the airport toilets.

Isolated in a cubicle, she put the barrel, firing pin and other metal parts of her Glock 21 among the screwdrivers and pliers in the tool box. Then she slid the tungsten bullets into the leaded containers, which block X-rays and make their contents totally invisible.

Sema was amazed at her own reflexes, at her gestures and know-how. Everything was coming back to her spontaneously. Her "cultural memory", as Ackermann had put it.

At five, she calmly boarded her flight, which arrived at Istanbul at the end of the day, without being bothered by customs.

In the taxi, she did not dwell on the surrounding countryside. Night had already fallen. A slight shower was casting its ghostly reflections beneath the street lights, matching the flow of her consciousness.

All she made out were details: a pedlar selling ring-shaped loaves; a few young women, their faces framed by headscarves, melding into the tiles of a bus shelter; a lofty mosque, grim and sombre, which seemed to be scowling over the trees; bird cages lined up on a bank side, like hives . . . It all murmured to her a language that was at once familiar and distant . . . She turned from the window and curled up on the seat.

She chose one of the most luxurious hotels in the city centre, where she merged in with a welcome flow of anonymous tourists.

At eight thirty, she locked her bedroom door and slumped down onto the bed, where she fell asleep with her clothes on.

The next day, Friday 22 March, she awoke at ten a.m.

She turned on the television at once, and looked for a French channel on the satellite network. She had to make do with TV5, the international service for the French-speaking world. At noon, after a debate about hunting in Switzerland, and a documentary about national parks in Quebec, she finally got to see TF1 news, broadcast the previous evening in France.

As she had expected, mention was made of the discovery of the body of Jean-Louis Schiffer in Père-Lachaise cemetery. But there was other news she had not been expecting: two other bodies had been found that same day in a mansion in the heights of Saint-Cloud.

Sema recognised the building and turned up the volume. The victims had been identified as Frédéric Gruss, a plastic surgeon and owner of the property, and a thirty-five-year-old police captain called Paul Nerteaux, attached to the First Division in Paris.

Sema was horrified. The commentator went on: "No explanation has yet been found for this double murder, but it may be linked to the death of Jean-Louis Schiffer. Paul Nerteaux had been investigating the murders of three women, committed over the past few months in the Little Turkey quarter. During his inquiries, he consulted the retired inspector, who specialised in the tenth *arrondissement* . . ."

Sema had never heard of this Nerteaux – a young, rather good-looking fellow with hair like a Japanese – but she could easily deduce what had happened. After pointlessly killing three women, the Wolves had finally found the right lead, which had taken them to Gruss, the surgeon who had operated on her during the summer of 2001. Meanwhile, this young cop must have followed the same path which led to the man in Saint-Cloud. He had turned up while the Wolves were questioning him. The situation had ended in a typical Turkish bloodbath.

Deep down, Sema had always known that the Wolves would eventually discover her new appearance. And, from that moment, they would know exactly where to find her. For an extremely simple reason. Their leader was Mister Corduroys, the lover of chocolate filled with marzipan, who was a regular customer at the Maison du Chocolat. She had made that incredible discovery as soon as she had recovered her memory. His name was Azer Akarsa. Sema remembered seeing him in an Idealist camp in Adana when she was a teenager, where he was already seen as a hero . . . Such was the final irony of her story. The killer who had been tracking her for months in the Turkish quarter had seen but failed to recognise her twice a week while buying his favourite confectionery.

According to the TV report, the events in Saint-Cloud had taken place the previous day, at around three in the afternoon. Instinctively, Sema sensed that they would wait until the next day before attacking the Maison du Chocolat.

In other words, *right now.*

Sema grabbed the phone and called Clothilde at the shop. No answer. She looked at her watch. Twelve thirty in Istanbul, so an hour earlier in Paris. Was it already too late? From that moment, she tried the number every thirty minutes. In vain. Powerless, she paced around her room, worrying herself to death.

At her wits' end, she went down to the hotel's business centre and sat in front of a computer. Via the Net, she consulted the electronic version of *Le Monde* of Thursday evening, reading through the articles devoted to the death of Jean-Louis Schiffer and the double murder at Saint-Cloud.

Absent-mindedly, she browsed through the other pages, and came across some more unexpected news. The article was entitled "Suicide of a Top Policeman". There, in black and white, was the announcement of the death of Laurent Heymes. The lines quivered before her eyes. His body had been discovered on Thursday morning, in his flat on avenue Hoche. Laurent had used his service revolver, a 38 mm Manhurin. As to his motives, the article briefly mentioned the suicide of his wife, a year before, and the fact that friends said he had been depressed ever since.

Sema concentrated on these densely worded lies, but she could no longer read the words. Instead, all she could see were pale hands, a slightly panicked stare, flaming blond hair . . . She had loved that man. A strange, disturbing love, mixed up with her hallucinations. Her eyes brimmed with tears, but she held them back.

She thought of the young cop, dead in that villa in Saint-Cloud who, in a way, had sacrificed himself for her. She had not wept for him. So she would not weep for Laurent, who had been one of her manipulators.

The most intimate one.

And, thus, the biggest bastard.

At four o'clock, she was chain-smoking in the business centre, with one eye on the television, and the other on the computer, when the bomb exploded. It appeared in the new electronic edition of *Le Monde*, in the "France-Société" section:

SHOOT-OUT ON RUE DU FAUBOURG-SAINT-HONORÉ

At noon on Friday 22 March, the police were still present at 225 rue du Faubourg-Saint-Honoré, after a gun battle in a shop called "La Maison du Chocolat". No explanation has yet been given for this spectacular shoot-out, which has left three people dead and two wounded, three of them from the ranks of the police.

From the initial reports, especially the testimony of Clothilde Ceaux, a shop assistant who escaped unscathed, the sequence of events was as follows. At 10.10, just after the shop opened, three men arrived. Some police officers in civilian clothes, who had been stationed just opposite, immediately intervened. The three men then produced automatic pistols and opened fire on the police. The gun battle lasted for only a few seconds, on either side of the street, but was extremely brutal. Three officers were hit, one fatally. The two others are in a critical condition. As for their aggressors, two were killed, while the third managed to escape.

They have been identified as Lüset Yildirim, Kadir Kir and Azer Akarsa, all Turkish nationals. The dead men, Lüset Yildirim and Kadir Kir, both had diplomatic passports. It has proved impossible to find out how long they have been in France, and the Turkish embassy has refused to comment.

According to the police, the two men were known to the Turkish authorities as members of an extreme right-wing group known as the "Idealists" or "Grey Wolves", and they had already carried out a number of contract killings on behalf of Turkey's organised crime cartels.

The identity of the third man, who managed to flee, is even more surprising. Azer Akarsa is a businessman, who has had an extraordinary success in the tree-farming sector in Turkey, and enjoys a good reputation in Istanbul. He is known for his patriotic views, but he backs a modern, moderate nationalism which is compatible with democratic values. He has never had any dealings with the Turkish police.

The involvement of such a person in these events suggests a political motivation. But the real reasons remain obscure. Why did these men go to the Maison du Chocolat this morning, armed with assault rifles and hand guns? Why were there policemen in civilian clothes (in fact officers from the Division Nationale Antiterroriste, or "DNAT") stationed over the road? Were they following the three criminals? It is known that they had had the shop under surveillance for the past few days. Were they preparing an ambush for the three Turks? If so, why take so many risks? Why attempt an arrest on a busy thoroughfare, in the middle of the day, when no warning had been given? The Public Prosecutor's Office is concerned about these anomalies and has ordered an internal inquiry.

According to our sources, one lead is being favoured. The gun battle on rue du Faubourg-Saint-Honoré could be linked to two other cases of murder, which were reported in yesterday's edition: the discovery on the morning of 21 March of the body of retired inspector Jean-Louis Schiffer in Père-Lachaise, then the bodies of Paul Nerteaux, a police captain, and of Frédéric Gruss, a plastic surgeon, later that day in a villa in Saint-Cloud. Captain Nerteaux had been investigating the murders over the last five months of three unidentified women in the tenth *arrondissement* of Paris, and for this reason had consulted Jean-Louis Schiffer, who specialised in the capital's Turkish community.

This series of murders could lie at the heart of a complicated affair, which is both criminal and political, that seems to have escaped the attention of both Paul Nerteaux's superiors and the investigating magistrate, Thierry Bomarzo. Further confirmation of a link lies in the fact that, one hour before his death, the captain had put out a wanted notice on Azer Akarsa and requested a search warrant for Matak Limited, in Bièvre, one of whose main shareholders is none other than Azer Akarsa. When his portrait was shown to Clothilde Ceaux, the main eye-witness of the shooting, she formally identified him.

The other key figure in this case could turn out to be Philippe Charlier, one of the commissioners of the DNAT, who clearly has some information concerning the assailants. Philippe Charlier is a major figure in the war against terrorism, but one whose methods have proved controversial. He has been summonsed later today by Judge Bernard Sazin, who is leading the initial enquiry.

This confusing series of events occurs in the middle of a presidential campaign, with Lionel Jospin planning to merge the Direction de la Surveillance du Territoire (DST) with the Direction Centrale des Renseignements Généraux (DCRG). This projected merger is aimed no doubt at reducing the sometimes excessive independence of certain police officers or secret service operatives.

Sema disconnected before making her own personal summary of the events. On the good side, Clothilde was safe, and Charlier had been summonsed by a judge. Sooner or later, he would have to answer for all these deaths, as well as the "suicide" of Laurent Heymes . . .

On the negative side, Sema placed just one point, but it outweighed all the others.

Azer Akarsa was still at large.

And this threat confirmed her decision.

She had to find him and, further up the line, discover who had put out this contract.

She did not know, had never known, his name. But she knew that little by little she would expose the entire pyramid.

At that moment, all she was sure of was that Akarsa would return to Turkey. He was probably already back. Being sheltered by his people. Protected by complacent policemen and politicians.

She grabbed her coat and left the room.

It was in her memory that she would find the path that led to him.

CHAPTER 68

First, Sema went to Galata bridge, near her hotel. She looked long and hard at the far side of the canal of the Golden Horn, the city's most famous panorama. The Bosphorus and its boats; the Eminönü quarter and the New Mosque; the stone terraces and flights of pigeons; the domes and arrow-like minarets, from where five times a day the voices of the muezzins poured out.

Cigarette.

She did not feel like a tourist, but she did feel that this town – her town – might provide her with a clue, a spark to give her back all of her memory. For the moment, she could still see the past of Anna Heymes, which was being gradually replaced by confused sensations, linked to her daily life as a drug smuggler. Snatches from an obscure trade, with no clear reference points, no personal details which could give her the slightest indication how to find her "brothers" again.

She hailed a cab and asked the driver to cruise through the city, at random. She spoke Turkish without an accent, and without the slightest hesitation. That language burst from her lips as soon as she needed it – like a source hidden in her inner self. So why was she thinking in French? Was it an effect of her psychic conditioning? No. This familiarity went back further than that. It was an essential part of her personality. During her life, her education, there had been this strange implant . . .

Through the window, she observed each detail: the red Turkish flags, decked with a golden crescent and star, which marked the town like a wax seal; the blue walls and the brown buildings, stained with pollution;

the green roofs and domes of the mosques, which oscillated between jade and emerald in the light.

The taxi drove along a wall: Hatun Caddesi. Sema read the names on the signposts: Aksaray, Kücükpazar, Carsamba ... They resonated vaguely inside her, evoking no particular emotions or distinct recollections.

Yet, more than ever, she sensed that something, anything – a monument, a sign, a street name – could stir up that quicksand and shift aside the memory blocks within her. Like wrecks lying on the sea bed, which you only need to brush against for them to drift back up to the surface ...

The driver asked: "*Devam edelim mi?*[1]"

"*Evet.*[2]"

Haseki. Nisanca. Yenikapi ...

Another cigarette.

The din of traffic, the tide of passers-by. The restlessness of the city drew to a height here. Yet, the overall impression was of gentleness. Spring was making the shadows quiver above this tumult. A pale light glittered though the iron-like air. A silver gleam hung over Istanbul, a sort of grey coating smothering any violence. Even the trees had something worn about them, a cinder coat that calmed and soothed the spirit ...

Suddenly, a word on a poster drew her attention. A few syllables on a red and gold background.

"Take me to Galatasaray," she told the driver.

"To the school?"

"Yes, the school. To Beyoglu."

CHAPTER 69

A large square, on the outskirts of the Taksim quarter. Banks, flags and international hotels. The driver parked at the entrance of the pedestrian precinct.

[1] Shall we continue?
[2] Yes.

"It will be quicker on foot," he explained. "Take Istiklal Caddesi. Then after about a hundred yards, you . . ."

"I know."

Three minutes later, Sema had reached the railings of the school, jealously protected by the sombre gardens. She went through the gate and dived into what was almost a forest. Firs, cypresses, eastern planes and lime trees, with their green blades, soft shades, shadowy mouths . . . Sometimes a patch of bark added some grey, or even black. On other occasions, a tip or bough split into a lighter line – a broad pastel smile. Or else, dry almost blue thickets with the transparency of tracing paper. The whole spectrum of vegetation was on display.

Beyond the trees, she spotted a yellow façade, surrounded by sports fields and basketball pitches. It was the school. Sema stayed hidden among the boughs and looked at the pollen-coloured walls. The cement surfaces with their neutral tones. The badge of the school, an S intertwined with a G, red trimmed with gold, on the navy blue sweaters of the pupils walking there.

But above all, she listened to the rising din. A sound that is identical in all latitudes: the joy of children freed from school. It was noon. Time for the lunch break.

More than a familiar noise, it was a call, a rallying cry. Sensations suddenly gathered around her, entwining her . . . Suffocated by emotion, she sat down on a bench and let the images of the past flood in.

First her village, in distant Anatolia. Beneath a limitless merciless sky, the wattle huts, clinging to the sides of the mountains. The rippling planes of high grasses. The flocks of sheep on the steep slopes, trotting along at an angle, as grey as filthy paper. Then, in the valley, the men, women and children living like stones, broken by the heat and the cold . . .

Later, the camp – a disused spa resort, surrounded by barbed wire, somewhere in the Kayseri region. The daily indoctrination, training and exercises. Mornings spent reading Alpaslan Türkes's *Nine Lights*, repeating nationalistic doctrines, watching silent films on Turkish history. Hours devoted to learning the basics of ballistics, telling the difference between detonating and incendiary explosives, shooting with assault rifles, handling knives . . .

Then suddenly, the French School. Everything changed. A suave, refined environment. But it was probably even worse. She was the peasant. The girl from the mountains, among the sons of notables. She was also the fanatic. The nationalist holding on to her Turkish identity and ideals amid middle-class, left-wing pupils all dreaming of becoming Europeans . . .

It was here, at Galatasaray, that she had fallen so much in love with the French language that, in her mind, she turned it into her new mother tongue. She could still hear the dialect of her childhood, those clashingly crude syllables, being gradually supplanted by these new words, those poems and books that modulated her slightest thought and moulded each new idea. The world then, quite literally, became French.

Then the time came to travel. Opium. The fields in Iran, set in steps above the jaws of the desert. The patches of poppies in Afghanistan between the fields of corn and vegetables. She could picture that name-less, undefined frontier. A no man's land of dust, dotted with mines, haunted by wild buccaneers. She remembered the wars. The tanks, the Stingers – and the Afghan rebels playing Buskashi with the head of a Soviet soldier.

She could also see the laboratories. Airless structures full of men and women wearing cloth masks. The white dust and acidic fumes, the morphine base and the refined heroin . . . Her real work had begun.

It was then that the face became clear.

So far, her memory had worked in only one direction. Each time, a face had acted as a detonator. Schiffer's appearance had been enough to bring back the previous months' activities – the dope, running away, concealment. Azer Akarsa's smile raised up the camps, nationalist meet-ings, men brandishing their fists, with their little fingers and indexes raised, screaming high-pitched wails or else crying "*Türkes basbug!*" – and had identified her as a Wolf.

But now, in the gardens of Galatarasay, the opposite was happening. Her memories revealed a leitmotiv character that crossed each frag-ment of her recollections . . . At first, a clumsy child, right back at the beginning. Then an awkward teenager, at the French School. Later, a fellow smuggler. In those underground laboratories, it was definitely always the same podgy figure, dressed in a white coat, that was smiling at her.

Over the years, a child had grown by her side. A blood brother. A Grey Wolf who had shared everything with her. As she concentrated, his face became clearer. Babyish features beneath honey-coloured curls. Blue eyes, like two turquoises placed among the rocks of the desert.

Suddenly a name emerged: Kürsat Milihit.

She stood up and decided to go inside the school. She needed confirmation.

Sema introduced herself to the headmaster as a French journalist and explained the subject of her report: old Galatasaray pupils who had become celebrities in Turkey.

The headmaster smiled proudly. What could be more natural than that?

A few minutes later, she found herself in a small room, its walls lined with books. In front of her, the files covering all the classes over the past few decades – names and pictures of former pupils, the dates and any prizes awarded each year. With no hesitation, she opened the register for 1988 and turned to the final year. Her year. She did not try to find her previous face, the very idea of looking at it made her feel ill at ease, as though she were touching a taboo subject. No. She looked for the portrait of Kürsat Milihit.

When she found it, her memories grew even more precise. The childhood friend. The travelling companion. Today, Kürsat was a chemist. The best in his field. Able to transform any gum-base into the best morphine, and then distil the purest heroin. His magician's fingers knew better than anyone how to manipulate acetic anhydride.

Over the years, she had organised all of her operations with him. During the final convoy, it was he who had reduced the heroin into a liquid solution. It was Sema's idea: they injected the smack into the air cells of bubble bags. If they put a hundred millilitres in each envelope, then only ten of them would be needed to transport a kilo – so two hundred for the entire load. Twenty kilos of Number Four heroin, in a liquid solution, concealed within translucent packaging containing banal documents, to be picked up at the freight terminal of Roissy airport.

She looked again at the photo. That large teenager with milky brows and copper curls was not just a ghost from the past. He now had a vital role to play.

He alone could help her find Azer Akarsa.

CHAPTER 70

An hour later, Sema was in a cab crossing the huge steel bridge over the Bosphorus. The storm broke just at that moment. In only a few seconds, as the car touched the Asian bank, the rain marked off its territory with violence. At first, there were needles of light hammering the pavements as though on tin roofs, then puddles, spreading, seeping. Soon, the entire landscape weighed down. Dark sprays swished up in the wakes of the cars, the roads swayed and drowned . . .

When the cab reached the Beylerbeyi quarter, snug beneath the bridge, the shower had turned into a downpour. A grey wave wiped out all visibility, mixing cars, pavements and houses into a shifting fog. The entire neighbourhood seemed to be dissolving into a liquid state – a prehistoric chaos of peat and mud.

Sema decided to get out of the cab on Yaliboyu Street. She slipped between the cars and took shelter beneath an awning along the row of shop fronts. She paused for a moment to buy an oilskin – a pale green poncho – then she tried to get her bearings. This neighbourhood was like a village – a scale model of Istanbul. Its pavements were as narrow as ribbons, its houses clumped together, its roads like pathways leading down to the riverside.

She dived down Beylerbeyi Street, towards the river. To her left, the cafés were closed, the bars shrunk back beneath their awnings, the stalls covered with tarpaulins. To her right, a blank wall, sheltering the gardens of a mosque. A red, porous rubble stone surface zigzagged by cracks sketching in a melancholic geography. Lower down, beneath the grey foliage, the waters of the Bosphorus could be heard, rumbling and rolling like kettledrums in an orchestra pit.

Sema felt overwhelmed by fluidity. Drops hammered on her head, beating her shoulders, swarming over her oilskin . . . Her lips tasted of clay. Her face seemed to become liquid, shifting, moving . . .

On the riverbank, the downpour intensified, as though freed by the open stretch of water. The land seemed about to drift away and follow the flow as far as the sea. Sema could not stop herself from shaking, sensing in the streams of her veins the pieces of the continent that were being shaken to their foundations.

She retraced her steps and looked for the entrance to the mosque. The wall she walked beside was flaking, pierced by the rusty bars of windows. Above it, the domes glistened and the minarets seemed to be launched higher by the rain.

As she walked on, more memories crowded in. Kürsat was nicknamed "the Gardener", because botany was his speciality, in particular poppies. Here, he cultivated his own wild species, concealed in the gardens. Every evening, he came to Beylerbeyi to inspect his Papavers . . .

Going through the gate, she entered a courtyard of marble tiles, with a rank of basins along the ground, used for ablutions before prayers. She crossed the patio, noticing a group of white and yellow cats curled up along the windows. One of them had an eye missing. Another had its nose covered in blood.

After a further gate, she at last reached the gardens.

The vision moved her heart. Trees, shrubs and undergrowth spreading chaotically. Overturned soil. Branches as black as liquorice. Thickets stuck with tiny leaves, tight as clumps of mistletoe. A luxuriant world, animated and tickled by the downpour.

She walked on, lulled by the scent of flowers, the dull odour of the soil. Here, the hammering of the rain became more muted. The drops bounced off the leaves in a dull pizzicato, streams of water slipped from the foliage like harp strings. Sema thought: *The body responds to music with dance. The earth responds to rain with gardens.*

Pushing aside the branches, she came across a large vegetable patch, hidden between the trees. Bamboo props stood high, squat tubs were full of earth, upside-down jars protected young shoots. It looked to Sema like an open-air greenhouse, or nursery. She took another step or two. The Gardener was there.

Kneeling on the ground, he was bent over a row of poppies, protected by transparent plastic envelopes. He was slipping a probe into the pistil, at the point where the alkaloid capsule is situated. Sema did not recognise the species in question. It was undoubtedly a new hybrid, which flowered early. Experimental poppies, right in the middle of Istanbul . . .

As though sensing her presence, the chemist looked up. His hood concealed his brows, barely revealing his heavy features. A smile rose to his lips, even more rapidly than the delight in his stare.

"Your eyes. I'd have recognised your eyes."

He spoke in French. It was a game they used to play – another mark of complicity. She did not reply. She imagined what he could see: a scrawny figure beneath a green hood, with emaciated, unrecognisable features. And yet Kürsat did not seem at all surprised. He knew about her new appearance. Had she told him? Or had the Wolves done so? Friend or foe? She had only a few seconds to decide. This man had been her confidant, her accomplice. So she must have told him about her plans.

Kürsat Milihit shifted about awkwardly. He was only just taller than Sema, and was wearing a cotton smock beneath a plastic apron. He stood up.

"Why have you come back?"

She said nothing, letting the rain mark the passage of time. Then, her voice muffled by her cape, she replied in French: "I want to know who I am. I've lost my memory."

"What?"

"I was arrested by the police in Paris. They made me undergo special mental conditioning. I'm amnesic."

"That's impossible."

"Nothing's impossible in our world. You know that as well as I do."

"You . . . can't remember anything?"

"Everything I know, I've found out for myself."

"But why come back? Why don't you just vanish?"

"It's too late for that. The Wolves are after me. They know my new face. I want to negotiate."

He carefully put down the flower, with its plastic hood, among the jerry cans and bags of leaf mould. He glanced at her rapidly.

"Have you still got it?"

Sema did not answer. He asked again: "Have you still got the dope?"

"I'm the one asking the questions," she replied. "Who's behind this operation?"

"We never know any names. That's the rule."

"The rules have been broken. When I went out on my own, I over-turned them. They must have questioned you. Some names must have been mentioned. Who commissioned that consignment?"

Kürsat hesitated. The rain slapped down on his hood, streaming across his face.

"Ismail Kudseyi."

The name struck her memory – Kudseyi, the grand master – but she pretended not to remember.

"Who's that?"

"I can't believe you've lost that many marbles."

"Who is it?" she repeated.

"The most important *baba* in Istanbul," he lowered his voice, in tune with the rain. "He was setting up an alliance with the Uzbeks and the Russians. The consignment was a pilot scheme. A test. A symbol. It vanished along with you."

She smiled through the crystal drops.

"Things must be rosy between the partners."

"War is imminent. But Kudseyi doesn't give a damn. What he's obsessed about is you. Finding you again. It isn't even a question of money. It's a matter of honour. He can't admit that he's been betrayed by one of his own. We are his Wolves. His creatures."

"His creatures?"

"The instruments of the Cause. We were educated, indoctrinated, brought up as Wolves. When you were born, you were nobody. A lousy peasant raising sheep. Like me. Like the others. The camps gave us everything. Faith. Power. Knowledge."

Sema needed to get down to the essentials, but she could not resist digging for more facts, further details.

"Why are we speaking in French?"

A smile inched its way over Kürsat's chubby face. A smile of pride.

"We were chosen. In the 1980s, the *reïs*, the chiefs, decided to set up an underground army, with its officers and elite soldiers. Wolves who could mingle with the highest social strata."

"Was it Kudseyi's idea?"

"He started the project off, but with everyone's approval. Emissaries from his foundation were sent to the clubs in Anatolia. They were looking for the most gifted, most promising children. The idea was to provide them with the best possible education. It was a patriotic project. Knowledge and power were being given back to the real Turks, to the children of Anatolia, instead of the bourgeois scum of Istanbul . . ."

"And we were chosen?"

The proud tone swelled even further.

"Yes, and sent to Galatasaray, along with a few others, thanks to grants from the foundation. How can you have forgotten all that?"

Sema did not answer. Kürsat went on, in an increasingly exalted voice.

"We were twelve years old. We were already little *baskans*, chiefs of our region. First we spent a year in a training camp. When we got to Galatasaray, we already knew how to use an assault rifle. We knew entire sections of *Nine Lights* by heart. Then suddenly we were surrounded by decadents, who listened to rock music, smoked cannabis, imitated Europeans . . . Fucking communists . . . To survive, we stuck together, Sema. Like brother and sister. The two bumpkins from Anatolia. The two paupers with their pathetic grants . . . But no one knew how dangerous we were. We were already Wolves. Fighters who had infiltrated a forbidden world. So as to struggle all the better against that red scum! *Tanri türk'ü korusun!*[1]"

Kürsat waved his fist, with his little and index fingers raised. He was doing his utmost to look like a fanatic, but he just came across as being what he always had been: a sweet, awkward child who had been conditioned into violence and hatred.

Motionless among the props and foliage, she asked: "What happened then?"

"For me, a science degree. For you, the modern languages department at the University of Bogazici. At the end of the 1980s, the Wolves took over the dope market. They needed specialists. Our roles had already been set down. Chemistry for me, transportation for you. There were many more Wolves in high places. Diplomats, CEOs . . ."

"Like Azer Akarsa."

Kürsat jumped.

"How do you know that name?"

"He was on my trail in Paris."

[1] God save the Turks!

He shook the rain off himself like a hippopotamus.

"They sent out the worst one of them all. If he's looking for you, then he'll find you."

"I'm the one who's looking for him. Where is he?"

"How should I know?"

The Gardener's voice rang false. At that instant, she was pricked by a suspicion. She had almost forgotten her side to the story. Who had betrayed her? Who had told Akarsa that she was hiding in Gürdilek's baths? But she kept that question for later . . .

The chemist continued, slightly too hastily: "Do you still have it? Do you still have the dope?"

"I've told you. I've lost my memory."

"If you want to negotiate, you can't come back empty-handed. Your only chance is to . . ."

She suddenly asked: "Why did I do that? Why did I try to double-cross everyone?"

"You alone know that."

"I involved you in my scheme. I put you in danger. I must have explained my reasons."

He gestured vaguely.

"You never accepted your destiny. You were always saying that they'd forced us to obey. That we had no choice. But what choice did we have? Without them, we'd still be shepherds. Bumpkins at the far end of Anatolia."

"If I'm a drug dealer, then I have money. Why didn't I just disappear? Why did I steal the heroin?"

Kürsat sneered.

"You wanted more. You wanted to screw them. To set one clan against the other. This mission gave you a chance to get your revenge. When the Uzbeks and the Russians get here, it'll be mayhem."

The rain slowed. Night was falling. Kürsat gradually sank into the shadows, as if he was fading away. Above them, the domes of the mosque looked fluorescent.

The idea of betrayal forced its way back. She now had to go to the bitter end. She had to get this over with.

"What about you?" she asked coldly. "How come you're still alive? They didn't come to question you?"

"Of course they did."

"And you told them nothing?"

The chemist seemed to shiver.

"I had nothing to say. I knew nothing. All I did was to transform the heroin in Paris, and come back home. Then no one heard from you again. Nobody knew where you were. Especially not me."

His voice was trembling. She suddenly felt sorry for him. *Kürsat, my Kürsat, how have you survived so long?*

The fat man went on at once: "They trust me, Sema. Really they do. I'd done my part of the job. I didn't hear from you again. After you'd hidden in Gürdilek's place, I thought . . ."

"Who mentioned Gürdilek? Was it me?"

She had now understood. Kürsat knew everything, but had revealed only part of the truth to Akarsa. He had saved his skin by providing him with her Paris address, but had said nothing about her new face. Thus had her "blood brother" negotiated with his own conscience.

The chemist stood there for a moment, his mouth agape, as though dragged down by the weight of his chin. The next moment, he stuck his hand beneath a plastic sheet.

Sema aimed her Glock from beneath her cape and fired. The Gardener crashed back between the shoots and the jars.

Sema knelt down. This was her second murder after Schiffer. But from the confidence of her movements, she realised that she had killed before. And in this way. With a hand gun, at point-blank range. When? How many times? She had no idea. On that point, her memory was still a sterile zone.

She looked at Kürsat, lying motionless among the poppies. Death had already smoothed out his features. Innocence was slowly rising back across his face, which was free at last.

She searched the corpse. Beneath his smock, she found a mobile phone. One of the numbers in its memory was labelled "Azer".

She stuck it in her pocket then stood up. The rain had stopped. Darkness had taken hold of the place. The gardens were breathing at last. She looked up towards the mosque. The drenched domes seemed like green ceramic, the minarets about to take off for the stars.

Sema remained for a few more seconds beside the body. Inexplicably, something clear and precise surged up inside her.

She now knew why she had done what she had done. Why she had fled with the dope.

To be free, of course.

But also to avenge a particular wrong.

Before proceeding any further, she had to check that.

She had to find a hospital. And a gynaecologist.

CHAPTER 71

All night spent writing.

A letter of twelve pages, addressed to Mathilde Wilcrau, rue Le Goff, Paris, fifth *arrondissement*. In it, she told her life story in detail. Her origin. Her education. Her job. And the last consignment.

She also provided names: Kürsat Milihit, Azer Akarsa, Ismail Kudseyi. She placed each person, each pawn on the chessboard. Describing their precise roles and positions. Putting back together each fragment of the puzzle . . .

Sema owed her these explanations.

She had promised her in the crypt at Père-Lachaise, but above all she wanted to make her story intelligible to that psychiatrist who had risked her life for nothing in return.

When she wrote "Mathilde" on the white hotel letter-pad, when she manoeuvred her pen around that name, Sema said to herself that she had perhaps never possessed anything so solid as those characters.

She lit a cigarette and paused to remember. Mathilde Wilcrau. A tall sturdy woman with a mane of black hair. The first time she had observed her bright red smile, an image had come to mind: the poppy stalks she used to burn so as to conserve their colour.

Today, now that she could recall her origins, the comparison had recovered its full meaning. That sandy landscape did not belong to the French moors, as she had thought, but to the deserts of Anatolia. The flowers were wild poppies – a hint of opium already . . . Sema used to shiver with excitement and fear when burning those stalks. She had sensed a secret, inexplicable link between the dark flame and the bright blooming of the buds.

That same mystery scintillated in Mathilde Wilcrau.

A burnt region within her reinforced the absolute redness of her smile.

Sema finished her letter. She hesitated for a moment. Should she add what she had learned in the hospital a few hours before? No. That was nobody's business but hers.

She signed the page then slid it into an envelope.

4.00 flashed on the radio-alarm in her bedroom.

She thought over her plan one more time. Kürsat had said: *You can't come back empty-handed.* Neither *Le Monde* nor the television news had mentioned that there had been heroin scattered around the crypt. So it was quite likely that Azer Akarsa and Ismail Kudseyi did not know that it had been lost. Thus Sema had a virtual object to bargain with . . .

She put the envelope by the door then went to the bathroom.

She turned on the tap in the basin and took up a cardboard box, purchased earlier that evening in a hardware store in Beylerbeyi.

She poured the pigment into the sink, contemplating its reddish swirls that faded in the water and froze into a brown mash.

For a few seconds, she looked at herself in the mirror. Her smashed face, broken bones and stitched skin. Under her apparent beauty lay another lie . . .

She smiled at her reflection, then murmured: "I've got no choice."

Gingerly, she dipped her index finger into the henna.

CHAPTER 72

Five o'clock.

Haydarpasa station.

A point of arrival and departure for both boats and trains. Everything was just as she remembered. The central building, a U surrounded by two huge towers, opening onto the straits like a greeting in welcome to the sea. Then, all around, the sea walls forming lines of stone, digging out a labyrinth of water. On the second one, a lighthouse stood at the end of the jetty. An isolated tower, placed above the channels.

At that time, everything was dark, cold, empty. Only a weak light quivered from inside the station, through the windows covered with a reddish, hesitant steam.

The kiosk of the *iskele* – the departure quay – was also glistening, reflecting a blue stain in the water, which was weaker still, almost mauve.

Shoulders high and collar up, Sema walked beside the building then alongside the sea wall. This sinister scene suited her. She had been counting on just this inert, silent desert, weighed down by frost. She went towards the jetty used by pleasure boats. The cables and sails followed her along with an insistent slapping noise.

Sema examined each yacht, each skiff. Finally she spotted a boat whose owner was asleep, curled up under a tarpaulin. She woke him up and started negotiating at once. The haggard man accepted the sum on offer. It was a fortune. She assured him that she would not go out further than the second sea wall, that he would never lose sight of his boat. He accepted, started up the engine without a word, then stepped out onto land.

Sema took the tiller. Drawing away from the quay, she steered between the other vessels. She followed the first wall, swerved around its far end, then went along the second one, as far as the lighthouse. There was not a sound as she passed. Alone, far away, the light from the bridged of a distant cargo ship broke through the shadows. Under the lights of the projectors, beaded with dew, shadows flittered. For a second, she felt at one with these gilded ghosts.

She drew up by the rocks, moored her boat and went over to the lighthouse. Without any difficulty, she forced open the door. The interior was cramped, icy and hostile to any human presence. The lamp was automatic and did not seem to need anyone's help. At the top of the tower, the huge projector revolved slowly on its pivot, giving off long groans.

Sema turned on her torch. The circular wall beside her was filthy and damp. The floor was dotted with puddles. Sema could hear the rushing of the water beneath her feet. It made her think of a stone question mark at the end of the world. A place of total solitude. The ideal location.

She got out Kürsat's phone and dialled Azer Akarsa's number.

A ringing tone. Then an answer. Silence. After all, it was only five in the morning . . .

In Turkish, she said: "It's Sema."

The silence continued. Then Azer Akarsa's voice sounded in her ear. "Where are you?"

"In Istanbul."

"Do you have anything to suggest?"

"A meeting. Just you and me. On neutral ground."

"Where?"

"At Haydarpasa station. On the second sea wall, there's a lighthouse."

"What time?"

"Now. You come alone. By boat."

There was a smile in his voice.

"So you can pick me off like a rabbit?"

"That won't solve my problems."

"I don't see what can solve your problems."

"You'll find out when you get here."

"Where's Kürsat?"

The number had presumably flashed up on the screen. There was no point lying.

"He's dead. I'll be expecting you. At Haydarpasa. Alone. And rowing."

She hung up and looked out through the barred window. The sea port was waking up. A slow movement, groggy from dawn, had started. A ship slid down the rails and rose up in the waves, before gliding under the arches of the brightly lit warehouses.

Her observation post was perfect. From there, she could keep an eye on both the train station and the jetties, the quay and the first sea wall. No one could sneak up on her.

Shivering, she sat down on the steps.

Cigarette.

Her mind wandered. A memory rose up, for no apparent reason. The warmth of plaster on her skin. The strips of gauze on her tormented flesh. The unbearable itching under the dressings. She remembered her convalescence, between waking and sleeping, dozy with sedatives. And above all the shock of seeing her new face, swollen fit to burst, black and blue with bruises, covered with dried scabs . . .

They'd pay for that as well.

Five fifteen.

The cold bit into her, almost like a burn. Sema stood up, stamping her feet and flapping her arms to ward off the numbness. Those recollections of her operation brought her back to her latest discovery, a few hours before, at Istanbul Central Hospital. In reality, it had merely been a confirmation. She could now remember clearly that day in March 1999 in London. A mild inflammation of the colon, which had obliged her to have X-rays done. And then to accept the truth.

How had they dared do that to her?

Mutilate her for life?

That was why she had fled.

That was why she was going to murder all of them.

Five thirty.

The cold dug into her bones. Her blood flowed towards her vital organs, gradually abandoning her extremities to chilblains and frostbite. Before long, she would be paralysed.

Mechanically, she walked as far as the door. She left the lighthouse stiffly, and forced herself to liven up her legs by walking along the wall. The only source of heat left was her own blood. She had to make it circulate, to fill her entire body once more . . .

Voices could be heard in the distance. Sema looked up. Some fishermen were landing on the first wall. She had not foreseen that. Not so early, at least.

Through the darkness, she could see their lines already flicking across the waters.

Were they really fishermen?

She looked at her watch. Five forty-five.

She would go in a few minutes. She could not wait for Azer Akarsa any longer. Instinctively she knew that wherever he was in Istanbul, half an hour would be enough for him to reach the station. If he needed more time than that, then it was because he was organising something, preparing a trap.

A slapping sound. In the shadows, the wake of a rowing boat opened out over the water. It passed the first wall. A figure was bending above the oars with slow, full, regular movements. A ray of moonlight flickered across his corduroy shoulders.

At last, the boat touched the rocks.

He got to his feet, picking up the mooring rope. His gestures and the sounds were so banal that they became almost unreal. Sema could not believe that the man whose sole aim in life was to kill her was now just two yards away. Despite the lack of light, she could make out his worn, olive-green corduroy jacket, his thick scarf, his mop of hair . . . When he bent over to throw her the rope, she even caught a fleeting glimpse of his mauve eyes.

She caught the rope and tied it to her own. Azer was about to step on to land, when she stopped him, brandishing her Glock.

"The tarpaulins," she whispered.

He looked round at the old sheets piled in the boat.

"Lift them up."

He did so. The bottom was empty.

"Come here. Slowly."

She stepped back, to allow him onto the wall. She motioned to him to lift his arms. With her left hand, she frisked him. No gun.

"I'm playing to the rules," he murmured.

She pushed him towards the door, then followed him. When she went inside, he was already sitting on the iron steps.

A transparent sachet had appeared in his hands.

"A chocolate?"

Sema did not reply. He took one out and lifted it to his lips.

"Diabetes," he said apologetically. "My insulin treatment causes drops in my blood-sugar level. It's impossible to find the right dose. Several times a week, I get violent attacks of hypoglycaemia, which are worsened by strong emotion. So I need sugar quickly."

The wrapping paper glittered in his hands. Sema thought of the Maison du Chocolat, of Paris, and Clothilde. Another world.

"In Istanbul, I buy marzipan wrapped in chocolate. A speciality of a confectioner in Beyoglu. In Paris, I found Jikolas . . ."

He delicately placed the packet on the metal structure. Whether it was feigned or genuine, his coolness was impressive. The lighthouse slowly filled with lead-blue light. The day was starting to come up, while the pivot at the top continued to moan.

"Without these chocolates," he added, "I'd never have found you."

"You never did find me."

Smile. He slid his hand once more towards his jacket. Sema lifted her gun. Azer slowed down his movement, then produced a black-and-white photograph. A simple group shot of students on a campus.

"The University of Bogazici, April 1999," he commented. "The only photo that exists of you. Of the old you, I mean . . ."

Suddenly, a lighter appeared in his hand. The flame burst into the darkness, then bit slowly into the glossy paper, giving off a strong chemical smell.

"Few people can claim to have known you after that period, Sema. Especially as you constantly changed your name, your appearance, your country . . ."

He was still holding the crackling picture. The sparkling pink flames flashed over his face. She thought she was having one of her hallucinations. It was maybe the start of an attack . . . But she was wrong. The killer's face was simply flickering in the fire.

"A complete mystery," he went on. "In some ways, that's what cost three women their lives," he stared at the blaze in his fingers. "They writhed in agony. For a long time. A very long time . . ."

He finally dropped the photo, which fell into a puddle of water.

"I should have guessed you'd had surgery. It was a logical step for you. The final metamorphosis . . ."

He stared down at the still-steaming pool.

"We're the best in our different fields, Sema. What do you have to offer?"

She sensed that he did not see her as an enemy, but as a rival. Even better, as his double. This pursuit had become far more than a mere contract. It was a personal challenge. A journey through the looking-glass . . . On an impulse, she provoked him: "We're just tools, toys in the *babas'* hands."

Azer frowned. His face grew taut.

"No, it's the opposite," he murmured. "I use them to serve our Cause. Their money . . ."

"We're their slaves."

A note of irritation entered his voice:

"What do you want?" he suddenly yelled, throwing his chocolates to the ground. "What do you have to offer?"

"To you? Nothing. I want to talk to God in person."

XII

CHAPTER 73

Ismail Kudseyi was standing in the rain in the gardens of his property in Yeniköy.

Beside the patio, among the reeds, he stared at the river.

The Asian side stood out in the distance, like a slender ribbon being frayed by the downpour. It was over a thousand yards away, and not a single vessel was in sight. The old man felt safe, out of range of any snipers.

After Azer's phone call, he had felt the need to go there. To plunge his hand in those silvery folds and soak his fingers with green foam. It was an imperious, almost physical craving.

Leaning on his stick, he walked along the parapet and cautiously went down the steps that led directly into the water. A salty smell assailed him, the spray soaked him at once. The river was in a frenzy, but no matter how agitated the Bosphorus was, there were always secret hiding places at the foot of the rocks, carved niches of grasses, where the waves rolled up in little rainbows.

Still today, at seventy-four, Kudseyi went back to this place when he needed to think. It was his real home. He had learned to swim there. He had caught his first fish. Lost his first ball made of tied-up rags that came undone in contact with the water, like the bandages of a childhood that had never entirely healed . . .

The old man looked at his watch. Nine o'clock. Where were they?

He went back up the steps and contemplated his kingdom: the gardens around his house. Along the crimson-red enclosure, which completely excluded the outside world, forests of bamboo shuffled like feathers, ruffled by the slightest gust of wind, stone lions with folded wings languished on the steps leading to the front door, swans threaded their way across circular pools . . .

He was about to go inside when he heard the noise of a motor. Because of the rain, it was more of a vibration under his skin than a real sound. He turned around and spotted a boat mounting to the assault of each wave, then flapping down with a jolt, digging out two furrows of foam behind it.

Azer was driving, with his jacket done up to his neck. Beside him, Sema looked tiny, wrapped up in the flapping folds of her oilskin. He knew that she had altered her face. But even at that distance, he recognised the way she stood. That slightly cocky air he had noticed twenty years back, among all those other children.

Azer and Sema.

The killer and the thief.

His sole offspring.

His sole enemies.

CHAPTER 74

When he moved off, the gardens came to life.

The first bodyguard appeared from a thicket. The second came from behind a lime tree. Two others materialised on the gravel drive. All of them were armed with MP7s, a close-defence gun loaded with subsonic shells capable of piercing body armour such as titanium or Kevlar at a distance of fifty yards. At least, so the salesman had told him. But did it all have the slightest sense? At his age, the enemies he feared most did not travel at the speed of sound and did not pierce polycarbon. They were inside him, carrying out their patient work of destruction.

He followed the path. The men at once gathered around him, forming a human quincunx. It was always the same. His existence was that of a precious jewel. But the jewel had lost its sparkle. He wandered around like someone under house arrest, never going beyond the limits of his gardens, always surrounded by his men.

He headed towards the mansion – one of the last *yalis* in Yeniköy. A summer house, made of wood, by the waterside, on tarred piles.

This lofty palace, decked with turrets, had the haughtiness of a citadel, but also the nonchalant simplicity of a fisherman's hut.

The weather-beaten laths on the roof gave off sharp reflections, as vibrant as a mirror. But the façades soaked up the light, producing sombre glints of infinite softness. All around this building, there was an atmosphere of transience, of floating, or departure. The sea air, the worn wood and slapping waters made the old man think of perpetual travel, of summer holidays.

Yet, when he drew nearer and examined the details of that oriental façade – the latticework on the patios, the suns on the balconies, the stars and crescents of the windows – he saw that this sophisticated palace was in fact quite the opposite. It was an elaborate, well-anchored, stable environment. The tomb he had chosen. A wooden sepulchre with a seashell's hush, where he could watch death approach while listening to the river . . .

In the hall, Ismail Kudseyi took off his macintosh and boots. Then he put on his felt slippers and a jacket of Indian silk, before examining himself in the mirror.

His face was his sole object of pride.

Time had inflicted its inevitable ravages, but beneath the skin, the bone structure still held up. It had risen to his defence, stretching his flesh and pulling at his features. More than ever, he had the profile of a stag, with his jutting jaw, and that perpetual pout of disdain on his lips.

He removed a comb from his pocket and tidied his hair. He was smoothing down his grey locks when he suddenly realised what he was doing, and stopped. He was being careful about his appearance for them. Because he was dreading seeing them. Because he was afraid of confronting the real meaning behind all those years . . .

After the 1980 coup d'état, he had had to go into exile in Germany. When he came back in 1983, the situation in Turkey had calmed down, but most of his fellows in arms, the Grey Wolves, were in prison. In his isolation, Ismail Kudseyi refused to abandon the Cause. On the contrary, he secretly reopened the training camps and set up his own personal army. He was going to give birth to a new generation of Grey Wolves. Even better, he was going to train a better race of Wolf, who would serve both his political aims and criminal activities.

So he left for Anatolia to choose the children of his foundation personally. He organised the camps, watched the youngsters being trained, kept files on them so as to select an elite group. Soon, he was totally absorbed. Even while he was beginning to take over the opium market, exploiting the opening left by the revolution that was going on in Iran, this *baba* was interested above all in bringing up his children.

He felt a visceral complicity develop with these peasant children, who reminded him of the street urchin he had once been. He preferred being with them to spending time with his own children – whom he had had late in life with the daughter of a former minister, and who were now studying at Oxford University or in Berlin – his privileged heirs who had become strangers to him.

When he came back home, he shut himself up in his *yali* and studied each file, each personality. He weighed up their talents and gifts, but also their will to raise themselves up, to tear away from their stony origins . . . He sought out the most promising profiles – the ones he would support with grants then bring into his own clan.

His quest gradually turned into an obsession, a mania. The pretence of a nationalistic cause was no longer enough to hide his own ambition. What excited him was moulding human lives from a distance. Manipulating destinies, like an invisible demiurge . . .

Soon, two names were to interest him more than the others.

A boy and a girl.

Two children of pure promise.

Azer Akarsa came from a village near the ancient site of Nimrud Dağ. He was exceptionally gifted. When only sixteen, he was already a hardened fighter and a brilliant student. But most of all, he displayed a real passion for old Turkey and nationalist convictions. He had enrolled in the secret Adiyaman camp, and had volunteered for commando training. He was already planning on signing up for the army, so as to fight on the Kurdish front.

And yet, Azer had a handicap. He was diabetic. But Kudseyi decided that this weak point would not prevent him from living out his destiny as a Wolf. He swore to provide him with the best possible treatment at all times.

The other file concerned a certain Sema Hunsen, aged fourteen. Born amid the rocks of Gaziantep, she had succeeded in winning a place at school with a state grant. Superficially, she was just another young, intelligent Turk set on breaking with her origins. But she wanted to go further than that and emigrate. At the Gaziantep Idealist Club, Sema was the only girl. She had applied for a course at the camp in Kayseri so as to be with a boy from her village called Kürsat Milihit.

He had at once been attracted by this teenager. He adored her head-strong wildness, her desire to better her condition. Physically, she was a rather chubby red-head, with a peasant-like appearance. To look at her, you would never have guessed how gifted she was, or how polit-ically motivated. Except for her stare, which she threw into your face like a stone.

Ismail Kudseyi was sure that Azer and Sema would turn out to be far more than mere scholarship students, or anonymous soldiers serving the extreme right-wing cause or his network of organised crime. They would be his protégés. But they would not know this. He would help them from a distance, from the shadows.

The years went by and the two chosen ones lived up to their promise. At the age of twenty-two, Azer had taken an MSc in physics and chem-istry at the University of Istanbul then, two years later, an international business degree in Munich. Meanwhile, Sema was now seventeen, had left Galatasaray school with full honours and had gone to the English University of Istanbul. She now spoke fluent Turkish, French, English and German.

Both of them had remained political militants, *baskans* who could have run local clubs. But Kudseyi pushed them towards different hori-zons. He had greater ambitions for his creations – projects linked with his own drugs empire . . .

He also wanted to cast light on certain darker regions. Azer's behav-iour revealed dangerous fault lines. While still at the French School, he had disfigured a fellow pupil during a brawl. The wounds were serious, and clearly not inflicted in a fit of anger, but instead with a terrifyingly calm determination. Kudseyi had to use all his influence to stop the boy from being arrested.

Two years later, Azer had been caught skinning live mice. Some female students also complained of the obscenities he addressed to them. They had later found the gutted bodies of cats rolled up among their underwear in the changing-rooms at the swimming pool.

Kudseyi was intrigued by Azer's criminal impulses, which he at once saw could be exploited. But he was still unaware of their true nature. A freak incident was to reveal it. While studying in Munich, Azer Akarsa was hospitalised after an attack of diabetes. The German doctors had decided to treat him in an unusual way: periods spent in a pressurised chamber so as to oxygenate his body better.

During these sessions, Azer had experienced the rapture of the depths and had started to rant. He had yelled out his desire to kill women – *all women!* – to torture and disfigure them, until he had reproduced the ancient masks that spoke to him in his dreams. When back in his room, this fit continued, despite the sedatives he was given, and he scratched effigies of such faces into the wall beside his bed. Mutilated features, with their noses cut off and bones crushed, around which he had stuck his own hair with his sperm – dead remnants, eaten away by the centuries, but with heads of living hair . . .

The German doctors alerted the foundation in Turkey which was paying the student's medical fees. Kudseyi himself made the journey. The psychiatrists explained the situation and suggested confining him at once. Kudseyi agreed, but had Azer sent back to Turkey the following week. He was sure that he could control, and even exploit, his protégé's murderous streak.

Sema Hunsen's problems were of a totally different order. Solitary, secretive and obstinate, she was constantly slipping away from his organisation. She had run away from school at Galatasaray several times. Once, she had been arrested at the Bulgarian border. On another occasion, at Istanbul's Atatürk Airport. Her independence and will to be free had become pathological, leading to aggressiveness and a constant desire to run away. Once again, Kudseyi had seen this as a plus. He would turn her into a nomad. An elite drug smuggler.

In the mid-1990s, Azer Akarsa the brilliant businessman had also become a Wolf, in the occult sense of the term. Via one of his lieutenants, Kudseyi had given him several missions of intimidation or escort, which he had carried out brilliantly. He was to cross the sacred line – of murder – without the slightest qualm. Akarsa liked blood. Too much so, in fact.

There was another problem. Akarsa had set up his own political group of dissidents, whose opinions were far more violent and excessive than the official party line. Azer and his companions showed their disdain for the old Grey Wolves, who had sold out, and even more so for nationalistic mafiosi like Kudseyi. The old man began to feel bitter. His child was turning into an increasingly uncontrollable monster . . .

He sought comfort by turning towards Sema Hunsen. But in a purely abstract way. He had never seen her and, since leaving university, she had practically disappeared. She accepted transport missions – aware of what she owed the organisation – but in exchange had demanded a quite exceptional isolation from her masters.

Kudseyi did not like that. Yet, each time, the dope arrived at its destination. How long would this reciprocal agreement hold up? But at the same time, he found her mysterious personality more and more fascinating. He followed her career, delighting in her abilities . . .

Soon, Sema was a legend among the Grey Wolves. She had faded away into a labyrinth of languages and borders. There were many rumours about her. Some said that she had been seen on the border with Afghanistan, wearing a veil. Others claimed to have spoken with her in an underground laboratory on the Syrian frontier, but she had been wearing a surgical mask. Others still swore that they had had dealings with her on the coast of the Black Sea, in a dark nightclub torn by stroboscopic lights.

Kudseyi knew that these were all lies. No one had ever really seen Sema. At least, not the original Sema. She had become an abstract being, changing her identity, movements, style and technique depending on the objective. A shifting being, with just one concrete aspect – the dope she was transporting.

Sema did not know it, but in fact she had never really been alone. The old man was always by her side. Not once had she conveyed dope for anyone else but the *baba*. Not once had she run a consignment without his men watching over her from afar. Ismail Kudseyi was *inside her*.

Unbeknown to her, he had had her sterilised when she had been hospitalised for acute appendicitis in 1987. Her fallopian tubes had been ligatured, an irreversible mutilation that does not disturb the menstrual cycle. The operation had been done using key-hole surgery via minute incisions in her abdomen. No traces. No scars . . .

Kudseyi had had no choice. His fighters were unique. They could not reproduce themselves. Only Kudseyi could create, develop, or kill his soldiers. Despite his certainty, he was always worried about that mutilation, with an almost holy dread, as though he had broken a taboo, had trodden on forbidden ground. Sometimes, in his dreams, he saw his white hands holding her innards. He vaguely sensed that a catastrophe would be born of that organic secret . . .

Today, Kudseyi had admitted his failure regarding both of his children. Azer Akarsa had become a psychopathic murderer, at the head of an independent group of activists – terrorists who made themselves up as ancient Turks, who were planning attacks against the Turkish state and those Grey Wolves who had betrayed the Cause. Kudseyi himself might well be on their list. As for Sema, she was more than ever an invisible messenger, both paranoid and schizophrenic, awaiting the moment to run away for good.

All he had done was to create two monsters.

Two rabid wolves ready to tear out his throat.

And yet, he continued to give them important missions, hoping that they would not betray a clan that thought so highly of them. Above all, he hoped that destiny would not inflict such an affront, such negation on him, who had invested so much in their lives.

This is why, last spring, when he had to organise a consignment which would inaugurate a new alliance in the Golden Crescent, he mentioned just one name: Sema.

This is why, when the inevitable finally happened, and the renegade vanished with the dope, he had chosen just one killer: Azer.

As he had never made up his mind to eliminate them, he set them against each other so that they would do the job for him. But nothing had gone to plan. Sema remained untraceable. And Azer had merely succeeded in sparking off a series of murders in Paris. His name was now on an international arrest warrant, and Kudseyi's own criminal cartel had sentenced him to death – Azer had become too dangerous.

Then, suddenly, something had upset the entire situation.

Sema had reappeared.

And asked to meet with him.

She was still leading the dance . . .

He took one last look at his reflection in the mirror and abruptly discovered a different man. A dotard with a burnt frame, his bones as sharp as blades. A charred predator, like that prehistoric skeleton which had just been dug up in Pakistan . . .

He slid his comb into his jacket and tried to smile at his reflection. It felt as if he was greeting a death's head, with hollow eye sockets.

He headed towards the stairs, and gave an order to his bodyguards: "*Geldiler. Beni yalnız bırakın.*[1]"

CHAPTER 75

The room he called his "meditation room" measured a good thousand square feet, with a parquet floor. He could also have called it his "throne room". On the top of the three steps of a dais, stood a long off-white sofa covered with cushions of golden braid. In front of it was a coffee table. On either side, two lamps shed arcs of shaded light on to the white walls, along which chests of carved wood were aligned like solid shadows, secrets sealed with mother-of-pearl. And nothing else.

Kudseyi liked this simplicity, this almost mystic void which seemed ready to receive the prayers of a Sufi.

He walked across the room, up the steps and stopped by the table. He put down his stick and picked up a carafe full of *ayran* – made of yoghurt and water – which was always there for him. He poured out a glass and drank it back in one. Savouring the freshness that was filling his body, he stared at his treasures.

Ismail Kudseyi had the finest collection of carpets in Turkey, but the true masterpiece was kept there, hung over the sofa.

This small ancient rug, just three feet square, glimmered with a dark red, trimmed with tarnished yellow – the colour of gold, of corn, of baked bread. In the centre was a blue-black rectangle, a sacred colour evoking heaven and infinity. Inside it, a large cross was decked with ram's horns, symbolising the male warrior. Above, an eagle spread out its wings, crowning and protecting the cross. Meanwhile, on the bordering frieze could be seen the tree of life, the saffron

[1] They're here. Leave me alone.

crocus, the flower of joy and happiness, a marijuana plant, offering eternal sleep . . .

Kudseyi could have examined this masterpiece for hours. It seemed to sum up his world of war, drugs and power. He also loved the mystery contained in the stitch of its wool, which had always intrigued him. Once again he asked himself the question: "Where is the triangle? Where is fortune?"

Firstly, he admired the metamorphosis.

That buxom girl had turned into a slender brunette, in the modern style of femininity – small breasts and narrow hips. She was wearing a black padded coat, straight trousers of the same colour and square-tipped boots. A true Parisian.

But above all he was fascinated by the transformation of her face. How many operations, how many incisions had been needed to obtain such a result? The desire to run away, to flee its own yoke, was written all over that unrecognisable face. It could also be read in the depths of her indigo eyes. Their blue gleam could barely be seen beneath her drooping eyebrows, and it pushed you away, like an intruder, an unwanted presence. Yes, behind these modified features, in those eyes he could make out the primitive hardness of his nomadic people, a wild energy born of desert winds and the burning sun.

Suddenly, he felt old, finished.

A charred mummy, with lips of dust.

Remaining on his sofa, he let her approach. She had been thoroughly searched. Her clothes had been examined. Her very body had been X-rayed. Two bodyguards were now standing beside her, holding MP7s, with the security catch off, bullets in the breech. Standing slightly behind them, Azer was armed as well.

And yet, Kudseyi felt vaguely apprehensive. His warrior's instinct whispered to him that, despite her apparent fragility, this woman was still dangerous. It made him feel slightly queasy. What was in her mind? Why had she given herself up like this?

She was looking at the rug, hung on the wall behind him. He decided to speak in French, to give an even more formal nature to their meeting.

"One of the oldest carpets in the world. Russian archaeologists discovered it in the middle of a block of ice, near the frontier between

Siberia and Mongolia. It must be nearly two thousand years old, and is thought to have belonged to the Huns. The cross, the eagle, the ram's horns are purely masculine symbols. It was probably hung up in the clan chieftain's tent."

Sema remained silent. A needle of silence.

"A carpet for men, except that it was woven by a woman, like all the *kilim* of Central Asia," he smiled and paused. "I often try to imagine the one who made it. A mother excluded from the world of warriors, but who managed to impose her presence even in the tent of the great Khan."

Sema did not make the slightest movement. The bodyguards drew closer.

"At that time, the weaver always concealed a triangle among the other patterns, in order to protect her rug from the evil eye. I like that idea. Patiently, a woman would produce a virile design, full of warlike symbols, while somewhere, on the border, amid a frieze, she would slip in a maternal touch. Can you see where the triangular charm is on this rug?"

Not a word, not a gesture from Sema.

He picked up the carafe of *ayran*, slowly filled a glass, then drank it even more slowly.

"You can't see it?" he said at last. "Never mind. This story reminds me of yours, Sema. A woman hidden in a world of men, concealing an object that concerns us all. An object that should bring us good fortune and prosperity."

His voice faded away with these words, then he suddenly yelled violently: "Where's the triangle, Sema? Where's my heroin?"

No reaction. The words ran off her like drops of rain. He was not even sure if she was listening to him or not. But then she suddenly said: "I don't know."

He smiled again. So she wanted to negotiate. But she went on: "I was arrested in France. The police brainwashed me, using special mental conditioning. I can't remember my past. I don't know where the dope is. I don't even know who I am."

Kudseyi looked over at Azer. He, too, seemed amazed.

"Do you think I'm going to believe such a ridiculous story?" he asked.

"The treatment was a long one," she continued calmly. "It's a method of psychic suggestion, using a radioactive product. Most of the people involved in the experiment are now either dead or in prison. You can check if you want. It's been all over the French newspapers these last few days."

Kudseyi weighed up these facts suspiciously.

"So did the police get hold of the heroin?"

"They didn't even know that I had a consignment of dope."

"What?"

"They didn't know who I was. They chose me because they found me in a state of shock, in Gürdilek's baths after Azer's raid. They finished off the task of removing my memory without knowing my secret."

"For someone with no memory, you seem to know a lot."

"I've been investigating myself."

"How did you find out Azer's name?"

Sema smiled, as rapidly as a camera shutter.

"Everyone knows it. Just read the Paris press."

Kudseyi remained silent. He could have asked further questions, but his mind was now made up. His long life had convinced him of an unbreakable law: the more the facts seemed absurd, the greater the chance they were true. But he still did not understand her attitude.

"Why have you come back?"

"I wanted to announce the death of Sema. She died with my memories."

Kudseyi burst out laughing.

"And you think I'm going to let you go just like that?"

"I don't think anything. I'm another person. I don't want to keep running because of the woman I no longer am."

He stood up and took a few steps. Shaking his stick at her, he said: "If you've come back empty-handed, then you really must have lost your memory."

"There's no guilty party any more. So there's no punishment."

A strange warmth entered his veins. Incredibly, he was tempted to pardon her. This was a possible conclusion. Perhaps the most original, most refined one . . . Just let this new creature fly away, take wing . . . Forget all about it . . . But he then stared straight into her eyes and said: "You have no face. You have no past. You have no name. You have become a sort of abstract being, that is true. But you have kept your ability to suffer. We will cleanse our honour in the stream of your suffering. We will . . ."

Ismail Kudseyi was struck dumb.

The woman was stretching her hands towards him, palms uppermost.

Each of them was covered by a henna design. A wolf, howling below four moons. It was a rallying sign. The symbol used by the members of the new movement. He himself had added the fourth moon, symbolising the Golden Crescent, to the three on the Ottoman flag.

Kudseyi dropped his stick, pointed at Sema and yelled: "She knows. SHE KNOWS!"

She seized on this moment of stupefaction. She leapt behind one of the guards, grabbing him brutally. Her hand closed on the man's fingers which were on the trigger of the MP7, sending a hail of bullets towards the dais.

Ismail Kudseyi felt himself take off from the ground, before being pushed to the foot of the sofa by the second guard. He rolled over and saw his protector spin in an explosion of blood, while his gun fired in all directions, blasting the chests into a thousand splinters. Sparks shot up like electric arcs, while the ceiling filled with clouds of plaster. The first man, who was being used by Sema as a shield, collapsed at the very moment she pulled his gun from his hand.

Kudseyi could no longer see Azer.

She dived towards the chests, and overturned them for protection. At that moment, two other men burst into the room. No sooner had they arrived, than they were already hit – the dull, isolated sound of Sema's shooting punctuated the rattle of uncontrolled automatic weapons.

Ismail Kudseyi tried to slip behind the sofa, but he could not move – the orders from his brain were no longer being relayed by his body. He was paralysed on the floor, inert. A signal rang though his body. He had been hit.

Three more guards appeared in the doorway, taking it in turns to shoot then disappearing behind the jamb. Kudseyi's eyes blinked at the fire from their guns, but he could not hear the shots any more. It was as if his ears and brain were full of water.

He curled up, fingers gripping a cushion. A painful convulsion ran through him, down to the pit of his stomach, pinning him into the foetal position. He looked down. His intestines were gushing out, unrolling between his legs.

Everything went black. When he came to once more, Sema was reloading her gun at the foot of the steps, beside one of the chests. He turned towards the edge of the dais and reached out his hand. One part of him could not believe what he was doing. He was calling for help.

He was calling to Sema Hunsen for help!

She turned round. With tears in his eyes, Kudseyi was waving his hand. She hesitated for a second then, bent below the continuing gun blasts, climbed up the steps. The old man groaned in thanks. He raised his shivering gaunt red hand, but she did not take it.

She stood up, braced herself and took aim, like a bent bow.

In a flash, Ismail Kudseyi understood why she had come back to Istanbul.

Quite simply to kill him.

To cut off that hatred at its source.

And perhaps also to avenge a tree of life.

Which he had had cut off at the roots.

He blacked out again. When he next opened his eyes, Azer was diving onto Sema. They rolled down to the foot of the steps, among the scraps of leather and pools of blood. They fought as waves of fire still continued to break through the smoke. Arms, fists, blows – but not a single cry. Just obsessive, obstinate hatred. The physical fight for survival.

Azer and Sema.

His evil brood.

On her stomach, Sema was trying to raise her gun, but Azer was pushing down on her with all his weight. Holding her by the nape of the neck with one hand, while with the other he pulled out a knife. She slipped from his grip and rolled onto her back. He lunged and stuck the blade into her belly. Sema spat out a muffled cry of blood.

Lying on the dais, Kudseyi could see it all. His eyes, like two slow valves, were beating in a counter rhythm with his arteries. He prayed that he would die before the end of the fight, but he could not resist watching.

The blade flew down, rose, then went down again, ferreting its way into her flesh. Sema arched up. Azer grabbed her shoulders and forced them back to the ground. He threw away his knife and plunged his hand into the open wound.

Ismail Kudseyi drifted far away into the shifting sands of death.

A few seconds before the end, he saw crimson hands stretched towards him, carrying their cargo . . . Sema's heart in Azer's fingers.

Epilogue

In Eastern Anatolia, the snow at high altitudes begins to melt at the end of April, thus opening a path to Nimrud Dağ, the highest peak of the Taurus mountains. Tourist excursions have not yet begun, and the site remains perfectly preserved, in total solitude.

After each mission, he looked forward to this moment when he would return to his stone gods.

He had taken a flight from Istanbul the day before, 26 April, and had landed at Adana in the late afternoon. He had rested for a few hours in a hotel near the airport, then, later that night, he had taken the road in a hired car.

He was now driving eastwards towards Adiyaman, having covered two hundred and fifty miles. Long pastures surrounded him like flooded plains. In the darkness, he sensed their vague, supple undulations. These rippling shadows were a first step, the initial shift towards purity. He remembered the beginning of a poem he had written in his youth, in old Turkish: *I have sailed the seas of greenness* . . .

At half past six, he drove past the town of Gaziantep, and the landscape changed. In the first glimmers of daylight, the Taurus mountains appeared. The fluid fields became stony deserts. Bare, abrupt, red spikes poked up. Craters opened in the distance, like dried sunflowers.

When confronted with this scene, the average traveller always feels rather apprehensive and vaguely anxious. But he loved these shades of ochre and yellow, growing deeper, brighter than the blue of the dawn. He was at home. This aridness had forged his flesh. It was the second stage of purity.

He remembered the next line of his poem:

I have sailed the seas of greenness,
Kissed the borders of stone, the empty eyes of shadow . . .

When he stopped at Adiyaman, the sun was struggling to rise. At the garage in the town he filled his petrol tank himself, while the employee was cleaning his windscreen. He stared at the pools of iron and bronze-tinged houses laid out as far as the foothills.

On the main avenue, he saw the Matak warehouses, "his" store-rooms, where thousands of tons of fruit would soon be stocked before being treated, turned into jams or exported. He felt no pride at all. Such trivial ambition had never really interested him. Instead, he sensed the approach of the mountains, the nearness of the ridges . . .

Three miles further on, he turned off the main road. No more asphalt, no more signs. Just a track cut into the mountain, snaking up through the clouds. At that instant, he truly felt that he was back on native soil, amid the flanks of purple dust, the spiky grasses forming aggressive clumps, and grey/black sheep parting just enough to let him though.

He passed his village. Women in headscarves decorated with gold walked by, with faces of red leather, fashioned like copper trays. Wild creatures, as hard as the earth, immured in prayer and tradition, just like his mother. There might even be some members of his family among them . . .

Higher up, he saw shepherds clustered along a slope, wrapped up in baggy jackets. He could see himself, twenty-five years before, sitting in their place. He still remembered the Fair Isle sweater he had worn as a coat, with its dangling sleeves, and his hands that pushed out a little further each year. The stitches in the wool were the only calendar he had.

He felt a tingling sensation in the tips of his fingers. The feeling of his shaved scalp when he was shielding himself from his father's blows. The softness of the dry fruit, as he ran his hands over the surface of the grocer's large bags on his way back from the pastures in the evening. The walnuts he gathered in autumn, whose juice stained his palms all winter . . .

He was now entering the veil of mist.

Everything became white, soft, damp. The flesh of the clouds. The first clumps of snow bordered the road. A special sort of snow, impregnated with luminescent pink sand.

Before going up the final section, he put chains around his tyres, then continued. He bounced on for about another hour. The snow-drifts shone more and more brightly, assuming the shapes of languid bodies. The final stage of the Pure Way.

> *I have caressed the snowy slopes*
> *Scattered with pink sand,*
> *Curved as a woman's body . . .*

Finally, he spotted the car-park at the foot of the rock. Above, the tip of the mountain remained invisible, shrouded in layers of mist.

He got out of his car and savoured the atmosphere. The silence of the snow weighed down on the scene like a block of crystal.

He filled his lungs with icy air. Here, the altitude was over six thousand feet. There were some thousand feet still to climb. In preparation for the effort, he ate two chocolates, then he set off with his hands in his pockets.

He passed the janitor's lodge, closed until the month of May, then followed the path of stones that barely emerged from the bed of snow. The climb became difficult. He had to make a detour, in order to avoid a steep slope. He advanced leaning sideways, his left hand on the slopes, being careful not to fall into the void. The snow crunched beneath his feet.

He started to pant. His entire body felt strained, his mind alert. He reached the first terrace – to the east – but did not linger there. Here, the statues were too eroded. He just allowed himself a few minutes' respite on the "altar of fire" – a platform of bronze-green frozen rock, which offered a hundred-and-twenty degree view of the Taurus mountains.

The sun at last graced the landscape. At the bottom of the valley could be seen red patches, yellow cracks, and also clumps of green, vestiges of the plains that had created the fertility of the ancient kingdoms. Light lingered in the craters, digging out white, shimmering pools. In other places, they seemed already to be evaporating, rising up in powder, reducing each detail to a myriad of spangles. Elsewhere, the sun played off the clouds, with shadows passing across the mountains like expressions on a face.

He was gripped by an inexpressible emotion. He could not convince himself that this was "his" land, that he himself belonged to that measureless beauty. It was almost as if he could see his ancestral hordes arriving over the horizon – the first Turks bringing their power and civilisation to Anatolia.

When he looked again, he saw that there were no men, no horses, but only wolves. Packs of silvery wolves, blending in with the reverberations of the earth. Divine wolves, ready to bond with mortals and so give birth to a race of perfect warriors . . .

He continued his path, towards the western slopes. The snow became at once thicker, lighter and smoother. He glanced back at his own footprints. They made him think of a strange script, translated from silence.

Finally he reached the next terrace, with its Heads of Stone.

There were five of them. Colossal forms, each measuring over seven feet tall. At the beginning, they had stood on huge bodies, at the summit of the burial mound itself. But earthquakes had knocked them down. Some people had then stood them up again, and they seemed to have gained extra strength on the ground, as though their shoulders were the very flanks of the mountains.

In the middle was Antiochus I, King of Commagene, who wanted to be buried amid these half Greek, half Persian gods, born of the syncretism of a lost civilisation. By his side, there was Zeus-Ahura Mazda, the god of gods, incarnate in lightning and fire, then Apollo-Mithras, who demanded that men be sanctified with the blood of bulls, Tyche, who, beneath her crown of corn and fruit, symbolised the kingdom's fertility . . .

Despite their power, they had youthfully placid expressions on their faces, mouths like fountains, curly beards . . . Above all, their large blank eyes seemed to be dreaming. Even the worn and snow-covered guardians of the sanctuary, the Lion, king of beasts, and the Eagle, lord of the skies, added to the docility of the parade.

It was not the right time yet. The mist was too thick for the miracle to happen. He tightened his scarf and thought of the monarch who built this sepulchre. Antiochus Epiphanes I. His reign had been so prosperous that he had thought himself blessed by the gods to the point of becoming one of them, and he had had himself buried at the top of the holy mountain.

Ismail Kudseyi had also mistaken himself for a god, imagining that he had the power of life or death over his subjects. But he had forgotten the essential point. He was a mere instrument of the Cause, just a link in the Turan. By neglecting that fact, he had betrayed himself and the Grey Wolves. He had broken the laws that he had once represented. He had become degenerate and vulnerable. That was why Sema had managed to kill him.

Sema. Bitterness suddenly dried his mouth. He had succeeded in eliminating her, but it had been no triumph. The entire chase had been a waste, a failure which he had attempted to redress by sacrificing his prey according to ancestral law. He had sacrificed her heart to the stone gods of Nimrud Dağ – those divinities which he had always honoured by sculpting their features into the flesh of his victims.

The fog was lifting.

He knelt in the snow and waited.

In a few seconds, the mist would drift away, wrapping those giant heads for a final instant, drawing them up with its lightness, implicating them in its movement – thus giving them life.

Their features would lose their clarity and contours, then float above the snows. It was impossible at such times not to think of a forest. Impossible not to see them advancing . . . Antiochus first, then Tyche and the other immortals behind him, surrounded, beautified and enveloped in icy vapours. Finally, in that moment of suspense, their lips would open and they would speak.

When a child, he had often witnessed this miracle. He had learned to catch their murmurings and understand their language, which was mineral, ancient, incomprehensible to anyone who had not been born there, at the foot of the mountains.

He closed his eyes.

That day, he prayed for the gods to grant him their forgiveness. He was also hoping for a fresh oracle. Misty words that would reveal his future. What would his stone mentors whisper to him now?

"Freeze."

The man did so. He thought he was hearing voices, but the cold muzzle of a gun pressed against his temple. The voice repeated, in French: "Freeze."

A woman's voice.

He managed to turn his head and made out a long figure, dressed in a parka and black ski trousers. Her dark hair, squeezed into her woolly hat, spilled out over her shoulders in two streams of curls.

He was baffled. How could this woman have followed him all this way?

"Who are you?" he asked, in French.

"My name is of no importance."

"Who sent you?"

"Sema."

"But Sema's dead."

He could not accept the fact that he had been jumped like this during his secret pilgrimage.

The voice went on: "I'm the woman who helped her in Paris. Who allowed her to escape from the police, to recover her memory, to come back to Turkey to confront you."

The man nodded. Yes, right from the start, there had been a link missing from the story. Sema Hunsen could not have eluded him for such a long time – someone must have helped her. He blurted out a question, at once regretting his haste: "And the dope . . . where is it?"

"In a cemetery. In funeral urns. *A little white powder amid all the grey powder . . .*"

He nodded again. He recognised Sema's ironic touch, the way she had practised her trade as if it was a game. It rang true – like a tinkle of crystal.

"How did you find me?"

"Sema wrote me a letter. She explained everything. Her origins. Her training. Her speciality. She also gave the names of her former friends – and current enemies."

As she spoke, he noticed a sort of accent, a strange lengthening of final syllables. For a second, he looked at the statues' white eyes. They had not awoken yet.

"Why are you getting involved in all this?" he asked, perplexed. "The story's over. And it finished without your help."

"It's true. I got here too late. But I can still do something for Sema."

"What's that?"

"Stop you from pursuing your monstrous quest."

371

He smiled and looked straight at her. She was a large woman, dark haired and very beautiful. Her face was pale, crossed by numerous wrinkles, but instead of lessening her allure, these furrows seemed to frame and define it. Such a spectacle took his breath away. She went on: "I read the newspaper articles in Paris. About the murders of three women. I studied the mutilations you inflicted on them. I'm a psychiatrist. I could give complicated names to your obsessions, your hatred of women . . . But what would be the point?"

The man understood that she had come there to kill him, that she had tracked him down so as to eliminate him. He was to die at the hands of a woman. But that was impossible. He concentrated on the stone heads. The light would soon bring them to life. Would the Giants tell him how to react?

"And you followed me all this way?" he asked to gain some time.

"I had no difficulty locating your company in Istanbul. I knew that you'd go there sooner or later, despite the arrest warrant, despite your situation. When you finally appeared, surrounded by your bodyguards, I kept you in my sights. I followed you, watched you for days. And I realised that I stood no chance of getting near you, and even less of taking you by surprise . . ."

A strange determination emanated from her words. She was beginning to interest him. He glanced at her again. Through the mist of her breath, another detail struck him. Her overly red mouth, made violet by the cold. Suddenly, that organic colour stirred up his hatred for women once more. Like the others, she was a blasphemous creature. An exhibition of temptation, sure of her power . . .

"And then a miracle happened," she continued. "One morning, you left your hiding place. Alone. And you went to the airport . . . All I had to do was follow in your footsteps and buy a ticket for Adana. I supposed that you were going to visit some underground laboratory, or training camp. But why go alone? I thought you might be visiting your family. But that seemed unlike you. The only family you now have is a pack of wolves. So what were you up to? In her letter, Sema described you as a hunter from the east, from the region of Adiyaman, who is obsessed with archaeology. While waiting for the departure, I bought some maps and guidebooks. I discovered the site of Nimrud Dağ and its statues. The cracks in the stone reminded me of those disfigured faces. I then realised that these sculptures are your model. The model that structures your insanity. You were going on a pilgrimage to this inaccessible sanctuary. Face to face with your own madness."

He had recovered his calm. Yes, he appreciated this woman's singular nature. She had succeeded in hunting him down on his own territory. She had, so to speak, entered into the significance of his pilgrimage. Maybe she was even worthy of being his killer . . .

He glanced one more time at the statues. Their whiteness now glowed in the sunlight. They had never seemed so strong to him – yet so distant. Their silence was confirmation. He had lost. He was no longer worthy of them.

He breathed in deeply and nodded towards them.

"Can you feel the power of this place?"

Still kneeling, he picked up a handful of pink snow and crushed it through his fingers.

"I was born a few miles from here, in the valley. At the time, there were no tourists. I used to come and sit here alone on the terrace. At the foot of these statues I forged my dreams of power and fire."

"Of blood and murder."

He nodded with a smile.

"We are working for the return of the Turkish Empire. We are fighting for the supremacy of our race in the East. Soon, the frontiers of Central Asia will break down. We speak the same language. We have the same cultural roots. We are all descendents of Asena, the White Wolf."

"You're just feeding your madness with myths."

"A myth is a reality that has become a legend. A legend can become real. The Wolves are back. The Wolves will save the Turkish people."

"You're just a murderer. A murderer who doesn't the know the price of blood."

Despite the sun, he felt numb, paralysed by the cold. To his left, he pointed at the ridge of snow, stretching away in the vibrant air.

"Long ago, on that terrace, warriors were blessed with the blood of bulls in the name of Apollo-Mithras. It is from this tradition that baptism derives – Christian baptism. Grace is born from blood."

With her free hand, the woman pushed back her black locks. The increasingly bitter cold was digging out and reddening her wrinkles. But that precise geography just made her all the more magnificent. She cocked her gun.

"In that case, this is a moment for rejoicing. Because blood is about to flow."

"Wait."

He still did not understand her audacity, her perseverance.

"No one takes risks like this. And especially not for a woman you saw for only a couple of days. What did Sema mean to you?"

She hesitated, then tilted her head slightly to one side.

"She was a friend. Just a friend."

As she spoke, she smiled. And that broad red smile, standing out against the bas-reliefs of the sanctuary confirmed the truth for him.

Her true destiny must also be at stake at that moment.

Just as much as his own.

They were both finding their precise positions in an ancient fresco.

He focused on her startling lips. He thought of the wild poppies, the stalks of which his mother used to burn so as to preserve their scarlet colour longer.

When the barrel of the .45 erupted, he realised that he was happy to die in the shadow of such a smile.